Lord Claybourne's hands covered Lily's shoulders, lightly massaging. Then bending, he covered her mouth with his in a slow, devastating, spellbinding kiss that sent searing heat arcing between them again.

"Don't you see?" he asked, his voice husky and low. "Whatever this is between us, it deserves exploring."

Dazed, Lily opened her eyes. Yes, she saw. She was aching with nameless longing . . . aching for *him*. Giving a frustrated groan, she slid out from his embrace and backed away, putting as much space as possible between them.

His lordship locked gazes with her, regarding her intently. With shaking fingers, Lily tucked a loose tendril of hair behind her ear and swallowed hard. Yet her voice was still a hoarse rasp when she finally spoke. "You are mistaken if you think I will meekly surrender just because you are a marvelous kisser."

"I think nothing of the kind," he said, his tone wry. "You haven't a meek bone in your lovely body, I'll warrant."

"No, and I will never accept your proposal of marriage, either," Lily said firmly.

The smile he gave her was utterly beautiful and utterly maddening. "We shall see."

By Nicole Jordan

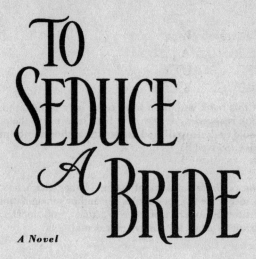

TO SEDUCE A BRIDE

A Novel

Nicole Jordan

BALLANTINE BOOKS • NEW YORK

To Seduce a Bride is a work of fiction. Names, characters, places, and incidents are the products of the author's imagination or are used fictitously. Any resemblance to actual events, locales, or persons, living or dead, is entirely coincidental.

A Ballantine Books Mass Market Original

Copyright © 2008 by Anne Bushyhead

Published in the United States by Ballantine Books, an imprint of The Random House Publishing Group, a division of Random House, Inc., New York.

BALLANTINE and colophon are registered trademarks of Random House, Inc.

ISBN 978-0-345-49461-0

Cover design: Carl Galian
Cover illustration: Aleta Rafton

Printed in the United States of America

www.ballantinebooks.com

OPM 9 8 7 6 5 4 3 2 1

To my wonderful rider friends:
Karen, Wyatt, and Kari.

Thanks for all the great times
and for taking such good care
of my "kids"!

Chapter One

❧

Lady Freemantle's matchmaking is vexing enough to drive a saint mad, and you know I am no saint.
—Miss Lily Loring to Fanny Irwin

Danvers Hall, Chiswick, England, June 1817

"I cannot understand why he flusters me so," Lilian Loring mumbled unevenly to the gray cat. "No man has ever unsettled me this way."

A soft purr was the only reply Lily received to her complaint.

"It is not merely because he is handsome, either. I am not ord'narily attracted to handsome noblemen." If anything she was highly wary of them. "And I care nothing for his rank and consequence."

Giving a woozy sigh, Lily stretched out in the straw as she stroked the cat's fur. She was hard-pressed to explain the deplorable effect that Heath Griffin, Marquess of Claybourne, had on her. Particularly since she had just met him for the first time this morning at her sister's wedding.

"The trouble is, he is too sharm . . . *charm*ing." *And virile. And vital. And powerful.*

Whatever his attributes, they made her absurdly breathless and agitated.

"Devil take 'im. . . ."

Lily bit her lip and fell silent upon registering how slurred her words sounded. No doubt the result of drinking three full glasses of champagne—which was at least two glasses too many, given how spirits of any kind went directly to her head. But the events of the evening had been dismaying enough to drive her to imbibe.

She wasn't *completely* foxed at the moment, yet it had probably been a mistake to attempt climbing up to the stable loft wearing a ball gown—an exquisite confection of pale rose silk—and dancing slippers. Weaving her way up the ladder in such narrow skirts while carrying a napkinful of tidbits had challenged her usual athleticism. But she had wanted to bring supper for Boots before she left the wedding celebrations.

Boots, the Danvers Hall stable cat, had recently given birth to a litter of kittens. Currently the family of felines was contentedly curled up in the box Lily had arranged in the loft to protect the mother cat and her new offspring from the home-farm dogs. Lily had left her lantern hanging on a peg below so as not to frighten the youngsters, and the muted golden glow contributed to the tranquility of the loft, as did the warmth of the night, since it was nearly summer.

The three kittens were little balls of fluff, their eyes barely open, but they were beginning to show their own unique personalities—much like the Loring sisters, Lily thought. The sight of the baby kittens blinking sleepily up at her roused intensely tender feelings in her chest, since she had a soft spot for the helpless and less fortunate.

If she was honest with herself, however, she would admit that she'd sought refuge in the stable loft as much to escape Lord Claybourne as to feed the estate cat and indulge in a bout of self-pity.

While Boots was nibbling delicately on breast of roast pheasant, Lily carefully reached inside the box and picked up one of the adorable kittens.

"Do you re'lize how precious you are?" she murmured, pressing her nose into its soft ebony fur. The black kitten was the rambunctious one, like Lily herself, and it swatted at her nose playfully.

Lily gave a low laugh, which helped staunch the ache in her throat at the poignant memories she was trying to hold at bay.

It had been a lovely wedding this morning in the village church, where her eldest sister Arabella had married Marcus Pierce, the new Earl of Danvers. An enormous wedding breakfast and ball had followed at Danvers Hall, with nearly six hundred guests in attendance. The celebrations had gone splendidly, due in large part to her middle sister Roslyn's untiring efforts and hostess skills.

The ball would continue for at least another hour or two, until after midnight, but Lily and Roslyn had said farewell to Arabella in private a short while ago, sharing tears of happiness and sadness.

It was extremely hard for Lily to bear, losing Arabella to marriage, but the evening had been made even more difficult by the meddlesome matchmaking efforts of their kindly patron, Winifred, Lady Freemantle. Several years ago, when the Loring sisters had been penniless and in desperate need of earning their own livings, Winifred had supplied the funds to start their Academy for Young Ladies for the daughters of the wealthy merchant class. All during the ball, Winifred had kept pushing Lily in the path of Marcus's close friend, the Marquess of Claybourne.

Eventually, much to her chagrin and dismay, Winifred cornered her and practically *forced* his lordship to dance with her.

"You will be delighted to have so desirable a dance partner as Miss Lilian, my lord, no mistake," the middle-aged matron assured him.

"Delighted and honored," Claybourne replied, smiling lazily down at Lily.

She felt color heat her cheeks. As her traitorous friend turned away, beaming with sly glee, Lily stared back at Claybourne, vexed and tongue-tied.

The marquess was tall and powerful, with an air of breathtaking virility that commanded attention. His hair was a tawny brown, his eyes a gold-flecked hazel, and he had an utterly masculine face that made countless feminine hearts flutter.

Lily discovered that she was no different. Deplorably aware of her quickening pulse and heightened senses, she stood there feeling awkward and fuming at Winifred's machinations. It was mortifying, being paraded before the very wealthy, very eligible marquess like a heifer at a fair.

She remained mute as she accepted Lord Claybourne's hand and let him lead her onto the ballroom floor. And when the orchestra struck up the opening bars of a waltz, she reluctantly moved into his arms. She did *not* like being so close to him, to his heat and vitality. Nor was she pleased at how conscious she was of his body, of his natural grace, his easy sensuality as he guided her to the lilting rhythm of the music. She had never observed such things about a man before. Normally she only noticed a man's potential for brutality, the size of his fists—

"Do you dislike dancing in general, Miss Loring?" Claybourne finally asked to break the silence between them. "Or do you object to dancing with me in particular?"

Lily was taken aback by his perceptiveness. "Why would you think I object, my lord?" she hedged.

"Perhaps because of that fearsome scowl you are wearing."

Feeling a fresh flush tinge her cheeks, she forced a polite smile. "I beg your pardon. Dancing is not my favorite pastime."

Those jeweled eyes glinted down from beneath heavy brows. "You do it quite well. I confess that surprises me."

She raised an eyebrow. "Why should it surprise you?"

"Because Marcus claims you are a spitfire and a hoyden. I understand you would rather enjoy a good gallop across a field than be caught dead in a ballroom."

That honest observation won a reluctant laugh from Lily. "Most decidedly I prefer riding to waltzing, my lord, although 'spitfire' is a bit harsh. Marcus thinks I am one because I frequently quarreled with him about Arabella when he was courting her. But I am fairly eventempered. However, I freely admit to being a hoyden—except when I play teacher at our Academy and must set a good example. Or upon occasions such as this, when I am required to endure the social niceties for my sisters' sakes. In truth, I find a certain pleasure in defying the dictates of the ton."

"I can admire a rebel," he said, his tone edged with

amusement. "You are very different from your sisters, are you not?"

His observation earned a sharp look from Lily. She regarded Claybourne suspiciously, unable to tell if he considered the difference favorable or not.

Not that she minded if his judgment of her was unfavorable. Nor did it bother her that she always fell short in comparisons with her sisters. Both Arabella and Roslyn were remarkable beauties with fair hair, creamy complexions, and tall, elegant figures.

Lily couldn't match their height or aristocratic bearing— in addition to having dark hair and eyes and a rosy coloring that made her seem a changeling in her blond, blue-eyed family. Moreover, her sisters were the epitome of grace and ladylike gentility, while her own high spirits and stubborn aversion to conforming to the absurdly stuffy precepts of the ruling elite regularly led her into trouble.

But Lily had no intention of apologizing to his lordship for her subversive tendencies. Indeed, to her mind, the less conversation she had with him the better.

He, however, did not appear inclined to take her hint and keep silent. "Did you enjoy the wedding ceremony this morning, Miss Loring?"

That topic was an extreme sore point with her also, although she managed to hide her wince. "Arabella made a beautiful bride," she said carefully.

"But you don't approve of your sister marrying my friend."

Lily's frown returned as she scanned the ballroom for the bridal couple and found Arabella and Marcus laughing together as they waltzed. "I fear she may be making a mistake, wedding so suddenly. They have known each other for barely two months."

"And yet they profess to be madly in love."

"I know," Lily said morosely. Watching the tender looks Belle and Marcus shared as they glided together in the dance, she had to admit they seemed very much in love. "But I worry that it won't last."

Claybourne smiled. "You sound very much like my friend Arden."

Arden, Lily knew, was Marcus's other close friend, Drew Moncrief, the Duke of Arden. The three noblemen—Danvers, Arden, and Claybourne—were as thick as thieves. "His grace did not want them to marry, either?"

"No, and for your same reasons."

"What about you, my lord? What is your opinion of their union?"

Claybourne's eyes glimmered with amusement. "I am reserving judgment for the time being, but I'm inclined to approve. They look remarkably happy now, don't you agree?"

"Yes. And I truly hope it continues. I don't want Arabella to be hurt."

That seemed to catch his attention. "And you think Marcus will hurt your sister?"

"That is what noblemen tend to do," Lily muttered under her breath, although his lordship evidently heard.

His gaze turned curious. "Not all noblemen are villains, Miss Loring."

"No . . . in all fairness, they are not."

At his mention of villains, she studied the marquess measuringly. He was a powerfully-built man, broad-chested and muscular. The top of her head barely came to his shoulder.

Ordinarily she was wary of powerful men. She tended to measure them by how they treated women, a habit ingrained in her when she was a mere girl. Yet surprisingly Lord Claybourne did not make her apprehensive. At least not for the usual reasons, because he was bigger and stronger than she.

He looked very strong, yet he didn't seem to be the kind of man who would use his strength against someone weaker.

Perhaps it was his easy smile. Or perhaps it was because of the tales she'd heard of him. The Marquess of Claybourne was legendary for the way women adored him.

He was said to adore women in turn, just not enough to marry any one of his numerous conquests. Which made it surprising that he didn't object to his friend Marcus's unexpected marriage.

"I trust you don't mean to condemn me out of hand," Claybourne observed, interrupting her intent perusal. "At least not until we are better acquainted."

Lily clamped down on her wayward thoughts. "There is no need for us to become better acquainted, my lord," she said lightly. "We don't move in the same circles, and as soon as the wedding celebrations are over, I plan to resume being a hoyden and never set foot in another ballroom except under pain of death."

His laugh was husky and charming—and quite disarming. "Marcus warned me you were unique."

Lily had a mutinous desire to resist that effortless charm. Tearing her gaze away from his amused one, she focused on a distant point over his shoulder.

She didn't *want* to admit her attraction to Lord Claybourne. He made her feel delicate and fragile and feminine—and she did not care for the sensations at all. Indeed, the sense of power, of vitality, about him, was overwhelming.

But oddly, his allure was due to more than his handsome features and masculine form. There was an aura about him that hinted at excitement. He looked like a bold adventurer. A traveler, an explorer. As if he should be captaining a ship, sailing the seven seas, or leading an intrepid expedition, probing the secrets of unknown lands.

Lily didn't know if he owned a ship, but she knew he was a sportsman. The stories of Claybourne's sporting exploits were repeated in all the drawing rooms. And Winifred had been singing his praises the entire day, attempting to rouse Lily's interest in targeting him for her husband.

She had absolutely no desire to marry the marquess, however, or any other man for that matter. Even though she was forced to admit that Claybourne was the most compelling man she had ever met—which was an ideal reason to keep away from him.

As soon as the waltz was over, Lily had extricated herself from his unnerving company.

She intended to leave the ball early in any case, to spend the night with her good friend Tess Blanchard, a genteel young lady who was also a teacher at the Freemantle Academy.

After saying farewell to Arabella and then drinking two more glasses of champagne in quick succession— Lily had needed the libation for fortitude and to hold back her tears of sadness—she made her way to one of the rear stable wings, formerly used for broodmares, to feed Boots and check on her kittens. It was blessedly quiet here, set away from the rest of the yard.

Her head was still swimming from the overindulgence of champagne, along with her potent memories of Lord Claybourne. The feel of him as they'd waltzed—sinewy and powerful, all lithe grace—had uncustomarily flustered her.

"But I trust I will never see him again after t'night," Lily muttered as she returned the black kitten to the box. "Or at least that I will never again be the victim of Winifred's humiliating mash . . . *match*making schemes."

It was then that Lily heard a faint noise from below, like a throat being cleared.

Wondering who had entered the stable, she shifted her position to look over the loft's edge. Her heart skipped a violent beat when she spied the broad-shouldered Marquess of Claybourne leaning against a post, his arms folded, his head cocked to one side.

When her head suddenly started spinning dizzily, Lily drew back in haste. *Oh, dear heaven.* Had he overheard her lament that he was too charming? What other incriminating observations had she made about him?

Holding a hand to her throbbing temple, Lily slowly peered over the side again. "M-my lord, what are you doing here?"

"I saw you leave the ball and wondered why you would visit the stables."

"You followed me?" Lily asked blankly.

Claybourne gave a bland nod. "Guilty as charged."

Her eyes narrowed. "So you were shamelessly eavesdropping?"

"I was curious. Do you always talk to yourself, Miss Loring?"

"Sometimes. But in this case I am speaking to the cat . . . Actually *cats*. Boots the stable cat recently had kittens."

"Would you care to explain what you are doing up there in the loft?"

"If you mush . . . must know . . . I am feeding her."

"You came here to feed the stable cat?" His tone held surprise and a hint of disbelief.

"Should I have let her starve?" Lily asked rhetorically. "Boots is an excellent mouser, but at the moment she has more important tasks to occupy her, namely taking care of her kittens."

His handsome mouth quirked. "Do you mean to remain there with the cats?"

"No. I will come down as soon as my head clears. I seem . . . to have drunk a bit too much champagne." To her chagrin, she was too dizzy just now to climb safely down the ladder to escape Lord Claybourne's unwanted presence.

"Then you won't mind if I join you," he said, moving across the aisle to put a foot on the lowest wooden rung.

Yes, she minded! Lily sat up abruptly, wondering how she could prevent him from imposing his company upon her. "You cannot climb up here, my lord!" she exclaimed, yet her protest obviously had no effect, since his head soon appeared above the ledge.

"I believe I can. I plan to keep you company."

With his torso in view, he paused to survey her with interest.

"You will get your coat dusty," Lily said lamely, eying his elegantly tailored evening coat of burgundy superfine—Weston, no doubt—that fitted those magnificent shoulders to perfection.

"My coat will survive." His gaze raked over her own attire. "What about you? You are wearing a ball gown."

"That is different. I don't care about clothing."

When his eyebrow shot up, Lily realized that her retort could have two meanings. "I d-don't mean that I like to go *naked* . . ." she stammered, feeling scalding heat flood her cheeks. "I only meant that I don't care about *fancy clothing* . . . ball gowns and shuch."

"How novel." His tone turned wry as he climbed the last few rungs and settled a hip on the loft's edge. "It strains the imagination. You must be the first female I have ever met who isn't interested in fancy gowns."

"But you see, I am not normal, my lord. I am very *abnormal.*"

"Is that so?" he replied, easing himself closer to sit beside her.

Even in the dim light, she could see that his hazel eyes were dancing. He was laughing at her!

Stiffening her spine, Lily opened her mouth to remonstrate, but he spoke first. "What is so abnormal about you, angel? You look exceedingly normal to me."

When his gaze drifted downward again over her body, Lily pressed her hands to her flaming cheeks and willed herself to calm down—which was deplorably difficult considering the fluttery, flustered sensations that were racing through her at his lordship's close proximity.

Stretching up to her full sitting height, she tried to appear regal and made her tone dampening as she replied. "I *meant* that I am not usual for a *female.*"

"I have little doubt about that."

She shot him an exasperated look. "The thing is, I should have been born male. I would have been mush happier."

"Oh, and are you so unhappy now?"

In her slightly inebriated state, her thoughts were more sluggish than usual, and she had to consider his question for a moment. "Well . . . no. I like my life quite well. But women have little of the freedom that men enjoy."

"What freedom would you like to enjoy, love?"

Lily bit her lower lip, abashed at how her tongue was running away from her. Yet she couldn't seem to help herself; the champagne had loosened her tongue deplorably. "Never mind. Don't listen to me, my lord. I don't hold my liquor at all well."

"So it would seem. What made you drink so much then?"

"I was drowning my sorrows, if you insist on knowing."

"What sorrows?"

"At losing my sister to matrimony. I was indulging in a bout of melancholy. But it was supposed to be *private*." When he didn't respond, Lily added pointedly, "That is a veiled hint for you to leave, my lord."

Instead of retreating down the loft ladder, he smiled and leaned back, casually resting his weight on his palms and crossing his long, satin-clad legs in front of him, as if settling in for a long stay.

Lily exhaled in a huff. "I don't think you comprehend the danger you are in, Lord Claybourne. It is a grave mistake for you to be alone with me. If Winifred knew, she would be ecstatic."

"Winifred?"

"Lady Freemantle. She is the main reason I left the ball early—to escape her scheming. She is trying to mash . . . match me with you. You must have noticed."

Her allegation didn't seem to alarm him as it should. "Perhaps, but her machinations are no worse than usual. I'm well-accustomed to eager mamas throwing their daughters at my head."

Lily grimaced in disgruntlement. "Perhaps *you* can dismiss her plotting, but I cannot. It is mortifying in the extreme. I am not a prize heifer, to be exhibited before an eligible gentleman and judged for my defects and qualifications."

His eyes were dancing again. "I should think not."

At his blithe reply, exasperation welled up in Lily full force. "Do you not *understand*? Winifred wants me to set my cap at you."

"But you don't intend to."

"Certainly not! I have no interest in marriage."

"That is quite a unique perspective for a young lady. Most women have made it their mission in life to find a husband."

"True. But you needn't worry about me hounding you, Lord Claybourne. Oh, I know you are a prime catch. You are disgustingly rich, you have a vaunted title, you aren't so shabby in appearance, and you are said to be irresistibly charming."

"But you aren't swayed by this delightful catalog of my attributes."

"Not in the least." Lily smiled faintly to soften the harshness of her observation. "No doubt you have a bevy of lovestruck admirers, but I will never join their ranks. And I have no intention of behaving like all the other flagrant husband-hunters you know. I won't chase after you."

"You relieve my mind, Miss Loring. I don't enjoy being chased." From the provocative laughter in his voice, he seemed to be enjoying himself far too much. "But I am quite curious to know why you have such a profound distaste for marriage."

Lily drew a deep breath. Hoyden or not, she normally would never dream of discussing her personal affairs with a perfect stranger. But in this case, she was eager to be rid of him, so a liberal dose of frankness might stand her in good stead.

"In my experience marriage usually leads to unhappiness for a woman," she said honestly.

"You speak from personal experience?"

Lily made a face. "Unfortunately, yes. My parents' union was hostile enough to give me an aversion to matrimony for life."

The gleaming light in Claybourne's eyes faded as he studied her. His searching perusal was more unsettling than his amusement, however.

"I don't need a husband," she hurried to add, "despite what proper society decrees for young ladies. I am financially independent now, thanks to the generous settlement Marcus made me. So I can have a fulfilling life without having to marry."

"Yet you implied you wanted more freedom."

She smiled uncertainly. "True." Her dream had always been to escape to a life of freedom and adventure. "I mean to use the funds to travel the world and explore new and exciting places."

"Alone?"

"Lady Hester Stanhope did it," Lily pointed out, mentioning the adventurous earl's daughter and niece of William Pitt the Younger who had sailed to the Middle East and eventually joined a settlement of Arab tribesmen.

"So she did. But she was significantly older than you."

"I am one and twenty, old enough to take care of myself."

"So . . . you won't marry because men often make their wives unhappy," Claybourne said slowly, as if testing the theory in his mind.

"Yes. First you make us too infatuated to think clearly, so we give over all control to you, and then you make our lives a misery." Unconsciously Lily ground her teeth. "I think it abominable that husbands have the *legal* right to be villainous toward their wives. I am not about to give any man that power over me."

To her surprise, Claybourne leaned forward and raised a hand to touch her cheek. "Who hurt you, angel?" he asked quietly.

Discomfited, Lily drew back. "No one hurt *me*. It was my mother who was hurt. And my eldest sister also, for that matter."

He was silent for a moment. "I understand your father was a champion philanderer."

Lily looked away, not wanting to recall the painful memories. "He was indeed. He flaunted his mistresses before my mother at every opportunity. It hurt her terribly. And Arabella's first betrothed betrayed her almost as badly. Belle *loved* him, but when my parents' scandal broke, he ended their engagement out of hand."

Lily was certain Lord Claybourne knew all about the terrible scandals that had befallen her family four years ago. First their mother had taken a lover because she was unable to endure her unhappy marriage any longer, and then was forced to flee to the Continent by her outraged husband. A fortnight later their libertine father gambled away the last of his fortune and was killed in a duel over one of his mistresses. The Loring sisters had been left penniless and homeless, at the mercy of their curmudgeonly step-uncle, the Earl of Danvers, who had taken them in most grudgingly.

"Is that why you didn't want Marcus marrying your sister?"

"In large part."

"You seem to harbor a strong prejudice against noblemen."

"I won't deny it. Noblemen can make the worst sort of husbands."

"Then I can take heart from the fact that your aversion is not directed at me personally."

Her brows drew together. "No, I have nothing against you *personally,* my lord. I don't even know you." *Thankfully,* she added to herself.

Claybourne remained silent for another dozen heartbeats before shifting his position to study the box's inhabitants. "I take it this is Boots," he murmured, reaching down to scratch the mother cat behind one ear. Surprisingly Boots didn't object but started purring at once, rubbing her head sensuously against his fingers.

Lily found her gaze riveted on his lordship's hands as he stroked the silky gray fur. He had strong, graceful hands, surprising in such a bold, masculine man.

"I think you are forgetting one important fact," he said finally.

She didn't immediately realize that Lord Claybourne was speaking to her. "What fact?"

"It is true that some men can be hurtful, but they can also give women great pleasure."

Warmth rose to her face. "Perhaps some men can, but that is beside the point."

Just then the black kitten pounced on his cuff and started chewing his knuckle.

"Hungry little fellow, aren't you?" he murmured with a smile. "And you as well," he added as the gray kitten attacked his thumb.

He drew out the tiny creatures, settling them in his lap. Almost at once the black kitten crawled up his chest, digging its claws into the gold brocade of his waistcoat.

"I am sorry, my lord," Lily said regretfully.

"It is no matter." When the black one scampered higher, Claybourne gave a soft laugh. The low, husky sound raked across Lily's nerve endings with undeniable potency.

"Here, let me help . . ." she hastened to say.

Leaning forward, she reached out to pluck the kitten off his chest, but the curling claws clung to his cravat. Lily tried to extricate the tiny claws from the fine fabric without damaging it and somehow wound up pushing the marquess back in the straw.

He lay there, looking up at her. Leaning over him, Lily froze at the expression on his face. He had gone quite still, but there was a soft fire in his eyes that made her heart beat faster.

"I am sorry," she repeated, suddenly breathless.

"I am not."

His fingers closing gently around the tiny black paws, he managed to free his cravat and set the kitten in the straw beside him. Immediately it bounded off toward the box, and the gray went scrambling after its littermate.

Even so, Lily couldn't look away from Lord Claybourne. When he reached up and slid his fingers behind her nape, her breathing faltered altogether. Then shockingly, he drew her mouth down to meet his in a featherlight contact.

She was unprepared for the rush of sensation that shot through her at the unexpected caress; his lips were warm and firm yet enticingly soft at the same time—and much too tempting.

Stifling a gasp, Lily pressed her palms against his chest and lifted her reeling head. "W-why did you do that?" she asked, her voice suddenly hoarse.

"I wanted to see if your lips were as inviting as they look."

His reply was not what she expected. "And were they?"

"More so."

Lily stared down at him, unable to move. Her gaze was riveted on his face. It was a strong face, arresting and beautiful in the muted glow of lamplight. He had a beautiful mouth also, even though she hadn't let herself acknowledge it before. His lips were chiseled and generous, and they curved now in a faint smile as he returned her regard.

"I expect you have no idea what you are missing, sweetheart. Passion between a man and a woman can be quite remarkable."

Lily cleared her suddenly dry throat, fighting her enchanted stupor. "Even so, I don't care to have anything to do with passion."

"What do you know about it? Have you ever even been properly kissed?"

Her brow furrowed cautiously. "What do you mean by 'properly'?"

His quiet chuckle was soft, husky, as he drew her face down to his again. "If you have to ask, the answer must be no. I think we should rectify the deficiency at once. . . ."

As the warm mist of his breath caressed her mouth, Lily braced herself for the renewed shock, but when his lips began to play over hers with exquisite pressure, she felt her resistance melting.

The effect of his kiss was spellbinding. The heady sensation he roused made her light-headed and giddy, much like the effect of the champagne.

When he left off this time, he reached up and stroked her cheek with a finger. "Did you find that pleasurable, sweeting?"

She couldn't utter a denial for it would be a lie. His kiss had left her breathless and dazed, and she felt a strange quivering between her thighs, a restless ache low and deep in her feminine center. "Y-yes."

"You sound unsure."

"It was . . . quite pleasant."

His mouth curved wryly. "Merely pleasant? I think I should be insulted."

"You know you needn't be. You are said to be a devil with the ladies, and you have countless conquests—" She paused, shaking her head in a futile effort to clear it. "At least now I can understand why everyone says women adore you."

"Who says so?"

"Fanny."

"Fanny Irwin? Ah yes, I recall your sister Arabella mentioning that you were childhood friends with Miss Irwin."

Fanny was one of the most sought-after courtesans in London. But as one of their dearest friends, she had attended Arabella's wedding celebrations today, much to the dismay of the ton's high sticklers.

Lily desperately wished Fanny were here now to advise her. How had she gotten herself into such a fix? What was she doing here in a secluded loft with this utterly beguiling stranger? Somehow she was sprawled all over Lord Claybourne, pressed against his hard, muscular body. Warmth radiated up from his chest, infusing her breasts with a delicious heaviness.

And that was *before* he raised a finger to the hollow of her throat and lightly stroked. "I think I should demonstrate."

"Demonstrate what?" she asked unsteadily.

His eyes smiled into hers. "The kind of pleasure a man can give a woman."

Her heart started thudding harder as he made good on his declaration. His hand cupping the back of her head, he drew her close again . . . yet this time his kiss held an even more delectable pressure. *This* kiss was slow and erotic and extremely thorough; parting her lips, his tongue slid into her mouth, creating an intense yearning inside her that only added to her light-headedness.

Lily fought the powerful urges in her body. Her head was still spinning from the champagne, but that didn't explain her overwhelming feelings of desire or her deplorable attraction to the seductive marquess.

She couldn't resist letting him continue, though. Not when he was assailing her mouth with such throat-stopping languor . . . molding, tasting, teasing. All her senses felt assaulted as his tongue stroked provocatively against hers, tangling in a sensual dance.

With a sound between a sigh and a whimper, Lily surrendered.

In response, his kiss only deepened.

Helplessly she raised her hand to his sun-streaked brown hair, which was amazingly thick and silky. His own hand cradled her throat, then slid lower to where the square decolletage of her evening gown exposed a generous amount of bare skin.

When his knuckles skimmed the upper swells of her breasts, Lily tried to draw in a shaky breath of air. But he kept on kissing her, arousing with silky strokes of his tongue, slowly driving, deliciously plundering.

She was achingly aware when he shifted beneath her, for one of his knees separated hers. Through her skirts she felt the pressure of his sinewed thigh against her femininity. At the same time his hand moved lower to lightly cup her breast.

Lily moaned at the feverish surge of pleasure that sensuous caress engendered. She felt overwhelmed with sensation, and when his fingertips discovered her nipple beneath her bodice, fire streaked through her body, flooding her veins with shuddering heat.

She had never felt anything like this captivating man's erotic assault on her senses. He was driving her mad with his caresses, encouraging her response, coaxing her, stirring the wildness that had always clamored in her blood.

Yet it was his tenderness that stunned her most. He knew his own strength, knew how to use it. He could be gentle, tender, that was evident. Moments earlier, the two kittens had swarmed over him, mewling and purring, disarming the caution that she had learned long ago, when she was sixteen.

That should have been a warning, Lily knew. Those

tiny creatures sensed no danger with him, which made him infinitely dangerous to *her*. . . .

Merciful heaven, what was she *doing*? She had to end this now, a desperate voice protested in her head. She couldn't let it continue.

Suddenly pushing against his chest, Lily tore her mouth away from his magical one and sat up. Her breath was coming in rapid bursts while her pulse raced wildly.

"That was quite a . . . demonstration, my lord," she murmured shakily, forcing a lightness to her tone. "But I imagine you were aided by the effects of the champagne." She lifted a hand to her temple. "I should never have drunk so much. I didn't know I would have to defend myself against you."

He didn't reply at once to her complaint. Instead his gaze was fixed on her, measuring, as he slowly pushed himself up on one elbow.

Lily had to look away from his penetrating regard. She still felt dazed, and their passionate bout of kissing had left her yearning for more—devil take him. She had to leave. She didn't trust herself to be alone with Lord Claybourne any longer.

Just then she heard a distant commotion out in the stableyard—the sound of carriages being readied, she realized. Some of the wedding guests would be leaving the ball early to return to London, a half dozen miles away.

"I must go," Lily said quickly, relieved to have an excuse to escape.

It was a moment before he spoke. "Can you make it safely down the ladder?"

"I . . . think so. I am almost sober now."

He corralled the two kittens and deposited them gently back with their mother and sibling. As they scurried down hungrily to root for their dinner, Lily eased her way toward the top of the ladder.

But Lord Claybourne wasn't finished with her, it seemed.

"Wait a moment. You have straw in your hair. You can't return to the ball looking as if you've been trysting in a stable."

Lily shook her head as he moved closer. "It doesn't matter. I am not returning to the ball. I am driving home with my friend, Miss Tess Blanchard, shortly. My sister Roslyn and I mean to spend the night at her house so as to give the newlyweds privacy."

"But you don't want Miss Blanchard to suspect you have been kissing me, do you?"

"Well . . . no."

"Then keep still while I play lady's maid."

Despite her reluctance, Lily obeyed as he plucked the straw from her upswept coiffure. She could feel his fingers in her hair like a soft caress, could feel his gaze lingering on her face.

"I had best hurry," she said as soon as he was done. "Tess will be waiting for me."

He put a hand on her arm. "Allow me to go first in case I must break your fall. I don't want you injuring yourself."

She couldn't argue with that, either, blast him. "Thank you, my lord," Lily murmured, allowing him to move past her.

He climbed down first, pausing partway to wait for her. Lily followed, lowering her feet to the ladder and holding tightly as she turned around to descend backward.

She made it down several steps, but then somehow her foot missed a rung. It was fortunate that Claybourne was below her, for when she slipped, his hand reached up and caught her hip to steady her. Her gasp, however, was due more to his touch on her body than her fear of falling.

"Easy," he murmured, guiding her foot back to the ladder.

The warm feel of his fingers as they wrapped around her ankle unsettled her even further. Unnerved by the intimacy, Lily bit her lip and descended the final rungs as quickly as possible.

"Th-thank you," she repeated as she reached the solid ground of the stable floor.

She remained there a moment, swaying a bit dizzily and trying to regain her composure. She was still shaken by his seductive kisses and eager to pretend that nothing had happened between them.

She expected Lord Claybourne to move away, yet he stood close behind her, his hands spanning her waist. His body felt hot and hard against her back, reminding her of his alluring caresses.

Her breath caught in her throat when he stepped even closer and nestled her buttocks against his groin.

Lily shivered. She knew what that male hardness meant. He was aroused from their brazen intimacy.

She was still keenly aroused as well, she admitted. Her body tingled all over, while the warm yearning in her feminine center continued to throb.

"You may release me, my lord," she whispered hoarsely. "I am quite safe now."

He gave a low, rough chuckle. "You truly think you are safe?"

Her throat went dry. "Please, Lord Claybourne . . ."

"Please what, Lily?" He spoke her name in a husky murmur as he bent his head to nuzzle her ear.

Her head jerked in alarm. "You cannot kiss me again!" she exclaimed, her voice high and breathless.

His exhalation was like a sigh. "I know. I would like nothing more than to climb back up there with you and spend the rest of the night showing you pleasure you've never dreamed of. But it wouldn't be honorable of me to take advantage of you in this weakened state . . . and Marcus would have my head on a platter if I tried."

Lily wasn't certain Marcus would view his role as her protector quite so fiercely. He had never wanted to be saddled with responsibility for the three penniless Loring sisters, and he'd only been their guardian for a few months, since becoming the new Earl of Danvers. Moreover, Marcus no longer technically held the office of guardian now, since he had granted his three wards their legal and financial freedom when Arabella won her wager with him. Yet Lily thought it wiser not to express her doubts to Lord Claybourne.

"So he would," she agreed unevenly.

Finally, after another moment, Claybourne stepped away from her, clearing a path to the stable door.

Grateful to be free, Lily let out the breath she'd been holding and quickly turned away from him. Without looking at him again, she hurried to the door. But then she came to an abrupt halt when she recalled what had driven her to the stable in the first place.

With reluctance, Lily glanced back over her shoulder, meeting his lordship's darkly glimmering eyes. "You must promise me you won't tell Lady Freemantle that I kissed you. If she knew, she would be planning our wedding."

His expression was enigmatic, unreadable, even in the bright glow of latern light. And he hesitated far longer than expected before replying. "Very well, I won't tell her."

Managing a faint smile, Lily picked up her skirts and fled, chiding herself all the way back to the Hall. She should never have let Lord Claybourne kiss her, she knew that now. Not when he was so dangerous to her willpower.

But from now on, Lily vowed earnestly, she would make a concerted effort to avoid him.

She had no choice. For the first time in her life she had met a man who might prove to be irresistible. The wisest thing she could do now was to keep far, far away from the handsome, alluring, seductive Marquess of Claybourne.

Chapter Two

❧

I would be forever grateful if you would allow me to take refuge in your boardinghouse, Fanny. I do not wish Lord Claybourne to find me.

—Lily Loring to Fanny Irwin

After her departure, Heath remained in the stable for quite some time, waiting for his blood to cool before he could return to the ballroom. Sporting a raging arousal when he was wearing satin evening breeches would no doubt appall the refined sensibilities of the wedding guests.

Heath's mouth curled in rueful amusement at the image, yet his smile soon faded.

He hadn't meant to let things go so far with Lilian Loring. Before she'd stopped him, he had been in serious danger of compromising her. But he'd been seduced by the tempting fire of her. Now he could only blame himself if the forbidden indulgence had left him hot and painfully hard.

His attraction wasn't the least surprising, Heath mused, even though he'd only met Lily this morning. For several months now his interest had been piqued by reports of the youngest Loring sister. He hadn't been put off by Marcus's accounts of her being a spitfire and a hellion. On the contrary. His usual pursuits had seemed so deadly dull of late that when he'd finally encountered the spirited, unconventional Lily, his interest had immediately been sparked.

Marcus was right; she was a lively beauty. She was certainly unique. And Heath had found himself unexpectedly enchanted.

Finally considering it safe enough, he left the stable, yet his thoughts were still centered on Lilian Loring as he crossed the yard and headed toward the Danvers Hall manor house.

She was as captivating as her elder sisters but wholly different. Her bold dark eyes and rich, dark-chestnut hair, in addition to her coltish grace, gave Lily a vividness that made her seem vibrant and alive.

She had marvelous eyes, Heath thought as he aimed for the rear terrace that flanked the ballroom. They were lustrous and expressive; warm and laughing one minute, indignant and defiant the next, heavy and slumberous when she was aroused.

She had a mouth like sin, as well. And he knew she would have a luscious body beneath that properly fashionable ball gown . . .

At the sudden memory of exploring her soft warm flesh with his searching fingertips, Heath felt a fresh rush of desire.

"Blast it, man," he swore at himself as he mounted the terrace steps. "You'd best bridle your lust before you do something even more inappropriate with her."

He sure as the devil couldn't deny wanting Lily, though.

Yet admittedly, one of her prime attractions was her laughter. He'd first heard it this morning while waiting at the church with Marcus and Drew for the wedding party to arrive.

When she drove up in the open barouche with her sisters, her laughter had been warm and tender. Later, at the wedding breakfast, it was lilting and musical during her animated conversation with her friends, Fanny Irwin and Miss Tess Blanchard. And then a short while ago, husky and delighted when she was talking to the kittens.

Laughter was important to him. It had been a big part of his childhood—an essential part, the best part—before his mother died when he was ten. His friends, Marcus and Drew, had supplied the laughter since then, all during his boyhood when they'd attended Eton and then Oxford together, and for the past decade as adults. But now that Marcus had taken a wife, that would change to a significant extent—

Cutting off that dark thought, Heath returned to ruminating about Lily Loring as he crossed the terrace. It was only natural that he enjoyed her laughter. But he also liked her forthrightness.

In his experience such honesty was unusual when dealing with females of any stamp. After all the mincing and coy flirtations he'd been subjected to from grasping debutantes over the years, her frankness was profoundly refreshing.

Lily's resistance to him, however, was wholly unexpected. He was not at all accustomed to female indifference. Bold seductions and relentless pursuit were the usual mode. As one of London's most eligible aristocrats, Heath had been the target of countless scheming husband-hunters for well over a decade.

Surprisingly, his disinterest in marriage hadn't stopped women from falling in love with him. Instead, they flocked to him, in large part because he knew how to satisfy their desires. . . .

Of necessity Heath's musings were brought to a halt when he entered the ballroom through one of the rear French doors, the same one he'd exited a half hour before. Almost at once a feminine voice called his name.

To his surprise, he saw Fanny Irwin approaching, as if she had been waiting for his reappearance.

Her expression did not look happy. "My Lord Claybourne," Fanny said in a low voice that held a note of urgency. "Perhaps you would be so kind as to give me a moment of your time?"

"Of course, Miss Irwin—" he started to say when she cut him off.

"In *private*, my lord, if you don't mind."

Although puzzled by her request, Heath had no objection to following her behind a bank of potted palms. He knew from Marcus that Fanny had been the Loring sisters' close neighbor and dearest friend in Hampshire during their childhood. He also knew that she was once a respectable young lady who had left home at sixteen to become one of London's most renowned courtesans. Her success now even rivaled the most fashionable Cyprian of them all, Harriet Wilson. Heath had never patronized Fanny, although he'd seen her at various entertainments they both attended.

The raven-haired, lush-figured Fanny was witty, beautiful, stimulating, and perceptive, and reportedly expert at satisfying her lovers in bed. In short, the ideal mistress.

At the moment, however, there was no sign of her usual sultry affability. Instead, she was surveying him with grave concern.

"I saw you follow Lily from the ballroom, my lord. You cannot deny it."

His brows drew together as he contemplated what he should say in answer. "Very well, I won't deny it, Miss Irwin. But is that a crime?"

"It would be if you seduced her."

Heath felt his gaze sharpen defensively. "My encounter with Miss Loring is a private affair, but you may be assured, I did not seduce her."

"No?" Fanny said acerbically. "It is obvious that you have been employing your usual seductive methods on *someone*. Your hair is tousled and flaked with straw, as if you've just been enjoying a roll in the hay with a farm milkmaid."

She reached up to pluck at a stray wisp from his hair. "Ordinarily I wouldn't dream of interfering with your conquests, Lord Claybourne, but I am Lily's friend, and I cannot sit idly by while you exploit her for your sport."

Heath took a slow breath, controlling his impatience. "I admire your concern for your friend, Miss Irwin, but you have nothing to worry about from me."

"How can I possibly trust your assurances?"

It rankled that she would question his word, yet realizing that Fanny was genuinely troubled, Heath decided to make allowances.

"What would you say if I told you I had just promised Danvers to keep an eye on Miss Loring while he was away on his wedding trip for the next month?"

That much was certainly true, Heath thought. A short while ago, when he and Drew had said farewell to Marcus and reluctantly drunk a toast to the demise of his bachelorhood, Marcus had coerced them into agreeing to look after the two younger sisters while he was gone.

But Fanny did not seem reassured. "*This* is how you

keep an eye on her?" she responded, her tone a bit caustic. "Trysting with Lily in a stable?"

"We weren't seen together, if it is any consolation."

"But someone could have discovered you. With your reputation, just being alone with Lily could give rise to gossip. Given their family history, she is more vulnerable than the usual lady of quality. She and her sisters are finally moving beyond the past scandals now that Lord Danvers has made such a concerted effort to reinstate them into society. But you could so easily ruin her."

"I certainly don't intend to ruin her."

"Then what *are* your intentions toward Lily, my lord?"

It was an impertinent question at the very least. And Heath didn't have an immediate answer, since he wasn't certain himself what his intentions were toward Lily. Before tonight, he would have said *none,* but after kissing her, holding her . . .

Admit it, man, you don't want to give her up. The thought came unbidden and made Heath frown.

When he remained silent, his gaze arrested as he distantly regarded the bank of palms, Fanny continued in a softer, more pleading tone. "You cannot seduce her, my lord. There would be no hope for her then. If you were to compromise her, her only recourse from disgrace would be marriage. And I know Lily quite well. She would never agree to marry you—or anyone else, for that matter."

Slowly he glanced back at Fanny. "What if I said my intentions were entirely honorable?"

Fanny looked startled at that. "Honorable? *You?* You are the worst heartbreaker in England, Lord Claybourne. You aren't the least interested in matrimony . . . *are* you?"

At her obvious shock, Heath's mouth twisted with wry humor. It was true that he had a reputation for breaking hearts, although he wasn't solely to blame for the fact that any number of women had fallen in love with him while he'd kept his heart whole. Although he loved the fair sex in general and delighted in their attentions, he'd never met the woman who could tame him and cause him to willingly relinquish his cherished freedom to settle down in staid matrimony.

But he had never encountered any woman like Lily, either.

"I am not suggesting that I propose this evening," Heath said slowly, testing the prospect in his mind, "but if I were courting her officially, there would be little gossip or risk of scandal."

"I suppose not. But you cannot honestly be thinking of marrying Lily."

"She might make me a good marchioness."

Fanny's laugh was uncertain. "She has the birth and the breeding, true, but you are forgetting one crucial detail. There is no possible way Lily would ever allow you close enough to court her. Not considering her fervent opinions about men and marriage."

Heath couldn't help but smile as he remembered Lily's adamant declaration about her aversion to matrimony. "Her notions *are* rather prickly. I discovered that just on our brief acquaintance."

"Indeed." Fanny shook her head firmly. "No, my lord. You should just abandon the whole absurd idea." Her gaze measured him. "I doubt you will mourn the loss, however. You have countless love-smitten females to pick from. You should choose one of them."

A smile tugged at the corner of his mouth. "But regrettably, I am not interested in any of them."

Fanny's gaze narrowed. "I hope you are not planning to pursue Lily simply because you relish a challenge."

He couldn't deny that the challenge greatly appealed to him. Among his boyhood friends, Heath had been the most adventurous and daring, the most willing to court danger. His need for thrills and excitement had led the three of them into escapades and scrapes more times than he could count. But the challenge Lily presented was not her major allure.

"That is only part of it," he replied honestly to Fanny. "My interest in her is due much more to her uniqueness. I find her novelty refreshing."

"I can see why someone so unconventional as Lily would intrigue you," Fanny said after a moment. "She has no compunction about thumbing her nose at society's strictures regarding the proper behavior of genteel young ladies. Indeed, she often behaves more like a man—she excels at any kind of physical activity such as riding and driving and archery. Compared to her sisters, Lily is the most passionate and expressive. However . . ."—Fanny's voice dropped and became earnest—". . . she is also the most sensitive. Of the three of them, Lily feels the most deeply. She was terribly hurt when her mother abandoned them to follow her heart, heedless of the scandal that ruined their futures. And Lily's bitterness toward men is deeply rooted in the past, in the way her father treated her mother."

He had sensed that vulnerability in her, Heath realized, feeling an odd tug at his heart. The emotion that

stirred in him was not one he usually felt for young
ladies. It wasn't pity, exactly. It was more tenderness.
Along with an undeniable lust that he hadn't experienced in a very long time.

Fanny broke into his thoughts again. "I would
imagine Lily is far more to your tastes than the typical
debutante—possibly enough to consider wooing. But
are you truly serious about matrimony, my lord?"

"A woman like that might induce me to marry," he
said slowly.

Fanny regarded him with worry. "Perhaps so, but I
pray you . . . don't even think about pursuing her unless
you are completely sincere about following through."

"That much I can assure you," Heath said with confidence.

Still looking uncertain, Fanny hesitated a moment
longer. "Thank you, my lord," she said finally. "And I
hope you will forgive me for my unwanted interference,
but I care deeply for Lily and don't want to see her
hurt."

"Your concern is duly noted, Miss Irwin," Heath
replied, keeping his tone easy. "But I am not in the habit
of hurting women."

A smile flickered on her lips. "Not intentionally, I
know. Indeed, your reputation for giving pleasure is legendary. But unintentionally? Please . . . just take care
with her, my lord."

"I will, I assure you."

With that, Fanny gave him a respectful curtsy and left
him.

Coming out from behind the palms, Heath returned
to stand on the ballroom sidelines, absently watching
the dancers. The Danvers wedding ball was a crush by

anyone's standards. The press of perfumed bodies, along with the candle flames from myriad glittering chandeliers, made the warmth of the ballroom oppressive. But the guests were clearly enjoying themselves.

Heath paid little attention to the gaiety and noise around him, however. His thoughts were too focused on his recent conversation about his matrimonial intentions.

Was he truly serious about pursuing Lily Loring?

Fanny's dire prediction didn't concern him overmuch, since he had always been able to have any woman he wanted. And he most definitely wanted Lily. If he set his mind to winning her, he was certain he could have her.

But did he want to win her?

His only option was marriage, of course. Seducing her was out of the question. His own honor wouldn't allow it, not to mention the certainty that Marcus would cut out his liver along with other more sensitive parts of his anatomy.

Until Marcus's engagement, he hadn't thought seriously of marriage. In fact, he'd earnestly avoided it, eluding the traps of countless matchmaking mamas and their grasping young darlings who saw him as prey.

He liked women immensely; he just had never wanted to be tied to a particular one, having her forever by his side until death did them part.

But perhaps it was time that he contemplated a foray into matrimony, Heath realized. He would eventually have to settle down to produce heirs to carry on his illustrious title, in any event. Just as Marcus had done.

Quite unexpectedly, Marcus had been the first to take the plunge. Before inheriting the earldom and assuming guardianship for the three impoverished Loring sisters,

Marcus had absolutely no desire to end his precious bachelorhood. In fact, he'd planned to discharge his unwanted duty as guardian by marrying his wards off to respectable suitors, despite their fierce objections. But his initial attraction to the beautiful eldest, Arabella, was so fierce that he'd wagered he could persuade her to accept his proposal of marriage—a wager that Arabella was just as determined he would lose. After several weeks of spirited battle, they had both fallen deeply in love.

Heath was sincerely pleased for his friend. It was not usual for a nobleman to find love and happiness in marriage. In the normal order of things, the aristocracy made unions of convenience to insure the best alliances of fortunes and bloodlines.

It was what his own parents had done, as had all the generations of his family before them.

Heath was not prepared to do the same. His parents' union had been such a wretched mismatch in terms of personalities and interests, he'd vowed he would never follow in their footsteps.

If he had to marry, he wanted a woman who could match him in the ways that counted most . . . in spirit and passion, in a craving for adventure.

Lily Loring might very well fit that bill.

Even her stubborn need for independence was appealing to him, Heath mused. He understood that need, for he felt it himself.

And admittedly, of late he'd begun to envy Marcus's newfound happiness. All his own relationships with women had been based on physical pleasure and mutual satisfaction, but he might relish having the kind of love and intimacy that Marcus now shared with his new bride. Marriage to a woman he could respect and enjoy and cherish.

In many other ways, Lily Loring would make a fitting candidate for his wife. Her birth and breeding, for one. More importantly, she would rarely bore him and would doubtless prove a delight in his bed.

Unquestionably he found her highly desirable, with her dark eyes, that lush mouth, those ripe breasts, her silken hair that shimmered with shades of russet and gold. Something about her called to him . . . something complex and compelling. Perhaps the way she pulsed with life and vitality. There was an inner fire to her, a fire that stoked the one inside him.

She was compassionate as well, Heath reflected. How many ladies of her elite station would concern themselves with the fate of the stable cat and kittens?

And there was that undeniable twinge of tenderness that kept pricking at his heart each time he learned something new about her.

Yes, Lily was suitable—and suitably intriguing enough—for him to consider wooing. Although most certainly he would need to use every ounce of charm and skill he possessed to overcome her reticence. She was afraid to give herself to any man in marriage, to trust that she wouldn't be hurt.

She wasn't cold-natured in the least, however. She only needed awakening. Heath knew that in his gut, had felt it in her innocently sensual kisses. Lily had responded to his embrace as if she'd never wanted before, never needed before.

She'd been shocked by the erotic fire between them, he could see it in her flushed cheeks and dazed eyes. He'd been more than a little jolted himself.

He couldn't recall ever being that powerfully, that savagely, attracted to anyone. She'd had a profound impact on his equilibrium.

At the recollection, Heath muttered a low oath. Remembering that passionate interlude in the loft with Lily was enough to arouse him again, so he turned away from the ballroom guests to hide the consequences.

And yet he couldn't regret the effect Lily had on him. It had been a very long time since he'd felt the rush of anticipation and expectation that was pumping through his blood now. An even longer time since his pulse had quickened at just the thought of coming to know a woman more intimately.

And as he stepped through the French doors onto the terrace so that the cooler night air could help calm his lust, Heath knew he had made his decision. He would pursue the enchanting Lily and see where a courtship could lead.

And if matrimony was the result? Well, he no longer found the prospect quite so unsettling or intimidating.

Indeed—amazingly enough—not intimidating at all.

"Perhaps I should come in just for a moment," Tess Blanchard said the next morning as she brought her gig to a halt before Danvers Hall's front entrance.

"No," Lily replied. "You are already dreadfully late for your appointment. I'm certain my sister is fine."

With a faint smile at her friend, Lily gingerly stepped down from the gig. She was exceedingly glad to be home, for several reasons. First, her head was throbbing from her lamentable overindulgence in champagne at the ball the previous evening. Second, her conscience was throbbing just as painfully. She hadn't slept much

last night at Tess's house; instead she'd been busy tossing and turning and mentally writhing at the memory of
the Marquess of Claybourne kissing her witless—and
her returning his enthralling kisses like a total wanton.

And finally, this morning they'd learned the dismaying news that her sister Roslyn and her friend Winifred,
Lady Freemantle had been the victims of a highway robbery shortly after leaving the ball.

Roslyn had not come to Tess's last night as planned,
but sent a dismaying note this morning explaining her
absence. Alarmed, Lily and Tess had immediately driven
to Freemantle Park, only to learn that Roslyn had already returned home to Danvers Hall. Winifred proceeded to detail the shocking events and claimed that
Roslyn had suffered no lasting effects, but Lily wanted
to see her sister for herself.

She went to the boot to unload her valise, not mind-
ing that no footmen or butler came out to help her. The
household staff was doubtless cleaning up after the massive wedding celebrations.

The bridal couple would have set out on their wedding journey by now, Lily knew. No one intended to tell
Arabella and Marcus about the robbery, since they
would likely have postponed their trip, and Roslyn was
adamant that her troubles not intrude on their hard-
won happiness.

Looking up, Lily offered Tess another brief smile.
"Thank you for letting me spend the night and for
bringing me home."

"You know you are welcome," Tess said warmly as
she gathered the reins. "I shall return shortly to see
Roslyn. Despite Winifred's reassurances, the experience
cannot have been pleasant for her."

"I will tell her to expect you for luncheon."

Tess was about to snap the reins at her horse when the sound of a carriage could be heard in the distance. Glancing beyond the gig, Lily spied a team and curricle sweeping up the gravel drive, driven by a lone gentleman garbed in a fashionable frock coat and tall beaver hat.

Her heart suddenly jolted when she recognized those splendid shoulders, and she voiced an oath under her breath. "What the devil is *he* doing here?"

"That is Lord Claybourne, is it not?" Tess asked.

"Regrettably, yes."

His lordship was the very last person she wanted to see, Lily thought as she stood there cursing her ill luck. If only she had arrived home five minutes earlier, she could have had the butler deny her presence at home. But now she would have to face Lord Claybourne when she was still flustered by the memory of his brazen kisses. And she was in no mood to do it alone.

"Please, Tess, stay another moment. Don't leave me here with him."

Her friend looked puzzled. "Do you not wish to see him?"

But there was no time to answer as the marquess expertly guided his team alongside Lily and brought the curricle to a halt.

Lily took a steadying breath as she locked gazes with him. She was much more herself this morning, in a rational state of mind. Or at least she was sober now. Without her head swimming, she could withstand his appeal.

Except that in the cold light of day, Lord Claybourne was still as devastatingly handsome as he'd been last night. And his slow smile was just as heart-melting as he greeted them both with a bow. "Good morning, ladies."

Deploring her stomach-tightening awareness, Lily managed a cool smile, although there was a breathless quality to her voice when she spoke. "What brings you here, my lord?"

"Why, I am merely paying you a morning call."

Her eyebrow rose. "You came all the way from London to call on me?"

He shrugged one powerful shoulder. "With a fast team, it is not much more than a half-hour drive. And these beauties"—he indicated the two grays before him—"are lightning fast."

His team was indeed magnificent, Lily noted in silent admiration. Obviously high-spirited but trained well enough to stand patiently while waiting for their master's commands.

But that didn't explain why Claybourne thought he had to call on her. "You should not have troubled yourself, my lord."

"It was no trouble. I've brought you a basket from my chef."

She looked at him blankly. "Your chef?"

"A few delicacies for Boots, and a remedy for your headache. I would imagine after last night your skull feels as if a drum took up residence inside."

Lily couldn't help but be impressed by his thoughtfulness, yet she was not about to let him know it.

"I imagine you speak from experience?" she said dryly.

"Of course."

Tendering her a grin of knee-weakening charm, he held up the basket. In order to take it, Lily had to set down her valise, which she did reluctantly.

"You are too kind," she said with forced politeness as

she accepted his offering. "Boots will no doubt appreciate your generosity. But you should not have come, my lord. And most certainly you should not be bringing me gifts."

"Why not, Miss Loring?"

Lily felt exasperation rise inside her. Lord Claybourne was being deliberately obtuse, since she had clearly warned him about Winifred's matchmaking machinations. "You know very well why not. Did you not hear a word I said last night?"

"Yes, I heard every word."

When Tess's gaze shifted between them at the undercurrents of tension vibrating the air, Lily modulated her tone, realizing she would do better to pretend indifference.

"Then you should have heeded my warning," she said more evenly. "You cannot bring me gifts without giving rise to speculation. Lady Freemantle will be in raptures."

"Lady Freemantle doesn't concern me."

"She will think you are courting me."

"So?"

At the casual question, Lily stared at him. "S-so . . ." She stammered to a halt as she understood his implication, since words failed her. "You cannot possibly be thinking of courting me."

"I beg to differ."

From his mild expression, he didn't appear to be ribbing her, yet he couldn't be serious.

"Lord Claybourne . . . that is absurd. You don't wish to wed me, and I most certainly don't wish to wed you."

His hazel eyes regarded her steadily. "How will we

know unless we explore the issue? And for that we must have the chance to improve our acquaintance."

He was making her unsettled now, and extremely vexed. Lily narrowed her gaze on him. "I don't know what sort of game you are playing, my lord, but I do not care for it in the least."

"It is no game, angel."

Lily tightened her jaw. "The polite response would be to thank you, Lord Claybourne, but—"

"But you are not the polite kind," he interrupted, his eyes dancing with provocative humor.

"No I am not!"

She could see Tess's brow furrow at her terse reply. Lily had little patience for the social niceties, but she was never overtly *rude*. She wasn't certain how to deal with a seductive nobleman showing her such marked attention, either.

He flashed her a lazy smile. "I am willing to make allowances for your testiness, Miss Loring, since I know the cause."

You are the cause of my testiness, Lily thought in frustration. *Not the aftereffects of the champagne.*

She wanted to be rid of the provoking marquess. Fortunately she had an ideal excuse. Drawing another calming breath, Lily forced a cool smile. "I would invite you to come in for refreshments, my lord, but I don't have time to entertain you this morning. I need to find my sister Roslyn and make certain she is all right. After the robbery last night, she will likely have little desire for company."

Lord Claybourne frowned at that. "What robbery?"

"Oh, hadn't you heard?" Lily felt a bit more confident now that she wasn't quite so much on the defensive.

"Last night Roslyn stayed late to direct the servants in setting the Hall to rights after the ball. Afterward, Lady Freemantle was driving her to Miss Blanchard's house when their coach was held up by a highwayman at gunpoint barely a mile from here."

His brows snapped together. "Were either of them hurt?" The sharpness of his tone was gratifying, Lily thought.

"Thankfully, no. But the footpad was likely wounded. The Duke of Arden happened along in time to foil the robbery and shoot the fleeing brigand. And now there is a massive search out for him."

"Where is Arden now?"

"At Freemantle Park. He stayed the night there to give comfort to Lady Freemantle and my sister. Perhaps you might wish to speak to him yourself."

Still frowning, Claybourne made no reply, and Lily realized that her gaze had somehow wandered to his mouth. She felt heat tinge her cheekbones as she recalled how the magic of that sensual mouth had burned into hers. . . .

Jerking her unruly thoughts back to the present, she said pointedly, "I am certain you don't want to keep your horses standing any longer, Lord Claybourne."

His frown easing, he raised an eyebrow at her. "Are you dismissing me, Miss Loring?"

Lily couldn't help but smile at his arch tone. No doubt a nobleman of his rank and consequence was rarely given a dismissal. "Make of it what you will, but you do not strike me as lacking in understanding."

His mouth quirked. "Perhaps you're right. I should speak to Arden and see if I can be of assistance. But I am not letting you off the hook so easily, sweeting. I will return at a more convenient time so that we may become better acquainted."

Lily eyed him in dismay. "There will never be a convenient time."

"Then I shall simply have to persuade you otherwise."

He had an utterly devastating smile, she thought, vexed at her own response. But no doubt he was well aware of his appeal, how irresistible he was to women.

When he picked up the reins and gave his grays the office to move forward, Lily held her breath, only letting it out when his lordship drove off. She was vastly relieved by his departure, but dismayed by his promise to return.

She was still watching his retreat when Tess's voice broke into her distracted thoughts.

"Do you plan to tell me what that was all about, Lily? I trust you had good reason for your incivility."

With a start, Lily offered her friend an apologetic look, having forgotten Tess was even there. "Indeed, I had good reason. I warned him that Winifred was doing her best to pair us together, but he completely disregarded my warning."

"What happened between you last night?"

"Well . . ." Lily hesitated. She would rather not have to confess about her wantonness in the stable loft with the marquess, yet she didn't like to keep secrets from her dear friend. "I encountered his lordship just before I left the ball with you. I had drunk three glasses of champagne because I was feeling sad at losing Arabella, so I'm afraid I was rather foxed when he found me."

Tess's gaze sharpened. "He didn't try to take advantage of you?"

"No . . . not exactly. But I may have tried to take advantage of *him*." Her mouth curved ruefully. "I wasn't thinking too clearly at the time. I fear I acted something of a wanton and gave Claybourne the mistaken impression that I am lacking in morals. And you saw the result this morning. I don't want him presuming he can add me to his long list of conquests."

"I imagine his intentions are more honorable than that," Tess replied with dry amusement. "He drove all this way to pay you a formal morning call. A gentleman doesn't do that if he has a nefarious purpose in mind."

"He *does* have a nefarious purpose in mind." Lily retorted. "You heard him just now. He intends to court me!"

Tess pursed her lips as if biting back a smile. "Lily, there is nothing criminal about him wanting to become better acquainted with you."

"There is if he thinks our closer acquaintance will lead to marriage."

Tess laughed outright at that, which made Lily grind her teeth. "This is not at all funny, Tess!"

"Actually it is, dearest. Not that Claybourne may be in the market for a wife, but that he seems willing to consider *you* for the position. If he knew your feelings on the subject of matrimony—"

"He *does* know my feelings. I told him so last night in no uncertain terms."

Tess's expression sobered. "Would it be so terrible to entertain his suit for a time? You are limiting your future significantly if you won't even consider the possibility of marriage."

Lily grimaced. "You only think so because you are a hopeless romantic—which I am not."

"He seems extremely charming."

"He is that." *And much too seductive,* Lily added to herself. Yet she had an entirely different plan for her future than marriage. A plan that did *not* include becoming the chattel of a husband, putting herself under his lawful control. Besides, no matter how charming and seductive and handsome a gentleman might appear on the surface, looks could be highly deceiving—as her own father had conclusively proved.

"Lord Claybourne's charm is entirely beside the point," Lily stated resolutely. "Nothing could tempt me to wed him, so there is no reason for him even to try to court me."

"So what do you mean to do about him then? I seriously doubt a man like Claybourne will give up easily."

That question stumped Lily. "I have no earthly idea." She had never encountered this sort of predicament, having to deal with a nobleman who might actually wish to marry her.

"Well," Tess commented at her silence, "I must go for now, Lily. As you said, I am dreadfully late for my appointment. But I promise I will return later and help you sort this all out."

"Yes, go, please. Your meeting is much more important."

Tess spent most of her time doing charitable works, focusing her efforts primarily on the Families of Fallen Soldiers, since she had tragically lost her betrothed to war two years ago at Waterloo. And she was currently occupied in persuading the local gentry to contribute to her cause.

When Tess had gone, Lily picked up her valise and his lordship's gift basket and turned to mount the front steps of the manor.

Recalling her friend's amused response to the prospect of Claybourne courting her, Lily shook her head in consternation. The notion might indeed have been humorous if it wasn't so alarming.

She knew she would be too vulnerable to him if she remained here at Danvers Hall while Arabella and Marcus were away on their monthlong wedding journey. Dealing with a nobleman like Claybourne was beyond her experience. He was completely, dangerously unlike any man she had ever known, with his easy smile, his heart-stirring charm, his breathtaking sensuality.

Yet she was not about to sit here waiting to be the victim of his unwanted courtship. She had to take action. If for no other reason than to prove that she was her own woman, in control of her own destiny.

Come now, be honest with yourself, a nagging voice in Lily's head chided. *You are afraid you will let your reckless nature lead you astray. That you will surrender to his unquestionable allure.*

A pained smile tugged at her mouth. That was the real trouble, Lily acknowledged unwillingly. The deplorable truth was, she didn't trust her ability to resist Lord Claybourne if he became her suitor. He would simply be too tempting.

Perhaps she would do well to leave home for a time. But where to go? Now that she had ample funds, she could pay a visit to her former neighbors and friends in Hampshire, but she had little desire to travel all that distance and be compelled to remain away from home like a fugitive.

What about going to London to stay with Fanny? Not Fanny's main residence where she plied her courtesan trade, of course. But she owned a boardinghouse in

London. . . . Coincidentally, they had discussed it just last night at the wedding ball.

Lily frowned as she let herself in the front entrance door. Fanny had not been her usual vivacious self at the ball, and when pressed, she'd confessed that she was worried about two of her close friends who were having financial difficulties.

Lily had pondered their problem during her sleepless night of tossing and turning, but she hadn't come up with any bright ideas for earning nearly thirty thousand pounds.

Perhaps by going to London, she might help Fanny determine a way to aid her friends, and solve her own problem of eluding Lord Claybourne at the same time.

It certainly deserved some serious consideration, Lily decided as she turned her valise and basket over to a footman and went in search of her sister Roslyn.

She found Roslyn in the morning room, cataloging the vast array of wedding gifts the guests had sent to the Earl of Danvers and his new countess, Arabella. Fortunately, Roslyn professed to be perfectly fine after her ordeal.

Despite her assurances, however, Lily wished she could have been there to help her sister last night, especially since *she* was probably better able to face down an armed highwayman. She at least knew how to fire a pistol with fair accuracy . . . although she was well aware that Roslyn's delicate golden looks were deceptive. There was a vein of fine steel in her sister's elegant aristocratic spine. And according to Winifred, Roslyn had comported herself with remarkable courage, saving her ladyship from being robbed of one particularly cherished piece of jewelry.

"It sounds as if you were very brave," Lily said after hearing Roslyn's abbreviated version of the tale.

"I was frightened out of my mind," Roslyn replied dryly. "But at least no one was harmed."

"Except for the brigand. I understand Winifred's bailiff has initiated a search for a wounded man."

Roslyn nodded. "Yes, although we don't hold out much hope of finding him." She studied Lily in turn. "Are you certain you are all right, Lily? You look as if something has upset you."

Though knowing her cheeks were still flushed from her encounter with Lord Claybourne, Lily decided not to confide the reason for her high color. Roslyn had enough to worry her, recovering from a highway robbery after nearly being shot. And she had worked her fingers to the bone for weeks, planning and preparing for Arabella's wedding celebrations.

And admittedly, Lily thought with a tinge of guilt, she didn't want to confess about her foolish lapse in judgment last night. After all her vows of never wanting anything to do with eligible noblemen, it smacked of hypocrisy to have enjoyed Lord Claybourne's stunning kisses so much.

"I am not upset," Lily replied. "I merely have a touch of the headache, and having Tess drive me home in her gig didn't help."

She told her sister about getting foxed on champagne, leaving out the part about being in the stable loft afterward.

But as usual, Roslyn was too perceptive. "Is that all that is wrong, Lily?"

She bit back a sigh, knowing she would have to offer

some valid explanation. "Well, perhaps not *all*. Winifred is still driving me to distraction with her maddening attempts at matchmaking."

"I know," Roslyn agreed wholeheartedly. "I was her target last night and again this morning. You were right about her wanting to pair me with Arden. It was mortifying in the extreme."

"Well, I don't intend to remain here to become Winifred's hapless victim," Lily said, coming to a decision. "I mean go to London and stay at Fanny's lodging house. She has room, and she has asked my advice in dealing with two of her friends who operate the house. I don't know if I can help them, but I would like to try."

Roslyn stared at her in surprise. "You intend to hide out in London in order to elude Winifred's matchmaking schemes? Are such drastic measures really necessary?"

Lily returned a wry grimace. "I am beginning to think so. If I can't be found, then I needn't worry about any unwanted suitors, do I? I cannot stay here in Chiswick, obviously. And no one will think to look for me at Fanny's place, including Marcus. You know he would not approve of my intimacy with her scandalous friends."

And Lord Claybourne will never find me there either. Relieved by the notion, Lily suddenly thought of another way to throw the marquess off her track and instantly felt more cheerful. "I have it! You can tell Winifred and anyone else who inquires that I have gone to Hampshire to visit friends at our old home."

Roslyn's brows drew together in puzzlement. "Why would you want her to think—"

She cut off her sister, not wanting to admit how irresistible she found the marquess. "Please, Rose, just humor me this once."

Roslyn's gaze became searching. "Lily . . . is there more you aren't telling me?"

"Not at all. Don't worry about me, dearest. It is nothing I cannot handle." Lily smiled reassuringly before adding under her breath, "I simply have absolutely no intention of allowing any man to court me, let alone wed me."

She had held that adamant view since she was sixteen, Lily reflected when eventually she left her sister and went upstairs to her bedchamber to unpack her valise and then pack again for an unexpected visit to London.

She'd sworn she would never let herself become so vulnerable—to be helplessly trapped in matrimony, at the mercy of her husband's whims, unable to escape. If a woman married, she legally *belonged* to her husband; she was his property to treat as brutally as he pleased. She would *never* give any man that power over her, Lily vowed.

Nor would she ever give her heart away, only to have it cruelly crushed, the way her mother had done in her first marriage, and as Arabella had done in her first, short-lived betrothal.

Thankfully, Arabella seemed to have a genuine chance for love and happiness with Marcus now, Lily admitted to herself, remembering the gentleness in their hands when they touched each other, the tender look in their eyes when they shared loving glances. And her mother professed to have finally found happiness in her second marriage with her French lover, Henri Vachel.

As far as Lily was concerned, however, marriage was

an odious word. She doubted she would ever overcome her lack of faith in men.

And she didn't need anyone but her sisters and her friends to be happy. She was mistress of her own life and content to stay that way forever. She knew what she wanted for her future, and it was *not* being shackled to a husband who would hurt her and betray her and use his power against her and make her so miserable that she cried into her pillow every night, the way her father had done her mother.

And now that she had her own modest fortune, Lily reminded herself, she could indulge in her long-held dreams. From the time she could read, she had pored over history tomes and geological maps and expedition accounts, in part as a way to escape her parents' battles. She had longed for the day when she could take control of her life; when she could fulfill her desire to travel the world and explore unknown lands and experience new adventures.

Oh, she might have someday liked to have children to love and cherish, but she would leave that to Arabella, and perhaps Roslyn. For herself, Lily was satisfied with teaching at the Freemantle Academy for Young Ladies, molding girls on the cusp of womanhood to stand up for themselves, despite their merchant-class origins, and providing them with skills to compete in the haughty world of the ton.

She had few duties at the Academy during the summer term, however, since most of the pupils had returned home to their families. So this was an ideal time to go to London—in more ways than one.

Most definitely she would be glad to escape Lord Claybourne's unwanted attentions. And she would find it very satisfying if she could help Fanny's fellow Cyprians solve their financial problems.

Just as gratifying, Lily reflected with a small frisson of pleasure, she would be starting a brand new chapter in her life. Now that the wedding celebrations were finally over, she could begin charting her own course for a life of freedom and adventure.

By the time Tess arrived and joined Lily in her bedchamber, she had written a note to Fanny, which she'd sent off to London by messenger, and had nearly finished packing.

"Roslyn doesn't seem to have suffered from her ordeal, thankfully," Tess said, taking a seat in a side chair. "But she tells me you are planning an excursion to London."

"Yes," Lily replied as she rummaged through her wardrobe for the final items she would need for an extended stay. "I mean to leave this afternoon."

"Surely that is a bit rash—fleeing home so you can escape Lord Claybourne's attentions."

"Not at all. But in truth, I have another very good reason to go. Fanny is in a bit of financial difficulty."

Tess frowned. "What sort of difficulty?"

"It is a matter of gambling debts, although not Fanny's. This past spring two of her oldest courtesan friends lost enormous sums at the Faro tables, and the gaming hell owner is demanding repayment now. Fanny is trying to keep her friends out of debtors' prison, or worse."

"You are speaking of Fleur and Chantel?"

"Yes. They took Fanny under their wing when she first came to London eight years ago, so she is not about to abandon them." Lily glanced back at Tess. "I didn't want to mention their troubles to Roslyn, for then she would feel obliged to get involved, and she deserves to rest after all her endeavors. But I hope to help Fanny myself."

Tess's frown deepened. "And you intend to stay at Fanny's rooming house? Lily, that place is little more than a home for lightskirts, run by two famous Cyprians."

"I suppose so."

Fleur Delee and Chantel Amour had been the most celebrated courtesans of their day, but they had passed their prime long ago and were now in their sixth decade. When their careers had waned and they'd had difficulty supporting themselves, Fanny had bought a large mansion to provide them a home. Not wanting to be a burden, they offset expenses by taking in boarders, mainly other members of the demimonde.

"But that," Lily explained, "is precisely why their boardinghouse could be an ideal hiding place for me. Claybourne is unlikely to find me there. And if he should happen to learn where I've gone"—Lily smiled a little—"I expect he will be too scandalized to discover me living with lightskirts to want me for his future marchioness."

Tess shook her head in exasperation. "You could be asking for trouble."

That comment made Lily laugh. "I wouldn't mind a bit of trouble to enliven my life. Indeed, that is part of my plan's charm. I mean to look upon it as an adventure . . . the first of many, I hope."

"You couldn't find another adventure besides taking up with Fanny's notorious friends?"

Lily arched an eyebrow. "You don't expect me to keep

away from them because of any prudish notions I ought to have?"

"I suspect," Tess said dryly, "there isn't a prudish bone in your body. But aren't you the least concerned about your reputation?"

"Not overmuch. I doubt I will be recognized, since I know few people in London. And I intend to remain as inconspicuous as possible."

"I should hope so. Advertising your presence there would not be good for your sisters—or for your continued career at the Academy, either."

"Indeed. So I must keep my location a secret. I will take refuge there and tell the world I have gone to visit my former home in Hampshire. Only you and Roslyn will know where I truly am. Certainly I don't want Winifred to know."

"You intend to deceive her?" Tess asked in surprise.

Lily's smile turned rueful. "I fear I have no choice. Otherwise she will doubtless tell the marquess I am in London, and then he will likely call on me there, and I don't want to have to deal with him. So you must help Winifred misdirect him and throw him off my trail."

Tess finally laughed. "Very well, if you insist. But just remember, I warned you. Is there anything I may do to help you prepare?"

"No, thank you. But you and Roslyn could handle my few classes at the Academy, if you don't mind?"

"Of course I don't mind. You have done the same for me numerous times."

Lily smiled, glad that her obligations would be taken care of. And their elderly butler, Simpkin, could be trusted to look after Boots and the kittens. She would say farewell to the felines before she set out for London this afternoon.

At the thought, Lily felt a swell of anticipation bubble up inside her. Living with Fanny's Cyprian friends should indeed prove an interesting adventure.

And in the meantime, she wouldn't be bedeviled by a handsome, devastatingly charming nobleman or have to worry about fending off his unwanted, thoroughly bewildering desire to court her.

Chapter Three

※

*I cannot believe that Lord Claybourne found me,
and worse—that he still means to court me!*

—Lily to Fanny

London, two days later

"I wish we could send that dastardly villain to
Hades," Chantel Amour muttered as she daintily sipped
her tea.

"He is not quite a villain," Fanny replied dryly. "He is
simply a keen businessman. And he wants payment for
the debt you and Fleur incurred in his gaming hell."

Fleur Delee gave an elegant sniff. "You cannot believe
Mick O'Rourke is anything less than odious, Fanny.
Not when he is coercing you to pay or else he will lay
charges against us to send us to debtor's prison."

"I never said he isn't odious. Just that we are in this
fix because you gambled away a fortune you didn't
have."

"But O'Rourke plied us with brandy and encouraged
us to play deep at the Faro table," Chantel complained.
"I have no doubt he arranged the entire episode because
of you, Fanny. He wants you to agree to be his *chère
amie*."

Fanny pressed her lips together. "I *know* what Mick

wants, but he won't get it. We will just have to think of another way to repay him."

Lily looked on as the three friends argued. When she'd shown up unexpectedly on the doorstep of Fanny's London home two days ago, she had been welcomed without much protest once she explained about needing to escape Lord Claybourne's unwanted attentions. An hour later she was settled here in the boardinghouse run by Fleur and Chantel.

To Lily's surprise, the mansion was quite large and unexpectedly elegant. She'd been given her own bed-chamber on the third floor and invited to use the own-ers' private sitting room on the floor below, as well as the communal drawing room and the two small parlors on the main floor.

This afternoon the four of them had gathered in Fleur and Chantel's private sitting room in order to discuss possible ways of earning enough money to repay the enormous gaming debt they owed.

Watching the women together, Lily had no trouble seeing the tremendous affection Fanny bore the aging courtesans. Reportedly they had taught Fanny every-thing they knew when she first entered the trade eight years ago, so she was determined to help them now.

Lily could also understand why the former Cyprians were once considered the toast of London. Though Fleur's auburn locks were now unnaturally aided by henna dye, and Chantel's blond tresses somewhat con-cealed the liberal strands of gray, they were still fascinat-ing women, despite their faded beauty. Lily found them exceedingly warm and charming, although a trifle dreamy-eyed and scatterbrained. It seemed to her that they spent most of their time lamenting their lost allure and reminiscing about their bygone glory when they had reigned over the London demimonde.

In the past two days, Lily had heard countless stories about their long-ago conquests, as well as the details of how they had come to be in such dire straits now: They'd spent a disastrous night at the Faro tables at Mick O'Rourke's gaming club and lost nearly *forty thousand pounds*.

Fanny, of course, had come to their rescue and paid off a quarter of the debt—ten thousand pounds, almost every penny she had saved—but they still owed the enormous sum of thirty thousand pounds. And they were exceedingly worried now, since O'Rourke was threatening to send them to prison.

He had offered to forgo the debt in exchange for Fanny's exclusive services as his mistress, but she was loath to accept. Fanny had a history with O'Rourke, since he'd been one of her first patrons when she set out on her career as a courtesan. But even though they once were lovers and he had since made a vast fortune by pulling himself up from his harsh, low-class origins and making a success of his gaming club, he refused to show leniency toward her friends.

Which was an unforgivable sin, to Chantel's mind. She had always viewed O'Rourke as uncouth and loutish, but now she considered him downright dastardly.

"I should think," Chantel mused aloud, "that you could apply to one of your current protectors for the funds."

Fanny shook her head. "Even if one of my gentlemen were inclined to such munificence—which I very much doubt—it would leave me uncomfortably obliged to him."

Lily had heard Fanny's rationale before this. She never allowed any of her patrons exclusive privileges, since she didn't want anyone having such power over her; for if her lover abruptly decided to end their arrangement, he could cut her off without a penny and leave her scrambling for her livelihood.

Lily could sympathize with her friend, since she herself was adamant about never giving any man control over her own fate.

"There is another possibility, Fanny," Fleur said, biting into a biscuit. "You could sell your memoirs."

"No, that is *not* possible."

"What memoirs?" Lily asked curiously.

Fanny gave a dismissive wave of her hand. "I don't even wish to discuss it."

Fleur leaned forward and whispered in a conspiratorial tone to Lily, "A publisher has offered to pay dearly for Fanny's memoirs if she will share titillating tales about her illustrious clientele."

"We are not that desperate," Fanny responded.

"I cannot fathom why you won't at least consider it," Chantel added plaintively.

"Because the sale would only cover part of your debt. More importantly, even if I wished to expose my former patrons in that distasteful way—which I do not—my memoirs would take time to write, and Mick has given us only one month, a concession he made very reluctantly after much pleading on my part, I might add."

"But have you considered," Fleur interjected, "how lucrative it could prove if you chose *not* to expose your lovers? There must be quite a few gentlemen who would pay handsomely to be left out of your recollections."

Fanny's gaze narrowed on the older courtesan. "You mean blackmail, do you, Fleur? That is totally out of the question. Not merely because it is unprincipled, but because I don't want to make enemies of London's elite set. Were I to do so, I could find it difficult to remain employed."

Fleur offered a graceful shrug of her shoulders. "Well, I do not see how we are to come about if you insist on being so virtuous. Beggars cannot afford to be choosers, Fanny."

"I am not reduced to begging yet," she said tartly.

"It is a pity our boarders cannot help us," Chantel lamented with a heavy sigh.

Fleur's scoffing sound was very much like a snort. "Indeed. But they earn a pittance compared to what we once did."

"Because they haven't our former skills *or* our former beauty," said Chantel.

"Or our refinement," Fleur added sagely.

Chantel gave a sad nod.

Lily comprehended what they meant by a lack of refinement. There were over a dozen female boarders lodging in the mansion, all from the lower classes, some who were just beginning to become established as members of the muslin company, or *demimondaines,* the polite term Chantel insisted on using instead of prostitute or harlot. Of the girls who roomed here, the majority were opera dancers and actresses who supplemented their meager incomes by becoming part-time mistresses. But several sold their wares in various clubs and pleasure houses in the nearby theater district.

Fleur and Chantel, on the other hand—and Fanny also—could claim superior birth and breeding, which had allowed them to excel at their profession and command a much higher class of clientele.

Looking despondent, the elder courtesans fell silent, until Fleur finally mused aloud. "What we need are some very rich men to come to our rescue."

"That goes without saying," Chantel agreed. "But how do we acquire such men? You and I have lost the ability to attract wealthy patrons."

"Alas, that is true. But several of our lodgers are beautiful enough to take our places. With the right guidance from us, they could be groomed to act in our stead."

"But what would be the point?" Chantel asked dismissively.

"Don't be such a slow top, love," Fleur chided. "If some of our boarders could land rich protectors, they could help us pay off our debt to O'Rourke."

"But how would they even meet any rich protectors?" Chantel huffed. "Such prizes are not scattered about waiting to be scooped up, you know."

"Of course not, but some could be found if we search hard enough. Just consider, Chantel. We could hold a soiree just like the old days. And we could invite everyone Fanny knows. She has valuable connections among the ton, and we still have a few ourselves."

For more than two decades Fleur and Chantel had reportedly held elegant soirees and entertained the cream of artistic and intellectual London society, even though they now no longer entertained at all.

"Well . . . I suppose we *could* hold a soiree," Chantel answered. "But the effort would be futile, since our boarders will never become more refined."

Fanny suddenly sat up as if her interest had been piqued. "Perhaps it would not be impossible with the right tutor." She cast a glance at Lily. "Do you think you could instruct some of our boarders in the social graces, Lily? Just as you do at your Academy for Young Ladies?"

Lily's brow furrowed. "Why do you ask?"

Fleur's expression also brightened as she regard Lily. "Because, darling," Fleur explained, "our boarders need cultivation if our plan is to succeed. Demireps from the lower orders cannot easily attract wealthy noblemen or gentlemen. Members of the Quality want refinement, not bawdy manners and coarse speech. The girls here would have been drummed out of our former soirees the instant they opened their mouths."

"Yes," Chantel chimed in. "Wit and charm are important, but proper diction and accent are crucial. Those and deportment are the biggest handicaps preventing them from acquiring wealthier protectors." Breaking off, Chantel suddenly stared at Lily as well. "*Could* you teach our girls, dear?"

Lily found herself frowning as she considered the question. The idea of helping young women sell themselves to rich men unsettled her more than a little, yet she didn't want to refuse outright. "Perhaps. It should not be much different from the academy my sisters and I started three years ago. We teach girls from the merchant classes how to become more refined and ladylike, so they can hold their own in genteel society."

"It might solve all our problems," Fleur admitted with enthusiasm.

"Is there some other way for them to help you repay the debt?" Lily hedged.

"Not such an enormous sum."

Lily couldn't dispute her. Respectable jobs as servants earned perhaps ten pounds per annum. Even the most elite positions open to women—housekeepers of large estates, governess to wealthy families—rarely paid more than fifty pounds.

"There is always my settlement," Lily suggested. When all three women looked blankly at her, she expounded. "The funds Lord Danvers settled upon me at my emancipation from his guardianship. It amounts to twenty thousand pounds, Fanny. You are welcome to have it."

Giving a little gasp, Chantel clapped her hands together in delight. "I knew you were a right 'un, Lily darling."

But Fanny frowned. "I could never take your money, Lily."

"Why not?"

"Because you have plans for those funds. In any case, your fortune isn't enough to satisfy the entire debt. We would still owe Mick an enormous sum, and you would be destitute again."

"I suspect Roslyn would gladly share her portion."

"Perhaps, but I have no intention of asking her. You both were virtually penniless three years ago, but now you are finally able to afford an independent life of your own. I won't spoil that under any circumstances."

It was Lily's turn to frown. "Fanny, if you think I will let you enslave yourself to a man you don't even like simply so I can spend a fortune I never expected on jaunting all over the globe, you have gone completely daft. What kind of friend would I be?"

"You know you have always wanted to travel."

"So I have, but the circumstances have changed. You need the funds far more than I do."

Fanny smiled faintly. "Thank you, dearest. I will consider accepting if the situation becomes truly dire, but not until then. Seriously, Lily, I believe Fleur's idea of helping our boarders to acquire wealthy patrons would serve far better. Raising their station holds such tremendous advantages for those girls, I'm certain they will agree to help us pay off the debt in exchange for the exceptional training we can provide. So what do you say? Could you teach them to speak and behave with more gentility?"

Lily pursed her lips in thought. Manners and deportment were certainly *not* her forte. She was far more at home coaching the Academy's pupils in sporting activities such as riding and archery, and physical skills such as dancing. But she could manage if the girls were willing to learn.

"Will your boarders be willing to apply themselves?" she asked.

"I have no doubt they will."

Her reticence must have continued to show, however, for Fanny murmured, "It is asking a great deal of you, I know. You needn't help if you are uncomfortable, Lily."

"No, of course I want to help," she said quickly, trying to control her squeamishness at participating so directly in the courtesan trade. "It is just that I wonder whether your boarders will be amenable to your plan to find them new patrons."

Intervening, Fleur offered Lily a sympathetic glance. "Our girls will be delighted to land rich men, darling, take my word for it. And you will be doing them a good turn. If they can attract a higher class of clientele, they can earn significantly better livings."

Lily nodded, knowing it wasn't fair to deny her help because of her own conflicted feelings. "Then we should begin at once."

The elder courtesans looked relieved, while Fanny smiled her thanks. "The question is, can we make sufficient progress in the next month?" she asked Lily.

"I believe we can if they are agreeable to attending classes for several hours a day."

"Good, because a month is all the time we have. We can perhaps put Mick off for a bit longer after that if we can convince him the debt will soon be repaid, but he could very well act on his threat to have Chantel and Fleur thrown in prison. So what do we do?"

Lily's brows drew together as she considered the problem. "I think we should conduct lessons in elocution and grammar to improve their improper speech, and in grace and deportment to improve their manners. We can use the drawing room as our main classroom, and we can clear one of the parlors to provide enough space for dance instruction. . . . But if we want to move quickly, I should begin devising a curriculum at once."

She glanced up at Fanny. "And it would be best if we divide up responsibilities. I can teach your boarders a number of useful subjects, but you and Fleur and Chantel could advise them on things I know nothing about, such as conversing with prospective patrons."

"Yes," Fanny agreed, "that would be wise. I can also send some of my servants here to assist with the additional workload, and my dresser to help the girls acquire suitable gowns to wear at the soiree."

"And I know Tess Blanchard will be glad to help,"

Lily said. "I also think we should ask Basil to teach diction."

Fanny's expression instantly shadowed. "Whyever would we ask him?"

Lily raised an eyebrow at her friend's curt response. "Because he is a Latin scholar and can speak four other languages as well. If anyone can teach proper speech, it is he. Moreover, he lives here."

Basil Eddowes was one of their few male lodgers—a tall, gangly young man about Fanny's age who clerked and translated Latin for a prestigious law office in the City. Although Lily hadn't seen Basil in four years, he'd been her bosom friend when she was a girl. Fanny also knew him well, since they'd all been neighbors in Hampshire together during their childhood.

The trouble was that Basil and Fanny had been at loggerheads ever since she'd taken up her scandalous new life. He severely disapproved of her occupation, which made it strange that he would choose to board here with so many fallen women, where he would be obliged to see Fanny whenever she visited the house, which was frequently.

"Basil is so disagreeable," Fanny said in a dark tone, "he will likely refuse just out of spite."

"Let me ask him," Lily offered.

"You may try, of course. He will be more willing if the request comes from you."

Fanny was still speaking when Fleur rose abruptly. "It is settled then, so we had best get started. Chantel, come with me. We will find the girls and discuss our scheme with them. And then we must begin planning the soiree. It will be such a pleasure to have an entertainment to look forward to."

Obediently Chantel stood and followed her colleague to the parlor door, but before she left, she glanced back at Lily. "We are delighted you have come, darling. Already our prospects are looking much brighter."

Lily returned a tentative smile. "I only hope we can make it work."

"It will, I feel sure of it."

When the two older women had gone, Fanny eyed Lily over her teacup. "Are you *truly* certain you want to involve yourself so intimately in our problems?"

"Yes, of course," Lily said at once. "I am happy to do it."

She was more than willing to try to help Fanny and her friends. And more importantly, she wanted to help the young women she had met during the past two days to improve their lot in life. Even if she had qualms about the purpose of the soiree, tutoring them in speech and deportment was a worthy goal and might allow them opportunities for respectable jobs that they could never hope for otherwise.

"You mustn't worry about me, Fanny," Lily assured her. "I wouldn't involve myself if I didn't wish to."

"I know." Fanny's smile suddenly turned humorous. "But when you came to London to escape Lord Claybourne, I doubt you expected to start a school for Cyprians and teach our boarders how to behave as proper ladies."

"No," Lily agreed lightly, hiding her wince at the mention of the marquess. "But this is an excellent use of my time."

And will provide an excellent distraction as well.

She had thought of the beguiling nobleman far too

often since that passionate interlude in the loft and his startling declaration the following morning.

Shifting uneasily at the memory, Lily picked up her own teacup. She simply *had* to stop dwelling on Lord Claybourne and his enchanting kisses. It was deplorable, how her thoughts were centered on a man she scarcely even knew. Especially since she suspected he had forgotten all about her the very next day.

By now his lordship would have moved on to more willing conquests, Lily was certain. Yet, vexingly, it would take her a good while longer to forget all about him.

One month later . . .

Lily still had not forgotten about Lord Claybourne four weeks later, but as she watched her pupils practice the proper use of silver and crystal one afternoon in the dining room, she felt pleased by the success of her "academy." Indeed, her classes were in high demand, since word had spread among the London demimonde.

There were twenty-two young women enrolled now, and the fees were waived for those who signed a voucher promising to donate a portion of their first year's income to Fleur and Chantel's debt relief fund.

In addition to speech and manners and deportment, the girls learned about proper dress, dining at table, pouring tea, conversing with the gentility, dancing, attending the opera and theater . . . the myriad skills needed to enhance their prospects of securing wealthy, well-born patrons.

Almost all of her pupils, Lily believed, would be ready for the soiree, which was to be held next week, although she was in truth surprised by their rapid progress. Yet as Fleur had predicted, the girls were eager for the chance to significantly improve their circumstances.

"For finding rich men to support them," Fleur had said more than once, "is the only way they will ever rise up out of poverty. It is the way of the world, Lily dear."

The courtesans' view was pragmatic by necessity. And admittedly, living here with them in their rooming house had opened Lily's eyes to an entirely different world, much of which was not pleasant or adventurous in the least. She'd thought she understood the plight of penniless females in society, since she and her sisters had faced destitution and homelessness after their family scandal. But some of the young women here were much worse off than she had ever been.

On the whole, however, her pupils were a cheerful bunch. Thanks to Fanny and the elder courtesans, they had safe, genteel lodgings to call home, which was more than most actresses and opera dancers could claim. And many of the girls actually seemed to enjoy their extra employment as ladies of the evening. They had *chosen* this life, just as Fanny and Fleur and Chantel had. Yet there were some who had been forced into the flesh trade unwillingly.

Those were the ones Lily wanted most to help. Those unfortunate incognitas who were trapped in a profession they despised. Lily had already managed to help two of them escape by sending them home to Roslyn at Danvers Hall to join the manor staff as chambermaids. It was menial labor, true, and the jobs paid less than the girls made as lightskirts, but they considered serving in a noble household better work by far than earning their livings in a brothel.

It had brought Lily profound satisfaction to provide the two girls new lives. And she understood now why Tess strove so hard for her special charities.

She'd recruited Tess as an instructor twice a week, and Basil Eddowes taught speech classes early each morning before leaving for his work. Fleur and Chantel had thrown their hearts into mentoring the girls, and Fanny had won their adoration by sharing her secrets of becoming desirable to men.

The girls seemed most grateful for Lily's efforts, which also gratified her. From the first moment of the first class, it had quickly became clear to her that these young women needed her far more than the rich daughters she taught at the Freemantle Academy.

Additionally, Lily felt a humbling gratitude for her own comparatively good fortune. She and her sisters knew what it was to be at the mercy of fate. It made Lily shudder to think that they might have been forced into prostitution themselves, had not their step-uncle felt obliged to take them in, however grudgingly.

As for Mick O'Rourke, he seemed to be biding his time, waiting for the agreed-upon grace period to be over.

Yet Fanny had been busy with another endeavor to raise money. Rather than writing her memoirs, she had penned a manuscript based on her recent letters to Roslyn, entitled, "Advice to Young Ladies on Capturing a Husband." The publisher anticipated brisk sales among the ton's debutantes when the book eventually went to print early this fall.

Lily's only regret now was that during the past month, Roslyn had fallen hopelessly in love with the Duke of Arden and become betrothed. If she'd remained at home to protect Roslyn, Lily lamented, perhaps she might have stopped her sister from making such a drastic mistake.

At least Arabella and Marcus still seemed to be happy. They had just returned to Danvers Hall from their monthlong wedding journey, according to Roslyn.

Lily yearned to see her sisters again, although not enough to risk encountering the Marquess of Claybourne.

Her gaze darkened as she remembered the dismaying letter Roslyn had sent her yesterday, warning that the marquess might not have lost interest in her. Reportedly Claybourne had made an unexpected trip to Hampshire in search of her.

He'd been directed there by Winifred, who was highly disgruntled to discover Lily was not visiting friends in her former neighborhood as she wanted everyone to believe.

Lily couldn't help but worry about his lordship's persistence. She'd been confident that she had escaped him. But apparently "out of sight" did not mean "out of mind" to him.

With any luck, though, he would never find her here, Lily thought as she moved from one elegantly set table to the next.

The score of female diners looked just as elegant as the place settings, all dressed in evening gowns even though it was barely two o'clock in the afternoon. They were practicing the art of drinking soup without slurping, and Lily had very few corrections to make.

She had just signaled the two manservants to clear away the soup plates and bring in the next course when she was approached by a chambermaid, who whispered in her ear.

"Beg pardon for intruding, Miss Loring, but you have a gentleman caller who wishes to speak with you."

Lily felt her heart skip a beat. No gentlemen of her acquaintance even knew she was here . . . unless. . . . *Surely* Lord Claybourne had not found her. "Did the gentleman give a name?"

"No, miss, but he looks like a fancy lord—and he acts like one, too. Said to tell you that he has 'enough patience to outlast you,' whatever that means."

Regrettably she knew exactly what that meant. Lily drew an uneven breath, alarmed at the thought of having to face the marquess again. "You put him in Miss Delee's sitting room, Ellen?"

"No, miss. He asked to be shown to your bedchamber."

"My *bedchamber*?" Her tone had risen in pitch, but when Lily realized that several curious pairs of eyes had turned in her direction, she lowered her voice. "My bedchamber is not the proper place for a gentleman caller, Ellen."

"I know, Miss Loring, but he wouldn't take no for an answer."

It sounded just like Lord Claybourne, Lily thought, torn between exasperation and vexation.

Vexation won out when Ellen added, "He said you would rather have a private interview there than have him come to the dining room with your pupils present."

At the implied threat, Lily pressed her lips together in irritation. Obviously she had no choice but to receive him in her bedchamber, since she didn't want him making a scene in front of an audience.

"Do you want me to fetch Miss Delee to deal with him?" the maid asked nervously at Lily's silence.

"No, I will see him, thank you, Ellen."

After politely excusing herself from her pupils for a moment, Lily left the dining room and took the back stairs. Deliberately ignoring the butterflies fluttering in her stomach, she climbed two flights to her own floor and marched down the corridor to her bedchamber. The door was shut, but she pushed it open—and came up short at the sight of Lord Claybourne.

He was actually lounging on her bed, his back propped up against the pillows, one booted leg casually drawn up as a prop for the book he was reading.

Her book, she realized, her mouth dropping open at his temerity. But it was the man himself who made her speechless. It was shocking how just being in the same room with him seemed to draw all the air from her lungs.

Then he looked up and locked gazes with her, and the flutter in her stomach suddenly became a riot.

Lily pressed a hand to her midriff, yet her defensive gesture did nothing to calm her smoldering awareness of him. Not when Claybourne was looking at her in that disconcerting way.

The gleam in his hazel eyes held a mix of triumph, sensuality, lazy amusement, and more—the promise of retribution.

"Come in, angel," he said in his low, rich voice. "We have a great deal to discuss, wouldn't you say?"

If he'd wondered how he would feel at seeing Lily Loring again, Heath had his answer now: Sensation shot through him, making his stomach clench and his loins tighten.

She felt the same spark of fire between them, he knew, watching her lustrous eyes widen and turn wary. It gave him a primal male satisfaction.

Marveling at the undeniable physical impact Lily had on him, he let the heat of his gaze travel slowly downward to her lush mouth. He couldn't forget the taste of those dusky-rose lips. Couldn't forget those amazing dark eyes, that rich chestnut color of her hair.

Yet in person she was even more vibrant than in his memories. And his visceral response to her was even more intense.

It wasn't mere lust, however. Something about her made his heart race. He hadn't imagined it, he knew that now.

Heath smiled inwardly at himself. The question of whether the spark would still be there between them had made the last four weeks seem interminable. His life had been utterly flat since meeting Lilian Loring. Certainly there hadn't been a single woman in the interim who'd captured his interest.

He hadn't expected to run his quarry to earth in a lodging house for lightskirts, though. He hadn't expected Lily to run from him, either. Or to put him to the trouble of chasing her. He'd never been compelled to exert himself to pursue any woman.

Admittedly he'd been piqued by her flight, yet exhilarated by the thrill of the chase. Which made his triumph at finally catching her all the more sweet, despite his reservations at finding her living in a residence owned by Fanny Irwin, with a pair of infamous highflyers and a score of other straw damsels.

"Do come in, angel," Heath urged. "And shut the door, unless you wish to broadcast my presence in your bedchamber."

That seemed to snap Lily out of her daze, for her beautiful eyes narrowed. "Your presence in my bedchamber is extremely ill-advised, my lord. You should not be here, you know very well."

"I wanted a place to be private with you."

"There are two parlors and a drawing room in the house. Any of those would be far more suitable for a gentleman caller."

"But not suitable for my purpose."

Her eyes turned wary again. "Just what *is* your purpose, Lord Claybourne?"

"I cannot tell you as long as you remain loitering out there in the corridor."

Lily obliged him, stepping into the room and closing the door behind her, but she obviously wasn't happy about it, for her hands went to her hips. "*Now* will you pray explain the reason for your delightful visit?"

Heath grinned at her acerbic tone. "Yes, if you will explain what the devil you are doing in a scandalous pleasure house."

She stiffened. "It is not a pleasure house precisely. The boarders don't entertain their patrons here."

Heath arched a skeptical brow. "You are saying they don't hold assignations with their lovers here?"

"Well . . . not frequently, at any event. The proprietresses frown upon it."

"And that should assuage my concerns?"

Her lips pressed together. "Assuaging your concerns is hardly my responsibility, my lord. But if you must know,

I am helping Fanny Irwin and her friends repay a rather large gambling debt."

"So I understand. I've learned a great deal about you over the past three days since I discovered your location. You have obviously been hard at work."

Her eyes widened. "You have been watching me?"

"In part. When I called yesterday, you were occupied in the drawing room, surrounded by a gaggle of beauties practicing the waltz. At least your friend Eddowes was willing to satisfy a measure of my curiosity."

"*Basil* told you about our endeavor?" She looked taken aback. "I cannot believe he betrayed my confidence! Or that you managed to persuade him to."

Heath smiled at her vexation. "You proved so elusive, I was forced to become more resourceful. Eddowes has your best interests at heart, you know."

"What did you tell him?"

"That I have your best interests at heart also. Actually, I think he was relieved to share his apprehensions with me. He doesn't quite approve of you being here." Heath's gaze narrowed on her. "Marcus would not approve either if he knew, I'll wager."

"I do not need Marcus's consent to be here," Lily replied stiffly. "He is no longer my guardian."

"But he is head of your family now. And Arden will soon be joining it as well. You know he and your sister Roslyn are betrothed?"

"I know," Lily said, her tone gloomy.

"So don't you think it would be detrimental to your sisters if your presence here became known?"

"I don't intend for it to become known. And if Basil Eddowes told you about our academy, then you must realize it is for a worthy cause. We are helping some unfortunate young women improve their speech and social graces so they can better their lives. It is immensely satisfying, seeing their progress day by day. And next week we plan to hold a soiree so they may meet a higher class of clientele. Hopefully they will be able to improve the deplorable circumstances under which they must earn their livelihood."

Her passion for her cause was obvious, Heath reflected, watching Lily's expressive face. Although it didn't surprise him, he wondered how many ladies of her class would become involved in helping prostitutes raise their standard of living, much less endure these rather spartan conditions for weeks on end. He glanced around the small chamber, which was bare except for a narrow bed and side table, a washstand and bureau, and a chair. Very unlike her bedchamber at Danvers Hall, he would imagine.

"Your compassion is highly admirable," Heath said mildly.

She regarded him with suspicion. "Are you roasting me, Lord Claybourne?"

"Not in the least. I am quite sincere in my admiration. And I understand why you began teaching here, but not why you came to be here in the first place."

That made her smile. "Why, I was avoiding you, of course. You made it clear that you wouldn't give up your absurd notion of courting me."

"I presumed as much."

Her look grew puzzled. "I confess I am astounded by your persistence in the face of my obvious reluctance to entertain your suit. Did you really go to Hampshire to look for me?"

His mouth twisted when he thought of his futile journey a fortnight ago. "I did. Imagine my surprise when I learned that you had not set foot there in four years. You merely put out that tale to misdirect Lady Freemantle and therefore me."

"It seems I was wise," Lily said wryly, "since you pursued me there. And here as well. How did you find me, if I may ask?"

"Your sister Arabella. When she and Marcus returned home from their wedding trip the other day, she accidently let slip that you were in London with Fanny. Once I had a general location, it was an easy matter to follow Fanny here."

Sitting up, Heath swung his legs over the side of the bed. "You led me on a merry chase, sweeting," he chided lightly. "I am not accustomed to women running from me."

"I imagine not," Lily replied, her tone dry.

"Did I frighten you that badly?"

She frowned a little, as if giving serious thought to the question. "Unsettled is a better word. I didn't like the feeling in the least."

"That is regrettable, because I am in no way giving up."

Lily stared at him a moment before her expression grew frustrated. "It makes no sense, Lord Claybourne. Why would you want to court me?"

"I beg to differ, love—it makes perfect sense. I will have to wed someday, and I think you might make a good match for me. But I need to ascertain if we have any chance for a future together. I already know I am powerfully attracted to you. And that you are just as attracted to me. Don't bother denying it."

Her mouth opened to protest but shut almost as

quickly. "Perhaps so, but that doesn't mean I want to *marry* you. Or that you want to marry me. We barely know each other."

"I intend to remedy that right now."

"Your lordship!" she exclaimed as he rose from the bed.

"Don't be alarmed. I only want to conduct an experiment."

Holding her gaze, Heath crossed the small room toward her. Immediately Lily tried to back away, but there was nowhere for her to run. Cautious, wary, she stood there looking up at him, her hands raised defensively in front of her.

Lifting his own hand, Heath let his thumb glide along her lush lower lip before he bent his head down to her.

"Lord Claybourne . . ." she said breathlessly.

"Hush, let me show you."

She inhaled sharply but remained frozen as Heath kissed her. Her lips felt soft and ripe under his . . . and oh so arousing. A jolt of pure desire sizzled through him.

No, he wasn't mistaken about Lily, he thought with a feeling of triumph and pleasure as he savored her. He felt that fire in her again, searing him. He felt the hunger in her. It was unconscious, instinctive, but there all the same, arousing the same intense heat that had ignited between them their first time together in the loft.

That fire and his own reciprocal response settled the issue for Heath. He'd never met a women who stirred his passion the way Lily did, certainly not a young lady who possessed the qualifications to become his marchioness. Ergo, he wouldn't let Lily go. Not until he proved to himself that she wasn't the right bride for him.

"There," he said softly when he at last raised his head.

"I wanted to see if my attraction to you was merely a passing fancy, and I now know it wasn't. You felt it, too, don't deny it."

She stared back at him, looking dazed, and wet her lips before finally finding her voice. "I felt *something*, but it was not at all pleasant."

Heath arched an eyebrow. "I never would have thought you were given to falsehoods, darling."

"I am being quite truthful, my lord. I did not enjoy kissing you. It made me too . . . disconcerted. Too flustered."

"You felt out of control, and you didn't like it."

"Yes, exactly! I am gratified you understand."

"But I don't understand. I am offering you pleasure beyond your wildest dreams, and you turn me down out of hand."

Her chin rose at his teasing. "I am not the least interested in pleasure."

"I expect I can change your mind."

Lily locked her jaw mutinously. "Your arrogance is astounding, my lord."

The amusement leaving his expression, Heath regarded her with all seriousness. "There is nothing arrogant about it, Lily. It is merely simple logic. I want you, but I cannot have you without the benefit of marriage. I am not interested in an affair that would only result in scandal. So I intend to court you honorably."

"Without my consent?" she asked, her eyes flashing.

"I hope to gain your consent. And I mean to start by kissing you again."

Looking alarmed, Lily pressed her palms against his chest. "I am not about to let you ravish me, Lord Claybourne!"

His gaze dropped from her face to her breasts. He would like nothing more than to draw Lily down to her chaste bed and ravish her to their hearts' content, but he was bound by the rules of honor.

Heath smiled. "It is broad daylight and you are surrounded by a houseful of people. I believe you are safe from ravishment for the time being. But that doesn't mean I won't use all the powers of persuasion at my disposal."

His hands covered her shoulders, lightly massaging them as he locked gazes with her. Then bending, he covered her mouth with his in a slow, devastating, spellbinding kiss that sent searing heat arcing between them again.

His sensual assault stunned Lily. She felt light-headed and dizzy; she couldn't breathe.

He was right, she thought with a feeling akin to desperation. The attraction between them was not a passing fancy. Nor could she blame her intoxication on champagne this time. His kisses still overwhelmed her senses even when she wasn't foxed.

Sweet shocks of reaction surged through her body, making her soften instinctively against him. As his lips moved over hers with exquisite pressure, she pushed harder against his chest, struggling for the will to resist, but he caught her lower lip between his teeth and tugged with soft nips.

When Lily responded with a little whimper, his tongue soothed the sensitive flesh before delving slowly, insistently, inside her mouth.

Filled with a strangled pleasure, she gave a helpless moan. She couldn't fight this hammering of her senses, couldn't fight his heat and hardness. Finding him impossible to resist, she gave a tiny, shuddering sigh of defeat and returned his kiss helplessly.

His mouth was magical . . . and so was his touch, Lily thought dazedly as his hand moved to caress her throat. While his kisses enchanted, his long fingers stroked the skin of her throat, gliding inexorably lower to the low, square neckline of her evening gown.

She whimpered once more as he feathered the peaks of her breasts with the backs of his fingers. Her nipples instantly hardened beneath the delicate silk fabric, while her breasts felt heavy and swollen.

And Claybourne was doing his best to increase her arousal, his knuckles slowly gliding over the crests, making Lily gasp at the sparks that shot through her. Then boldly, he brought both hands to her bodice, molding the contours of her breasts, making her knees go weak. Fire radiated from his hands and bloomed between her thighs, shocking her.

Lily closed her eyes against the undeniable pleasure. It was maddening the way he drew out each brazen caress, yet she didn't want him to stop. His touch was so tender, so wicked . . . so right. The sensations left her shaking inside, kindling a heavy ache deep in her lower body. . . .

It was some time before she realized that he had left off kissing her, although he was still cupping the ripe swells of her breasts.

"Don't you see?" Heath asked, his voice husky and low. "Whatever this is between us, it deserves exploring."

Dazed, Lily opened her eyes. Yes, she saw. She was aching with nameless longing . . . aching for *him*. She couldn't deny it, couldn't hide it.

But the emotional turmoil inside her was even

stronger. She didn't *want* to want him. She couldn't bear to risk subjugating herself to a man's domination for a fleeting taste of passion, no matter how delicious it promised to be.

Giving a frustrated groan, Lily slid out from Lord Claybourne's embrace and backed away from him. When he took a step toward her, she held up her hands defensively and retreated farther across the small bedchamber, putting as much space as possible between them.

Claybourne stopped then, regarding her intently.

With shaking fingers, Lily tucked a loose tendril of hair behind her ear and swallowed hard. Yet her voice was still a hoarse rasp when she finally spoke. "You are mistaken if you think I will meekly surrender just because you are a splendid kisser."

"I think nothing of the kind," he said, his tone wry. "You haven't a meek bone in your lovely body, I'll warrant."

"No, and I will never accept your proposal of marriage, either," Lily said firmly.

The smile he gave her was utterly beautiful and utterly maddening. "We shall see."

Lily started to reply but gave a start when a sharp rap sounded on her bedchamber door. Then she froze as Fleur pushed open the door and swept into the room.

The courtesan took one look at Lily's flushed face and passion-bruised lips and turned to regard the marquess with a baleful eye. "I trust you mean to explain yourself, my lord. Miss Loring is under our protection, and we will not stand for you seducing her!"

Chapter Four

✲

*I must be mad to have agreed to his courtship, but
the potential benefit to our boarders outweighs the
risk to me . . . or so I sincerely hope.*

—Lily to Fanny

Lily was vastly relieved for the interruption, but Lord
Claybourne did not look chagrined in the least by
Fleur's irate accusation.

Instead, he gave the courtesan a graceful bow. "How
delightful to see you again, Miss Delee. Pray accept my
apologies for alarming you, but I did not come here to
seduce Miss Loring."

"No?" Fleur asked with marginally less rancor. "Then
what does bring you here, my lord? Fanny would never
forgive me if I allowed anything untoward to befall Miss
Loring while she is dwelling under this roof."

"I assure you my intentions toward her are entirely
honorable. I wish to court her."

Fleur blinked in surprise. "You want to court her? So
you can *wed* her?"

Claybourne glanced at Lily, his eyes assessing her with
a tinge of knowing mirth. "Well . . . perhaps 'wed' is
premature, since she professes to be so set against marriage, but I hope for the opportunity to determine if we
might make a good match."

"My heavens," Fleur said with a mix of wonderment and delight. "That does change things, my lord."

"I thought it might," he murmured under his breath, so low that only Lily heard him. To Fleur, he said aloud, "I would like to solicit your assistance, if I may. Miss Loring insists on eluding my attempts even to speak to her, but if you would be so kind, you could convince her to at least entertain the idea of my suit."

In disbelief, Lily stared at the marquess. The nerve of him, using her friends against her.

Fleur, on the other hand, gave him a fond smile. "Yes, indeed, Lord Claybourne. I would be pleased to help. Shall we repair to my sitting room to discuss the matter?"

"Fleur," Lily said in exasperation as the elder woman turned to leave the bedchamber. "There is nothing to discuss."

"Certainly there is, darling. I mean to satisfy my curiosity if nothing else."

Lily's continued protests fell on deaf ears. Thus, when the marquess accompanied Fleur from the room and down the corridor, Lily trailed after them, not trusting what he might say behind her back.

Fleur chatted graciously with him as she led him down a flight of stairs to the elegant second-floor sitting room she and Chantel claimed for their own. Chantel was lounging on a settee, reading a volume of poetry, but she perked up when she spied their caller. It was rare these days that she received visitors, especially a nobleman so handsome and distinguished as Lord Claybourne.

Chantel flushed becomingly when he bent over her hand to kiss her fingers lightly, but her blue eyes widened when Fleur repeated what he'd told her about wishing to begin a courtship.

"You are a sly puss," Chantel chided Lily. "You never told us you have a noble suitor."

"Because it isn't true," she insisted.

"But I hope to make it true," Claybourne said mildly.

"So your intentions are genuinely honorable, my lord?" Fleur asked.

"Completely."

"Then do please sit down and tell us why you might wish to wed Lily."

He didn't take the seat he was offered, however, since Lily resolutely remained standing. But he did explain some of his motivation.

"To begin with, I have never met anyone quite like Miss Loring. I last saw her a full month ago but I couldn't forget her."

To her chagrin, Lily found herself flushing. She had not been able to forget Lord Claybourne either, but she hoped he wouldn't divulge the reason—because he was her first romantic tryst.

Fortunately Fleur spoke before he could expound. "Even so, marriage is a serious step, my lord."

"Indeed," he murmured, his tone wry. "The avowed bachelor in me is trembling. But since my good friend Danvers recently wed Miss Loring's eldest sister, I'm willing to view the marriage noose with more favor. And of course I will need heirs eventually. But the chief reason I am interested in her is that I think we might make a good match."

Lily grimaced, not caring for the way they were discussing her as if she wasn't even present. It was time for her to put an end to this foolishness. "You are obviously lacking in discernment, Lord Claybourne. I would make you an utterly unsuitable wife."

He shifted his gaze to her. "How so?"

"There are numerous reasons. I am highly independent, for one thing."

"But that is a point in your favor, since I dislike limpets. I don't want a wife who would forever be clinging to me."

She gave him a dulcet smile. "I daresay I would be just the opposite. I have a mind and a will of my own. And I have no intention of calling any man 'lord and master.' "

"Nor would I expect you to. As my wife, you would be free to do as you please."

Lily raised a skeptical eyebrow. "*Anything* I please?"

His own half smile was slow, direct. "Anything within reason."

"But it is *your* definition of reason that counts."

"I imagine we could set mutually agreed-upon limits to your behavior."

"I doubt it," she rejoined. "I don't conform well to the dictates of society."

"So you have told me."

She couldn't help but note the teasing glint in Claybourne's eyes, which miffed her further. "Did I also tell you that I am something of a bluestocking? My sister Roslyn is the scholar in our family, but I like to study history and geography."

"I can appreciate a well-informed intellect," he replied, unperturbed.

Realizing she was unlikely to ever win this argument as long as Claybourne was pretending such forbearance, Lily shook her head. "It scarcely matters what you appreciate. I am not at leisure to entertain your suit. I am quite busy teaching our boarders."

"I won't interfere with your efforts."

"No? I find that hard to believe."

"As you said, it is for a worthy cause."

Her smile turned cool. "Then you understand why I have no time to indulge your eccentric whims."

He looked perfectly solemn except for the devils dancing in his eyes. "It is hardly eccentric for a gentleman to decide to take a wife."

"In your case it is. You are the greatest Lothario in England."

The marquess gave a mock wince of pain. "Your accusation is rather harsh, sweeting. I am no libertine, even though I like women exceedingly."

"You won't like *me*."

"You are gravely mistaken if you think that."

"I am nothing like your usual conquests."

"Quite true. You are more thorn than rose."

"Precisely. And I am certain you will find my tart tongue uncomfortable. I tend to speak my mind."

"Good. I can't endure simpering, vacuous women." Claybourne paused a moment, holding her gaze. "But in your eagerness to list your drawbacks, Miss Loring, you are forgetting one chief advantage you hold over every other potential candidate for my bride."

"Oh. What is that?"

"My attraction to you. I find you lovely and fascinating."

Lily raised her gaze to the ceiling, and yet some small feminine part of her was foolishly pleased by his compliment.

Vexed by the very thought, she exhaled in a huff of

exasperation. "Regardless . . . this entire discussion is meaningless, my lord. The simple truth is, I do not wish to marry you."

"How do you know unless you put the issue to a true test?"

Chantel interrupted their exchange at that juncture. "Yes, Lily, darling, just consider. You would be a marchioness!"

Lily softened her reply to the kindhearted older woman. "I know, Chantel, but a title is of little importance to me. I care nothing for his lordship's rank and consequence."

The marquess responded with a rough chuckle. "Actually I find that reassuring. If you wed me, it will be because you want me, not my title or my fortune."

Fleur entered the dispute then. "Lily, his lordship could be the ideal husband for you."

Lily turned to eye her in dismay. "You mean to take his side?"

"Not entirely. But I do believe you may be well-matched. Lord Claybourne is a man of passion and daring, very much like you. And I think you should allow his courtship for a time."

"Yes," Chantel seconded her. "There are tremendous advantages to becoming Lady Claybourne, Lily. We can see it, even if you cannot at this stage in your life."

"But Chantel, I have no desire for a title."

"I am not merely talking about the title. A woman needs someone to protect and care for her. When you come to be our age, you will be glad to have a husband and family. Surely you don't want to end up poor and lonely in your later years as we have?"

Lily bit back her instinctive retort. She knew the two

Cyprians worried deeply about financial security, but she hadn't had any notion they were lonely. Even so, their circumstances were very different from her own. She had her sisters and close friends to ward off loneliness, and a modest fortune to insure she wouldn't have to sell herself in order to survive, either in marriage or out of it.

"Lily," Fleur remarked in a cajoling tone, "even if you don't wish to wed his lordship now, you should give his courtship a chance. It is not every day that you find so alluring a suitor." She sent the marquess a coy look from beneath her eyelashes. "So handsome. So charming. So masterful."

"Yes," Chantel said dreamily. "I could die for a man like that."

"I could kill for a man like that," Fleur said with more frankness. "Trust me, Lily, there are countless women who yearn to be in your shoes. Just look at him. How can you resist such a marvelous courtier?"

Lily found their observations totally exasperating, but she did look at Lord Claybourne. She couldn't deny he had a commanding presence that was made even more compelling by his aura of virile, vital energy. Add to that his strikingly handsome features and effortless charm, and he became a lethal weapon against feminine hearts.

She could easily see why the marquess was a great favorite with females of every stamp, and why adoring admirers flocked to him in droves. But his legendary achievements as a lover were a prime reason for her to avoid Lord Claybourne entirely. She most certainly didn't want to be among the legions of lovelorn women who surrendered their hearts and bodies to him.

Indeed, she should be wise enough by now to be inured to his admittedly undeniable appeal. So why did his mere nearness play havoc with her composure? Why did his slow smile make her pulse race and her stomach turn somersaults? Lily wondered as her eyes were drawn irresistibly back to his.

The amused gleam she saw there in the hazel depths suggested he understood her deplorable attraction to him.

Vexed, Lily swore a silent oath. *That* was the most damning reason to refuse his request to court her: She feared succumbing to Claybourne's captivating allure. She had already proven how susceptible she was to his stunning kisses.

When she remained stubbornly mute, Fleur addressed the marquess with a regretful sigh. "I am sorry, my lord, but I fear your quest might be hopeless. Lily is completely immune to masculine charm, even yours."

"I am not willing to give up just yet."

"There may be a way to solve this impasse, Fleur," Chantel said slowly. "The game."

Fleur immediately brightened. "Do you think she would agree?"

"We could try to convince her."

Lily's exasperation welled up again. "Convince me of what?"

Fleur regarded her with a measuring look. "We frequently played a game with our prospective patrons, back in the day when we had numerous gentlemen vying for our favors."

"It was great fun," Chantel chimed in. "Our gentlemen would woo us for a specified time, usually a fortnight, while we rated their creativity and effectiveness as courtiers. Then the two winners were awarded our exclusive favors for the next quarter."

Fleur smiled as if recalling a fond memory. "The competition not only provided us a delightful diversion from boredom, it caused the gentlemen to strive harder to win us."

Lily felt bewildered. "Whatever does your game have to do with me?"

"It could be a solution to your present standoff," Fleur replied. "You would play the game with Lord Claybourne. In essence, it would be a competition between the two of you."

"But of course Lily could not take him as a lover at the end," Chantel pointed out.

Fleur nodded. "Of course not. The stakes must be different. She must give Lord Claybourne a fortnight to court her . . . but in exchange for what?"

Having no desire to let their deliberations continue, Lily shook her head. "I am not about to play any kind of game with him," she stated firmly. "The very idea is absurd."

"I think it an intriguing idea," Claybourne countered. "How would it work in our case?"

"Well," Fleur answered thoughtfully, "we customarily awarded points to each competitor and tallied the score after a fortnight. We could use that same method now. For instance, my lord, you might bring Lily a gift of some kind to win points. Sonnets worked well for Chantel, since she is extremely fond of poetry."

"Yes, sonnets were my very favorite gift," Chantel murmured. "Even better than jewels."

"Which is why you have little left to show for your

success after so many years," Fleur said dryly. "You never did have a head for business."

Chantel's rouged mouth turned down in a pout. "Alas, that is true. I was swayed more by a handsome face and a romantic address."

"And you always had your favorites."

"Mmmm. Lord Poole, do you remember, Fleur? Now *he* was a splendid courtier. He always won the most points of any of my lovers."

"The very best," Fleur agreed.

"So I would have to earn points to win our game?" Claybourne asked.

"Yes, exactly. You would woo Lily and be awarded for your effectiveness and creativity." Fleur's brow furrowed. "I suggest that to keep the play impartial, Chantel and I should set the rules and act as judges, since Lily is unlikely to consider any of your endeavors worthy of reward. As for the stakes, if you earn a certain number of points in the next fortnight—say ten—then Lily must agree to your formal courtship for a full quarter. If not, then you will end your suit forever and award her a prize of her choosing. We can begin tomorrow. Her sister Roslyn's wedding is two weeks from then. That should be ample time to see if you truly want Lily for your bride, shouldn't it?"

The word *bride* was enough to make Lily cringe. "No, absolutely not," she objected. "I won't participate for any length of time. I couldn't endure his lordship's courtship for one day, let alone a fortnight."

"But don't you see the advantages, darling?" Chantel said. "You can demand whatever you want from him."

"But I don't want anything from him!"

"Nothing at all? Just think about it for a moment.

Surely there is something you desire that Lord Claybourne could provide you."

The question suddenly made Lily pause. *Was* there something of value he could provide her? Not for herself, perhaps, but for her friends?

When she didn't answer, Claybourne made a *tsk*ing sound. "I expected you to have more mettle, Miss Loring. You are afraid I will win."

At his light taunt, Lily felt her spine stiffen. She was indeed afraid of his winning, yet her pride wouldn't let her turn tail and run from him like a weakling again. Nor could she ignore Claybourne's challenge, even knowing that he was trying to goad her into agreeing.

"I have plenty of mettle, my lord," she said tersely. "I was attempting to decide what would be worth my while to have a vexing rogue breathing down my neck for so long a period."

His smile showed in his eyes. "Name your price," he said easily.

Now that she considered it, there *was* one thing she wanted from him. It would of course be impossible to ask even the supremely wealthy marquess to hand over thirty thousand pounds to pay off Fleur and Chantel's debt. Not only would such magnanimity make Lily uncomfortably beholden to him, she doubted anything short of her pledge to wed him would induce him to part with so vast a sum. Besides, there was another favor that would benefit even more needy souls.

Yet did she dare risk letting him court her? Lily asked herself. What did she have to fear, after all? She didn't believe his lordship's pursuit would last for an entire fortnight. If he was like most nobleman of means, he had far too much idle time on his hands. Undoubtedly his current preoccupation with her was merely his way of relieving boredom. She was a diversion, nothing more. But perhaps he would lose interest in her if she went along with the game.

"Please, Lily, darling," Chantel implored while she debated. "You will relieve my conscience and Fleur's as well. We couldn't bear to think we hurt your chances for a prosperous match simply because you are so devoted to helping us."

Still silent, Lily caught her lower lip between her teeth as she argued with herself. There were indeed some advantages to agreeing. At least Claybourne would have to play by set rules. And she could use the opportunity to show him precisely why he didn't want to marry her; to prove that she was much too independent for him. Most importantly, her sacrifice would be for a very good cause.

Furthermore, she seriously doubted she could be rid of him any other way.

Two weeks was not so very long, if she considered it. She would be busy with her classes for much of that time. Surely she could maintain her defenses against him for a fortnight, Lily reflected. She wouldn't be in danger of falling in love with him in such a short period, surely . . .

It was imperative, however, that he not win the game, since she was unlikely to withstand his potent charm for an additional three months of a formal courtship.

"Very well," Lily said, taking a deep breath. "I do have something I want from you, my lord. We are holding a soiree here next week so that our boarders can exhibit their hard-won skills to attract prospective new patrons. I would like you to arrange for some of your wealthy bachelor friends to attend their debut. And you must weed out unsuitable candidates beforehand—anyone who would be cruel or domineering toward our young women. We only want those who will be considerate and kind. If you can promise to bring a dozen such eligible gentlemen to the soiree, then I will agree to play your game."

Claybourne hesitated for a moment before amusement twisted his mouth. "You drive a hard bargain, angel."

"Then you accept my terms?"

"Yes, of course."

She could hear Fleur's sigh of relief, while Chantel clapped her hands.

"That is very clever, Lily," Chantel said with admiration. "Lord Claybourne's support should insure our soiree's success."

"I sincerely hope so," Lily murmured, placing a hand over her suddenly queasy stomach as realization sank in. She had actually agreed to let the marquess woo her. What the devil had she done?

Claybourne might have sensed her dismay, for he kept his tone mild when he spoke. "If I have only a fortnight, then I must begin at once. Are you free tomorrow morning to accompany me on a ride in the park, Miss Loring?"

Frowning, Lily pursed her lips. A ride in a public park seemed innocuous enough. And as long as she could avoid being alone with him, she should be safe. "What time? We must make it before my classes begin at nine, and I doubt you will want to rise so early."

"Is seven o'clock convenient?"

It surprised her that he was willing to disturb his comfort in order to accommodate her schedule. "Seven o'clock will do well enough."

Chantel let out a small moan. "I never rise before ten, but you may report back on your excursion afterward."

Lord Claybourne nodded in agreement, then turned to Lily. "I will take my leave now. If your lovely friends"—he bowed to each of the courtesans—"are to grade my performance, then I had best think of something to impress them."

"Oh, I'll wager you will do quite well, my lord," Fleur said, returning a flirtatious smile. "Indeed, I believe we should award you two points now."

Lily's brows drew together. "Two points? That hardly seems fair."

"Oh, but it *is* fair, darling. He deserves at least one point for hunting you down here, since it shows excellent resourcefulness. And a second point for soliciting our help in persuading you to accept his courtship. That was very clever of him."

"But then he only has to earn eight more, and I will be starting out at a disadvantage."

"Perhaps, but he still has a long way to go. And keep in mind, he could *lose* points if we judge it fitting. However, by the same token, Lily, you must give him a sporting chance to score points," Fleur warned. "You must allow him time each day to advance his suit."

"Yet truly, Lily," Chantel added quite seriously, "I am certain you will enjoy yourself. The mating dance is the most pleasurable game in all the world."

Lily's grimace clearly showed her disagreement.

"Do you want to renege already?" Claybourne asked when she hesitated, his tone provocative.

Yes, was Lily's instinctive response. "No, I do not

wish to renege," she said aloud. But she lifted her chin as she met his amused gaze. "You should not be so confident, however, my lord. You will quickly learn you don't want me as your wife."

"I very much doubt that. But I won't underestimate you again."

Stepping toward her, he took her hand and gave her fingertips a chaste kiss. Lily drew a sharp breath at the heat that sizzled across her skin from the mere touch of his lips.

Perhaps she had made a serious mistake after all, she thought in alarm.

But the battle lines were drawn now, and she had no intention of allowing him the victory.

Chapter Five

❧

I intend to show his lordship I am far too independent for him to want me as his bride.

—Lily to Fanny

Still piqued by her friend Basil Eddowes's betrayal, Lily hunted him down early the next morning before his class on diction. She suspected he'd been deliberately avoiding her, since he hadn't dined with the boarders the night before or taken tea with them afterward in the drawing room. And when Basil opened his bedchamber door at Lily's knock, the guilty look on his face only confirmed her suspicions.

"Now don't be angry with me, Lily," he said, holding up his hands defensively.

"*Whyever* would I be angry?" she asked with false sweetness. "Merely because you have done untold damage to my life by divulging my personal secrets to a near stranger?"

Wincing, he shoved a shock of blond hair out of his eyes. Tall and lanky, wearing his usual dark frock coat and spectacles, Basil looked very much like the scholar he was, although the unruly hair that tumbled over his forehead was rather endearing and softened his lean, hungry appearance.

Basil possessed a keen mind but few social skills, and

it was that lack that Lily took issue with now. "I did not think you capable of such perfidy, Basil."

"I only hoped to do you a favor."

Her eyes narrowed. "What favor?"

"Why, to provide you a proper alternative to the life you are leading now. I don't want you following in Fanny's scandalous footsteps."

"*Basil* . . ." she said with mingled vexation and exasperation. He had never gotten over his fierce anger and disappointment at Fanny's decision to join the flesh trade, but he should know better than to think *she* wanted that same life. "You know I have no intention of becoming a Cyprian."

"But you should not be living here in a place like this, continually exposed to the seamier side of nature."

"*You* choose to live here."

"But I am a man, not a genteel young lady."

Her frown deepened. "I thought you supported my efforts to help our boarders, Basil."

"I do, but when Lord Claybourne said he wanted to court you, it seemed providential. The chance for you to become a marchioness is too splendid to pass up. I *care* what happens to you, Lily."

Hearing the genuine concern in Basil's voice, Lily bit back the scoffing retort she was about to make. She couldn't hold on to her vexation, despite his unwanted interference. They had been close friends since childhood.

In character, Basil was more like her sister Roslyn, his nose usually buried in a book. But he'd been Lily's faithful companion in sporting endeavors, climbing trees and galloping across the countryside like wild Turks and caring for the animals on the home farms of the Loring family estate. He had also been her unwilling partner in crime for many of her youthful escapades.

"I have no doubt you care for me, Basil," she said more gently. "And you know the feeling is mutual. I just wish you had found some other way of showing your affection than to betray me to Lord Claybourne."

"Well"—a sheepish grin wreathed Basil's mouth—"his lordship *was* very persuasive."

"I have no doubt about that either," Lily said dryly. "So you agreed to his courtship?"

"Under duress, yes," she muttered. "Because he promised to aid our boarders. But I must endure him only for the next fortnight. I am to go riding with him in a few moments."

Basil's brown eyes surveyed her approvingly. "I am glad you at least thought to take a veil. The damage to your reputation will be unavoidable if you are discovered to be living here in a house of low repute."

Along with her own riding habit, Lily was wearing a borrowed shako hat equipped with a veil so she could avoid advertising her identity. She didn't want to be easily recognizable by anyone she encountered during her ride with the marquess.

"The possible benefits to our pupils," she said, "are well worth any risk to my reputation. But Basil, in future *please* do not do me any more favors that involve you playing matchmaker."

He grinned. "I promise. Enjoy your ride."

"Oh, I will. I mean to show his lordship that I would make him an extremely unsuitable wife."

Basil frowned as she turned away. "Lily," he called after her, "just what devilish scheme are you planning?"

She laughed lightly as she continued down the corridor. "Nothing more mischievous than usual. I shall return in time for my class at nine."

"You know coves like Claybourne don't like mannish young ladies, Lily. You will put him off if you insist on outriding him and outshooting him and outthinking him."

"That is precisely my intention!"

Ignoring Basil's muttering, Lily made her way through the house to the front entrance. But when she stepped outside and saw Lord Claybourne waiting on the street for her, accompanied by a groom holding the reins of two magnificent bay horses, she came to an abrupt halt.

"Oh my heavens," she murmured to herself. How had he known she couldn't resist such superb horseflesh? She would be delighted to ride a spirited mount any time, but particularly now, when she'd been deprived of her favorite pastime during the entire month she'd been in London.

Stiffening her spine, Lily gathered her composure and continued down the steps. Clearly the marquess was not going to play fairly. But there was no need for panic. Indeed, she was counting on their absurd game to aid her cause, even if it meant being compelled to spend time with him. For she was convinced that if Lord Claybourne came to know her better, he would soon realize that he would not be at all happy with her as his bride.

Heath felt his loins tighten at the sight of Lily looking as fresh and lovely as the summer morning. She ignored him completely, however, and instead had eyes only for his horses.

Going directly to the smaller of the two bays, which sported a lady's sidesaddle, she spoke softly to the mare, stroking her face and receiving an affectionate nicker in return.

When Lily finally deigned to notice *him,* her lively eyes held appreciation. "I must say one thing for you, Lord Claybourne. You do have excellent taste in horse-flesh."

"Is that actually a compliment, Miss Loring?" Heath responded.

"I give credit where it is due . . . although I'm certain you are merely trying to score points with our judges."

"And with you as well. I thought you might have missed riding and hoped to disarm you by providing you an excellent steed."

"Well, I admit you succeeded," she said with rueful amusement. "I have rarely been privileged to ride such a wonderful animal."

"You may consider the mare a gift. After all, you are here in London without a mount because of me."

She shook her head. "I cannot accept so expensive a gift."

"A loan, then."

Lily gave the mare's face another fond stroke. "Thank you, my lord. I will love riding this beauty. Shall we be on our way?"

Heath had thought she might be reluctant to share his company this morning, yet she looked as though she was anticipating their outing with relish. But then, he should have known he wasn't dealing with any meek-mannered miss. Lily would throw herself into every challenge that confronted her, their courtship game in-cluded.

"I am trusting that you can handle a spirited horse," Heath said as he moved closer to help Lily mount.

Her vibrant smile left a dimple in her cheek. "You needn't worry about that. You should be more concerned about handling *me*."

Her sparkling dark eyes enchanted him, while her beauty and vitality made him want to touch her. It was with great pleasure that Heath put his hands on Lily's waist and lifted her onto the sidesaddle. The mare jigged a little, but Lily easily brought her under control, then adjusted her skirts and pulled down her filmy lace veil, which regrettably covered all of her face but her mouth. Then without waiting for him, she set off down the street.

Heath quickly swung up into his own saddle and gave orders to his groom to await him here, before urging his gelding after her.

"I thought we would ride in Green Park," he said when he caught up to her. "It is closer and won't be as crowded as Hyde Park."

"That will do nicely," she said in approval. "We can have a good gallop."

Green Park was only about a half mile from Fanny's boardinghouse on Gerrard Street, although in a busy part of London. The route they took to get there was congested by vendors hawking wares and all manner of traffic—drays and carriages, sporting vehicles and other riders. Heath kept a watchful eye on Lily, yet she dealt with the spirited mare so skillfully, he was soon able to relax and simply enjoy her company.

Heath found his mouth twisting with rueful amusement as he wondered how he'd wound up in this utterly alien situation—courting a woman he wanted for his bride who clearly didn't want him.

He had never courted anyone before. Certainly he'd

never had to expend such extreme effort just to gain a woman's attention. With his wealth and power, he needed merely to show a modicum of interest for her to become his. And not in his wildest dreams would he ever have expected to have to woo Lily under the eagle eyes of her protective courtesan friends.

Yet he was looking forward to the most intriguing challenge he'd encountered in years.

He had every confidence that he could eventually change Lily's mind about not wanting to marry him. His powers of persuasion were legendary, with charm and persistence being primary weapons in his arsenal.

In truth, winning had always come easily to him, Heath reflected—and he had every intention of claiming victory in their courtship.

But since Lily was so unconventional, he knew conventional methods would be ineffectual with her. If he hoped to keep her off balance, he needed to be creative and enterprising. Thus the superb Thoroughbred mare he'd bought for her late yesterday.

His instincts told him the way to Lily's heart would not be through jewels and other feminine gewgaws. And from her pleased reaction to the mare, he knew he'd succeeded in winning their first skirmish.

However, the first words out of Lily's mouth were not those of a young lady eager to win his own heart:

"I wish you would believe me, Lord Claybourne, when I say I will never marry."

Heath cocked an eyebrow. "You mean to remain a spinster your entire life? I just cannot see it."

"I can, quite easily. I imagine I will find spinsterhood delightful," Lily contended. "Besides, two married women in one family is more than enough."

He chuckled. "You haven't yet forgiven your sisters for falling in love."

"I have not." Since Lily's face was mostly veiled, he couldn't see her eyes, but her luscious mouth was curved in a half smile. "I suppose they have a right to choose their own futures, however. And I *am* very glad they are happy. As for me, I was perfectly content before Marcus inherited the title from our late step-uncle and came into our lives."

"Even living under the taint of scandal as you were?"

When her smile faded, Heath was sorry he'd brought up the subject. "It is highly regrettable that you and your sisters had to bear the brunt of your parents' ignominy."

Lily's shrug was nonchalant. "You needn't pity us, my lord. We quickly realized there was a silver lining to the disgrace. We were no longer expected to behave like perfect ladies."

"Which you rarely did in any case."

Her smile returned. "Indeed. But the scandals liberated us in a way." She sighed. "You have no idea how frustrating it is to be shackled by the restrictions deemed proper for genteel young ladies. Frankly, I envy Fanny the freedom she enjoys."

"But society permits more freedom for married ladies to behave as they please than single ones."

She laughed. "Possibly, but that still won't induce me to marry you."

Heath very much liked the sound of her husky laughter. "What objections do you have to wedding me, other than your desire for independence?"

Lily waited until they had negotiated their mounts across a busy avenue before she answered. "Your reputation, for one thing. You are infamous for your amorous conquests, and I have no wish to become one more of their number."

"As my wife, you would hardly be my conquest, sweeting. In fact, some would say *you* would be making the conquest."

"Oh, yes, I know," she said sardonically. "You are a great matrimonial prize. But you have plenty of admirers pursuing you. And since I don't like to imitate sheep, I mean to resist you on general principle. I am stubborn-minded that way."

"I can see that," Heath remarked, amused. "But would you really allow stubbornness to dictate your entire future?"

She didn't respond at once, and when she did, her tone was thoughtful. "Do you keep a mistress, Lord Claybourne?"

The question surprised him for its boldness, but he gave her an honest reply. "Not regularly, no."

"But you have had countless lovers."

His mouth curved. "You give me too much credit. The number is not countless. Even I haven't that much fortitude."

"Nevertheless, I expect you are a bit too much like my father for my tastes."

Fixing his gaze on Lily, Heath regarded her intently. "I'll have you know, I mean to remain faithful to our marriage vows after we are wed."

Her pause spoke volumes. Because of the veil, he couldn't see her arched eyebrows, but he heard the cynicism in her voice when she replied. "I find that very difficult to believe."

He would never overcome her doubts by arguing with

her, Heath knew, so he settled for a mild reply. "I can see that teaching you to trust me should be my first goal."

"You are welcome to try," she said without much conviction.

"I realize it won't be easy, given your low opinion of noblemen."

Lily nodded seriously. "I've had good reason to think ill of your ilk just recently, my lord. Two of our boarders were in service to noble households and were seduced by their masters, then thrown out onto the streets and forced to sell their bodies to survive." Her tone turned dark. "It is appalling, what they endured. Can you even imagine facing such an horrific experience?"

Since her question seemed rhetorical, Heath didn't answer, nor apparently did Lily expect him to, for she went on ardently. "And then they were roundly condemned for the sin of prostitution! It isn't fair," she said with real anger in her voice.

"No it isn't."

She finally looked over at him again. "Are you simply being agreeable because you wish to impress me?"

"No," Heath said solemnly. "I admire your passion. It's clear you are a very compassionate and caring woman."

Lily seemed to relax a measure. "Not as compassionate as my friend Miss Blanchard. Now *she* is truly good. She has the kindest soul I've ever known. I am not particularly good or kind. I just feel sorry for the vulnerable and helpless, especially the unfortunate women who must use their bodies as merchandise. Thankfully I was able to find those two girls employment with the household staff at Danvers Hall, even though Marcus didn't need any more servants."

Heath raised an eyebrow. "You sent your two boarders to Marcus?"

Lily hesitated. "Actually, I sent them to Roslyn. At the time I couldn't ask Marcus to take them in, since I didn't want him to know I was in London." From her tone, he suspected Lily's cheeks were flushing, but she gave him no chance to reply before continuing. "I could not simply ignore their plight, though. They needed someone to stand up for them. To help them to escape that awful life."

He studied her thoughtfully. "And yet you are actively preparing your pupils to attract wealthy patrons at the soiree."

Lily grimaced. "I know. But my friends convinced me it was the best course. If our boarders have a large enough income, they will have a greater measure of control over their lives, more choices for their futures. They won't be quite so trapped and powerless as they are now. I am still concerned for them, however—which is why I asked you to find suitable candidates from among your bachelor friends. Our boarders deserve patrons who are kind and gentle. Widowers, perhaps, who need companionship more than passion. Or gentlemen like my friend Basil, who are amiable and tolerant, even bashful. Men who won't behave like brutes simply because they control the purse strings."

"Your pupils are fortunate to have you champion them so earnestly."

For a few heartbeats, Lily eyed him as if trying to judge his sincerity. "I suppose you deserve some of the credit, Lord Claybourne."

"Credit?"

"For causing me to come to London in the first place.

If not for you wanting to court me, I never would have become involved with our boarders."

"Now *that* is a novel notion," Heath murmured with a tinge of wryness.

Lily stiffened. "I am completely serious, my lord."

"I can see that, angel. And I commend your efforts. I was simply laughing at the irony of my courtship driving you to such lengths."

"It *is* rather ironic," she said more softly. Her mouth twisted without humor. "No doubt I can sympathize with their difficulties because of what my sisters and I went through after our family scandals erupted. We could easily have wound up in the same dire circumstances as our boarders."

Heath found himself frowning. He didn't like thinking of Lily at the mercy of fate like that. He hated to imagine her as a needy young girl, forced into prostitution to survive.

"And *someone* needs to help them," Lily added. "They will get little assistance from most members of our class. Take yourself, for example. You are a gentleman of leisure. You treat life as a game."

Perhaps that was true, Heath acknowledged. Pursuit of pleasure and excitement had been his aim for much of his life.

"Before meeting our girls, I was a good deal like you," Lily continued. "I didn't worry much about the lower classes or consider how they managed to survive. And we were so sheltered from the realities of life, I never even knew women like our boarders existed. Except for Fanny, of course, and she is certainly not typical of the demimonde. But now I feel as if I have finally found a calling."

Heath nodded thoughtfully. He'd never given much consideration to the plight of fallen women. Oh, he'd always behaved with honor toward his servants and ensured their welfare. But otherwise, he rarely involved himself in their lives.

He could admire Lily for her newfound passion. She had channeled her rebellious spirit into striving for a worthy cause.

Just then, however, they arrived at the entrance to the park.

Lily visibly shook herself before giving him another glance. "Do forgive me, my lord. I have bored you to tears."

"You haven't bored me in the least. In fact, I can honestly say you are the least boring woman I have ever met."

When he smiled, she made a face. "Well, it certainly was not my intention to entertain you. Perhaps we should ride?"

Entering the park, they guided their horses onto a wide gravel path flanked by elms and oaks. But they had gone barely ten yards when they saw two riders approaching.

Recognizing both gentlemen, Heath paused politely to greet them, but Lily urged her mare past them, leaving him to deal with his friends.

And as soon as he caught up to her, she broke into an easy canter.

"I'm certain you understand why I would rather not meet anyone in your illustrious circles," she explained before he could take her to task for riding on without him.

"Yes, but I would prefer that you wait for me next

time," Heath chided. "You should have an escort when you ride anywhere in London."

"A pity that I cannot oblige," she replied sweetly, spurring her horse into a faster canter. "You see, I mean to leave you in my dust."

Heath couldn't help but grin at her provocation. "Is that a challenge to race, Miss Loring?"

"Most certainly," she called over her shoulder.

Bending over the mare's neck, she asked for more speed, and Heath knew that if he wanted to keep Lily in sight, he would have to accept her challenge.

He dug his heels into his mount's sides, and soon they were both galloping along the path, heedless of the impropriety of racing through a public park.

He managed to close some of the distance between them, yet he was distracted by the simple pleasure of watching Lily ride. She was a hellion in the saddle, that was strikingly clear. And then she threw her head back and laughed with sheer exuberance.

At the sound of her joyful laughter, Heath felt a sharp tug of sheer lust rippling in his gut.

Realizing that he would never win their race if he didn't focus, though, he put all his effort into the match. Even so, she gradually drew away from him. And when they finally reached the end of the path at the far end of the park, Lily was ahead by nearly two lengths.

When she pulled up, her spirited mare was snorting and prancing in excitement, and Lily herself was a bit breathless.

"That was utterly delightful!" she exclaimed, patting the mare's neck.

Heath drew rein ruefully, aware that he hadn't been bested that badly in a horse race since he and Marcus and Drew were boys. He was even more aware of his ex-hilaration at watching Lily. *She* was utterly delightful, Heath thought. Delightful and vibrant and intoxicatingly alive.

He couldn't see the upper part of her face because of that damned veil, but her ripe mouth alone was enough to rouse a stimulating fantasy in his mind: making love to Lily and setting all that marvelous passion free. He had no doubt what she would be like in his bed. Hot, passionate, eager, wild.

The thought made him hard at once, which regrettably made his doeskin riding breeches painfully tight. Hence, Heath was glad for the slower pace when they turned back the way they had come and kept to a walk to cool their sweating horses.

They had reached the juncture of a new path when Heath found himself hailed again by more of his acquaintances. This time it was two ladies driving a dashing phaeton.

"You are quite popular this morning, my lord," Lily murmured, flashing him a mischievous smile before turning her horse down the side path.

By the time Heath had suffered the ladies' effusive regards, Lily was nowhere in sight. Impatiently he set out after her, a niggling concern for her safety chafing at him. Even though she seemed well able to take care of herself, an unaccompanied young lady could be a target for any manner of riffraff.

He followed the path Lily had taken, moving off it now and then to make certain she wasn't hiding behind a thicket or concealed in a stand of trees. But there was no sign of her anywhere. She had disappeared.

Heath combed the entire park twice to no avail.

Twenty minutes later, he finally returned to the park entrance and found her patiently waiting for him.

His relief vied with vexation, although her enchanting smile almost made him forget his ire.

"What kept you, Lord Claybourne? I have been waiting for simply ages."

Her tone was teasing, provocative, and it made Heath want to drag Lily off her mare and onto his lap so he could kiss her senseless. But he settled for saying mildly, "I was searching for you, of course. I couldn't credit that you would be so unwise as to ride alone. It can be dangerous for you."

"Perhaps, but I decided to start as I mean to go on. I won't make it easy for you to win points by always acquiescing passively to your tactics, my lord." Her saucy smile broadened. "What will our judges think when you confess that you lost your quarry? It should prove amusing, seeing you explain how I managed to escape your escort."

"It will hardly be amusing for me," he said dryly.

She laughed at his exasperation. At that husky, glorious laughter, Heath felt a rush of heat arrow through him.

I want you, sweet Lily, he thought. *I want you beneath me, beside me, sharing your vibrant passion with me. I want your laughter surrounding me.*

"I expect you won't find it amusing, my lord," Lily agreed. "But I warned you, remember? This is what you can expect if you insist on continuing our game. Are you willing to give up yet?" she asked sweetly as she turned her horse toward the street.

"Not on your life."

He wasn't about to give her up now, Heath reflected

silently. He wanted this bright-eyed spitfire who radiated vibrancy. And the only honorable way to have her was through marriage.

The prospect was growing more appealing by the moment. He could imagine Lily as his wife now. He could even imagine willingly spending time with her once they were wed.

Long pleasurable nights filled with passion. Delightful days filled with laughter and adventure.

However, it would be a tactical mistake to suggest any such future to Lily, Heath knew. "You will find that challenges only spur me on to greater lengths," he said instead.

"They do the same for me," she replied.

"See, I've been trying to tell you we have a great deal in common."

Her smile returned. "I don't deny that, but my love of a challenge will prove very uncomfortable in a wife."

"Actually I think it will prove exhilarating. And I think you are utterly enchanting."

That made her smile falter. "I wish you wouldn't do that, Lord Claybourne—shower me with empty flattery."

"It is not empty, believe me."

"Well, I don't want your compliments."

"Very well, if it makes you uneasy, I will stop."

That was another difference between Lily and most other women he knew. She was so unassuming about her beauty. And she had no idea how desirable he found her.

But he did find her utterly desirable. There was a fire in her, and he wanted to be burned.

He had never expected to encounter a woman like

Lily, Heath reflected. She continually surprised him, even if she left him exasperated and very determined to win their battle. She was feisty, clever, tart-tongued, generous, with a lively sense of adventure.

His mother had possessed her same high spirits, he recalled. In truth, he saw something of his mother's vividness in Lily . . . except that his mother had been rather gay and flighty, always living for the moment.

Camilla was always laughing, also. He still missed the laughter she'd instilled in his childhood. She had died in childbirth when he was ten, dealing Heath a severe blow.

It had been a blow to his father as well, surprisingly enough. Before Camilla's death, his father had been a staid, boring, deadly dull stick in the mud. And afterward, Simon had become more like a corpse, as if the very life had drained out of him. He'd withdrawn even further into his shell, closed himself off to any kind of joy or pleasure.

Heath was adamantly determined never to turn out like his father, which was why he'd pursued his own pleasures all those years—to prove he was totally different from his illustrious sire.

His desire for excitement and adventure had been a chief source of argument between them when Heath was in his salad days. His father had put great store in responsibility and duty, perhaps because he had so little in his life to fulfill or gratify him.

The fact that his parents had been so unsuited to each other in personalities and temperament was a prime reason Heath had resisted matrimony in the past. His greatest fear was that he would end up wedding an insipid, spiritless gentlewoman merely to sire necessary heirs.

But he certainly needn't fear that with Lily. She was the first woman he'd ever met who could lure him into wanting to give up his freedom. If he'd had any doubts about wanting to wed her, they had been vanquished during their ride.

He wanted her. And he intended to have her. As his wife. Nothing less.

It wasn't a rash decision, made with his usual impulsiveness. There were several practical reasons to choose her for his bride. In terms of birth, breeding, and compatibility, Lily would make him an ideal marchioness. Moreover, it would save him the trouble of having to search for a wife in the near future.

But mainly his decision was based on sheer instinct. He feared if he didn't act now, he would let something precious slip through his fingers.

It remained for him to convince Lily, however. An immense challenge, Heath was well aware.

But fighting it would do her no good—

"You there! Stop that at once!"

Her sudden shout startled him abruptly out of his reverie.

Lily was staring down an alley they were passing, Heath realized an instant before she suddenly whirled her mare and took off down the narrow lane, leaving him in her dust again.

Chapter Six

❦

*Perhaps my agreeing to play the game was a mistake
after all. At this rate he could very well win.*

—Lily to Fanny

Heath muttered an oath under his breath, but when
Lily shouted once more, her fury told him this was not
another attempt to elude him and make it harder for
him to win points in their game.

Her mare's hooves clattering on the cobblestones, she
charged down the alley toward a gathering of brawny
youths at the far end. It took Heath another moment to
understand what had infuriated her so: The ruffians
were brandishing thick sticks at a dog, taking turns
beating the animal's cringing body.

Voicing a more vivid curse, Heath turned his horse
and set off after Lily. He was hard on her heels when she
drew rein and practically threw herself from the saddle.

His heart in his throat, he watched as she waded into
the throng of rowdies, her fists flailing, her cries of outrage startling the lads.

"Stop tormenting that poor creature, you *louts*! Stop
this instant!"

Since she had the advantage of surprise, every one of
the half-dozen toughs staggered back defensively, clearly
stunned by the Fury who had descended in their midst.

But when they realized their attacker was only a woman—and a genteel lady at that—the rabble turned on Lily in unison, waving their sticks threateningly.

She got the better of the nearest one, ferociously kicking him in the shins just as Heath flung himself off his horse and entered the fight. Fear and fury flooding him, he grabbed the shoulder of a muscled lummox, dealing a punishing blow with his fist and knocking the oaf to the cobblestones.

Seeing another burly youth raise his stick high to strike Lily, Heath jerked the wood from his grasp and swung it like a club at his gut, landing a powerful whack that elicited a sharp cry of pain. Clutching his belly, the lout reeled backward and then lunged off, groaning.

In the face of Heath's relentless wrath, the other bullies capitulated at once. And when they raced away, their fallen accomplice struggled to his feet and limped off after them.

"Yes, run, you worthless mawworms!" Lily shouted in their wake.

She had sunk to her knees, Heath saw, and was cradling the trembling dog in her arms, shielding it from harm with her body. She had lost her hat and veil in the melee, and her dark eyes were giving off sparks.

His own fury ebbing a small measure, Heath joined Lily on the ground as she bent over the shaking animal and crooned softly.

"Oh, you poor, frightened sweetheart. No one will hurt you now, I promise."

The dog was a mongrel bitch, Heath realized, mangy and flea-bitten and clearly battered. Her brown fur was matted with blood while a nasty gash welled over one eye.

As Lily stroked the ragged head gently, Heath ran his hands carefully over the mutt's body. When he reached the ribs that stuck out beneath her coat, she whimpered at his touch, but that seemed to be the most serious of her injuries.

"Her ribs are bruised but likely not broken," Heath said, finishing his examination.

"Thank heavens," Lily breathed, even as she glanced murderously back down the alley. "But those sorry wretches may return to torment this poor creature. We cannot leave her here." She glanced down tenderly at the dog. "And her wounds need tending."

The "poor creature" seemed to understand Lily's intent, for she licked her hand feebly in gratitude, the brown eyes looking up at her with adoration.

"I shall take you home with me," Lily said, bestowing a soft smile on the animal.

"To the boardinghouse?" Heath asked dubiously.

"Yes. She can stay in my room."

He couldn't quite picture Fleur and Chantel welcoming the dirty mongrel into their elegant abode. "Your friends will hardly thank you."

"I know, but this sweet beastie needs a safe place to live. And food. She looks as if she is starving."

"And a bath," Heath murmured dryly.

"Yes, of course."

There was no point in arguing with Lily, he realized, since she had her mind set on rescuing the dog. So he rose to his feet. When Lily had carefully gathered the animal in her arms, Heath helped her rise and went to collect their horses, which surprisingly were standing docilely nearby.

Leading the two horses to Lily, he reached for the dog. "I will take her."

But Lily shook her head. "No, she trusts me. I can hold her while I ride."

Having seen her skill on horseback, Heath repressed the urge to argue and lifted her into her sidesaddle, then helped arrange her position so that she cradled the trembling dog in her lap while clutching the reins one-handed. But he kept a wary eye on them both as he swung up into his saddle and led the way back down the alley. And he remained close on the chance that she needed help controlling the spirited mare.

Offering reassurance to the dog, Lily spoke softly to her for the first few minutes as they rode down the busy streets, ignoring Heath completely. When the animal seemed finally to relax, however, she glanced over at him with a faint smile.

"I haven't properly thanked you, my lord. I could never have overpowered those brutes alone. You were truly magnificent."

When Lily's marvelous eyes regarded him with gratitude, Heath felt a strange lurch in the vicinity of his heart. *She* was the one who was magnificent, plunging into the fray, heedless of her own safety. It was one of the braver things he had ever seen.

Yet that didn't mean he condoned her rash leap into danger.

"You left me little choice but to follow you," Heath replied. "I lost a year off my life, seeing you attack that riffraff. It was valiant of you, but foolhardy as well. You could have been seriously hurt."

Lily shrugged. "But I wasn't hurt because you were

there to save us. Not many noblemen would bother to help a stray dog."

"Nor would many ladies," he pointed out.

He'd been given yet another glimpse of Lily's compassionate nature . . . and her single-minded zeal. She was passionate even in her faults. That inner fire was evident in everything she did, Heath thought, surveying her still-flushed cheeks and overbright eyes. And it made him want her even more fiercely.

Yet he didn't believe her courtesan friends would share her desire to rescue a mangy mongrel. "Can you honestly see your friends deigning to take in your new canine companion?" he queried.

Lily's smile was rueful. "I will just have to convince them. Thankfully she will be much more presentable once she is clean and her wounds are tended."

"I doubt that will be a significant improvement."

"Well, she is obviously not an aristocrat like you."

"Indeed."

Lily smiled at his dry tone. "But she is very sweet. Just look at that darling face."

"I would not exactly term it 'darling,' " Heath remarked, examining the bloodied features.

"Perhaps not, but I am not about to turn her back onto the streets. Although. . . ."

"Although what?" he asked at her pause.

"London is no place for a dog." Lily frowned thoughtfully. "She would probably be happier living in the country. Perhaps I should send her to Danvers Hall . . . but no. She needs special care, and Roslyn is in the midst of planning for her wedding, and Arabella is extremely busy helping."

"I expect I could take the dog off your hands," Heath said slowly.

Turning to survey him, Lily appeared skeptical. "*You,* my lord? What would you do with a stray with no pedigree?"

He sent Lily a glance of humorous reproach. "I am not offering to make her my personal pet. She could have a home on the farms at my family seat in Kent."

Still Lily hesitated. "I would rather not be so beholden to you."

"I know—you wish to remain unequivocally independent of any man. But think of the poor dog. She would be better off living in the countryside than in the city, you said so yourself."

"I suppose you are right. And doubtless you have an army of servants who could look after her."

"Yes. She will be well cared for there."

Lily gave him a searching look. "You would do that for her?"

"I would do it for *you,* since you are so concerned about her welfare."

"Your kindness would be much appreciated," Lily said finally. "By both of us." She gazed down at the dog lovingly. "We will have to think of a suitable name for you, won't we, sweetheart?"

"How about *Fortune*—the French word for lucky?" Heath suggested.

Her brow furrowed. "Why that choice? She seems terribly *unlucky* to me."

"Until now, yes, but she is highly fortunate that you decided to come to her rescue."

"And you as well. Very well, 'Fortune' it is."

She included Heath in her warm, endearing smile, and

he couldn't regret his impulsive offer to take responsibility for the dog, even when Lily returned all her attention to the mutt.

When they arrived back at the rooming house, his groom went dutifully to their horses' heads.

"You can hand Fortune over to my man," Heath told Lily. "He will take her to the stables so she can be bathed and bandaged and fed."

Rather than complying, however, Lily tightened her arms around the dog and regarded Heath with an imploring look. "She might be frightened of a stranger. Won't you see to her care, my lord? I will happily tell our judges about your magnanimity. Just think, you could win another point or two in our game."

Heath couldn't help but chuckle at her devotion to her new charge, yet it was a significant step that Lily had actually asked him for something.

Therefore, even though he would have preferred to hand the animal over to his footman, Heath nudged his horse close to Lily's and reached out for the dog. "Come here, little mutt. It seems you are coming home with me."

The dog licked his fingers once, then scrabbled over onto his lap. Heath winced as her claws dug into his loins, and felt relieved when she finally flopped down across his thighs.

Lily's eyes danced. "She likes you."

"Animals usually do. As do women."

He could see Lily's effort to repress a rejoinder at his quip. Instead she merely said sincerely, "Thank you, my lord. You have my profound gratitude."

Her soft, husky tone raked across his nerve endings. Locking gazes with her, Heath went very still. For a span of several heartbeats, he stared at her, desire rushing though him like a warm tide.

He wanted to kiss her. He wanted to take down her hair and see how it would look tangled after their love-making. He could picture Lily breathless with passion, her skin glowing, her eyes languid with sensuality, her ripe mouth parted.

He craved that sweet mouth under his. He craved her luscious body beneath his.

He was sorely tempted to carry Lily off right then and take her someplace where he could spend days teaching her about the delights of passion that she so ardently denied wanting.

But now was certainly not the time, when he had the dog's welfare to see to.

The moment would come, he had no doubt. He would make Lily his wife and have a long future ahead with her, enjoying the pleasures of their marriage bed.

Even so, subduing his lust required a greater struggle than anticipated, and his voice was unexpectedly husky when he spoke. "I will find a way for you to reward me when I return this afternoon. And we still must score this round of our game, remember?"

Although looking a trifle wary, Lily nodded. "If you will call this afternoon at three, I will see that our judges are there to welcome you."

"Three o'clock, then."

Allowing his groom to help her down from her sidesaddle, Lily reached up to gently stroke Fortune's head once more. Then flashing another ravishing smile at Heath, she turned and ran lightly up the front steps.

Heath remained sitting there, totally immobile, as she disappeared inside the house. His mouth had gone dry, while his loins had tightened at the impact of that breathtaking smile.

A wet tongue licking his hand suddenly recalled him to his surroundings.

"I trust you do realize how lucky you are, my girl," he said, glancing down at the dog, "garnering such singular attention from your new mistress. Would that I could say the same."

Another lick was the response he got.

Repressing a wry grin, Heath waited while his groom took the mare's reins so as to lead her and mounted the hack.

Only then did Heath turn his gelding away from the house.

The desire to make love to Lily was still stinging his body. But he promised himself that it wouldn't be long before he fulfilled his urgent need for her.

Lily was more upset by her confrontation with the brutish youths than she let on, for the encounter had forced her to recall an even uglier memory. One that was branded into her heart and soul.

But once her rage dissipated, she was determined to put it from her mind.

She was exceedingly glad, however, that the marquess had been with her when she'd impulsively charged down that alley. He had dealt with those louts in heroic fashion, not stopping to question that he was risking injury or worse to help her rescue a mongrel dog. And she trusted that he would provide for the injured animal's welfare.

She had considerably less trust, Lily admitted as she

sought refuge in the calming privacy of her bedchamber, in her own ability to withstand his masculine allure.

She'd found herself enjoying his lordship's company far too much. He was delightful to converse with, charming and witty and interesting. He made her laugh, and he made her think.

What was more, she felt completely at ease with him.

Which was patently absurd. How could a man make her feel safe and so unsettled at the same time?

Lord Claybourne had only to look at her to make her heart beat faster. And when he smiled at her in that captivating way . . . There was something in his smile that made her feel special, appreciated, valued.

Perhaps that was the secret of his devastating success with the fair sex. He treated women as individuals in their own right, not simply as objects of desire.

Yet she had to remember he was only employing his well-honed amatory skills. She had to keep in mind the danger of letting herself become spellbound by his appeal.

And she would have to do better to resist him. He was winning their competition thus far, Lily acknowledged. And once she reported back to their judges about the events of the morning, he would be even farther ahead.

The judging went much as she predicted.

By the time Lord Claybourne was shown into the courtesans' private sitting room that afternoon where Lily was waiting for him with Fleur and Chantel, she had truthfully recounted what had happened in the park and the alley.

And her friends were charmingly effusive in their welcome.

"Hail the hero," Chantel declared, fluttering her eyelashes provocatively at the marquess when he bent over her hand in greeting.

"Indeed," said Fleur just as fervently. "It was splendid, how you championed Lily in that brave manner, my lord."

"You give me too much credit," he responded lightly, shooting a glance at Lily. "Miss Loring was the brave one."

"And foolhardy, too," Fleur added tartly. "Who knows what would have happened to her had you not been there to save her from her own recklessness?"

Subduing her own absurd pleasure at seeing him again, Lily resumed her seat in a wing chair so he couldn't kiss her hand as he'd done her friends. "Did you have any trouble caring for Fortune, Lord Claybourne?"

He smiled at her swift change of subject but remained standing. "Your canine has been bathed and doctored. And I personally fed her half a mutton chop in bite-sized pieces. She will be given the other half this evening. I thought it wise to take her recovery slowly, since I doubt she is accustomed to such rich fare."

"Thank you, my lord," Lily repeated sincerely.

"So, ladies," he said, looking at the two courtesans who had settled on the settee. "I presume you mean to judge my first performance?"

Fleur took the lead. "We are all agreed, my lord—even Lily. You won a point for bringing her such a lovely horse to ride. But you lost one for letting Lily escape your escort in the park. And we are awarding you *two* points for helping her rescue the dog and sending those bullies fleeing."

"And yet another point for being so generous as to give the animal a home," Chantel chimed in.

"Yes," Fleur said with a mock shudder. "I wanted to grant you an extra bonus point for keeping that mangy animal out of *our* house, but we decided that would be a little much this early in the game. In any case, you still have nearly a fortnight to earn the rest of your ten points."

Chantel smiled. "So your total is now five, my lord, if you count the two you earned yesterday."

"And you agreed to that tally?" Claybourne asked Lily.

"Yes," she replied, knowing she couldn't begrudge him what he honestly deserved, even if it was rather alarming that he'd already collected half the number of points he needed to win. "It is only fair."

"Speaking of fairness . . ." Fleur interjected, "we have reminded Lily of her agreement to permit your courtship, my lord, and clarified the rules for her. She can resist, but she cannot deliberately sabotage your efforts to woo her. If we discover otherwise, we may grant you extra points to make up for her hindering you unfairly."

Lily saw him smile at that agreeable announcement. "Then I would be within my rights to claim my reward?"

"What reward?" Chantel asked curiously.

"Yes," Lily seconded. "What reward?"

He shifted his attention to her. "The one you promised me for taking your dog home with me."

Her gaze turned wary. "What reward would you like, my lord?"

"A simple kiss, that is all."

Color rushing into her cheeks, Lily shot a tentative

glance at her friends, wondering if they would allow so brazen a ploy. But neither of them responded.

She dragged her gaze back to Claybourne. "You want to kiss me?"

"Very much," he answered, his eyes glinting wickedly. "I have since our very first meeting."

"But right here in front of an audience?"

"Would you permit such a liberty any other way?"

"Well, no."

"Then I will take what I can get."

Lily shot her friends another anxious glance. "You don't intend to object?"

Fleur answered for them both. "We are merely judges, Lily darling. We are not supposed to interfere in your game unless it is necessary for your safety."

"*Did* you promise to reward his lordship?" Chantel asked. "If so, you must honor your word. But if you wish, we will leave the room."

"No!" Lily protested. I don't want you to leave."

She had not promised to kiss Claybourne, but she supposed it would be an innocuous enough payment for his earlier generosity. After all, what could he do to her when they had witnesses?

"Very well, my lord," Lily murmured.

She regretted her capitulation the instant he moved toward her.

"Stand up, sweeting," he urged, taking her hand.

Feeling a sizzle of heat arc up her arm, Lily rose unsteadily to her feet. Claybourne smiled slowly, devilishly, as if knowing exactly what impact he was having on her.

Then he raised her hand almost to his lips. His breath fanned the edge of her palm, yet his mouth never touched her skin. Instead he reached out and slipped his fingers beneath her jaw, cradling her chin.

Her respiration grew shallow as he stood gazing down at her, while her pulse pounded in a heavy, uncertain rhythm.

After a dozen heartbeats had passed, though, Lily had had enough. "Pray hurry and be done with it, my lord."

He made a *tsk*ing sound. "Such impatience. A kiss should be savored, not rushed."

"Yes, indeed," Chantel agreed, her tone dreamy.

Lily gritted her teeth, willing herself to remain calm. Even so, her nerves were on fire by the time Claybourne's mouth at last descended to hers.

It was the lightest of caresses. His lips barely moved against hers, yet the impact was searing. His kiss was warm, tender, magical . . . and oh so devastating, just as she'd expected.

Lily felt hot and breathless and dazed when he finally let up.

While she tried futilely to regain her wits, Chantel applauded his performance with delight. "That kiss was perfectly lovely, Lord Claybourne."

"And quite romantic," Fleur said with a sigh. "I think you should have another point added to your tally."

"Fleur!" Lily protested. "It really was not so extraordinary."

"I might be wounded, love," Claybourne said, amused, "if I thought you believed that."

She had only to look into those gold-flecked eyes, gleaming with wicked knowledge, to realize she hadn't fooled him in the least. He knew very well that even a simple kiss from him was captivating.

"Well, it certainly was not worth a full point," she complained.

The marquess eyed her thoughtfully. "What do you say we strike a compromise? I will relinquish any points for my kissing skills just now in exchange for a few moments of privacy with you."

Lily narrowed her gaze on him. "Why do you want privacy?"

"Because as charming and lovely as your friends are"—he bowed gracefully to the courtesans—"their presence does put a damper on my courtship."

"Having to be alone with you was not part of our game."

"Very well, if you want me to accept another point—"

"No!" Lily exclaimed.

Rising, Fleur nodded as if coming to a decision. "I think you have earned the right to a little privacy with Lily, my lord. You may have five minutes with her, no more."

"You cannot be serious," Lily objected.

"Oh, but I can," Fleur replied. "A measure of intimacy will go a long way toward loosening you up, my dear. And his lordship is just the man to do it. You will find very few gentlemen with his prowess. Moreover, if you become better acquainted with him now, you will be better informed to make a decision about wedding him." Fleur's mouth twisted as she contemplated Lily. "I happen to think you are a fool to resist his suit, my darling, but you are the one who must live with the consequences."

"I agree, Lily," Chantel announced as she also rose. "If I were twenty years younger, I might try to steal him from you."

"You may have him with my blessing," she muttered under her breath.

When the two women had left the sitting room and shut the door behind them, Lily regarded the marquess nervously. "Just what do you think you are doing?"

"I intend to kiss you again. That brief taste wasn't nearly enough. For me or for you either, I suspect."

"It was more than enough for me."

He smiled. "Then look at it as gaining more knowledge upon which to base your decision."

She didn't want any more knowledge of him! Certainly not the sensual kind of education he had in mind. Lily edged away from Lord Claybourne, determined to put some distance between them, but he reached out to lightly grasp her wrist.

"You are hardly playing fair," she said, futilely trying to free her hand.

"Perhaps so, but you know the saying . . . all's fair in love."

"This has nothing whatever to do with *love*! You only want to win this absurd game . . . and perhaps to gain a broodmare for your heirs."

He shook his head. "I want a *wife*, Lily, and I am laying claim to you."

Her exasperation turned to frustration. "You cannot just claim me as if I were the spoils of war."

"*You* are the one who has made this a war. I am exerting my best effort to woo you."

"Well, I wish you would cease plaguing me this vexing way."

Claybourne released her hand but held her gaze. "One kiss, and then I will go."

That made her pause. "Just one?"

"Yes. And you can end it whenever you choose."

It was incredibly dangerous to kiss him again, Lily knew. His kisses set her senses aflame and made her head spin so that she couldn't even think straight. And yet she knew there was no other way to be rid of him.

She dragged in a deep breath. "Very well," she said mutinously. "Since you leave me no choice."

Ignoring her reluctance, he gently caught hold of her shoulders, bringing her close to him.

He didn't kiss her at once, however. Instead he reached up with one hand to caress her. His fingers lightly rubbed the erratic pulse in her throat, then explored the warm hollows of her ear.

Lily wanted to flee, to run, but his golden gaze held her prisoner. Something hot and molten unfurled inside her at that look in his eyes. She couldn't speak, couldn't move. She could only feel.

His other hand slipped behind her and skimmed up her spine, then stroked her nape before cupping the back of her head. A heartbeat later, he finally bent and sealed his mouth to hers.

He kissed her thoroughly this time, his hot, clever, tongue slowly penetrating and exploring the deepest recesses of her mouth. Her breath gone, Lily felt herself melting in his embrace. Urgency flared at the searing warmth he roused inside her, and that was before his hand cupped her breast with shocking possessiveness.

His brazen caress suffused her body with heat and a liquid heaviness, and she found it impossible to control the small moan of pleasure that rose to her lips.

Her moan deepened when he caught her more firmly about the waist, drawing her even closer. She should have been shocked by the hard length of his arousal pressed against her abdomen, yet somehow the knowledge only excited her.

Then his knee moved against her skirts, nudging her own knees apart. Lily was unprepared for the sharp, erotic rush of feeling from his thigh against her woman's mound.

Her moan turned to a helpless whimper as the pulse quickened between her legs. Encouraging her further, he moved his palm downward to mold her derriere and went on kissing her.

Yet now she didn't want him to stop, couldn't bear the thought of his sublime mouth leaving hers. Clutching at his broad shoulders, she gave in willingly to the glorious madness.

The madness eventually ended, however. His hard thigh still was nestled between hers when his devastating kiss at last broke off and his lips moved to nuzzle her ear.

"I want you, Lily," he murmured, his voice a husky rasp. "I want you in my bed. I want your lovely hair on my pillow, your soft breath on my skin, your luscious body writhing beneath mine."

She should not be thrilled by his admission, but it made her tremble and ache with longing. When he drew back to gaze down at her, she stood there staring back, wide-eyed and dazed.

"Just think how hot and sweet it would be between us, bright-eyes."

Her heartbeat hammering in her throat, Lily swallowed hard. She doubted she would be able to think of anything else.

His eyes tender, he reached up to caress her cheek.

"That should give you something to ponder until we meet again. Shall we ride tomorrow morning?"

A shaky laugh escaped her; she couldn't help herself. How could he remain so calm and unaffected when she was in such turmoil?

"I cannot ride tomorrow morning," she said. "I am scheduled to teach an early class to our boarders. There is less than a week before the soiree, so they must make use of every moment to practice their social graces."

"Perhaps tomorrow afternoon then?"

"You may come for tea." That way she would have company to protect her from being alone with him.

"As you wish."

With one more tender smile, Claybourne lifted her fingers to his lips for a farewell kiss, then bowed himself out, leaving Lily standing there dazed, her body still thrumming, her knees weak.

Sinking into a chair, she brought her fingers to her throbbing lips. She had wanted Claybourne's enthralling embrace to go on and on. Yet the emotional aftershock was even more powerful than the physical. Not only could she finally envision what passion with a man could be like, for the first time she actually found herself craving it.

At the realization, Lily half laughed, half moaned, and lowered her forehead to her hands. She certainly wouldn't tell Fleur and Chantel how his lordship's kiss had affected her. They were likely to award him even more points for his prowess.

And while his easy success made her again question the wisdom of playing the game, she renewed her resolve to finish it. Her pupils needed Lord Claybourne's help in attracting potential patrons to the soiree next Monday.

She would just have to be stronger, Lily decided, shaking her head at her own weakness. Already she was struggling against the urgent desire to throw herself into his arms and let him teach her the exquisite pleasures she was missing. But she was not about to let that irresistible man drive her to reckless behavior. He would *not* make her lose her head.

Even so, the sooner she convinced him she wasn't the right bride for him, the sooner she could be free of his alluring temptation.

Chapter Seven

❧

Today's contretemps vividly reminded me why I never intend to marry.

—Lily to Fanny

Smiling, Lily watched as her three favorite pupils practiced the fine art of subtle flirtation with Fanny. Lily had come to know several of the boarders fairly well, and these three in particular—Ada Shaw, Peg Wallace, and Sally Nead—had applied themselves so diligently to their lessons that they deserved extra guidance.

Ada was an actress with a propensity for bawdiness, which Fanny was endeavoring to tone down. Peg, on the other hand, was a ballet dancer who was painfully shy and had to be coaxed into attempting even the mildest banter with a gentleman. And Sally, also an actress, was a delightful minx—a little plain in appearance but lively and clever enough to attract notice.

Sally, Fanny believed, stood the best chance of landing a wealthy patron at Monday's soiree.

Lily ardently hoped they would all be able to improve their situations significantly. For their sakes, she wanted the upcoming evening to be a success. And knowing how hard their lives had been put her own troubles into prospective. Because of them, Lily reminded herself, she was willing to suffer the persistent Lord Claybourne and his unnerving courtship.

The small class broke up just then, with Ada and Sally excitedly chattering as they rose to leave the drawing room.

Peg, however, tarried long enough to say shyly to Lily, "Thank you again for buying our gowns, Miss Loring. I've never owned anything so beautiful."

Lily felt her heart swell at the girl's simple gratitude. She herself had little interest in what she wore, but the blue lace confection that Fanny's modiste had created for Peg emphasized her blond delicacy to perfection.

"You look lovely any time, Miss Wallace, but you are perfectly stunning in your new costume."

Peg blushed at the compliment and curtsied before following the other pupils from the room.

Watching her go, Lily repressed a sigh. They addressed each other by their surnames so as to increase the girls' self-esteem, an attribute that was sorely needed. Peg had been a lady's maid before embarking on a dance career with the Royal Opera, and she found it difficult to break her old habits of subservience. And while her beauty truly was remarkable, a stylish gown would go a long way toward presenting the image of an alluring Cyprian.

Lily had spent her own funds outfitting all of the twenty-two students in the academy with proper evening gowns. And Fanny's modiste was working unflaggingly to have their costumes ready by Monday. Since the girls had attended a final fitting this morning, however, it had decreased their much-needed practice time on social conversation. Hence, the special private sessions with Fanny and Lily.

As if reading Lily's thoughts, Fanny shook her head as soon as they were alone. "I'm certain Sally will be ready by Monday, but I wouldn't vouch for any of the others."

"I know," Lily agreed. "But they are oceans beyond where they were a few short weeks ago."

"True. You have done a remarkable job, Lily."

"Much of the credit goes to you, and Tess as well. And Basil has been a tremendous factor in improving their diction."

Fanny instantly grimaced at the mention of Basil Eddowes. "I suppose so, but he has contributed to our cause with extremely poor grace."

Lily couldn't help but smile at her friend's complaint. "You only think so because you two are always at loggerheads."

"That is hardly my fault," Fanny said darkly. "Basil is critical of my every effort because of the 'sinful' life I lead. It is beyond irksome." She made a scoffing sound. "I should give up my livelihood simply because *he* disapproves? What does he know? He is a lowly law clerk, for heaven's sake. I have noblemen fighting for my favors. I don't require *his* approval."

Hearing the disgruntled resentment in Fanny's tone, Lily tried to offer some consoling words. "Basil adores you, he always has."

"Well, he has a fine way of showing it. Just this morning he accused me of putting too much emphasis on beauty. And him as tall and gangly as a scarecrow. If I looked a fraction as homely as he does, I would starve to death."

"I think perhaps he is envious of your patrons," Lily said thoughtfully.

Fanny stared at her. "I don't believe it," she stated

flatly. Then less strongly: "I would never take Basil on as a client, even if he could afford to keep me, which he can't. I enjoy men who make me laugh, and Basil certainly does not. Now, if he had an ounce of Lord Claybourne's charm, I could better deal with him."

Lily's brows drew together at the leading comment. "What are you saying, Fanny?"

"Just that I think you should at least consider Claybourne's proposal of marriage."

It was Lily's turn to grimace. "Did Fleur and Chantel press you to coerce me?"

"No, not at all. But I must say I agree with them. There are significant advantages to you becoming Claybourne's marchioness."

Her exasperation rising, Lily narrowed her eyes on her traitorous friend. "It amazes me that you would take their side. *You* never wished to marry."

"No . . ." Fanny replied slowly. "Our childhood in Hampshire was so deadly dull that all I could think of was escape. I wanted to be wild and gay, to fill my life with excitement and pleasure, not settle down as some fat squire's broodmare. But I sometimes wonder if I made the right decision. I do get lonely at times, Lily, despite the gaiety. And having a husband and family might be the antidote to my doldrums. At least marriage is looking more and more appealing as I grow older."

She was entirely serious, Lily realized with astonishment. Yet Fanny's possible change of heart regarding matrimony had nothing to do with *her*.

Lily shook her head. "Being lonely is better than suffering the pain my mother endured all those years of marriage."

"You might be happy with the right husband."

"I don't intend to risk it. Now, may we *please* change the subject?"

Smiling ruefully, Fanny obliged. "Very well. Do you mean to attend Lady Freemantle's garden party on Saturday?"

"Yes . . . even though Lord Claybourne will likely be there and Winifred is sure to throw us together. I want to see my sisters. It has been over a month since I've even laid eyes on them. And now that his lordship knows my location, I have no reason to keep away from home."

"Lady Freemantle kindly invited me," Fanny disclosed. "So would you like to ride with me in my carriage?"

"Yes, indeed," Lily replied, "since I have no transportation of my own here in London—"

Just then Ellen the maid hurried into the drawing room, wringing her hands on her apron in obvious agitation. "Beg pardon, Miss Irwin . . . Miss Loring . . . but I think you should come at once. There's a gent in Miss Delee's sitting room who won't leave. Mister O'Rourke is his name."

Her face paling, Fanny jumped up and made for the door, and Lily immediately followed her. Mick O'Rourke was the gaming hell owner to whom Fleur and Chantel owed thirty thousand pounds. Most likely he had come to demand the return of his money, and to possibly renew his threat to send them to debtors' prison.

"What will you tell him?" Lily asked as they quickly mounted the front staircase in the entrance hall.

"I don't know," Fanny said worriedly. "I will have to implore him to grant us a little more time, since we don't have the means to pay him just yet. And once I explain our plans for the soiree, perhaps he will be amenable. Mick always was an astute businessman."

Upon reaching the top of the stairs, they hastened down the corridor. Lily was directly on Fanny's heels when they reached the sitting room. But what she saw when they entered made her blood run cold.

While Chantel cowered on a corner of the settee, a ruggedly built, ebony-haired man stood menacingly close to Fleur, clutching her arm and growling down at her. "I have been lenient so far, woman! I gave you extra time, an entire month. But my patience is at an end. I want my money now, or Fanny will answer to me."

Fleur, however, only raised her chin imperiously to stare O'Rourke down. "You ill-bred oaf, I would not give you the time of day! You will not get a single half-pence as long as you continue to behave in this boorish manner. I demand you leave at once!"

His face mottled with anger. "You dare to call *me* ill-bred?"

"Yes, you brute!"

In response to her aspersion, his grasp on Fleur tightened and he twisted her arm behind her back hard enough to make her cry out.

"Mick, please! Let her go!" Fanny exclaimed in alarm.

But Lily didn't stop to plead or even to think. Rage welling up inside her at seeing her friend's pain, she lunged across the room in three strides and began pummeling O'Rourke's back with her fists. And when he abruptly released Fleur's arm and turned to face Lily in startlement, she aimed a blow at his jaw, connecting with a powerful enough impact to make him stumble backward.

"What the bloody devil . . . ?" he exclaimed, raising his arms to protect his face.

"Don't you dare hurt her!" Lily declared furiously, still attacking with flailing fists.

Yet when O'Rourke saw the size of his opponent, he stopped retreating and stood his ground, easily blocking her blows.

Realizing her disadvantage in size and strength, Lily hastily glanced around her for a weapon, her gaze alighting on a thin bronze statue of a naked Aphrodite on a nearby table.

Picking it up, she brandished it at O'Rourke. "Get out! Get out of this house this instant!"

When he took a threatening step toward her, his eyes narrowing dangerously on her, Lily swung the statue at his shoulder and managed to hit him squarely on the joint.

O'Rourke gave a shocked yelp of pain and fell back again, clutching his shoulder.

"Get out, I say!" she repeated in a fierce hiss.

He held up both his hands defensively, but his tone remained belligerent. "No one tells Mick O'Rourke what to do, Missy."

"*Now!* I mean it!" Lily demanded again, raising the statue to swing again.

Practically grinding his teeth, O'Rourke brushed past her and stalked from the room.

Fanny immediately went to Fleur to offer comfort, while Lily followed O'Rourke to make certain he left the house entirely.

He stomped down the corridor, his fury obvious, but as he started down the flight of stairs, he called over his shoulder, "You haven't heard the last of me! Prison will be the least of their worries, I promise you."

Wrath vibrated in his tone and in Lily's retort as well as she moved to the head of the staircase, still wielding her statue. "We will find your money somehow! But you are not welcome here!"

"I am leaving, you bloody madwoman," he blustered, "but you'll regret this, no mistake."

It registered on her that Lord Claybourne was mounting the stairs at the same moment and had paused halfway up, arrested by the commotion. But she only had eyes for O'Rourke.

Lily stood there watching as he bounded down the lower steps and flung open the front door, then fled outside to the safety of his carriage.

When he finally was gone, her gaze shifted blindly to Claybourne. He looked taken aback to have seen her drive O'Rourke from the house, yet it was hard for her to focus on him since she was so enraged, she was shaking.

Then just as suddenly, her rage left her and her knees went weak. Reaching out, she grasped the balustrade with her free hand to keep from falling.

In three strides, the marquess had sprung up the remaining stairs and caught her about the waist to steady her.

"Sit," he urged, guiding her down to sit on the top step.

Having no strength left, she obeyed, even though she wanted to protest when he settled close beside her. But she seemed to have lost her voice. Her breath was coming in short gasps, while her body still trembled.

He waited as she tried to gather her composure, although he pried the statue from her grasp and set it on the carpet.

By then several people had gathered below—boarders and servants alike—and Claybourne gave them all a dismissive look as he said tersely, "You may go about your business."

His order instantly cleared the entrance hall, leaving Lily alone with him.

"What happened?" he asked gently.

"He was hurting Fleur," Lily rasped.

Muttering a sharp invective under his breath, he glanced sharply down at the front entrance door, as if he wanted to go after O'Rourke himself. But all he said was, "And you came to her rescue."

"Yes." She had leapt to Fleur's defense a moment ago, just as she had her mother all those years ago. Except that then it had been her father who had acted the brute, cruelly using his greater male strength against a smaller, weaker woman.

Still shivering, Lily wrapped her arms around herself as the awful memory swept over her. Doubtless that was why she had reacted so fiercely this time—because she'd dealt with similar physical violence before.

When she remained silent, Claybourne spoke again. "I take it that was O'Rourke, here to collect the gaming debt owed him."

She emitted a short, humorless laugh. "I believe so. I didn't take the time to ask. When I found him threatening Fleur, all I could think about was stopping him."

Claybourne searched her face as his jaw hardened. "I will be more than happy to deal with O'Rourke for you."

It touched her that he was so ready to step in to protect her, Lily thought as his perceptive eyes regarded her intently. There was concern there in the hazel depths, along with anger. Anger she knew was on her behalf.

Her own anger had mostly dissipated by now, but a darker emotion compressed her chest, welling up inside her with suffocating force. She couldn't ward off the grim memories of that summer day when she was sixteen, when she'd intervened in her parents' worst battle.

For most of her childhood, Lily had taken refuge in the stables whenever they fought, but that particular day she had returned to the house unexpectedly. Upon hearing screams, she rushed into the drawing room, only to find her father striking her mother in a violent rage, pummelling her body . . . her breasts, her ribs, her stomach.

For one horrified moment Lily stood frozen with heart-pounding fear, unable to breathe. Then hearing another helpless cry from her mother, she stumbled blindly forward and reached for the only weapon at hand—a knife used to pare quill pens. Her stomach roiling, she raised the blade high, brandishing it at her father threateningly, swearing to stab him with it if he didn't leave Mama alone.

Thank God he had heeded her.

Despite his shock and fury, Sir Charles appeared to believe her warning. He spun on his heel and stalked from the room, leaving Lily to console her bitterly sobbing mother.

To her knowledge, her father had never again raised a hand to her mother, but Lily had vowed then and there never to let any man hurt her like that.

Shutting her eyes, she shuddered at the raw remembrance that still burned deep inside her. She still recalled the horror she'd felt. The gut-wrenching helplessness. The revulsion. The fear. She had hated her father in those few moments. And she had never forgiven him for his brutality.

Lily could feel Claybourne's penetrating gaze on her now, even before he spoke again in a quiet voice. "What is it, sweetheart? Something has upset you, and I don't believe it was only that you had to chase a bully from the house."

Perhaps she should explain. . . . But no. She had no desire to share her most intimate fears with the marquess. She already felt too vulnerable to him.

Why, she had never even told her sisters about the dreadful incident when she'd threatened to kill her own father; her mother hadn't wanted them to know. Basil was the only one who had learned the ugly truth, and that was because he'd happened upon Lily shortly afterward, when she was still too upset to stop herself from spilling the sordid details.

Indeed, she had tried to block them from her memory for years. But a woman's natural fear of physical violence from a bigger, stronger male had always stayed with her.

Which was why, when Claybourne raised a hand to touch her cheek, Lily flinched and drew back sharply.

At her instinctively fearful response, he stilled and lowered his hand. "You should allow me to help," he said quietly.

His gentleness made her feel even worse, since she knew she had greatly overreacted.

Biting her lip, Lily dragged in a deep breath. "Thank you, but I think we can deal with O'Rourke ourselves."

"At the very least I can make certain he won't call here again."

Perhaps so, Lily thought, *but I don't wish to be so deeply obligated to you.* "I think it might be better if Fanny deals with O'Rourke. They once were lovers, so she is most likely to persuade him to give us more time. I suspect he won't look kindly on your interference, especially after you witnessed what I just did to him."

Claybourne hesitated. "Even so, he needs to know that your friends have a protector."

Lily's mouth curled. "I'm afraid that won't help much. They still owe O'Rourke an enormous sum."

"Ah, yes, the thirty thousand pounds."

His pause was longer this time, and when it ended, his tone was thoughtful. "I have a proposition for you. I will pay off their debt if you will agree to marry me."

Her gaze swung back to him, her eyes narrowing. "You cannot be serious."

A hint of rueful amusement flickered in his own eyes. "Why do you always refuse to believe me, love? I know my own mind. Thirty thousand pounds for your hand in marriage. Some might think it a very fair bargain."

Lily locked her jaw, vexed that he thought he could simply buy her for his wife. She was anxious to help her friends, yet she didn't wish to make *that* immense a sacrifice, entering into a marriage of convenience to absolve their huge debt. Yet hopefully she wouldn't have to.

"We don't require such magnanimity from you, my lord," she eventually replied. "If we are fortunate, we will have the funds within a few weeks. You know of our plans for the soiree. Our boarders should be able to help pay off the debt to O'Rourke shortly."

"What if he insists on being paid now?" Claybourne

asked. "You don't want your friends to wind up in prison."

Lily pressed her lips together. "I won't let that happen. Marcus settled twenty thousand pounds on me. If need be, they can have that."

He raised an eyebrow, evidently surprised. "You would donate your entire fortune to save them?"

"It is far better than the alternative."

"What about the other ten thousand they owe?"

"I will prevail upon Marcus or Lady Freemantle to loan me the money. They are both rich as nabobs. And Fanny has written a book that will be published next month. The publisher believes the subject—advice to young ladies who are searching for husbands—will be in great demand, and if so, the income will help her repay O'Rourke."

"But I can fund the entire debt now."

His persistence made Lily smile, albeit briefly. "You are exceedingly generous, my lord, but I must decline your proposition. At some point I may be desperate enough to consider it, but not just yet."

She doubted she would ever be that desperate, she added to herself. Her fracas with O'Rourke a few moments ago had forcibly reminded her exactly why she didn't want to turn control of her fate over to a husband. She couldn't, wouldn't, trust any man enough to marry him and give him that kind of power over her.

Lord Claybourne might not be the sort who would ever strike a woman, but that didn't mean he couldn't hurt her just as badly if she were legally tied to him, unable to escape. If she were trapped in a union where she was considered his property to do with as he pleased, just as her mother had been her father's property.

Uncomfortable with Claybourne's searching look, Lily changed the subject. "Speaking of the soiree . . . have you invited some of your acquaintances as you promised?"

"I have begun issuing invitations, yes."

"And were you able to find the sort of gentlemen I hoped for? Bachelors who are kind and gentle and who are wealthy enough to provide our boarders with good lives?"

"Your standards are not easily met, but I am making progress. I expect to bring close to a dozen suitable candidates."

"Good." She exhaled a sigh. Although her tremors had stopped, her chest still felt heavy, and there was still the grave issue of how to deal with O'Rourke to be determined.

"I must go," Lily said. "I need to see how Fleur is after her ordeal, and to help Fanny decide what must be done about O'Rourke."

She rose, but when Claybourne stood also, she hesitated. "Forgive me, I forgot. I promised you tea. You are welcome to remain if you like, or you might prefer to return tomorrow when things should be more settled."

His smile was wry. "I'll stay now, thank you. I can't afford to turn down an invitation to be with you. I only have a fortnight to win our game, remember?"

His light tone made Lily relax a little; she felt infinitely more comfortable returning to their game than dealing with his tenderness. "I will be sure to tell Fleur and Chantel of your generous offer to pay their debt. They will likely award you another point."

"The points don't concern me as much as knowing whether O'Rourke will be bent on retaliation. He won't thank you for showing him up, even if you were entirely in the right."

Lily wrinkled her nose. "I know. I suppose I should write him a note of apology and assure him that we plan to repay his debt . . . although my first inclination is probably best. We should let Fanny deal with him. She knows far better than I how to soothe a man's wounded pride."

When she began moving down the corridor, Claybourne accompanied her. "True. But if you mean to keep attacking men who are much larger than you, you should learn how to fight."

Her gaze arresting, she glanced up at him, wondering if he was just making idle conversation. "Are you offering to teach me fisticuffs, my lord?"

His chuckle was low and amused. "The thought gives me palpitations. I would far rather you cease tilting at windmills and endangering yourself so frequently . . . but I suppose that is too much to ask."

"Indeed it is," Lily said sweetly. "But I have always wanted to learn how to fence. Mama wouldn't hear of it when I was growing up. My virtually living in the stables was bad enough for her. I understand that Marcus and you and your friend Arden are expert swordsmen."

"We do well enough," he acknowledged. "We practice regularly . . . or we did before Marcus and Arden lost their hearts to your sisters."

Lily eyed him thoughtfully. "If you were to give me fencing lessons, I could learn how to defend myself better. I know how to shoot but not how to wield a rapier."

Claybourne laughed outright at that. "Will I earn points for instructing you?"

Her answer was slow in coming as she debated whether it was worth giving him such an easy chance to increase his score. Yet she wished she had known how to wield a sword when she was sixteen. And she very much wanted to know now how to deal with brutes like Mick O'Rourke and those bullies they'd encountered in the alley who had been beating a helpless dog. "If you insist."

"Very well, then. We can begin tomorrow if you can make time in your busy schedule."

"I am certain I can spare an hour around two in the afternoon, my lord."

"Can you devote another hour? I have a salon at home designed specifically for fencing matches."

Lily shook her head. She didn't want to be alone with Lord Claybourne for that length of time, certainly not in his domain. "Can't we hold my lesson here? The parlor we used to teach dancing should be large enough."

He nodded. "That will serve better than my salon, I expect. It could harm your reputation to be seen at a bachelor's residence, engaged in a man's sport."

They had reached the sitting room door by then, so Lily paused just outside. "I don't care much about my reputation, you know."

"But I do, sweeting. I will bring my practice foils with me when I call. Only . . . I have one condition if I'm to teach you."

"What condition is that?"

"That you call me by my given name instead of 'my lord.' My name is Heath."

Heath watched her struggle to decide if the familiarity of using first names was worth her desire to learn the art of swordsmanship.

"Very well," she finally said. "I shall call you Heath. But your lessons had best be stellar, or you will go back to being 'my lord.' "

He grinned as she turned to enter the sitting room, congratulating himself on winning a minor battle. Yet Lily had won one of her own by convincing him to suspend his better judgment and tutor her in fencing.

Still, he had gotten the best of the bargain. Not only would he enjoy spending time with her; it would allow him the chance to intensify his campaign to woo her. He had a much more interesting lesson in mind than teaching her the rudiments of fencing.

Shoving a hand through his hair, Heath laughed softly to himself upon realizing just how calculating and manipulative he'd become with Lily. He was no better than many of the debutantes who had relentlessly pursued him over the years.

But she had given him little choice, he thought, following her into the sitting room.

When she went directly to her friends to embrace them, however, Heath stood back to permit them some time together. Fleur seemed to be holding up well after her confrontation with O'Rourke, but Chantel was trembling and making weak, fluttering gestures with a silk fan. Fanny, on the other hand, was obviously trying hard to control her temper.

When the four women began talking at once, Heath kept his gaze fixed on Lily. She was a fascinating maze of contradictions, infuriatingly headstrong and stubborn, yet amazingly generous and compassionate and loyal. She wouldn't give an inch in their courtship game, yet she was ready to give away her fortune to her friends if they needed it.

Lily was also delightfully novel and intriguing. And courageous and tenacious to the point of being foolhardy. Heath remembered her feistiness when she'd chased O'Rourke with that bronze statue. It might have been humorous if he hadn't feared what a man like O'Rourke might do in revenge.

Even so, he couldn't fault Lily entirely for her passion in defending the weak. It was one of the things he admired most about her.

She had her own weakness, though, Heath was coming to realize. Not for the first time he'd sensed vulnerability beneath that firebrand demeanor. He'd seen the tormented look that had crossed her features once she had won her skirmish with the gamester. Something wounded had flashed behind her eyes, a haunted glimmer that had made Heath want to hold her, to comfort her.

The powerful feeling wouldn't leave him. Lily aroused his protective instincts as well as his body, although he knew she would swallow nails before accepting any man's protection.

But someone had hurt her before this, he was certain. Perhaps that was why she was so unattainable now.

He wasn't about to let anyone hurt her again, Heath vowed. He protected what was his, and Lily was his now. Even if she hadn't accepted it yet.

Tenderness ran through him, irrevocably strong, as he watched her console her friends. He intended to discover why Lily was so self-protective, so defensive. And he was more determined than ever to succeed in winning her.

Lily thought she didn't need men, didn't need *him*, but he would show her how very mistaken she was.

Chapter Eight

❦

Lord Claybourne most certainly does not play fair!
—Lily to Fanny

Heath stared as Lily lightly skipped down the front staircase toward him the following afternoon. She had managed to surprise him yet again, this time because her shapely form was garbed in men's breeches and boots and cambric shirt. With her hair worn long and tied back with a ribbon, she looked the complete hoyden—and she knew it, judging by her arch expression.

"Good afternoon, Heath," she said blithely in greeting as she reached him.

Since her challenging smile dared him to object to her choice of apparel, Heath kept his response mild. "So what is the point of your unusual costume, sweeting?"

"I can hardly learn to fence dressed in skirts, can I? Breeches allow me comfort and freedom of movement. Moreover, they should make it easier for you to pretend I am a man."

His eyebrows shot up. "Why the devil would I want to pretend you are a man?"

"So you won't treat me as a mere female and coddle me as a weakling."

She was gravely mistaken if she thought for one instant that he could ever think of her as a man. Those breeches only called attention to the lithe, feminine curves of her hips and legs, while her shirt molded the ripe swells of her breasts.

"You are not just dressing outrageously in order to put me off?"

Her laugh was low and delighted. "I confess the thought had crossed my mind. You don't want a marchioness who wears such scandalous attire."

Heath shook his head. Lily's scandalous attire didn't daunt him in the least. In truth, it was enjoyable, finding a woman who was more rash and rebellious in nature than he was. "You will discover that I am rather broadminded. I don't plan to dictate your wardrobe when we are wed."

"But society would care and condemn me as a Jezebel."

"Not necessarily. The wealthy nobility are held to different standards than most denizens of society. If you wear breeches as my marchioness, you'll more likely be termed an eccentric."

His observation made Lily's expression turn thoughtful, and Heath pressed his point. "Furthermore, as my wife, you will enjoy much more freedom than you are permitted now as an unmarried young lady. And I can assure you, life with me would never be dull. We can hold fencing bouts every day if you wish."

Her nose wrinkled. "Not even that delightful prospect can tempt me, my lord."

"You are to call me Heath, remember?"

"Oh, yes, then . . . Heath. Are those rapiers?" she asked, indicating the long leather case he carried.

"Yes, my practice foils. The blades are kept dull and the points are buttoned with leather safety tips."

"Good." She flashed him a bright smile. "I would not want to skewer you accidently."

She could still catch him off guard with her smile, Heath thought, arrested by the dazzling sight. Indeed, her sparkle and vibrancy impacted him like no woman he had ever met.

Yet Lily seemed completely unaware of her uncommon charms. "Come," she said, "the makeshift salon is this way."

He followed her from the entrance hall toward the rear of the house, admiring the gentle sway of her derriere. The parlor she led him to was a fairly large room. The floor had been cleared to practice dance steps, the chairs and tables all pushed against the walls, the carpet rolled up to expose a shining wood surface.

"Will this suffice for my lesson?" Lily asked.

"It will do very well."

Shutting the door behind him, Heath quietly turned the key in the lock. This was a rare opportunity to be alone with Lily, and he wanted no interruptions.

He intended to give her a much more potent lesson than mere fencing, though. For all her passionate nature, she was sexually innocent and badly needed awakening. Teaching her about physical pleasure, he surmised, would soften her defenses and make her more willing to wed him.

Smiling to himself in anticipation, Heath set his rapier case down on a table, then casually removed his coat and waistcoat and cravat.

"So where do we begin?" Lily wondered aloud as he opened the case.

"With the basics. Stance and handwork first. Then the fundamentals of movement and hitting. And finally simple attacks and defense. In some future lesson, we'll cover tactics and strategy for beating your opponent, but for today we will keep it elementary."

Withdrawing a long, slim foil, he let her examine the button that kept the sharp steel point from becoming deadly. Then he showed her the proper position for her body—right arm extended, foil raised, left arm bent upward. Next he demonstrated the basic elements—thrust and parry, feint, riposte, recovery, counter-parry, lunge—and had her practice each technique.

Heath enjoyed that he was able to touch her frequently, and admired the fact that Lily caught on quickly because of her agility and natural athleticism.

Lastly, he stood opposite her and taught her how to advance and retreat.

"Fencing is not unlike our game," Heath commented as they slowly moved back and forth across the floor. "You engage and disengage and try to score a hit while keeping up your own defense."

"I can see that," Lily replied a little breathlessly. "Your skill is amazing," she declared a while later when he allowed her to rest.

"A little more practice and you will be ready to take me on."

She laughed outright. "It will take me a lifetime of practice to ever be a good enough match for you."

Heath couldn't agree with her. Lily was easily a match for him already. Not with foils, of course. But her zest for living, her spontaneity, her endearing high spirits, delighted him down to his soul.

It was remarkable, the bond he felt with her after such

a short acquaintance. Marcus's younger sister Eleanor was the only other woman who'd ever engendered such sentiment in him. And in truth, Lily acted toward him much the way Eleanor did, as if he were her older brother, her demeanor friendly and platonic.

Heath intended to change that very shortly, but he relished the feeling, in large part because it reminded him so much of his closest friends. He had distant relatives still living, but no immediate family, yet he thought of Marcus and Drew as his brothers. He cherished the bond he'd shared with them over the years. The joys and sorrows, the camaraderie, the friendship.

He would greatly miss that closeness now that they had each found brides. But seeing their happiness made him wonder what he could have with Lily.

If she were his wife, he would be able to spar with her regularly, to laugh with her, to tease her and provoke her and challenge her as he was doing now. And he could have her in his bed. It was highly pleasurable to imagine awakening with her beside him every morning, making love to her slowly and thoroughly. . . .

He wanted to take her right now, Heath thought, gazing down into her laughing eyes. She was so utterly desirable, he wanted to bury his hands in her lustrous hair and back her against the wall and make a delectable feast of her.

But he would not allow himself. He didn't want a hurried affair; he wanted Lily for his wife. More crucially, a careless seduction would surely wound her, no matter how it might assuage the stinging needs of his body. And then there was her reputation to consider. Lily had lived under a cloud of scandal for years, and he wouldn't make it worse for her.

No, he intended to leave her a virgin until she was his bride. But that didn't mean he couldn't use passion to persuade her to accept his hand in marriage. He wanted more than her surrender, however. He wanted her to know the blissful pleasure that could exist between a man and a woman. . . .

Heath didn't realize he had gone still until Lily looked up at him quizzically. "Is something wrong?"

"Not at all. But it is time for your next lesson."

"What lesson?" she asked, her expression suddenly a bit wary.

Not replying at once, Heath stepped toward her and took her foil from her, then set both rapiers down on a side table. When he returned to stand before her, the need to have his arms filled with her was almost overwhelming.

"I mean to teach you about arousal," he said as he drew Lily against him.

Her breath catching audibly, she raised her hands to push against his shoulders, but Heath refused to release her.

"Have I mentioned that seeing you in those breeches makes my imagination run riot? I'm afraid it has had the opposite effect than the one you intended."

"What effect has it had?" she demanded, her voice nervous and uneven.

"You have aroused me quite painfully," he said, his gaze locking with hers.

"I most certainly don't mean to."

"And you can't deny that I arouse you."

Lily's mouth opened as if to do just that, but then she closed it again. "Of course you arouse me. You are a renowned lover who can seduce anything in skirts. But my response doesn't mean a thing. It is purely an involuntary physical reaction."

"You dismiss physical pleasure readily enough when you know little about it."

His hands moving to her waist, Heath held her flush against him, enjoying the fine tremor of her body. "You are a woman of great passion, Lily. Too passionate to live the rest of your life as a spinster. Too warm-blooded and intense. And I mean to prove it to you."

Her chin lifted stubbornly. "I think passion is highly overrated."

"I know you do. But you won't after today."

Lowering his hands to her hips, he slipped one knee between hers, parting her legs. With a soft gasp, Lily tried to pull back, but his tightening grip pressed her abdomen into his loins.

The contact sent a surge of desire rocketing through Heath, purely masculine, primal and urgent, yet he clamped down fiercely on his own urges. This moment was for Lily, not for him.

Deliberately rubbing his thigh against her woman's mound, he lifted her slightly to make her slide against him. Her breathy inhalation turned to a moan just before he bent his head and captured her lips.

Lily went rigid at his bold assault, but Heath went on teasing, coaxing, playing, exploring . . . showing her that he found her mouth incomparably special.

After a long moment's hesitation, he was rewarded when she began to respond ardently, as if she couldn't help herself. The riveting sweetness took him off guard and made exultation rip through him. She kissed with an enthusiasm and hunger that set his blood soaring, her mouth willing and wild, almost abandoned.

Heath let himself get swept away by her eagerness, feeling the effects of the kiss as if it were his first. He himself was breathless by the time he forcibly drew back.

Lily stared at him, looking dazed and beautiful, her hair tousled, her cheeks flushed, her eyes bright. The sight made him want her with a kind of primitive ferocity he'd never experienced before. But he forced himself to go slowly.

Pulling her with him, he backed toward the chairs lining the wall and sat in one. Then he eased Lily down to straddle his knee.

Her eyes widened, but she didn't protest when he opened his shirt to bare his chest, or when he caught her wrists and placed her palms against his warm flesh.

But when his hands began revolving in lazy, widening circles over her shoulders and along her arms, she finally murmured his name. "Heath . . ."

"What, love?"

"You have to stop this."

"What an amusing notion. We have barely begun."

His gaze dropping to her breasts, he parted the front of her cambric shirt. She wore a linen camisole beneath, and her nipples were blatantly outlined beneath the fine fabric.

Tugging down the edge of the undergarment, he freed the lovely mounds to his perusal. Then slowly Heath ran his hands upward till his fingertips barely brushed the uprise of her breasts. The rose-hued buds were ruched and taut, begging for his attention, yet he ignored them, instead tracing the silken ivory skin surrounding them.

Lily quivered, muscles tensing, and when he cupped

her fullness, cradling the weight in his palms, she drew a shuddering breath.

Her heated softness was a sensual delight. Wanting to learn her by touch, he began gently kneading, molding. He relished the feel of her, the enchanting contrast of feminine firmness and softness—both her ripe breasts and her thighs nestling the harder flesh of his leg.

Her breathing was shallow by the time he circled the peaks with his thumbs. Her nipples were highly sensitized, he suspected, lifting his fingers to lightly stroke. He lingered on the engorged crests, introducing her to sensation, then plucked at the straining buds, caressing, teasing.

Lily inhaled sharply, while her deepening flush told him he was successfully arousing her. And that was before he bent to lick one nipple with his tongue. It was hard and tight, and he prodded it to even stiffer erection with slow erotic circles, laving with tender care.

"I have dreamed about doing this for weeks," he murmured, finally moving his mouth to her other nipple. "Tasting you, suckling you . . ."

He set his lips to her soft flesh, nibbling, tantalizing, and elicited a shivery gasp from Lily with his sensual assault. When he drew the tip deep into his mouth, she whimpered and clutched at his shoulders.

Heath savored her for long heated moments, until Lily pleaded with him hoarsely. "Heath . . . you have to stop."

"Not until you beg me," he replied.

She would do no such thing, he knew very well, since she clearly didn't want him to stop. And he wasn't letting her go. Her lithe, supple body was ripe for his touch, eager even. She felt warm and intensely vital in his arms, and the feel of her skin heating under his hands and mouth was enough to drive him mad. Already his erection was throbbing, rigid and swollen with need.

And to his delight, Lily was growing hot and restless at his erotic suckling. Evidently wanting more, she twined her fingers in his hair and pulled, trying to bring his mouth even closer.

However, he eventually brought his delicious feast to an end. Giving her nipples a final kiss, Heath drew back to meet her gaze.

Lily stared at him in dismay as she sat astride his hard thigh, her eyes darkened and wide. Her pulse was pounding in her throat, he could see it.

"Is that the end of your lesson?" she asked breathlessly, disappointment rife in her tone.

Heath smiled. "No, there is much more." Reaching up, he pulled the ribbon from her hair, letting the glorious chestnut mass cascade over her shoulders. "But we must be circumspect. You look delectable in your breeches, and the thought of peeling them off you is quite devastating, but regrettably we must do with making love fully clothed."

"Is that possible?" Her expression turned dubious.

"Yes, indeed. I will show you."

He brought his hands to her hips and shifted beneath her slightly, lifting her up and raising his knee so that she slid toward him.

Lily sucked in a huge, shaky breath at the friction, while her hips instinctively rocked against him.

"That's right, love . . . ride me."

Her mouth parted in surprise when she realized what he wanted from her, but she didn't protest when he drew her even closer so that her naked breasts rubbed hot and damp against his bare chest.

His hands guiding her, he moved her lower body in a slow deliberate rhythm. She caught on quickly, and began to rock of her own accord, yet she shut her eyes as her arousal grew.

"No, look at me, angel. I want to see the pleasure in your beautiful eyes."

He could indeed see pleasure in the dark depths when she obeyed. Pleasure and dazed arousal, as if she didn't quite know what was happening to her.

She writhed against the hard flesh of his thigh, arching in his arms, which made Heath grip her hips harder.

Desire ran through him like fire as her ragged breaths reverberated in his ear. He wanted to drive himself inside her, plunging in hard and deep. She would be slick and swollen and so incredibly hot. . . .

His chest tightened at the image, while his cock throbbed painfully.

His arms shifting to wrap around her, he found her lips again, his thrusting tongue tangling roughly with hers. Her response was urgent and needy. She opened to him fully, letting him ravish her mouth while he rocked her faster, grinding her woman's cleft against him.

Lily felt as if her body was afire. As his thigh moved powerfully against her aching core, her hips surged forward, seeking some nameless relief. She was panting, flushed, feverish with the storm of heat building inside. Her primal instincts had taken control, yet the result still shocked her: The sudden, intense rush of sensation was overwhelming.

She arched convulsively as the world careened around her, sinking her nails into Heath's shoulders. The tide of feeling surged and crashed through her, eliciting a wild cry of abandon from deep in her throat.

When the last shudders quivered through her, Lily collapsed limply against him, her face buried in the curve of his shoulder. Her breasts rose and fell against his naked chest as she tried to make sense of the sensual explosion her body had just endured.

She was amazed by the pleasure. Stunned. Her whole being felt gloriously hot and languid.

And she was certain Heath knew it. He was holding her in his arms, one hand tenderly stroking her hair. When she finally found her voice, it came out in a weak rasp. "That was *not* the lesson I asked for, my lord."

She felt his lips curve against her hair. "No, but that was the lesson you needed. You can now see what you are missing by swearing off men and marriage."

"What I see," Lily retorted feebly, "is that I was mistaken to wear breeches this afternoon. You would not have been so brazen if I were dressed as a lady."

She heard his smothered laugh. "Loath as I am to contradict you, darling, I couldn't care less what you wear. I would lust after you if you were garbed in sackcloth and ashes." His mouth pressed a kiss against her temple. "I am more painfully aroused now than I've ever been in my life."

Suddenly aware of the hard bulge of his swollen manhood through their clothing, Lily tried to ease away, but his arms tightened around her, refusing to release her. "So what did you think of your first taste of passion?" he murmured, nibbling her ear.

Lily's face warmed with embarrassment. "I found it . . . interesting."

"Merely interesting?" he repeated skeptically.

"Very well . . . perhaps it was incredible."

His laughter this time held satisfaction. "I am gratified. It makes a man swell with pride, to know he has given his lover pleasure."

She frowned against his smooth bare skin. "We are not lovers."

"I plan to remedy that very soon."

Lily sat up to eye him narrowly. "I believe I have some say in the matter."

"Of course you do. But I suspect after this you won't be quite so stubborn about refusing my offer of marriage."

"My stubbornness hasn't changed one whit, my lord."

"Call me Heath."

It was difficult to think of so illustrious a nobleman in such familiar terms, but she *had* agreed to address him by his given name as a condition of his fencing tutelage. "Very well, but I must warn you, Heath. Seducing me won't make it any easier for you to win our game."

He smiled lazily. "If winning was easy, I wouldn't enjoy it half so much—and neither would you."

That was regrettably true, Lily lamented. She found it exhilarating, matching wits with him. Even if she frequently came out the loser, as she had just now.

How had he turned their fencing lesson to his advantage so quickly? Lily wondered with disgust. No doubt because she was an utter weakling where he was concerned. She'd had every intention of withstanding any sensual overtures he made, but her resistance had melted instantly under the searing heat of his kisses.

Heath leaned forward now to place a slow, lingering kiss on her lips, catching her by surprise. He had a wicked mouth—one he kept using to fluster her, Lily thought distractedly as her senses heated again.

Realizing how easily she was surrendering, she forcibly broke away, although when she tried to climb off him, Heath once more prevented her.

"I cannot believe I let this go so far," she muttered.

"It was the next logical step in our courtship. We both knew it would happen. I'll go so far as to say you wanted it to happen."

She couldn't deny there was a measure of truth to that accusation, also. She had wanted to know what carnal pleasure was like—and had discovered it beyond her wildest imagination.

When she remained silent, Heath held her gaze intently. "We *will* become lovers, Lily, I have no doubt about it. But when we make love, it will be because you want me for your husband."

She splayed her hands against his muscular chest, refusing to accept his declaration. "You are indulging in fantasies."

"If so, they are supremely blissful fantasies. It is even more blissful to contemplate having you in my bed. When we are wed, I will delight in teaching you all about pleasure and passion."

His pledge conjured wild and reckless images in her mind, but Lily fought their allure. "*When* we are wed?" she repeated. "Your arrogance is astounding."

At her scoffing tone, challenge glimmered in his hazel eyes. "I can safely promise that you will enjoy our marriage bed. It isn't an exaggeration to say that I am rather gifted at lovemaking." As if to prove his point, he bent to tauntingly kiss her left nipple.

The sizzle of desire that shot through Lily made her

arch and shiver. Alarmed, she pushed at Heath's chest more determinedly this time.

When he at last let her go, she scrambled off his lap and unsteadily turned away to set her camisole and shirt to rights, covering her brazenly exposed bosom. Heath would be a magnificent lover, she had absolutely no doubt.

"I suppose you mean to tell Fleur what transpired between us," Lily said crossly, "so she will award you more points."

He was calmly restoring his own clothes to order, she saw out of the corner of her eye. "Certainly not. A gentleman never discusses his amorous accomplishments. This will remain strictly our affair."

Without responding, she went to the door and unlocked it.

"Does this mean we are finished with our fencing lesson for today?" Heath drawled behind her.

Lily shot a glance over her shoulder at him. "Yes, indeed. I don't care to have any more lessons of any kind from you. I don't trust you."

He raised an eyebrow. "You don't trust *me*? Or is it that you cannot trust yourself when you are alone with me?"

Lily didn't answer his deplorably perceptive question. But as she flung open the door and stalked from the room, she couldn't shake the shocking realization that she wanted passion with that enticing, maddening rogue after all.

Chapter Nine

I can now understand why the marquess makes women swoon, but falling in love with him—or any other man—is anathema to me.

—Lily to her sisters

If Lily hoped to avert any more perilous encounters with Heath in the near future, her desire was thwarted that evening when Fleur pointed out that their pupils needed a real live gentleman upon whom to practice their newfound social skills.

As long as he was beleaguering her, Lily decided, she might as well put her unwanted suitor to good use. Thus, she swallowed her disquiet and sent Heath a message at his London town house, enlisting his aid for a class at ten o'clock the next morning.

By surrounding herself with the other boarders, Lily persuaded herself, and avoiding being alone with him, she stood a better chance of resisting him.

She should have realized her ambition was wishful thinking. Seeing Heath so soon after her stunning carnal experience with him brought a host of sensual memories cascading into her mind and body. And although she determinedly pretended disinterest upon greeting him, she couldn't forget a single sensation of yesterday's erotic interlude: The play of rippling chest muscles against her palms. The feel of his hard, powerful body beneath her.

The heat of his mouth as he suckled her nipples. The stunning firestorm he had started inside her . . .

She now understood firsthand why women leaped into his bed and fought for his favor.

Fortunately Fleur and Chantel were there to take the lead in their class, introducing Lord Claybourne to the girls and setting the scene for the upcoming soiree.

Lily hadn't expected his impact to be so remarkable, however. She watched as Heath effortlessly charmed the entire gathering of females, putting them at ease and making them laugh. By the end of the session, they were practically swooning over him. Yet he parried Ada Shaw's brazen overtures expertly and fended off Sally Nead's flirtation good-naturedly.

He could woo the birds out of their trees, Lily thought morosely.

It was his effort with shy Peg Wallace, however, that warmed her heart. Peg's timidity melted under his gentle attentions, and Lily felt compelled to thank him for his kindness when the class ended.

She did so by drawing Heath aside a little way. "I think it only fitting," she added reluctantly, "that Fleur award you another point for helping our pupils today."

"Are you certain you wish to be so generous?" he asked, his sensual lips uptilting in amusement. "With the point they granted me for your fencing lesson yesterday, that will bring my total to seven. At this rate, I may very well win our game."

Lily winced. She most certainly did not want him to win the right to extend his courtship for three more endless months. But she felt she needed to be fair. "You deserve to be rewarded in this instance."

"I am willing to exchange some points if you will accompany me to a play at Drury Lane this evening."

She couldn't help but smile at his persistence. She had no doubt that his invitation to the theater was a ploy to get her alone in an even more intimate setting. "Sadly, I must decline. I don't wish to be seen in public with you, remember? Besides, you have already used up your allotted time with me today."

He gave her a smile of heart-stopping charm. "I had to try. Then I will see you tomorrow at Lady Freemantle's garden party? I would offer my escort, but I suspect it is too much to ask for you to ride with me in my carriage."

"Thank you, but I am riding with Fanny," Lily was glad to say. Chiswick was some half dozen miles from London's Mayfair district, and under no circumstances did she want to be alone with Heath for so long. Just standing this close to him in a roomful of people was unsettling enough.

And a new tension filled her stomach when he brought her hand to his lips and lightly kissed her fingers.

Lily forced herself to remain calm, not wanting to give him the satisfaction of knowing he had so much power over her. But when he took his leave, she stood there for a deplorably long moment afterward, feeling the warm tingling in her fingers where his lips had brushed.

When Saturday dawned cool and cloudy, Lily hoped the rain would hold off for Winifred's garden party. After conducting morning classes for the academy, she donned a fashionable gown of pale green sprigged muslin with a matching bonnet for the occasion.

Fanny was dressed even more stylishly, Lily saw when the carriage arrived to pick her up, no doubt in order to face the supercilious gentry who were sure to attend.

But the guests were not Fanny's chief concern; instead it was Mick O'Rourke.

"I wrote a long letter to him, explaining our plan to repay the debt," Fanny told Lily as soon as they were on their way, "but I never received a reply. I admit it worries me."

"Do you expect him to retaliate for what I did the other day?" Lily asked, frowning.

"I don't know. It's possible he is waiting for me to come to him on bended knee to beg him to relent."

"You should not have to prostrate yourself before him," Lily declared militantly. "Especially when the debt is not even yours."

"I know. But I may have no choice if he wants his money at once."

Lily's frown deepened. "If you like, I can sound out Winifred this afternoon to see if she would be willing to contribute the funds immediately."

"You might mention it to gain a feel for her willingness," Fanny replied. "But hopefully, after the soiree on Monday we won't need her financial backing."

They spoke about preparations for the soiree then, and discussed last-minute details. Fanny intended to send her dresser to the boardinghouse to help the girls with their gowns and hair, and Lily wanted her three favorites to have special attention to improve their chances of landing new patrons.

When she and Fanny arrived at Freemantle Park, Lily found her sisters already there before her, on the terrace overlooking the magnificent gardens. Immediately upon spying her, Arabella and Roslyn left the gathering to embrace her warmly. And after a fond reunion with Fanny, they drew Lily inside to a quiet parlor so they could have some privacy.

Lily was rather surprised to discover how fervently glad she was to see her sisters. They had written to each other frequently in the past weeks since Arabella's wedding, but it wasn't the same as being able to talk and laugh together in person. Moreover, a good deal had happened since then. Particularly Roslyn's betrothal to the Duke of Arden.

Arabella looked beautiful and sophisticated as usual, Lily thought, but Roslyn's pale golden beauty was even more exquisite since she was positively glowing.

"Are you certain you have made the right choice about marrying Arden, Rose?" Lily asked once the elementary details had been recounted. "You still have time to change your mind. There are ten more days before your wedding, when your decision becomes irreversible."

Roslyn smiled wryly while Arabella laughed.

"That is exactly the attitude we expected from you, dearest Lily," Arabella said. "We know how much you despise the very thought of marriage. But Roslyn has always been more open to the idea than either you or I."

Because Roslyn had not been witness to their father's physical brutality as *she* had, Lily thought to herself. Nor had Roslyn been forsaken by a fiancé who professed to love her, as Arabella had been during her first betrothal.

"I must say you *seem* happy, Rose," Lily admitted.

Roslyn's smile softened. "Ecstatically so. What about

you, Lily? Are you happy, living in London with Fanny's friends and boarders?"

"Yes, indeed," she answered truthfully. "It is extremely fulfilling, being able to teach those women and improve their self-esteem. I can actually see them blossom day by day. They are far more eager to learn than our students at the Freemantle Academy ever were. Possibly because they know how hard life can be, having to earn their own livings instead of being born to wealth and comfort."

"So what about Lord Claybourne?" Arabella wanted to know.

"What about him?" she hedged.

"How is your courtship progressing? I doubt you welcomed his romantic attentions."

"Of course not. I am only enduring him so he will bring some suitable gentlemen to the soiree on Monday evening."

"But Claybourne is a delightfully charming man," Roslyn pointed out. "Clever and quick-witted and charismatic. I should think you would find the challenge he presents at least a little exciting."

Lily couldn't deny that Heath was dynamic and exciting. Around him she felt exhilarated, her wits and senses alive and on full alert. And since he'd begun his pursuit, her life was far livelier than it had ever been.

Which was what made him so dangerous. If she felt this way about him after less than a week, how could she fight her deplorable attraction to him if he actually won their game?

"Perhaps, but I won't even consider accepting his proposal. I am perfectly content as I am. Especially now that I've begun to reconsider my future. I want to find a way to aid women like our boarders. To help them seek better lives."

"That is certainly an admirable goal," Roslyn remarked, "but helping indigent women and having a husband are not mutually exclusive."

Lily eyed her sisters with growing impatience. "If you mean to quiz me so relentlessly about Lord Claybourne, I think I will leave."

"Don't be absurd," Arabella chided amiably. "It is just that we both fell in love with our ideal mates, and we want you to have the same chance at happiness. You should at least give Claybourne's courtship a chance."

Lily shook her head adamantly. She never wanted to fall in love, and she never wanted to marry. She had vowed never to let any man have such irrevocable power over her, and she wouldn't change her long-held beliefs simply because one possessed a nearly irresistible charm.

"I cannot trust him enough," Lily said simply.

"He may be nothing like our father. Marcus certainly isn't."

"Nor is Drew," Roslyn chimed in. "Lord Claybourne seems nothing like Papa, Lily."

No, Heath seemed very different, Lily acknowledged. She could see the kindness in him, the gentleness, the humor. And he hadn't tried to control her or dictate to her, the way their father had ruthlessly done their mother. Nor had he physically threatened her. Instead he had protected and defended her—

"I cannot imagine that you are *afraid* of him, Lily," Arabella commented thoughtfully.

No, it was her response to him that made her afraid. She was frightened of the desire he made her feel. She had never wanted that kind of intimacy with a man, but now she found herself thinking of it constantly.

The irony was almost amusing. Just a few short months ago, she had warned Arabella about giving in to Marcus's masculine allure. But now she understood the powerful temptation her sister had faced.

"You really should not condemn all men simply because of what Papa did"—Arabella smiled ruefully— "even though I felt exactly that way before I fell in love with Marcus. I know many noblemen have been raised to be selfish and uncaring, and such men are not even capable of love, but Claybourne could prove to be another exception."

Lily had no idea if Heath was capable of love. She had seen glimpses of his magnanimity in the past few days— although that could be merely because he was trying to win their game.

But the state of his heart didn't matter to her in the least, she reminded herself, stiffening her spine. "Belle, I truly don't wish to discuss this any further."

Her eldest sister pressed her lips together, as if wanting to argue, but then her expression softened. "You are right, of course. You must discover love on your own, Lily. So we won't push you any further. But you do realize that Winifred is still set on matchmaking? She knows all about Claybourne's courtship of you."

Lily's brow furrowed. "How did she find out?"

"I have no idea. Perhaps he told her."

It would be just like him to secure Winifred as an ally, Lily thought in exasperation.

"Regardless of Winifred's intentions," Roslyn interrupted, "we should rejoin her party. You haven't met

Constance yet, Lily, or the children. You will love the children, I'm sure."

From Roslyn's letters, she had heard the remarkable story of how Winifred had taken in her late husband's mistress and three illegitimate children. In fact, the garden party was being held in honor of Constance Baines, to introduce her to the local gentry. Reportedly Constance was almost completely recovered from the grave illness that had nearly taken her life.

"I very much want to meet them," Lily said, linking arms with both her sisters. "And I brought the children presents, Rose, so I can spoil them as you suggested."

Roslyn's laughter was soft and tender. "They desperately need a bit of spoiling, they've had so little of it in their lives."

Lily was more than happy to focus all of her attention on coming to know Constance and the children this afternoon, since it would give her an excuse to avoid a particular charming nobleman. But as soon as she stepped out on the terrace, she spied Heath with his two close friends, the Earl of Danvers and the Duke of Arden.

Like Heath, they were strikingly handsome aristocrats, with the virile look of avid sportsmen. The duke was darkly blond, his tall frame one of lithe elegance, while Marcus had ebony hair and a more powerful physique than Arden. But they each had eyes only for their ladies; it was clear they cherished Arabella and Roslyn dearly.

Heath, Lily noticed, was regarding her with a gleam of interest in his own eyes. Deplorably, her heart gave a leap of delight when she met his gaze, so she turned away quickly and detoured toward her friend Tess, who was talking and laughing with a small group of youngsters.

She would have to do much better, Lily scolded herself, if she hoped to get through the afternoon unscathed.

She did indeed relish meeting Constance and her three children.

Constance was a beautiful woman, although she still possessed the pallor of an invalid. And her two young daughters, Sarah and Daisy, showed signs of becoming just as lovely someday.

Her sixteen-year-old son, Benjamin, was less refined, with the strong, wiry build of a boy who'd been employed in menial labor for much of the past four years.

Ben pretended nonchalance at being in such illustrious company, but the little girls were dancing with excitement at attending their first party, anticipating the treats they'd been promised. Winifred had arranged for them to taste ices for the first time and to enjoy various entertainments and games. Later, they would take rowboats out on the ornamental lake under adult supervision.

Several other children had been invited to provide company for the Baines offspring, and Lily willingly volunteered to assist Tess in taking command of the infant troop.

Thus, for the first hour she managed to keep her distance from Heath while she played Pall Mall on the side lawn with Sarah and Daisy, showing them the art of hitting the wooden ball through a wicket with a mallet.

When they moved back to the gardens for a game of hide-and-seek, however, she couldn't help but notice

Heath. There was a genteel crowd of more than a hundred guests, and Lord Claybourne was clearly a favorite among them, with his charming manner and easy smile.

It surprised Lily immensely, then, when he left his peers to join her and the children.

"Lady Freemantle has recruited me to organize the boating," he informed her.

Lily cast her friend a narrow-eyed glance across the gardens before responding to Heath's casual remark. "It is an obvious ploy to throw us together."

"Naturally. She is well aware that you've been avoiding me ever since you arrived."

"Well, you needn't make such a sacrifice. Surely you cannot have any interest in taking children on boat rides."

"Oh, but I can. Especially if it will allow me to share your enchanting company."

Lily rolled her eyes, but Heath appeared to be entirely serious about his desire to entertain the children. He enlisted Benjamin Baines as his chief assistant and corralled the others to follow him through the gardens and across the elegant lawns down to the lake.

Several of the adults joined in the fun, so five boats were soon being filled with the assistance of several strapping Freemantle footmen. Lily stood on shore, helping the passengers settle into their seats, and then watched the ensuing laughter and gaiety as they ventured out onto the water.

It amazed her to observe Heath with the children. He was just as congenial and charming with the youngsters as he had been with her academy pupils. Sarah and Daisy in particular were spellbound by his presence as he rowed them back and forth across the lake and patiently showed them how to man the oars.

Winifred came up to Lily just then and wrapped her in a fond embrace before drawing back to scold her. "I have a serious bone to pick with you, my girl. What do you mean, haring off to London so that delightful marquess couldn't find you? It was very bad of you to deceive us that way."

Lily smiled affectionately. "You know your scheming drove me to it, Winifred."

"Pah," the plump, matronly lady retorted. "I had only your best interests at heart—and I still do. You led Claybourne on a wild-goose chase. I expect you to make it up to him."

"What do you mean?" Lily asked warily.

"You must allow him to give you a boat ride after the children are done, just the two of you. It will be quite romantic"—she gestured at the lovely landscape—"in this idyllic setting."

"Winifred—"

"I insist."

When Lily scowled, Winifred held up a hand. "Very well, I know better than to insist with you. But I don't believe it is too much to ask." Her ladyship mimicked a pout. "Please, dear, just indulge an old woman's whims this once."

Lily gave a huff of exasperation. "You aren't old in the least."

"I am old enough to be your mother," Winifred retorted. "What's more, I have a great deal more experience than you do. Trust me, you don't want to end up alone in your old age, unloved and unwanted, as I am."

Biting back further argument, Lily gave in reluctantly and agreed to a boat ride with Lord Claybourne.

The adults in the company were satisfied with short excursions on the lake, but it was nearly an hour later before the children had had their fill of boating and Heath returned to shore with his last group of young passengers. Lily hoped he might have lost interest in taking her out, but once the children had debarked and had been led away by Tess, he turned to her expectantly. "At last it is your turn."

Lily started to step into the rowboat, but Heath held out his hand. "Allow me to be chivalrous for once," he said, laughter lurking in his deep gold eyes.

Knowing how the contact would affect her, she didn't really want him to touch her. But she had little choice other than to give him her hand and allow him to support her. Yet she snatched her hand away as soon as she was settled on the bench opposite him.

"You put Lady Freemantle up to this, didn't you?" Lily asked as Heath picked up the oars and began to stroke.

"She scarcely needed encouragement. She wants us to have the opportunity to be together. So just relent with good humor, love, and pretend you are enjoying yourself."

Lily felt her mouth curve wryly. It *was* rather humorous, letting herself be maneuvered so expertly.

"I am perfectly capable of rowing myself, you know," she declared, not wanting to give in too easily. "You needn't treat me as a helpless blossom."

"Believe me, I am laboring under no such misapprehension. You are much more like thistle." Heath chuckled softly when she made a face. "You may take a turn with the oars in a moment, but for now, sit back and savor this romantic interlude."

She arched an eyebrow. "Surely you don't expect me to simper and flirt with you?"

"What a singular notion. You are too forthright to possess any feminine wiles."

Lily tore her gaze away from his winning smile, and instead focused on the scenery. She had to admit she was enjoying herself. It was pleasant being out on the water, despite having to endure this charming rogue's company . . . or perhaps because of it. The sun had come out from behind the clouds, and it was turning into a beautiful summer afternoon, even though the breeze had picked up significantly.

She felt a welcome contentment steal over her—until they neared the middle of the lake, when Heath stowed one oar and reached out to tug on the ribbons of her bonnet.

Giving a start of surprise, Lily clasped his wrist to stay his hand. "What the devil are you doing?"

"You look too prim and proper," he said provocatively as he loosened the ribbons completely and plucked the bonnet off her head. "You need to feel the wind in your hair."

She glanced back at the shore, but no one seem to be paying any attention to his vexing mischief. Leaning forward, Lily snatched back her bonnet and placed it on her head where it belonged. Yet before she could find the ribbons to retie them, a sharp gust of wind came up and caught the wide brim. Instantly, the bonnet lifted and went sailing over the side of the boat.

It was purely a reflex action on Lily's part: she lunged sideways after it. To her dismay, not only did she miss, but her left arm sank shoulder-deep into the water.

She gasped at the sudden chill and grasped wildly at the boat's edge with her free hand, her balance precarious. For a heartbeat, she hung there suspended. Behind her, she felt Heath grab at her skirts to keep her from falling completely overboard. But his added weight on that side tilted the little rowboat so that Lily lost her frail grip and went tumbling headfirst into the lake.

She heard Heath swear violently a second before the water closed over her. The shock of the cold made Lily open her mouth, which then made her inhale a mouthful.

Near panic, she came up choking and flailing and gasping for air. But almost immediately she felt a powerful arm slide around her waist as she struggled.

There was fear in Heath's voice when he urgently said her name, although his tone soon gentled. "Easy, I have you," he murmured soothingly, treading water while he held her.

He had plunged in after her to save her, Lily realized as she endured a helpless fit of coughing.

When she finally managed to catch her wheezing breath, he drew her even closer against him. "Are you all right?" he asked, concern in his eyes.

His face was very near hers, and she was clutching at his shoulders. Although she didn't want to let go, Lily forced herself to relax her death grip.

"Yes," she rasped hoarsely. "I'm fine."

His mouth curled. "You don't look fine."

"I will be once I can breathe."

As if to dispute her declaration, another bout of coughing overtook her. Heath continued to support her until she found her voice again.

"Thank you," Lily said finally. "You didn't need to get wet, though. I could have saved myself."

"I thought you might drown."

"I know how to swim. Basil Eddowes taught me when we were children. It was just the shock of falling in that paralyzed me for a moment." She paused, suddenly aware of his body pressing against hers. "You can release me now. I can manage on my own."

"You may find it hard to swim in long skirts and petticoats."

"I can manage," Lily repeated.

He still seemed reluctant to release her, so she pushed away from him. He was right, Lily quickly learned. She could float somewhat, but she wasn't very buoyant. Her skirts felt like a ship's anchor, pulling her down. And when she tried to kick her legs to swim, she discovered they were tangled in swaths of muslin.

It was a struggle, but she made it over to the rowboat several yards away. Reaching up, she grasped the edge and clung.

She waited a short while to regain her strength before attempting to climb in, but then found it impossible; the weight of her sodden gown dragged her down, and every time she attempted to haul herself up, she tilted the rowboat into the water.

"Do you need my help yet, sweeting?" Heath asked mildly when she muttered an oath of exasperation.

Pushing a strand of dripping hair from her eyes, Lily glanced back at him. He was enjoying her dilemma, she could tell. And he wanted her to admit defeat. But she wasn't about to give him the satisfaction of asking him for help.

By now a group of people had gathered on shore and were calling to her in alarm, demanding to know if she was all right.

"Yes, don't worry," Lily called back. "I am coming."

Releasing her hold on the little boat, she struck out for the nearest shore to her left, swimming slowly because of her entangling skirts.

Judging by his tone, Heath didn't seem to approve of her decision. "Just what do you think you are doing, Lily?"

She continued making small strokes, despite the frustration of only inching along. "I am saving myself. I don't want you to earn any points for rescuing me. You only need three more to win as it is."

"What if I relinquish any claim to points this time? Will you return to the boat and let me help you?"

"Thank you, your lordship, but I find the exercise stimulating."

"Lily . . ." he said, amusement warring with exasperation.

When she wouldn't give up, Heath caught up to her and swam alongside her, matching his strokes to her much shorter ones. "Did anyone ever tell you how stubborn you are, Miss Loring?"

"Yes, quite frequently. You have yourself. But I warned you of that, remember?"

Several of the people on land realized what she was doing and started hurrying around the lake to meet her. Benjamin was in the lead, followed swiftly by three footmen. And Winifred panted after them, her larger bulk preventing her from maintaining the same speed.

Lily's arms and legs were growing tired, but thankfully she shortly reached shallower water where her feet could touch bottom. Standing upright, however, was an exercise in futility. She had lost both her slippers, and her stockinged feet had difficulty finding purchase in the sandy mud. And even when she eventually managed to find her footing, climbing out of the lake was like dragging chains behind her.

Once, she almost fell, and when the water was waist-deep, she stepped on a sharp piece of gravel that cut into her toes. When she let out an exclamation of pain, Heath exhaled in disgust.

"Enough is enough," he stated, closing the distance between.

Without waiting for her permission, he scooped Lily up in his arms to carry her the rest of the way.

She gave a yelp of protest but was forced to cling to his neck as he plowed through the water, up the sloping bank to the shore's edge.

"Put me down!" she insisted when the water was knee level.

"Gladly," he replied. "You weigh as much as a beached whale."

No sooner had he spoken than he stumbled and went down on one knee. Although he easily kept hold of her while she clutched his neck more tightly, they voiced the same oath at the exact same instant.

The humor of it struck Lily and Heath at the same moment. Laughter echoed from them both as they met each other's eyes.

When eventually he stood up, holding her safely, their laughter faded to a shared breathless smile.

"It's damned hard playing the hero with you, sweetheart."

Lily's mouth curved with mirth. "Some hero you are. If you hadn't loosened my bonnet, we would not be in this fix."

By the time they reached dry land, the small group of spectators had joined them.

Winifred was out of breath, but she spoke first. "How wonderful of you, my lord. You saved her life."

"You give me far too much credit, my lady," he answered, his tone dry.

"Yes," Lily added wryly. "I believe I had something to do with my deliverance."

He grinned at her while Winifred shook her head. "But it was still quite romantic," she insisted.

Ignoring her friend's gushing, Lily instead addressed Heath. "Pray put me down now, my lord. You have been chivalrous enough for one day."

When he obliged, setting her on her stockinged feet, Lily winced at the feel of the rough ground against her tender soles.

Seeing her pain, Winifred frowned. "Lily, you cannot walk back to the house with no shoes."

"I don't plan to return to your house, Winifred. I shall go home to Danvers Hall instead, so I may change out of this sopping gown."

A light of speculation suddenly entered her ladyship's eyes. "Yes, of course you must change at home. I don't have any gowns that would fit you. And you must accompany her, Lord Claybourne. You need dry clothing, and Lord Danvers should have ample choices in his wardrobe."

Lily wanted to argue, yet they were both dripping wet, and she was beginning to grow chilled.

In any event, Heath took the decision from her. "My carriage will take us to the Hall, Lady Freemantle. We shall go directly to the stables so we needn't importune your guests."

Although nodding happily, Winifred cast a measuring glance at Lily's bedraggled form. "I suppose I should send a footman to fetch some blankets for you. . . ."

"There are carriage rugs in my coach," Heath assured her. "Please accept our apologies for leaving so precipitously, my lady."

With a brief bow to their hostess, he picked Lily up again without regard to her sharp inhalation and strode toward the stableyard.

Lily knew protesting would be futile, yet she scolded him all the same once they were out of earshot. "You are taking shameless advantage of Winifred's scheming."

"Perhaps, but conventional methods of wooing won't work on you, so I must act when I have the chance."

The sound she made was between a scoff and an amused *humph*. "You cannot possibly consider this farcical comedy romantic, as she does."

"No, it is hardly romantic. You look like a drowned rat."

Lily's eyes widened in mock insult. "My, my. First a whale, now a rat. How delightfully complimentary you are."

He grinned at her. "You aren't the kind of female to cherish compliments—I learned that within my first moments of meeting you."

Even though she knew better than to encourage him, Lily found herself smiling back. She couldn't deny the pleasure, either, of being held in Heath's strong arms, pressed against his warm, powerful body. The sun had disappeared behind the clouds, and her wet garments were raising goose bumps all over her skin.

But she tore her gaze away and stared at a point over his shoulder as his long strides ate up the distance.

When they reached the stableyard, he carried her directly to his coach. His servants sprang to do his bidding, opening the door for him so he could set Lily inside.

Struggling to arrange her dripping skirts, she settled on the leather seat and felt herself shiver as the clammy, cold fabric molded to her limbs and back.

After giving orders to his coachman, Heath climbed in to sit beside her, carrying a heavy woolen carriage blanket. She was grateful when he arranged the blanket over her lap and shoulders. But when he put his arm around her and drew her close, Lily stiffened. "My Lord Claybourne—" she began quellingly.

"Hush and let me warm you. Otherwise you'll be frozen by the time we reach the Hall."

Reluctantly, she allowed him to tuck her against the curve of his body. She could scarcely believe she had let Heath manipulate her into this vulnerable situation, although she couldn't help but admire his initiative, the way he always countered any move she made to avoid his wooing. Shaking her head, she laughed softly at him and at herself.

Heath put a finger to her chin and turned her head to face him. "I like your laugh." His gaze appraised her tenderly. "I like how your laughter makes your eyes sparkle."

Lily felt breathless all of a sudden.

The coach began to move just then, jostling her against him. Stirring uncomfortably, Lily looked away. She couldn't ignore him, however, for his thumb slid to the side of her neck, brushing. Tingling sensation skittered up her nerve endings, making her shiver again.

"That is quite enough, my lord."

"I beg to differ, angel. You need warming, and I intend to do it by kissing you."

When he pressed his lips to her nape, creating an excited flutter in her chest and stomach, Lily glanced back at him sternly. "You cannot want to kiss a drowned rat."

His grin was slow, potent, and incorrigibly infectious. "How many times must I tell you, I don't care how you look? You are utterly desirable in any condition."

He didn't look any less desirable for his own dousing in the lake, Lily thought, staring up at his handsome face. His wet hair had darkened and curled a little, making her want to reach up and slide her fingers through it. And how could she resist such a sinfully sensual smile?

Doubtless that was why she didn't pull away when Heath bent his head. He kissed her softly, warming her mouth as he'd promised, along with other even more sensitive parts inside her. Deploring the shameful way her blood thickened, Lily gave a little sigh as damp heat pooled between her thighs. She knew she should stop him, but his wicked mouth could kidnap a woman's common sense. . . .

Then one of his hands pushed aside the blanket and came to rest on her breast, closing possessively. Lily broke away determinedly, striving to gather her scattered wits.

"You cannot possibly be thinking of making love to me in broad daylight in a carriage," she exclaimed breathlessly. "Not even you would be so scandalous."

"I could indeed be thinking of it."

"It is barely a mile to the Hall."

"I told my coachman to go slowly in deference to the shock you endured from falling in the lake. Trust me, we have time for what I have in mind." He lifted a finger to her throat, trailing it down to the neckline of her gown. "But I promise, I won't arouse you to climax this time. I don't want your cries of pleasure to be overheard by my servants."

At the thought of Heath making her cry out with pleasure as he'd done yesterday, Lily felt her throat go dry. She sat there, torn, as his thumb moved maddeningly in light caresses over her skin. His body was giving off a powerful heat, making her yearn for him, while sensual awareness spread to all of her nerve endings. She could scarcely believe how much she wanted him to make love to her.

Lily squeezed her eyes shut. Heath was so very bad for her. He roused the very recklessness that she was trying to control.

With a sound of self-disgust, she extricated herself from his hold and moved to the opposite seat, facing him, letting the blanket drop to her waist in her haste. "You are a devil, trying to make me forget all my sense of propriety."

"Which has never been very great to begin with."

That much was true. There had always been a wild streak inside of her, and now Heath was encouraging it, urging her to behave with rash abandon, just as she longed to. But she wouldn't give in to her longings this time, Lily vowed.

It didn't help, however, that his gaze was slowly raking over her.

"Will you *please* stop looking at me that way?" she demanded in exasperation.

"What way?"

"As if you want to undress me."

"But I do want to undress you, darling." His smile was roguish, sensual. "Can I help it if I lust after you? That muslin gown of yours is hiding few of your charms at the moment."

She glanced down at herself to see that her nipples were showing even through the wet bodice of her gown and undergarments. Feeling color warming her cheeks, Lily dragged up the carriage blanket to cover her bosom, shielding her breasts from his avid gaze.

Heath gave a pained sigh. "If you won't oblige me, I suppose I can make do with fantasizing."

Lily regarded him suspiciously, wondering what he would do next. She didn't trust the devils dancing in his eyes.

She was right not to trust him, she realized the next moment, for he reached down and unbuttoned the front placket of his pantaloons. Lily's breath faltered altogether when he opened his drawers and freed his rampant male member to her shocked gaze.

"Have I robbed you of the power of speech? Fancy that."

Lily swallowed. "You are utterly wicked," she said hoarsely.

"I can be. You will find I am a very physical man."

Her eyes widened as he cradled the rigid shaft in his palm. He was greatly aroused, judging from the way it jutted out, thick and long and swollen.

She had never seen a man's naked loins before, except for those on marble statues. And Heath was far larger and more virile than any statue. Fascinated, her gaze riveted, Lily stared as he lightly stroked his tumescence.

"I would much rather you be doing this to me."

When she remained speechless, he bent down and, much to her startlement, reached beneath the blanket to take hold of her left ankle and peel off her stocking. Lifting her foot onto his lap, he lightly massaged the sole, warming it, then drew it closer to contact his naked flesh.

She sat enthralled, unable to look away. The hot, granite thickness of his manhood felt strangely erotic against her bare foot.

"Lily," he called softly. "Come and sit beside me."

She lifted her gaze to his, instinctively understanding what he was asking of her. "You want me to . . . caress you?"

"Very much." His smile tantalized, his eyes seduced. "You know how pleasurable it feels when I arouse you, so you can imagine how pleasurable it can be for me when you arouse me."

Her heart began to pound, but she didn't have the willpower to deny his scandalous request. Drawn by the wicked gleam in his alluring hazel eyes, she rose and resumed her seat next to him, the blanket completely forgotten as it slipped to the coach floor.

Without waiting, Heath guided her palm to his naked loins. Lily inhaled a sharp breath as her fingers closed around his hardness, feeling the life of him pulse and leap at her touch.

Tension spiraled within her, but Heath merely leaned casually back against his seat. Keeping a light grasp of her hand, he coaxed her to fondle him, letting her cup the heavy sacs beneath his arousal, tracing the blunt, velvety head, until finally he curled her hand around his turgid length. Demonstrating how to give him pleasure, he began moving her hand slowly up and down, stroking.

A shameful thrill raced through Lily, kindling her senses, igniting a fluid rise of heat inside her. She was inflamed by the feel of him, by the lazy passion glowing in his eyes.

"Harder, love. You won't hurt me." His voice sounded slightly breathless as he increased the pace of their strokes.

Shortly his face became taut, the skin flushed, while his eyes shimmered with a hot, primal haze of desire.

His jaw locked as their fingers kneaded harder, sweeping up and down in short, rough motions. His breath was harsh and uneven by now, his fingers clenching around hers. But the moment before his climax, he released her hand and cupped his own around the head of his shaft.

Clenching his teeth, he shut his eyes as his pulsing seed spurted into his palm. The resultant explosion made his hips arch convulsively.

Lily watched wide-eyed as Heath shuddered and went still.

Finally opening his eyes, he smiled at her. "Our private trysts could well become the delight of my life," he said huskily.

Unable to respond, she simply sat there, her lips parted, her own breath shallow, reduced to speechless, quivering pudding.

When she stayed silent, he took out a handkerchief from his coat pocket and wiped his hand clean, then calmly rearranged his clothing, covering himself and rebuttoning his pantaloons.

Lily wet her dry lips. "That is all you mean to do?"

"Did you expect more?"

"Well . . . yes." She expected him to try to seduce her at the very least. Instead he had left her hot and aching, her senses on fire.

"Alas, we don't have time. We should be reaching Danvers Hall shortly."

At his blithe tone, Lily frowned at him, suddenly comprehending his intent. "You did that on purpose, didn't you?"

"Yes, love. It was another lesson in passion. Now you know what it feels like to be painfully aroused with no hope of fulfillment . . . which is the state you continually leave me in."

He had deliberately titillated and excited and aroused her, only to keep her frustrated and hungry and craving more.

"That is hardly fair," Lily muttered. "Rather underhanded, in fact."

His half smile was enchanting. "You have the power to change your fate. All you need do is say you will wed me, and I will be more than happy to satisfy your carnal desires anytime you wish. Until then, your virtue is safe with me."

There was laughter in his eyes, but a challenge, too.

A challenge Lily had no intention of taking up.

Not for the first time she voiced a silent oath at the vexing, tempting Lord Claybourne—on this occasion for using the lure of incredible carnal pleasure to try and persuade her to accept his hand in marriage.

"I suppose I will just have to suffer then," Lily declared, moving away from him again in a fit of pique before bending to retrieve the blanket and her discarded stocking. "But I will say one thing: This absurd game cannot be over soon enough for me!"

Chapter Ten

❦

I see now the incredible lure of having a tender lover.
— Lily's reflections to herself

"I believe we should call it a draw," Fleur announced the following afternoon after hearing the tale of Lily's unexpected swim in the lake. "What do you think, Chantel?"

Lily saw Chantel give Lord Claybourne an apologetic smile. They had gathered in the courtesans' sitting room in order to judge his performance, but Chantel was so softhearted that she never liked to disappoint anyone, particularly handsome noblemen.

"Regrettably I agree, my lord," Chantel murmured. "No points should be awarded to you or taken away in this instance. You managed to inveigle Lily into your boat, but she fell overboard while under your care. And she did not require your assistance to save herself. Furthermore, you escorted her to Danvers Hall so she could change her gown, but you also benefited, in that you were provided with dry clothing. Have we summarized the facts correctly?"

"I would call that a fair assessment," Heath said mildly—much to Lily's relief. She had almost expected him to mention his amorous exploits in his coach. When he met her gaze, she knew he was remembering that scandalous incident and was very glad that he held his tongue.

And in truth, there was nothing more to report about yesterday that might affect the outcome of their game. For the remainder of the afternoon, Heath's behavior had been perfectly unexceptional and circumspect. They had changed their attire at the Hall and returned to Freemantle Park to rejoin the garden party.

Of course, Winifred had been eager to learn any juicy details when she privately pressed Lily to be more accommodating to his courtship. But only under pain of death would she have confessed to their passionate tryst.

It was bad enough that Winifred still took every opportunity to push her in the marquess's path. When Lily had sounded out the wealthy widow about possibly helping Fanny with her friends' debt, Winifred, in yet another obvious attempt to play matchmaker, had quickly declined, saying that Lily should apply to Lord Claybourne for the funds—which she most certainly was not willing to do.

"So, my lord," Fleur said, bringing the judgment to an end. "I believe your total points to date are seven. You still must earn three more."

"Perhaps this will improve my score," Heath said, reaching for a side table to retrieve the package he had brought with him.

When he handed the package to Lily, who sat beside him on the settee, she took it warily. It was wrapped with expensive gilt paper and tied with a ribbon.

"Oh, a present!" Chantel said with delight. "It looks like a book of some type. Do open it, Lily."

Lily removed the ribbon and wrapping to uncover a leather-bound book.

"What is it?" Chantel asked. "A volume of sonnets?"

"No," Lily answered as she read the title. "*Travels in the South Sea Islands* by George Wilkins."

"I thought you would prefer this to sonnets," Heath commented. "Wilkins is a member of the Royal Society and a protégé of Sir Joseph Banks. His recollections of the native cultures in the Pacific make for some very intriguing reading."

Chantel looked puzzled. "Why would Lily care about the condition of heathens in some foreign sea?"

Heath's amused gaze met Lily's again. "Because she claims to be an adventurer at heart," he answered.

"Is that true, Lily?" Chantel queried in a tone that expressed dismay.

Lily smiled. That tone was the same one her mother had regularly used when lamenting her daughter's thirst for adventure. "I am afraid so, Chantel. But you needn't worry; it isn't contagious. How did you come upon this book, my lord?"

"Wilkins is a colleague of mine. And I am honored to call Sir Joseph a friend."

Lily couldn't help but be impressed, although her friends didn't recognize the significance.

"Who is Sir Joseph?" Fleur wanted to know.

Lily glanced over at her. "He is the president of the Royal Society, Fleur." The Royal Society was a learned organization for the promotion of the natural sciences and had arranged various scientific expeditions around the globe over the past several decades. "Sir Joseph also once sailed with Captain James Cook in the *Endeavor* to explore the Pacific and the coast of Australia."

"And you are interested in such things?"

"Well, yes. But I confess surprise that Lord Claybourne is."

Beside her, Heath leaned back in his seat. "My friend Arden is an avid member of the Society, and I became involved at his urging. My chief interest is in exploration. I've helped fund three expeditions of research vessels thus far, including this most recent one of Wilkins's."

Lily eyed him in admiration, recalling that her first impression of Heath had been as a bold adventurer and explorer. "I didn't realize you were interested in exploration."

"There is a great deal you don't know about me."

Fleur broke in once more. "I would say this gift is surely worth a point, Lord Claybourne, since it is quite thoughtful and inventive. A conventional courtier would have brought Lily poetry. It shows that you are attuned to her true desires."

"I most certainly have her true desires in mind," Heath murmured so softly that only Lily could hear.

At his deliberately provocative remark, she sent him a quelling glance and resolved to change the subject, not wishing to dwell on the disheartening fact that he now needed only two more points to win the game. "Thank you for the book, my lord. I shall be pleased to read it. Now would you care to report on your efforts to find attendees for our soiree tomorrow evening?"

"I count thirteen who have promised to make an appearance."

Chantel clapped her hands together with delight. "That is capital, my lord! With your candidates as well as Fanny's, we should have nearly thirty eligible guests in attendance."

Heath's smile was modest. "One of the candidates purports to be an old acquaintance of yours, Miss Amour. Viscount Poole."

"My heavens! I haven't seen Poole for a donkey's age. His wife objected to his . . . er . . . liaison with me, so he gave me up."

"He is widowed now," Heath informed her.

"Yes, I had heard that." Chantel gave a bemused sigh, as if remembering her colorful past. "Lord Poole always was one of my favorite courtiers. Not the most original lover but a jolly sort and by far the best poet. He regularly won the contests for my favors by composing sonnets for me, do you remember, Fleur?"

"I do remember." A speculative look entered Fleur's eyes. "Perhaps you can turn his attendance tomorrow night to your advantage and renew your former association with him."

"I will certainly try. But it will be delightful to see him again, in any event."

"You will have to look your very best," Fleur advised. "Age has not been our friend, as you well know."

"Yes, but Fanny's dresser can work miracles with cosmetics and coiffures. And Lily has sprung for marvelous new raiments for me." Chantel smiled at Lily. "I wish your own gown was half so fine, my dear."

"I shall make do with a simple evening gown," Lily replied. "Our pupils are the ones who must shine."

She felt Heath's frown as he turned his gaze on her. "Surely you won't be attending the soiree?"

Her brow furrowed. "But of course. What did you expect?"

His frown never wavered. "The company will not be what you are accustomed to."

"If you are concerned about the impropriety, I plan to come in disguise—a mask and turban—so no one will recognize me."

"Even so, you don't need to be there."

Lily's eyes widened at his obvious disapproval, until she realized that he was worried that his bachelor friends would think her among the muslin company. "But I must be there, my lord, to help our boarders if necessary. Surely you see that I cannot abandon them now? This soiree is far too important to their futures. Not to mention that a successful outcome of the soiree should help us to repay the debt owed O'Rourke."

Heath didn't argue but sat silently regarding her. Uncomfortable with his penetrating gaze, Lily rose to her feet. "Thank you for the gift of the book, my lord, but if you will forgive me, I have another class scheduled in a few moments. Shall I see you at the soiree tomorrow evening at eight? Regrettably I won't have time before then, since we will be making preparations all day."

"Till tomorrow at eight," Heath said as he also stood.

He offered her a polite bow before she turned away toward the door, although he didn't appear at all happy with her, Lily noted.

Yet his happiness was not her chief concern now—or at any other time, for that matter, she added mutinously to herself.

Her only concern now was holding a successful soiree so that her pupils could acquire new patrons who would care for them and give them better lives than they could ever hope for otherwise.

Heath was indeed severely unhappy with Lily's decision to attend Monday evening's event. He most certainly didn't want his future marchioness at such a risqué gathering, exposed to the blatant overtures of his friends and fellow bachelors.

Thus he arrived early at the soiree, prepared to keep a close eye on Lily.

He was restless and impatient, however, as he watched her mingle among the company. She had indeed worn a three-quarter mask, which concealed all of her face except for her mouth and chin, as well as an elegant turban to hide her lustrous hair. No costume could disguise her essence, though. She was vibrant and alive, pulsing with life and sensuality. Every man in the room noticed her—which was quite a feat, considering how much competition she had.

The soiree was an elegant affair, comparable to any glittering fete held at Carlton House by the Prince Regent's tonnish cronies. The drawing room was filled to overflowing. Every one of the young women on display looked and spoke like ladies, and Heath couldn't help but be impressed, knowing that Lily's "academy" had turned them into beauties worthy of becoming London's finest courtesans.

Fleur Delee and Chantel Amour looked on like proud mother hens. Fleur was garbed in scarlet silk and black lace, while Chantel was resplendent in purple satin and matching ostrich plumes, although he suspected her amethyst and diamond jewelry was made of paste.

For the first hour, Heath hovered protectively near Lily, but she moved from group to group, ignoring him. After that, she latched on to the elderly Lord Poole and spent the next hour laughing and flirting and drinking champagne with him.

And if that wasn't bad enough, the evening was barely half over when Lily was approached by a pair of eager young bloods.

Heath felt his fists clench when one of them kissed her hand, but it was only when Lily laughed up at the young man that he could take no more. In two strides, he was standing before her.

"Ah, there you are, darling," Heath said through gritted teeth as he took her elbow and drew her away from the company.

When he would have led her from the drawing room, however, she pulled back, resisting. "What do you think you are you doing, my lord?"

"Taking you away from here."

"You cannot. I told you, I must remain in case our pupils need me."

"No, you will not. In fact, I forbid it."

"You *forbid* it?" she repeated, her voice rising in disbelief.

"Yes," Heath insisted, his fingers taking tighter hold of her upper arm. "You are coming with me, sweetheart."

"Of all the arrogant, high-handed—"

Her sputtering faltered when she noted numerous pairs of eyes watching their altercation. Fuming in silence, she allowed Heath to escort her out of the drawing room and up two flights of stairs to the floor where her bedchamber was located.

The corridor was dimly lit by a single wall sconce, Heath saw, and her bedchamber wasn't lit at all, he discovered when he shut the door hard behind them. Yet since the curtains and windows had been left wide open, his eyes quickly adjusted to the moonlight streaming into the small room.

Lily had ripped off her mask and whirled to face him, her hands on her hips. And judging from her expression, she was clearly irked by his possessiveness.

"You cannot tell me how to behave, Lord Claybourne! You do not own me."

Her declaration only raised Heath's ire. He rarely lost his temper, but he could feel it turning flame-hot. "You are wrong, Lily. You *are* mine. And I won't stand for you carrying on with other men like the veriest trollop."

"Carrying on?" Her voice rose nearly an octave. "What, pray, was I doing to warrant that unfounded accusation?"

"You have been simpering and flirting with Poole since he arrived."

She looked half astonished, half infuriated. "Because I quickly determined he was the only man here who was safe for me to be with." Her eyes narrowed. "You cannot possibly be jealous of Lord Poole! Why, he is old enough to be my grandfather. Moreover, he isn't the least interested in *me*. He spent the entire time reminiscing about Chantel's former glory days. He is quite smitten with her—and completely harmless to me."

"Those two leering bucks aren't harmless. They want nothing more than to have you in their beds."

"What if they do? You have no right to be jealous!"

In one distracted part of his mind, Heath acknowledged the novelty of the fierce emotion he was feeling. He never became jealous over a woman. Yet both Poole and his younger rivals had made him livid with it. Or rather, he was livid at the attention Lily had shown them. Her consorting had roused a primal male urge to carry her back to his lair and keep her safe from all his competition.

How had this spirited hoyden managed to do what no other woman ever had?

Lily was glaring at him as if she wanted to box his ears. "This is positively absurd. I am returning to the soiree this instant. Let me pass."

"No."

"*No?*"

"No," he repeated as the air between them crackled with tension. He'd had enough of her resistance, enough of her denials. Lily didn't want those lecherous blades, she wanted *him*.

Determined to prove it to her, Heath stepped forward and hauled her into his arms.

It started as a kiss of mastery and domination, with no hint of gentleness. His need was all about possession as he plundered her mouth . . . ruthless, relentless, his tongue thrusting with a hunger that was angry, thorough, and devastatingly passionate.

Lily felt his hunger as his strong hands pulled her even closer. Her resistance lasted another heartbeat before she gave in entirely. With a seizure of need she melted against Heath, kissing him back with ruthless abandon.

She reveled in his fierceness . . . yet what had started as angry and intense quickly turned hot and tender; their kiss became wild, delicious, and stunningly sensual. Lily gave a helpless whimper at the sheer power of it.

Her heart was hammering and her breath came in ragged pants when Heath finally drew back to stare at her. Desire throbbed in the air, along with a telling pulse between her thighs.

Lily's heart pounded harder. He meant to make love to her, she could see in his eyes, in the intent expression on his face, illuminated by the pale glow of moonlight.

"I want you, Lily," he stated, his voice a low, husky rasp. "And I know you want me."

"Yes," she said simply.

Sliding one hand around her nape, he stroked the base of her neck in a light, tantalizing massage before reaching up and relieving her of her turban. Making short work of the pins that held her hair up, he spread the dark mass over her shoulders.

Then his hands began to move gently over her body, exploring her with enthralling seductiveness, tracing her shape through her gown and causing Lily to shudder with longing.

"Will we leave our clothes on this time?" she asked in a breathless murmur.

Heath flashed a smile that came close to taking her breath away. "Not this time, love. I want to see and feel and taste all of you . . . and for you to do the same with me."

He undressed her then, not allowing her to help. Lily was excruciatingly aware of his slow movements, the erratic rhythm of her heartbeat, the heavy pinprick of sensations in her body.

When he had dispensed with her last garments, he stood back to take in her nakedness. The expression on his face was almost reverent as his gaze caressed her. "I have imagined this countless times . . . how perfect your body would be, how exquisite. How it would feel to make love to you with nothing standing between us."

She had imagined it, too, which was why she felt surprise and disappointment when Heath led her to the bed and sat her down, then left her there.

But he was only stepping back to remove his own clothing, Lily realized with gratitude, watching as he began with his coat and waistcoat. His cravat and shirt came next, before he moved on to shoes and stockings and satin knee breeches.

Her breath caught in her throat when she saw his body completely naked for the first time. He looked utterly perfect himself, she thought, her enthralled gaze wandering over his magnificent shoulders, his wide chest, his narrow waist and hips, his long, powerful legs.

Muscles rippled and played beneath the satiny skin of his broad frame, while his arousal thrust out thick and swollen from the juncture of his thighs.

The sight made Lily's mouth go dry. She stared, hypnotized, as Heath came to stand before her. When he put a finger under her chin, lifting her gaze, she found herself drowning in the shadowy glimmer of his eyes.

She shivered as he urged her back upon the narrow bed, and when he joined her, stretching out his full length beside her, the muscles in her stomach clenched in anticipation.

Lily drew another sharp breath as their naked flesh touched. He felt amazing, warm and smooth and hard and muscular. Her senses came alive at the exquisite, profoundly male textures. The softness of his bare flesh, the heat and steel beneath. And his loins . . . His erection pulsed and strained against her abdomen, she could feel the scorching heat of it.

Stirring restlessly, Lily pressed her body against his, wanting to be even closer.

"No, keep still and let me pleasure you," Heath murmured.

Obediently, she lay back and let him have his way, but it wasn't easy to remain still when he began to stroke her, his hand wandering over her skin, his touch skimming like a breath.

Her nipples were excruciatingly taut, and when his palms barely brushed over the pouting buds, a spark of fire kindled inside her and flowed downward to her female center.

Lily bit her lip hard as she surrendered to the deft expertise of Heath's hands. She was enchanted by the pure sensuality of it . . . his magical touch, the quiet hush of the night, the muted moonlight pouring over them like liquid silver.

His hands left her breasts and tangled in her hair, while his mouth joined the tender assault on her sanity. His feathery kisses were a tantalizing caress on the underside of her throat before moving upward over her jaw to her cheekbone. Then, with the slow eroticism of a dream, his lips settled on hers.

Lily made a soft sound like a sigh as his mouth enthralled hers. For long heated moments, she lay there beneath him, drinking his breath, absorbing his taste, savoring his enveloping warmth, his masculine scent. Her sigh became a soft whimper as his fingers spread deliciously through her hair, guiding her even deeper into his kisses.

She was enraptured . . . held spellbound by his gentleness, paralyzed by his sweetness.

He continued to feed her the thick, dreamy pleasure, dazing her with his mystical power. Just now there was nothing in the world but the two of them, and yet her body yearned with the need to know more of him, stung with a hunger for greater fulfillment.

She was infinitely grateful when his hand returned to the naked swell of her breasts. Her nipples were aching and throbbing, and when he pinioned one between his thumb and forefinger, fiery sensations pulsed inside her, throbbing through her belly.

Then he cupped the mound in his hand and took the peak into his mouth, suckling, laving with his hot tongue. Lily dragged in a shuddering breath as melting heat began to blaze throughout her body. When he went on rousing her with pleasure, she sank her fingers into his hair, holding his head to her breast.

Heath, it seemed, was not content with merely tormenting her nipples, however. Breaking free of her clutching fingers, he trailed his mouth down to her abdomen.

Lily burned where his lips pressed, but she went rigid when he nuzzled her nest of curls at the vee of her thighs.

"Easy," Heath murmured. "I won't hurt you."

Her heart feverishly pounding, she strove to be still, waiting while his large hands framed her thighs, holding her legs apart, exposing the heart of her to his touch. Then deliberately, he set his lips to her soft flesh, pressing a long, hot kiss against her feminine center, dredging a breathless gasp from deep within Lily's throat.

Heath paid her no mind. Instead, he lapped at her slowly, teasing the folds of her cleft in deep, velvety strokes, sending lashes of heat to the very core of her.

He seemed to savor her, his attentions first long and slow and languid, then more intense . . . his tongue alternately delicate and butterfly light, then firm and rough and urgent.

Her breathing grew increasingly ragged, racing with her heart at the devastating stimulation. Her body was raw with wanting, the pleasure sharp and riveting, a feast of sensation. But Heath prolonged the delicious torture until Lily was faint with bliss.

Eventually he increased his rhythm, wringing a moan from her parted lips, and when he slid one finger partway inside her, wild desire flared through her.

Thrashing beneath his hot mouth, Lily gave in with fierce abandon. It was too much . . . too hot, too intense, too overwhelming. Emotions stormed her senses, desire and pleasure and want and need. She bucked and cried out, reeling with the shattering ecstasy.

When the firestorm finally receded, she became aware that Heath had stretched out beside her again and was watching her. As she looked up into the glimmering gold of his eyes, she saw myriad emotions reflected there: sexual hunger, tenderness, possessiveness, supreme satisfaction.

When his fingers strayed to her face, caressing her with the lightness of a drifting shadow, Lily found herself suddenly swallowing against the strange ache that had formed in her throat. Heath's passion had called to the wildness within her, yet aroused a profound emotional turmoil as well. His tender intimacy stunned and awed her even more than the carnal release he had given her.

Feeling the foolish prick of tears behind her eyelids, Lily ducked her head and hid her face in the warm skin of his chest. She had never known such tenderness with a man, certainly not the kind that brought tears to her eyes. She hadn't realized such a thing was possible. Her parents had warred constantly, their marriage a battle-ground.

She had little defense against tenderness.

Not wanting to accept it, Lily forcibly quelled the ache in her chest and eased away from Heath, purposely breaking the poignant feeling of intimacy between them.

He evidently sensed her withdrawal, though, for he reached out to pull her closer, fitting her body to his. Lily stiffened with resistance, even as her traitorous senses relished the contact with his virile warmth.

He held her like that for a long moment, his lips tenderly kissing her hair, his fingertips skimming over her arm, her back, her hip, her thigh. She could feel the rigid length of his manhood pressed against her belly, yet he made no move to seek his own carnal release.

"Don't you . . . intend to do more?" Lily finally asked hoarsely.

"Not now." His hushed murmur caressed her ear. "I want to, believe me. I want nothing more than to stay here with you and make love to you all night long, to show you that lovemaking can be even better when it is fully consummated. But I won't until you agree to wed me."

He was in pain from his intense arousal, she knew that much from his recent lessons. And she thought it only fair that she offer to assuage his discomfort. "I can attend to you . . . if you wish. The way we did in your carriage."

There was a pained smile in Heath's voice when he responded. "I would rather wait for the real thing, Lily. I demonstrated what I needed to tonight, so I am satisfied for now."

The trouble was, *she* wasn't satisfied. Heath had given her remarkable pleasure, but she still felt . . . incomplete somehow.

When she was silent, his hands returned to cradle her head—the same gentle hands that had stroked her body to such arousing effect—and tilted her face up to his so that she had to look at him.

"I wanted you to know passion, sweetheart, so you will understand what you are giving up by eschewing marriage. You don't want to remain a spinster all your life, wasting your nights in emptiness, alone in your chaste, virginal bed. And someday soon I hope to make you believe it."

She already did believe one thing, Lily acknowledged to herself. She didn't want to remain a virgin forever. Not after experiencing the stunning passion Heath had showered upon her.

Lily squeezed her eyes closed at the undeniable realization. Heath's strategy had succeeded. The truth was, she wanted to be this man's lover.

Even if she didn't wish to marry him, even if she didn't want his tenderness, she wanted to know the magical mysteries of passion and desire that he could unveil to her.

Chapter Eleven

❧

I was eager to divert his lordship's attention away from me, but I never expected to kindle my own jealousy.

—Lily to Fanny

Lulled by the sensual haven Heath had created for her, Lily fell asleep in his arms, physically sated yet with her thoughts in turmoil. And when he woke her sometime during the night, whispering that he didn't want to be discovered in her bed, the parting kiss he gave her aroused her turmoil all over again, along with her deplorable longings.

Dismayed by her weakness, Lily rose and donned her nightdress before returning alone to her bed. But she spent the remainder of the night tossing and turning, unable to sleep, powerless to forget Heath's touch, his scent, his warmth, his tenderness. And she rose early, bleary-eyed and fatigued and muttering invectives against her lamentable response to his cunning tactics.

Not only had he given her a taste of wonder, he'd left her craving his passion and fighting the temptation to take their relationship even further.

Trying to crush the scalding memory of his lovemaking, Lily washed and dressed as she considered her dilemma. Regrettably, she couldn't think about leaving London just yet in order to avoid Heath. Even though her tutorial services wouldn't be needed now that the soiree was over, she had agreed to play the courting game with him, and honorably, she would have to see it through to the conclusion, particularly since he had fulfilled his part of the bargain by bringing suitable candidates to the soiree. Besides, her friends' debt to O'Rourke still remained unpaid.

But clearly, Lily reminded herself, she couldn't afford to let down her guard with Heath any more than she already had. Most certainly she had to stop herself from such foolishness as yearning to be his lover.

Perhaps she should even start preparing for the disturbing possibility that he might actually win their game. He had an entire week left to earn only two more points and the right to court her publicly for another quarter.

Which meant it was imperative that she begin building an emotional wall between them, Lily realized. Otherwise she would leave herself much too vulnerable to him.

Lily was still contemplating how to improve her defenses when she went down to breakfast. To her surprise she found the dining room occupied by both Fleur and Chantel in addition to Ada Shaw. It was rare that the elderly beauties rose before ten.

Ada looked as contented as the proverbial cat who'd drunk an entire pot of cream, while the older courtesans were smiling broadly.

"Our soiree was a grand success, Lily," Fleur said at once. "Fourteen of our girls made arrangements for new patrons."

"Yes," Ada chimed in. "And *I* made the best conquest

of all. I found a rich earl who will be setting me up as his mistress."

"And I," Chantel added happily, "believe that Lord Poole is interested in me once more. If I play my cards right, I may be able to persuade Poole to contribute to our debt fund."

"You forget," Fleur drawled wryly, "that cards are what got us into this predicament in the first place."

"Of course I have not forgotten," Chantel retorted. "It was simply a figure of speech. Or perhaps you are merely jealous that I have found a beau after all this time?"

Fleur made a scoffing sound. "Of course not! I don't begrudge you a beau, darling. Especially not one who is old and fat and creaks when he bends. Poole wears more corsets than I do."

When Chantel's expression turned miffed and pouting at the same time, Lily hastened to intervene, expressing her delight at the success of the soiree—which fortunately sent the courtesans off into raptures about how splendid the evening had been and detailing which pupils had garnered the chance to improve their circumstances and move up in the world of the demimonde.

By the time Fleur and Chantel finished breakfasting and exited the dining room together, they were fast friends again.

Left alone with Ada, Lily sent up a silent thanks that they had been too busy last evening to notice her absence or her failure to return to the drawing room. She did *not* want to have to confess the wanton, scandalous things she had been doing with Lord Claybourne in her bed during the final hours of the soiree.

Thus, her thoughts were greatly distracted when Ada spoke.

"Lord Claybourne seems quite taken with you, Miss Loring," Ada commented.

"Why do you say so?" Lily answered absently as she sipped her coffee.

"He won't so much as look at any of us girls when you are around . . . nor when you are absent, either."

"I wish he *would* look at someone else," Lily muttered in a low undertone.

"Truly?" Ada's tone held surprise. "You want him to look elsewhere?"

Realizing she'd spoken her thought aloud, Lily looked up to find Ada watching her shrewdly.

"Most women," Ada pointed out, "would rightly sell their souls to have the attention of such a magnificent man."

Feeling her cheeks warm, Lily occupied herself with spreading marmalade on her toast. "Perhaps, but I am inclined to keep my soul for my own."

"I heard that his lordship wants to wed you," Ada added leadingly.

"So he claims, but I don't want to wed him."

"You don't want to be a marchioness?" Her eyes widened as if she couldn't comprehend such a sacrilege. "I would give up my new protector in the blink of a pig's eye if I thought I had a chance at winning Lord Claybourne's patronage." Then she sighed. "But I would never poach another girl's man. At least not one who has been so good to me, as you have been, Miss Loring."

"Lord Claybourne is not *my* man, Ada," Lily assured her.

A calculating gleam lit Ada's eyes. "Then you would not mind if I tried my hand at attracting his notice?"

Frowning, Lily wondered how she would feel if the beautiful young courtesan tried to seduce Heath. She would not like it at all, she decided. But then, she didn't have the right to prevent Ada from pursuing him, nor did she even want that right.

"I have no claim to him," Lily repeated.

"Then if you truly don't mind . . . I may give it a try. Not that I have much of a chance of succeeding. Most gents are not so hard to seduce, but Lord Claybourne is said to be a splendid lover. I've heard tell he can make a woman weep with joy. It won't be easy to pleasure such a man, or persuade him to take me on, not when he can have any woman he wants." Ada tossed her head. "But if I cannot do it, then no one can."

Lily had to agree with her assessment. With her fiery hair, lush curves, and earthy beauty, Ada should appeal even to a jaded nobleman of Heath's discriminating tastes, especially since Ada had learned to temper her vulgar mannerisms over the past month and her speech now sounded almost genteel when she worked at it. Heath might well be attracted to the sensual young siren.

"I expect you are right," Lily said with a faint smile.

Ada dimpled. "And if I can't, I fancy it could prove his devotion to you."

"What do you mean?"

"Why, just that if his attention can be turned to me so quick, then you'll know he won't be faithful to you in the long run. 'Tis better to know a man's stripes before you throw your lot in with 'im, I always say."

"True. My father was an inveterate rake, and I have no desire for a husband who is anything like him."

Lily found her mouth curling at the remembrance of her father's libertine ways. She doubted Heath was much like her profligate father, but if he readily gave in to the temptation the lightskirt presented, it would indeed prove he didn't want her all that much after all.

And in truth, if Ada *could* seduce him, Lily rationalized, it could solve her own problem of his courtship. If his carnal needs were filled by someone else, he was less likely to be lusting after *her*.

"You needn't worry that I will stand in your way, Ada," Lily murmured. "In fact, Lord Claybourne is coming to call at eleven. You are welcome to greet him in my place."

"Why, thank you, Miss Loring. I believe I know just how to go about it."

Ada's plan was relatively simple: Upon the marquess's arrival, she would descend the front staircase and contrive to fall at his feet, so that he would have no choice but to assist her. Ada was an actress, after all, and she intended to put her thespian skills to good use.

Lily was beginning to have second thoughts, however. Even though she'd voiced no objection to Heath's possible seduction, she felt strangely anxious for the entire remainder of the morning. And she found herself watching the mantel clock in Fleur's sitting room as eleven o'clock approached.

When eventually she heard the front door knocker sound, she slipped out into the corridor and edged toward the head of the stairs where Ada was poised to begin her performance.

All went perfectly according to the courtesan's plan, Lily saw, watching clandestinely from above. Moments after Lord Claybourne turned over his hat to the houseboy, Ada twisted her ankle on the bottom stair and fell gracefully to the parquet floor directly in front of him.

At her small cry of pain, Heath immediately came to Ada's rescue. And when she professed a need to lie down, he was compelled to carry her into the nearest room with a sofa, which happened to be the first floor parlor.

Unfortunately, Lily soon discovered, from her position on the second floor landing, she couldn't see or hear what was transpiring between Ada and their noble guest.

Five minutes passed before Lily's impatience won out over her better judgment. Descending the staircase, she slowly made her way down the corridor toward the parlor door, yet she could hear little there either, save for the murmur of voices.

Fighting the urgent need to rush in after them, Lily instead forced herself to stand in the corridor, although chiding herself all the while. She couldn't believe she was hovering about in this pathetic manner. She didn't give a fig if Heath was kissing Ada, or touching her, or stroking her, or bringing her to pleasure the way he'd done *her*—

Lily stifled a groan at the tormenting image of him making love to the beautiful Cyprian, and after another moment, admitted that it was futile trying to fool herself. She *hated* to think of Heath with another woman. She didn't want him kissing anyone but her, pleasuring anyone but her.

When the low rumble of his voice was followed by his

amused chuckle, Lily stiffened. She had to stop Ada from seducing him, despite her original assent to the plan!

Bracing herself for what she might find, Lily tried to keep her steps unhurried as she moved to the door, but when she entered the parlor, she came up short.

Ada was indeed lying on the sofa, lounging back against a pillow in a languid, seductive pose, while Heath sat at the lower end with the girl's bare foot in his lap, her slipper and stocking gracing the carpet. He was massaging her ankle gently, much as he'd done to Lily's foot in his carriage the afternoon of the garden party.

A pang of dismay shot through Lily, along with a fierce sting of jealousy—both of which she tried to quell as she loudly cleared her throat.

Ada glanced up with a start. "Oh, Miss Loring. I did not expect you."

Lily forced a smile. "I was supposed to meet his lordship at eleven but was delayed."

Heath, she noted, seemed not a bit discomfited that she had caught them together. In fact, he didn't even stand in her presence, as any gentleman normally would.

"Ada, my dear, are you in pain?" Lily asked, pointedly regarding the courtesan's bare foot.

"Well, I *was*—I sprained my ankle quite dreadfully— but Lord Claybourne has taken all the pain away." Ada fluttered her kohl-darkened eyelashes up at him. "I vow, 'tis splendid for a girl to have such a gallant savior."

"Yes," Lily responded in a dust-dry tone, "his lordship does enjoy playing the hero."

He also looked as if he was enjoying the beauty's attention, Lily thought, feeling piqued. "Ada, I will ring for Ellen to bring you a cold compress if you like."

When she started to move across to the bellpull, however, Heath's easy drawl followed her. "Have the compress delivered to Miss Shaw's bedchamber. I intend to carry her there since she cannot walk."

"Oh, *thank* you, my lord," Ada breathed in a husky murmur. "I don't know how I would have managed if you had not rescued me."

"I cannot let you suffer, now can I?" he said with a caressing smile.

Although clenching her jaw, Lily had no choice but to comply with his request. By the time the maid Ellen came scurrying into the room, Heath had scooped Ada up in his arms and was smiling down into her eyes while she clung to his neck and gazed back up at him in adoration.

When he strode from the parlor with his feminine burden, Lily quickly gave instructions to Ellen, then snatched up Ada's shoe and stocking and followed Heath up the front staircase.

Ada's bedchamber was on the second floor at the rear of the corridor, and Lily managed to reach it before him, in time to open the door for him. He carried the courtesan inside and gently set her down on the bed. Ada kept her arms twined about his neck, though, while she whispered something in his ear that made him laugh softly.

Lily realized she was grinding her teeth, and she willingly admitted relief when Heath disengaged himself from the beauty's hold and gallantly took his leave of her.

When he accompanied Lily out into the corridor, however, she was surprised that he took her elbow in a firm grasp. "Where may we be private, angel?" he asked in a deceptively pleasant tone.

Lily sent him a narrow glace. He almost sounded angry at her. "Will Fleur's sitting room do?"

"Well enough," he said tersely.

Wondering what had roused his wrath, Lily led the way. She felt herself tense when Heath shut the door sharply behind them. After last night, she most certainly didn't want to be alone with him again.

Yet he obviously didn't have in mind a repetition of last night's lovemaking. His gaze pinned her for a long beat before he moved toward Lily, stopping barely a foot away. Despite his intimidating stance, her body's response to his nearness was immediate: She found it difficult to breathe, let alone think, when he was that close.

"You endorsed Ada's attempt at seduction, didn't you?" Heath demanded in a curt tone. When she remained silent, a muscle ticked in his jaw. "Don't bother to deny it, sweeting. Ada confessed your role."

Lily's eyes widened as comprehension dawned. "You persuaded her to tell you, didn't you? You *charmed* a confession out of her."

"Guilty as charged," he shot back.

"How did you even guess?"

"I thought her behavior strangely forward, even for her. And I've learned to spot a ruse when I see it."

"Oh, yes, I forget," Lily rejoined. "Females have been throwing themselves at your feet for aeons. So that display of concern for her injury—your rubbing her ankle so tenderly—was all for show, for my benefit?"

"Indeed. Her ankle is perfectly sound."

Lily felt her fingers curl into fists as she remembered her fierce feelings of jealousy a moment ago. And Heath had deliberately stoked them, pretending to be interested in the beautiful other woman.

Apparently he was not finished upbraiding *her*, though. "You admit that you approved Ada's little scheme. What I want to know is *why*."

"I should think it obvious," Lily retorted, starting to feel uncomfortable with his piercing regard.

"According to Ada, you meant to prove that I am like your late father—eager to chase anything in skirts."

"That is part of it, yes."

Her answer made sparks flare in his eyes. "And you thought you could be rid of me by pawning me off on some other woman? Bloody *hell*, Lily."

When she winced at his fury, Heath's jaw locked with the visible effort to control his temper. "What the devil were you thinking? Did you actually believe she could succeed in enticing me? That I would ever want a woman like her when I could have you?"

Lily wrapped her arms around herself defensively. "Truthfully . . . yes. I thought that if she satisfied your carnal desires, you wouldn't want me any longer."

"Dammit, Lily . . ." In frustration, he raked a hand through his hair. "I don't merely want sex with you. I want you for my *wife*. If fucking was all I wanted, I could find any number of willing women to indulge me."

"I know," Lily said in a small voice, feeling rather chastened by his argument.

"And I am perfectly capable of finding my own mistress if I want one. I do not need your assistance. And I most assuredly don't appreciate your deceit or your plotting."

Moving across to the sofa, she sank down. "I am

sorry. I never should have allowed Ada to try and seduce you. Besides," Lily added, biting her lower lip, "I never even considered the risk she was taking. She has a new patron, and it could have ruined her chances if he discovered she was dallying with you."

To Lily's relief, Heath's tone was a trifle less harsh when he spoke. "Is that the reason you interrupted us? Because you worried she might spoil her chances with her new protector?"

"Ummm . . . not exactly."

"Then what, exactly?"

Lily risked a glance at Heath. His jaw was still set in anger, she saw. "I . . . didn't want you kissing her."

He stared for a moment before the hard line of his mouth eased. "You were jealous."

Feeling a betraying blush rise to her cheeks, Lily ducked her head. "Well . . . yes."

Silence reigned for a time. Then Heath came to sit beside her on the sofa. "I suppose I should be flattered. And encouraged. I must be making progress in my courtship if you were roused to jealousy."

The faint hint of humor in his tone made Lily stiffen. "Don't raise your hopes too high, my lord. I still have no intention of marrying you."

She felt his gaze intensify on her again. "You acknowledge your jealousy, but you won't consider my proposal? That makes little sense. Why are you so damned set against marrying me, Lily?"

"I told you why."

"Because your parents' union was hostile. It doesn't follow that ours will be so."

Squaring her shoulders, Lily looked up. "If you had

experienced their battles all during *your* childhood, you would not be so eager to wed, either."

His gaze bored into hers. "So you believe our marriage would be a battleground, like theirs was."

"I . . . don't know," Lily finally said. "But I am not willing to risk it. I don't wish to be miserable for the rest of my life, the way my mother was."

A muscle flexed in Heath's jaw. "You are equating me with your father again." When Lily refused to comment, he made a sound like a growl. "What did he do to your mother that was so terrible?"

Lily swallowed, her stomach clenching with the old, old pain. "I don't wish to discuss it."

"Damn and blast it, Lily! How can I defend myself as being different from your father if I haven't a clue what he did?"

"Very well. . . ." The pain welled up inside as she choked out the words. "If you must know . . . he struck her! He beat her with his fists and felled her to the floor and then kicked her till she screamed. And I couldn't bear it. *I couldn't bear it!* So I grabbed up a knife and told Papa to leave her alone or I would kill him. And I meant it. I would have *killed* him had he raised his fists against her again. Is *that* what you wished to hear?"

Her voice had risen practically to a shout, and when she ceased, her breath came in hoarse, uneven pants.

Heath stared at her, his expression arrested. Lily stared back, gritting her teeth fiercely, refusing to look away. But her chest felt hard and heavy and tight, while the back of her throat ached and her eyes stung with tears.

His expression softened then, and she read sympathy in the perceptive hazel depths.

Swallowing hard, Lily averted her gaze from Heath's suddenly gentle one. She didn't want his sympathy, his pity. She didn't want his tender touch, either—yet she was given no choice. She felt the warm, sliding pressure of his fingers as they raised her chin, compelling her to regard him.

"So you were forced to protect your mother from your father's violence," he said, his tone very gentle.

Nodding, Lily sat there rigidly, struggling to hold on to her composure. Her voice was a tearful rasp when she finally spoke. "My greatest regret was that I couldn't help her further. A year later Mama finally took a lover to allay her misery, and then she was banished from her home and even her country. You . . . you know about the resulting scandals."

For a span of several heartbeats, Heath remained silent. Then he reached up to capture her face carefully between his palms. "I would never strike you, Lily. *Never.* I would never be physically violent with a woman, no matter the provocation."

She searched his face, his intent expression, and could give him no argument. Somehow she was certain Heath would not hurt her physically . . . but emotionally was another matter altogether.

"Even so, I won't allow any man to have that kind of power over me. As your wife, by law I would be little more than your chattel. If you chose to beat me—or even kill me—I would have no recourse."

Reflexively, Heath clenched his jaw at the ludicrous notion that he would ever raise a hand to Lily, although he supposed he could appreciate her perspective, even if it frustrated the devil out of him. But he forced himself to hide his frustration as he smoothed the knuckles of his hand across her cheekbone.

Seeing her dark eyes so big and bright with incipient tears, he felt a fierce surge of protectiveness toward her—along with an intense, burning need to dig up her father from his grave and punish him for what he'd done to his wife and daughter.

At least now, however, Heath better understood Lily's fervent desire for independence. Her determination to carve out her own destiny. Her fear of putting her fate in any man's hands. Even her stubborn determination to place him in the same category as her bastard father. With her bitter experience, she couldn't trust that he would be any different.

When his hand slid lower, giving a delicate massage to the curve of her neck, Lily stiffened and pulled back, obviously discomfited.

"If you will pray excuse me . . ." Dashing a hand over her eyes to wipe away any trace of tears, she rose abruptly to her feet. Her fingers knotting together, she glanced down at Heath. "I am sorry if I made you angry by allowing Ada to attempt your seduction, but perhaps it was for the best. Now you know why I can never consent to be your wife."

With that barely audible murmur, she turned and quit the room, leaving him alone with his thoughts.

Heath sat there for a long while after she had gone, contemplating his courtship of Lily and how he should respond to her revelation.

For one thing, he would have to show her indisputably that he was far, far different from her father, or any of the other men she'd known who treated women like chattel or used violence to hurt and dominate.

Heath's jaw hardened. He couldn't stop thinking about that haunted pain in Lily's eyes when she'd confessed about threatening her father in order to save her mother from assault. He remembered seeing that same look last week when Lily had chased O'Rourke from the house, brandishing a statue at his retreating back. And when she'd flung herself against the gang of bullies in the alley to defend a mongrel dog.

It also explained why she'd insisted on kindness as a qualification for the candidates he invited to the soiree. And why she was so irate about the injustice done to some of the young women she'd taken under her wing here at the boardinghouse. And why she'd put herself out to help two of them escape a life of prostitution by finding them respectable jobs in her own home.

Lily's actions reflected her ferocious desire to protect the weak and helpless, which touched Heath with tenderness for her.

Yet after learning about her father—after witnessing the pain in her eyes and hearing it in her voice—Heath finally realized just how difficult a task he faced, trying to win Lily's hand in marriage. She would never let down her guard because she was afraid to give herself to any man, lover *or* husband.

He would have to teach her about tenderness, about intimacy, about trust, that much was certain to him. She was like a wild woodland creature, cautious, wary, in need of coaxing, of gentling.

He'd made a start last night when he'd held her in his arms, Heath decided. He would wager half his fortune that Lily had never felt such emotional closeness with a man before him.

He'd never felt that kind of shared tenderness, either, and he knew it was very special.

At the memory, Heath closed his eyes momentarily, recalling the naked feel of her pressed into the curve of his body, her warmth, her fragrance. He knew instinctively that Lily's passion was something he alone could kindle—a thought that gave him primal satisfaction. But he wanted more than merely to control her body. Much more.

He wanted Lily for his wife.

Attaining that goal, however, would be the biggest challenge he'd ever faced. The decision to marry him had to be Lily's. He couldn't force her to accept him. She would have to take him for her husband because she *wanted* to.

And very likely, the only reason she would want to was if she loved him enough to overcome her doubts and fears about him.

Which meant he must strive to make her fall in love with him.

Heath frowned darkly in contemplation. Perhaps using his sexual prowess was not the best way to win her heart after all. Nor was wooing Lily with marriage in mind. As long as she felt pursued and hounded by his courtship, she would keep her defenses unassailable.

But what if he were to back off his campaign? What if he were to cease pursuing her?

Admittedly, he could benefit from a respite himself. Every morning he woke with a painful arousal that wouldn't cease. And each time he touched Lily, kissed her, held her, became more and more tormenting. If he had to endure another chaste night with her, making love to her without really making love to her, he feared he wouldn't be able to hold back. He would give in to his fierce desire for her and make his possession irrevocable.

But if he retreated, Heath mused, perhaps he could bring some discipline to the fire in his senses and manage a semblance of control over his hunger.

It seemed a very wise step to avoid any further sexual intimacy with Lily at least. And an even wiser step to stop wooing her for now. To give her time to sort things out for herself instead of constantly pressing her to marry him.

Meanwhile, Heath thought, slowly nodding with resolve, he would use the opportunity to determine how to earn Lily's trust and respect, to show her a better, more admirable side of his character, so she would have no doubt that he was utterly and completely different from the kind of man she despised and feared.

Chapter Twelve

❧

*It is very strange. He seems to have abandoned the
game.*

—Lily to Fanny

It surprised Lily when she saw nothing of Heath the
following day. He had called on her so regularly that
she expected him to continue the same pattern. Yet she
didn't hear a word from him on Wednesday, not even a
note.

She heard nothing from him on Thursday, either, and
was greatly puzzled to learn that he had invited Fleur
and Chantel to share his box at the theater that evening
without even mentioning the invitation to her.

Lord Poole was to accompany them, Lily discovered.
Since the night of the soiree, the viscount had practically
lived at the boardinghouse, and was obviously enamored of Chantel—a development that delighted the
aging beauty and warmed Lily's heart.

Having declined Heath's invitation to the theater once
before, Lily could hardly object to being excluded this
time, but when he arrived to collect the courtesans, he
said barely a word to her.

Fleur and Chantel didn't seem to notice, they were so
excited about the treat Lord Claybourne was offering

them. They bustled about the entrance hall, laughing and chattering gaily as they collected wraps and fans.

When they had gone—after telling Lily not to wait up since they were to dine at a fashionable hotel after the play—the echo of their gaiety made the house seem rather quiet.

Her spirits sinking as a consequence, Lily wandered into the drawing room in search of something to read. She felt at loose ends now that the soiree was over, since her time was much less occupied. Oh, she was still teaching lessons to several of her pupils at their request, but the urgency was gone for most of the girls, at least those who had secured new protectors.

Seeing a copy of the daily newspaper, *The Morning Post*, lying on a table, Lily began skimming the pages. Fleur and Chantel subscribed to both the morning and evening papers, since they liked to pore over the society and fashion sections. Normally the items about books, Parliamentary proceedings, foreign news, and shipping reports interested Lily, but just now they failed to hold her attention.

Instead, she kept wondering if Heath had abandoned his courtship of her. Perhaps he considered their game not worth finishing, given that she'd made her position about marrying him so clear.

Strangely, the possibility disappointed her rather than relieving her. She should be very happy to be rid of him.

Her regret was only temporary, Lily told herself. Heath's absence would create something of a void in her life at the moment, since he'd been underfoot so much of late. But she would adjust. She couldn't deny, however, that she had missed his presence over the past two days.

Missed him teasing her and provoking her and arousing her—

Determinedly Lily cut off that train of thought. There was no point in dwelling on Heath's plans for their courtship. Even so, she couldn't help but wonder if their night of passion together had opened his eyes to her deficiencies. She knew very well, from Fanny and other sources, that a man's carnal needs required fulfilling. And she was likely too inexperienced, too unskilled, too *virginal,* to satisfy a renowned lover like Heath.

Indeed, it was surprising that he had abstained for as long as he had.

Lily felt herself scowl as she remembered his terse declaration that he could find a mistress on his own, without her help. Perhaps he would do so now if he'd decided she wasn't worth pursuing any longer.

The notion of him making love to a new mistress made Lily's stomach churn and lowered her spirits even further.

Chiding herself for being a fool, she set down the newspaper and rose, deciding to go up to her bedchamber to fetch the book Heath had brought her about travels in the South Seas. She had read it through once but had had little time to study it in depth, and the narrative was indeed fascinating, just as he'd promised.

However, as she mounted the front staircase and reached the second floor landing, Lily heard the unmistakable sound of sobbing coming from down the corridor on her right. Turning that way, she followed the sounds to an open door.

It was the bedchamber that Peg Wallace shared with two other lodgers. To her surprise, she found Peg sitting on one of the beds, her arm around a weeping young woman—one of the boarders who hadn't found a patron at the soiree, Betty Dunst.

Betty was crying inconsolably, low racking sobs that seemed to be dredged up from the bottom of her soul.

When Lily entered tentatively, Peg looked up, her eyes bleak with sadness. "We are sorry to disturb you, Miss Loring. I meant to shut the door."

"Is Betty injured?" Lily asked quietly, approaching the bed.

Peg gave a savage grimace, while Betty wailed harder and buried her face in her hands. "You might say so," Peg replied. "She is with child."

Lily hesitated, not having any experience in such matters. "Is there any way I may help?"

Grimly Peg shook her head. "I doubt so, Miss Loring. You are too fine a lady. But you are kind to offer," Peg added quickly.

Sitting beside Betty, Lily placed a gentle hand on the girl's shoulder. "At least tell me what is upsetting you so terribly."

Nodding shakily, Betty drew several deep breaths in an effort to control her weeping and wiped at her streaming eyes with the handkerchief she held clutched in her hand. "It is just . . . that I . . . don't know what to do. I can't keep the child. What will become of me if I try? When my belly swells too big . . . I cannot work."

Betty, Lily knew, was employed at a nearby gentleman's club that was little more than a high-class brothel, and had worked there for two years. Betty was the daughter of the head gardener on a large estate in Dorsetshire. When she'd let herself be seduced by a groom at the estate, her father had cast her out of his house, so she came to London. She'd nearly starved before finding a position selling her body in a pleasure house. It was that or perish.

"And the father?" Lily asked. "Could he help?"

Betty gave another hoarse sob. "I don't know who the father is. It could be any one of a dozen coves. And none of them would care a fig about a bastard whelp."

Lily bit her tongue, realizing how naive her question had been. And she was at a loss for something further to say.

Betty went on tearfully lamenting her plight. "I'll have no blunt to pay for my board, and no income for months, and Miss Delee will throw me out on the streets, and I will have nowhere to go—"

"She will do no such thing, Betty," Lily murmured.

"But even if she allows me to stay, what will I do with a baby? How can I care for it?"

When her voice broke again, Peg interrupted softly. "Betty knows she will have to visit a midwife soon. That is why she is crying."

Comprehending what Peg meant, Lily felt her stomach clench. "You want to have the baby, Betty?"

"Yes . . . even if I don't know who the father is. But I don't see how. I can't go back to the streets. I can't put an innocent child through that. I don't want my baby to know what it is like to be so hungry, your stomach feels as if it is caving in. To be so desperate you want to die. I *cannot* do that, Miss Loring. I would rather kill it now."

When Betty began weeping into her hands again, Lily stroked her back gently, trying to offer comfort. Her heart ached for the girl, and she knew she couldn't allow Betty's misery to continue.

"Betty . . . you must stop crying before you make yourself ill. Listen to me. We will find a solution somehow. I have friends whom I can persuade to help you. We will find someone to take you in so that you may have the baby and not worry about his future."

Betty's sobs arresting suddenly, she looked up, her expression half fearful, half hopeful. "Oh, Miss Loring . . . do you think you *could*?"

"I am certain of it," Lily said convincingly. "If nothing else, I will supply the funds myself for you to raise your child."

"Oh, Miss Loring," she breathed. "You are an *angel*. No one is so good as you. But I could never ask you to pay my way. I can work—I am happy to work for my living."

Lily searched the girl's blotched, earnest face, recognizing the sentiment: Betty wanted independence, not charity. Just as the Loring sisters had always wanted.

"Then I think we must find you gainful employment," Lily said. "What sort of work are you best suited for?"

"I am good with flowers . . . growing them, I mean. I was used to acting as my da's assistant from the time I could walk."

"Well, I will see what I can do. For now, why don't you wash your face and lie down? Weeping cannot be good for the baby."

"I know." Her tears had quieted by now, and Betty sniffed as she wiped her eyes with the handkerchief. "But I cannot lie down, Miss Loring. I am supposed to report to work in a short while. The madam will turn me off for cert if I am late, and then I will be in a worse fix than I am now."

Frowning, Lily shook her head. "You cannot continue to work there when you are with child. No, Betty, you are not to return to your club. Tomorrow you can give notice, but just rest now and don't worry about the future. I will let you know as soon as I think of something."

Fresh tears sprang to Betty's eyes as she looked at Lily almost reverently. "*Thank you,* Miss Loring. I cannot thank you enough—"

"You needn't thank me, my dear. It is no more help than a very kind lady once offered my sisters and me," Lily said, thinking of Winifred and how, because of her generosity in funding the Freemantle Academy for Young Ladies, they had been able to have lives far different from the one poor Betty had endured. "I am only trying to extend her kindness."

Patting Betty's shoulder comfortingly, Lily rose and started to turn toward the door. But then Peg's quiet voice stopped her. "Miss Loring?"

"Yes?"

Lily waited while Peg slowly stood up. She seemed hesitant, her gaze lowered as she plucked at her skirt. Finally she swallowed. "Miss Loring . . . do you think it would be possible . . ." She cleared her throat. "That is, would your friends . . . be willing to find respectable employment for me, perhaps?"

Lily regarded Peg with a quizzical look. Her tale was somewhat similar to Betty's in that both girls had found themselves on the streets, forced to fend for themselves. Except that Peg had worked in a noble household in London as a lady's maid. When her lordly master had cornered her in a drunken stupor and kissed her against her will, his lady-wife had caught them together and dismissed Peg without a character. Unable to find respectable work without proper references, Peg had found employment as a ballet dancer with the Royal

Opera, although she'd been hired for her exquisite beauty rather than her meager dance skills.

Peg's request was puzzling, however, since she had just garnered a very wealthy baronet as a protector.

"I thought you were pleased with the arrangement you made with Sir Robert," Lily said slowly.

"I *am* pleased, Miss Loring. I mean . . . Sir Robert is a better patron than I ever hoped for. But I . . . I don't really want to be his mistress. Truth to tell, I hate it," she said in a low ardent voice. "I was a good girl before I became a demirep. And when I must sin that way . . . Sometimes I want to die, too."

Lily felt herself flinch as a sharp knife of guilt stabbed her. She had thought Peg was merely painfully shy, not that she was so dreadfully unhappy.

"I never realized, Peg," Lily murmured, feeling a little sick inside. "I am sorry I encouraged you to join our lessons, or helped prepare you for the soiree. I thought it was what you wanted."

"Oh, *no,* Miss Loring . . . that wasn't my meaning! I don't want you to think I didn't appreciate your lessons. I *did.* If I must earn my living on my back, it is far better to serve a rich gentleman. No, you were wondrous, teaching us all how to better ourselves. But if I could quit this life, I would, and gladly. And if you could help me . . . I would be ever so grateful."

Lily couldn't speak for a moment; her throat had closed with the threat of tears when she considered the plight of these poor women. Their lives were a constant struggle; they had no family, no future, with little hope of happiness or joy. But she could change that.

"Of course I will help you, Peg," Lily declared, her

voice thick with emotion. "There is no question that I will do everything in my power for you."

Peg's lips quivered in a tremulous smile. "I have learned one useful skill recently, at least. I've become very clever with a needle, sewing costumes for my fellow dancers. I could perhaps work in a modiste's shop as an apprentice . . . or as a dresser's assistant."

"Yes, Miss Loring," Betty broke in earnestly, despite her own troubles. "Peg has a splendid eye for fashion. Why, she could create her own designs if she had the chance. You should see her sketches. They put *La Belle Ensemble* to shame."

"I didn't realize," Lily said, impressed.

Peg blushed. "Well, I have no *real* training, but I designed a morning gown for Miss Delee last season, which she professed to be very pleased with."

"I will arrange something, I promise you."

It was a promise she would do her utmost to keep, Lily vowed moments later as she climbed the stairs to her own bedchamber, where she sat and stewed about what to do for Betty and Peg.

An even greater tragedy, Lily reflected with anger and dismay, was that there were countless other young women just like them who faced similar bleak futures. Girls who found themselves destitute and defenseless, with no one to turn to and no friends or family to depend on.

In the long term, Lily resolved, she would set her mind to determining how she could help some of those poor unfortunates find shelter and support. Somewhere they could be safe, where they could learn a trade so they wouldn't have to turn to prostitution merely to survive.

But that could wait, Lily knew; her friends needed help now.

She was confident she could find suitable employment for Peg, but with a child on the way, Betty was a much more serious problem.

She would have liked to talk the situation over with Fleur and Chantel—now, at once. The sooner she could find positions for the girls, the sooner they could begin their new lives and leave the ones they hated.

But the elderly courtesans were still attending the play with Lord Claybourne and Lord Poole. And Basil was out with his chums and fellow law clerks at his favorite tavern. After the success of the soiree, Basil had been eager to return to his former life, since his tutelage was no longer required by their pupils.

Asking Winifred to help Betty, however, would likely be futile, Lily suspected. Ordinarily the wealthy widow sympathized with the working class, since she came from the same origins. Winifred could usually be counted on to be magnanimous with the vast fortune her late industrialist father had amassed from his manufacturing and mining enterprises. But in this instance, Lily surmised, Winifred would just tell her to apply to Lord Claybourne.

She could perhaps ask Marcus for assistance, since he was now her brother by marriage as well as her former guardian. But Marcus had done more than enough for her by taking in the two boarders she'd already sent to Danvers Hall last month.

"You know what you must do," Lily murmured to herself.

She worried her lower lip as she came to a reluctant conclusion: Even though she disliked asking Heath for help because she didn't want to be indebted to him, he was her most logical choice. She shouldn't let her aversion to being dependent on a man stand in the way of doing what was best for Betty.

As a wealthy nobleman, Heath had significant resources she didn't have, including several estates and a vast servant staff. Moreover, he had voluntarily found a home for a stray dog. He might be willing to do the same for a deserving young woman and her unborn child.

And as her sister Arabella had recently pointed out, Lily reflected, Heath didn't seem to be the typical selfish, uncaring nobleman—although in her case, his generosity toward her had doubtless had a purpose, trying to earn points to win their game.

Deciding she ought to approach Heath first, Lily put her mind to developing the argument she would present to him in order to persuade him.

Three hours later, nearing the time when she could reasonably expect his carriage to return from the theater, she went downstairs and took up a position in the entrance hall on a footman's bench, passing the interval reading *Travels* by the light of a wall sconce.

As soon as she heard the sound of carriage wheels out on the street, Lily threw a shawl around her shoulders and went to the front door.

It was indeed Lord Claybourne bringing his party home, she saw upon stepping outside. Night had fallen, but the carriage lamps illuminated his tall, powerful figure as he stood on the curb, saying farewell to his guests.

In the event he didn't plan to accompany them inside, Lily descended the steps and moved down the sidewalk toward the street.

Lord Poole noticed her first. "Ah, Miss Loring, I did not expect to see you again this evening. The play was splendid, just splendid. You should have come."

Chantel had explained to her new beau that Lily didn't want to attract notice by going out in public, but the elderly viscount was a bit absentminded, so he tended to forget.

Lily murmured something polite in response to Lord Poole's comments, but her attention was on Heath, whose eyebrow was arched in question as he asked, "Is something amiss, Miss Loring?"

"I wondered if I might I have a word with you in private, my lord."

After a moment's hesitation, he nodded. "Of course. Shall I accompany you inside the house, or would you prefer to use my carriage?"

Glancing at his carriage, Lily flushed as she remembered what had happened the last time she was alone with him there. "The house, please."

They had followed the Cyprians and Lord Poole inside when Fleur stated, "We will be in our sitting room when you are finished, my dear."

Nodding, Lily led Heath to the nearby parlor.

"May I offer you some wine or port?" she asked as soon as he shut the door behind them.

His penetrating gaze surveyed her. "Why so formal, angel?"

"I suppose because I am nervous."

"You? Nervous?"

"Well," Lily replied, ignoring the hint of amusement in his tone, "the stakes *are* rather high. You see . . . I have a very large favor to ask of you."

Heath regarded Lily another moment before repeating slowly, as if in disbelief, "You wish to ask me a favor."

"Yes, although it isn't for myself."

The corner of his mouth curved dryly. "It never is."

"Would you care to have a seat?"

"I prefer to stand. Why don't you just come out with it, Lily? What favor do you need?"

Deciding it would be easier to explain if *she* was seated, Lily moved over to a wing chair and perched on the edge. "The thing is . . . one of our boarders is facing a difficult dilemma. Do you remember Betty Dunst?"

"Petite, dark hair, blue eyes?"

Lily wasn't surprised that as a connoisseur of women, Heath recalled the pretty lightskirt. "Yes, that is Betty. Unfortunately she is expecting a child."

When Lily briefly told him about Betty's circumstances, she grew angry all over again at the injustice of it all—a young woman being thrown onto the streets and forced to work in a brothel, and then being gotten with child by one of her many customers.

"It is hardly her fault that she is *enceinte*," Lily said in a tight voice. "But now that she is, she wants to have the baby—although only if she can provide him a decent future."

Thankfully, Heath seemed to take her request very seriously. "Does Betty want a marriage arranged for her, so the child won't be born out of wedlock?" he asked. "Securing a husband for her would be the customary course."

The question made Lily hesitate, since she hadn't even considered that option. "I don't know, actually. But I don't believe she wants to marry—and she should not be forced to wed if she doesn't choose to," she added adamantly. "Being trapped in an unwanted marriage could be nearly as bad as her current situation, possibly even worse."

Her fierceness brought a faint smile to Heath's lips. "I am well aware of your feelings on the subject of matrimony, sweeting. But Betty may hold a different opinion from yours."

"She told me she wants to work for her living. Her father was a chief gardener on a large estate, and she claims to be good at growing things. I was thinking that you might find a place for her on one of your estates, where she might raise her child in safety. A baby would fare better in the country than in London."

To her relief, Heath nodded. "The housekeeper at my family seat may be amenable to taking her in, but I want to speak to Betty first, to ascertain her true wishes."

"Thank you!" Lily said, rising to her feet. "I will fetch Betty at once—"

Heath held up a hand. "There is no need to interview her this late at night. But you needn't worry. I will take care of the matter." He cocked his head at Lily. "You realize this will likely earn me another point in our game?"

"I expect so, but it is worth the price if Betty can be free of a life she despises."

"Very well, then," he murmured. "If that is all you require of me . . . ?"

Heath glanced over his shoulder toward the door, as if impatient to leave, but Lily found herself wanting him to stay. She hadn't planned on mentioning Peg's troubles to him, yet she found herself blurting out a request for him to wait.

"There *is* one more thing," Lily said, taking a step toward him.

He regarded her expectantly. "Yes?"

"It concerns one of our other boarders . . . but the matter is somewhat indelicate."

When Heath merely waited politely for her to explain, Lily rushed on. "You said you have had several mistresses in the past, so I hoped you might know the modistes they frequented."

"I beg your pardon?" His eyebrow had shot up, and he was looking at her as if he had misheard.

She felt color rise to her cheeks. "Well, you see . . . Peg Wallace is dreadfully unhappy having to work as a courtesan. And even though her new patron could improve her circumstances significantly, she wants out of that life. So I promised I would try to find her employment as a modiste's apprentice. And I thought that if you had spent a fortune on clothing for your former mistresses, you might have some sway with their modistes, and you could persuade one of them to consider Peg for a position."

When Heath remained silent, simply gazing at her, Lily added hastily, "I cannot ask Marcus about his former mistresses now that he is married to my sister."

"But you can ask me? Should I be honored?"

Lily flashed him a reluctant smile. "I don't think so. I just would rather spare Arabella the discomfort of bringing up her new husband's rakish past. And you are the only other gentleman with experience in such matters whom I know well enough to approach with such an improper request."

His mouth twitching, he shook his head slowly in disbelief. "You never cease to amaze me, darling Lily."

At his response, Lily began to feel uncomfortably awkward. "Well then, please forget I mentioned it. I can doubtless find a position for Peg on my own. . . . Although the modiste who fashioned new wardrobes for me and my sisters this summer is a high stickler and would be unlikely to hire a former courtesan. I can ask Fanny's dressmaker, but she caters mainly to the demi-reps of the theater and opera, and I would rather give Peg a chance to break with her old life, if possible—"

"I will see what I can do," Heath broke in.

Lily stopped to eye him warily. "You will consider helping Peg?"

"Yes, I will help Peg if I can. But I pay little attention to such things as modistes. I will speak to Eleanor Pierce, though. She should know the best course to take."

Lily frowned. She had greatly enjoyed meeting Marcus's younger sister at Arabella's wedding last month. Lively and beautiful, Lady Eleanor was a significant heiress who dressed in the height of fashion. But she was also a single gentlewoman with a reputation to protect.

"Lady Eleanor?" Lily said skeptically. "She might not care to become involved with the fortunes of a light-skirt."

"She won't mind," Heath assured her. "Nell is no shrinking violet. I will ask her tomorrow morning when I see her."

"You will be calling on her tomorrow?" Lily asked, highly curious about his relationship with Lady Eleanor.

"Yes. We are riding in the park together. I escort her on her daily rides with some regularity, particularly now that Marcus is spending so much of his time at Danvers

Hall. She is an avid horsewoman, although perhaps not quite as zealous as you."

Lily found herself wishing that she could join them—but of course she could do no such thing if she wanted to keep her encounters with Heath to a minimum. Her inability to ride was no doubt the cause of the twinge of jealousy that rippled through her. She didn't care that Heath seemed to be on excellent terms with Marcus's sister. Nor did she care what he did in his free time when he wasn't here courting her.

Her only concern was what he could do for her courtesan friends—which reminded Lily of the subject at hand.

"I would be grateful if you would ask Lady Eleanor then," she told Heath, "although I hope it won't be too much of an imposition on her."

"It won't be. She is sure to admire your desire to help Peg. I will let you know what she says about a modiste. So is there anything else I may do for you?"

Lily blinked, realizing he was eager to be gone. "No, but please let me thank you—"

"I don't want your thanks, Lily," Heath said, his expression enigmatic.

Then, with a brief bow, he turned away and exited the parlor, leaving Lily staring after him, torn between gratitude for his generosity and regret that he hadn't wanted to remain in her company even a moment longer.

"Most certainly I will help," Lady Eleanor said as soon as Heath explained what he wanted. "And I have just the modiste in mind. The same one who created this riding costume for me."

He glanced critically at Eleanor, who rode beside him

along the Row in Hyde Park. She was garbed in a stylish emerald green habit and jaunty military hat that set off her short raven curls and rosy complexion to perfection. "You look quite fetching," he said approvingly.

Marcus's irrepressible younger sister dimpled. "Thank you for the pretty compliment, but Madame Gautier deserves the credit. Not only can she work wonders with her needle, she has a marvelous sense of fashion. And as it happens, she was remarking just last week how she despaired of finding skilled seamstresses. Madame will be in raptures if this Peg has an aptitude for designing as well as fine stitching. I will arrange an interview and notify you about the particulars."

Heath smiled his appreciation. "I knew I could count on you, love."

Eleanor shook her head. "My contribution will be of small moment compared to Miss Loring's efforts. I think her compassion for those women is exceedingly admirable. I didn't realize she was so involved in philanthropy, however, although I knew her friend, Miss Blanchard, advocates for several charities."

Heath had to admire Lily's compassion as well. This was just the latest instance of her championing the helpless and the downtrodden, he reflected, remembering how her eyes had sparked when she spoke of the young women she had befriended.

"Lily says the same thing about Miss Blanchard," Heath commented.

"Perhaps I will ask Miss Blanchard how I might aid her charities," Eleanor said thoughtfully, before she sent Heath a curious glance. "So does this mean your courtship of Miss Loring is prospering?"

Heath shrugged. "Well enough."

"*Well enough?*" The raven-haired beauty flashed a mock scowl. "Is that all you mean to tell me? You are too cruel, Heath! I am *dying* to know if I may soon wish you happy."

He couldn't help but chuckle at her teasing. A lively minx, Eleanor was like the sister he had never had. He'd known her since she was born, and she had managed to wrap him around her finger from the time she was a toddler.

In some ways she reminded him greatly of Lily, for they shared many of the same qualities; both young ladies were charming and endearing, forthright, independent, and generous in nature. At twenty, Eleanor was actually a year younger than Lily, but she had far more experience with the courting game, having been on the Marriage Mart for two Seasons. And since her comeout, Nell had been betrothed twice. Both times she'd broken off the engagement, much to the dismay of her aunt, Lady Beldon.

"As soon as I have anything of consequence about my courtship to report," Heath offered, "you will be among the first to know."

"That doesn't sound very promising. Are you certain you don't need my help in wooing Miss Loring? I was able to advise Drew on how to romance Roslyn."

"For someone who has jilted two suitors, Nell, you make a odd matchmaker."

Eleanor smiled impishly. "Indeed. But merely because I have resolved to remain single, doesn't mean I cannot aid the course of true love."

"Ah, yes. You are a hopeless romantic."

"So I am. Which is precisely why I ended my betrothals—because neither of my fiancés could love me the way I wished to be loved. But miraculously, Marcus and Drew found love, so I still hold out hope for myself, and for you as well."

Heath had no ready reply for her. He'd never lost his heart, but the notion that Lily could inspire that particular malady had a definite appeal. If anyone could tempt him to fall in love, it would be Lily. He wondered if he could tempt her to love him in return. . . .

"Perhaps," he drawled in response to Nell's observation, "you should concentrate on your own affairs of the heart and not worry so much about mine."

Eleanor made a face at him. "I expected you to say that. But I still am rather stunned that you are considering donning marriage shackles."

He was a little stunned as well, Heath reflected. He'd never wanted to be tied down to just one woman. Until recently he had been a dedicated bachelor, devoted to a life of freedom and adventure, resolutely determined never to be locked in a tedious, insipid, passionless union merely for the sake of carrying on his illustrious title. But since his courtship of Lily, he had come to the realization that he could be content with the chains of matrimony if she were his jailor.

"But I *can* comprehend," Eleanor continued, overriding his thoughts, "why you would be attracted to Miss Loring. And from what I know of her, I think she might make an ideal match for you. The two of you seem highly compatible."

That was certainly true, Heath agreed. He'd never expected to find a wife who could be such a perfect match for him, as Lily would.

His own parents had been poorly matched, nearly opposites in character and outlooks on life. His mother had been gay and charming and full of laughter; his father staid and proper and dull to the point of grimness. A grimness that only compounded after Lady Claybourne's death as the marquess retreated further into himself.

As a child, Heath had cherished his mother's joie de vivre, although admittedly she had been concerned with her own pleasure above all else. Unlike Lily, who was concerned for everyone *but* herself.

Whether or not he could have a love match with Lily, however, he wanted her for his wife. Not just to bear him heirs, as he'd first planned. Not merely to alleviate his boredom or to grace his bed, either, although those were excellent reasons to wed her.

No, he wanted Lily for herself. Her liveliness, her intensity, her passion for life called to him. As did her fierceness, since it was tempered by warmth and softness and compassion. Lily stirred him like no other woman ever had.

Yet it would be unwise, he warned himself, to let his feelings for her grow any stronger when she had closed off her heart to any possibility of love. For the first time in his life he had met a woman whose defenses might be insurmountable.

Which frustrated the devil out of him, since he wanted his union with Lily to be much more than the cold marriage of convenience his parents had known.

He wanted more from his courtship of Lily, as well. He wanted to be able to venture out in public together, to ride with her in the park as he did with Eleanor, to attend plays and garden parties and enjoy all the other small intimacies that normal suitors were permitted. Most of all, he wanted to claim Lily for his own.

Yet that moment seemed a long way off.

Hell, perhaps his decision to stop overtly wooing Lily was a mistake. He had visibly slowed his pursuit of her to allow time for her feelings toward him to soften, reasoning that he could lower her resistance if she felt less pressured by his courtship. But his strategy might be having no effect at all.

Shaking off his frustration, Heath returned his attention to his charming companion. As close as he was to Eleanor, however, he didn't want to discuss his relationship with Lily any longer.

"You stun me also, Nell," he said to change the subject. "Since when would you rather amble along at this snail's pace, chattering about matrimony instead of enjoying a good gallop?"

"You make an excellent point," Eleanor replied, gathering her reins.

"Shall we race to the end of the lake?" he challenged.

"You are on!" Eleanor exclaimed, digging her heel into her horse's side, leaving an amused Heath to eat her dust and make yet another comparison with his spirited Lily.

He called on Lily that afternoon to report on Eleanor's progress: A meeting had been arranged for Peg with Madame Gautier the following morning. When summoned to the parlor to hear the news, Peg was overjoyed at the prospect of finding respectable employment at the modiste's shop, and she thanked Heath profusely.

Betty's response, however, was altogether different at first. The girl appeared nervous and intimidated when Heath questioned her about her wishes for her future, stammering out her replies. Yes, milord, a husband might be welcome at some point, and yes, she would be very happy to return to the country. But for now she only wanted safety for herself and the chance to bear her baby without fear of finding herself on the streets again. When Heath offered her sanctuary at his family estate under the aegis of his housekeeper, Betty stared at him for a long moment and then burst into tears.

Lily immediately wrapped her arm around the girl in an effort to ease her distress, but startlingly, Betty eschewed the proffered comfort and got down on her knees to Heath instead.

"Oh, milord!" she sobbed, taking his hand to kiss it fervently. "You are a saint, just like Miss Loring. You won't regret taking me in, I swear it. And I will repay you somehow, every penny."

Disconcerted by her abject display of gratitude, Heath gently drew the girl to her feet, assuring her that he didn't want recompense, that serving his housekeeper well would be payment enough.

When Betty could at last be pried away from him and had left the parlor, still sniffling with joy, Lily stood there gazing at him, her expression soft.

"I cannot thank you enough, Heath," she murmured in a voice rife with gratitude.

Heath stilled as he became lost in those melting dark eyes of hers. Struggling against the urge to take Lily in his arms, he merely shrugged. "Don't refine on it."

"Of course I will refine on it. You may possibly have saved her life, and you undoubtedly saved her baby's life." Lily hesitated. "Such generosity is rare, especially coming from a nobleman."

His mouth twisted at her unconscious disparagement

of his class. "You may make a philanthropist out of me yet," he said lightly.

Lily cocked her head as she studied him thoughtfully. "I imagine that would be a very good thing. Just think, Heath, you could put your enormous wealth to noble purpose. There are so many people who could benefit . . . not to mention the immense satisfaction of doing a kindness for others."

It was even more satisfying to win her regard, Heath reflected. When Lily looked at him that way, he was willing to give away his entire fortune.

Heath shook his head mentally at the image of him doling out alms to the poor and oppressed, yet the thought of sharing Lily's cause held surprising appeal. She had accused him of wanting to play hero, and it was true; he wanted to be a hero in her eyes. And he wanted the right to slay her dragons.

"Will you stay for tea?" she asked in that same soft voice.

He hadn't meant to remain, but he found himself agreeing. And as Lily led the way upstairs to Fleur's sitting room, her words about putting his wealth to noble purpose echoed in his mind.

The possibility hadn't seriously occurred to him before now. No doubt because he'd been wrapped up in his own pursuits.

Perhaps, however, it was time to take stock of his life. Seeing Lily's concern for the less fortunate, Heath couldn't help but question his own goals and desires.

He had been born to vast privilege and wealth, receiving too much, too easily, with too few responsibilities to keep him grounded. His doting mother had spoiled him as a child, and like her, he'd been more concerned with his own selfish gratification.

And after losing his mother when he was ten, he'd taken refuge from his anguish in anger, rebelling against his father's dictates at every opportunity, sometimes on sheer principle, recklessly pushing the boundaries of civilized behavior to the point of physical danger.

But even as he grew older, he hadn't used his talents or resources very wisely. He'd treated life as a game, with the quest for pleasure and excitement his primary aim. He'd been adamant that he wouldn't become like his sire, mired in a grim, joyless, passionless existence.

But Heath could see now that he'd gone overboard trying to repudiate his father's influence. And he realized he ought to make more of his life.

Indeed, Lily was the first thing he'd ever had to work for, to strive to win—and the challenge had opened his eyes. Thanks to her inspiration, he wanted to contribute something productive to society, to a cause greater than himself. She made him want to do better, to be better, to prove himself worthy of her.

Perhaps when he returned home, he would pen a message to Tess Blanchard and ask how he could aid her charities—

Heath's ruminations were interrupted just then when they reached the sitting room. Surprisingly, Fanny was there with Fleur and Chantel. The women had been speaking in low tones, but all conversation stopped when Heath entered behind Lily.

And when Fanny turned her face toward them, Lily went rigid with shock.

The Cyprian's lower lip was split and bloody, Heath

saw, while bruises in the shape of fingerprints disfigured the creamy skin covering her jaw.

"Good God, Fanny—whatever happened?" Lily exclaimed in tones of anger and dismay.

Obviously embarrassed, Fanny ducked her head. "It is nothing, Lily, truly."

"What do you mean, *nothing*? Someone *struck* you!"

"It wasn't like that. . . . Mick just didn't realize his own strength."

Lily took a step forward, her fists curled in rage, and Heath knew she was moments away from exploding.

Chapter Thirteen

I have no intention of wedding him, but I confess that the notion of becoming his mistress has a certain appeal.

—Lily to Tess Blanchard

"Mick O'Rourke?" Lily demanded, clearly appalled and furious. "*He* did that to you, Fanny?"

Heath saw Fanny wince. "Yes," the Cyprian replied, "but I doubt he meant to hurt me. When I refused his patronage again, Mick became angry and tried to kiss me."

"Of course he meant to hurt you!" Lily retorted. "That brute hurt Fleur when she ordered him from the house last week—"

"Because she called him an ill-bred oaf. It incenses Mick when he thinks someone is insulting his origins."

"It incenses *me* when I see a man assaulting a much weaker woman!"

"I know, Lily," Fanny said soothingly. "But he doesn't know any better. He was raised in the London stews and always had to fight for whatever he wanted, so he has different notions of civilized behavior than we do."

Heath felt his jaw tighten at that unpersuasive justification, while Lily stared at Fanny in disbelief. "Are you actually making excuses for that lout? I cannot credit it!"

"No," Fanny said a trifle defensively. "I only thought to explain his point of view."

"I don't give a fig for his point of view! He has no right to brutalize you."

Fanny's smile was pained. "Mick doesn't see it quite that way. He believes I am spurning him because his money isn't good enough for me, which is not the case at all. It is his possessiveness that I dislike. But truly, I am not concerned for myself. I am worried for Fleur and Chantel. Mick says he will make good his threat to put them in debtors' prison. I went to his club to ask him for another fortnight to repay the funds, but he wouldn't listen."

"Well, he will listen to me!" Lily declared, turning abruptly toward the door. "I will *make* him listen."

Not liking her implication, Heath stepped into her path, blocking her exit. "Just what do you intend, Lily?"

"To go down to that brute's gaming club this instant and confront him—give him a piece of my mind at the very least."

"You will do no such thing."

"What the devil do you mean?" she demanded, her fists clenching.

Lily was practically breathing fire, she was so angry, but she obviously was not thinking clearly. "I mean that you will allow me to handle O'Rourke. He will take me far more seriously."

She looked as if she would dispute him, but then she hesitated, as if knowing he was right.

Taking advantage of her fuming silence, Heath pressed harder. "You can sheathe your sword for now, angel. I promise to deal with him."

Lily gazed up at him warily, clearly reluctant to accept his help. "This really is not your concern, you know."

"I am making it my concern." Heath's gaze intensified. "You don't want to fight me on this, Lily. You won't win."

"You promise to stop O'Rourke from hurting Fanny again?"

"You have my solemn word."

He waited as Lily debated with herself, feeling an overwhelming need to wrap her in his arms and protect her from herself. She was magnificent in her fury, and he admired her loyalty to her friends, but he wanted to know that she was safe. Accosting O'Rourke in his lair was only asking for trouble, if not actual danger, and he was not about to let her attempt it.

When Lily nodded once, brusquely, Heath tucked a tendril of hair behind her ear and hid a smile of relief and satisfaction.

He had wanted the chance to slay dragons for Lily. It was merely that the opportunity had arrived much sooner than he'd planned.

O'Rourke's gaming club was situated just off Bond Street, not far from the boardinghouse, so Heath's carriage reached it shortly. The decor was expensive with pretensions to gentility, he saw when he was admitted by a well-muscled bruiser. He found O'Rourke in his office at the rear of the gaming rooms, sitting behind his desk.

Sporting ebony hair and a burly build, O'Rourke somewhat resembled the ruffians Lily had confronted in the alley last week. His facial features were square and rugged, with a nose that had been broken at least once.

When Heath was shown in, the gamester's expression registered surprise and wariness, but he rose politely.

"Lord Claybourne . . . to what do I owe this honor?" he asked, taking obvious care with his diction.

"I gather you know who I am," Heath replied.

"Naturally. I make it my business to know all the nabobs in London." O'Rourke hesitated. "And I saw you at the jades' house last week."

Heath raised an eyebrow. "Jades?"

"Fleur and Chantel. You were on the stairs as I was leaving."

"When you were unceremoniously evicted, you mean."

A muscle flexed O'Rourke's jaw, but he held on to his temper as he gestured at a wooden chair set in front of his desk. "Would you care to be seated, milord?"

"Thank you, no. My business won't take long."

Heath had kept his hat and walking stick upon being admitted, and O'Rourke surveyed the stick measuringly before locking gazes again with his guest. "I'll wager I know the purpose of your visit, milord."

"Do you?"

"You've come on behalf of those bawds."

"In part. I am more concerned about your mistreatment of Miss Irwin."

The heavy black brows snapped together. "What do you mean, mistreatment? I never laid a hand on Fanny."

"Indeed? You split her lip and left bruises on her jaw from your grip."

His expression turned bewildered. "I never meant to. I would never hurt Fanny. I love her."

"You have a curious way of showing love."

"Is that so?" O'Rourke's tone held a hint of belligerence. "What is it to you, your lordship? Fanny hasn't taken up with you, has she?"

"If you mean, am I enjoying her services, then no. But she is under my protection all the same. Miss Irwin is a friend of a friend."

Nodding as if in understanding, O'Rourke sank back into his chair. "So that's the way of it? You're hot for that little firebrand who attacked me."

Heath felt his mouth twitch at the suitability of the term for Lily. "You might put it that way. I hope to make that little firebrand my wife someday, and the well-being of her friends is of grave importance to her, and therefore to me."

"Did she send you here?"

"I volunteered." Heath smiled rather coldly. "You should consider yourself fortunate that I stopped her from coming here herself. She was quite eager to have your blood."

"And you are not?"

"Let us say I am willing to settle for a warning. If you hurt Miss Irwin again—if you so much as damage a hair on her head—you will answer to me."

The gamester stared back. "What will you do, your lordship, call me out? That would hardly be fair, considering that you're one of the premiere swordsmen in London."

"I daresay in England," Heath returned mildly. "And I am accounted a fair shot as well." In truth he was a deadly shot, as he suspected O'Rourke would know.

The man glanced down to where Heath had rested his hands on the gold knob of his walking stick. "That is a swordstick, or I miss my guess."

"I make it a policy never to confront an opponent unarmed."

"I am not your enemy, milord."

"You will be if you persist in ill-using Miss Irwin."

O'Rourke visibly clenched his teeth. "So you will meet me at dawn some morning?"

"That is one possibility," Heath replied. "Or I could pursue an alternate course. It might pain you more to be forced to close the doors to your club."

The threat made O'Rourke scowl harder. "You mean you would drive me out of business."

"If I must. I have no compunction about crushing a man who abuses women." Heath paused to let that sink in before saying in a leading tone, "A gaming hell's reputation is a fragile thing, wouldn't you agree, Mr. O'Rourke? If word were to get out about certain dishonest dealings. . . ."

"I run an honest establishment!"

"So I understand. But rumors of cheating are difficult to quell."

His anger was evident, but he merely demanded, "What do you want of me, Lord Claybourne?"

"I told you. I want you to keep your hands off Miss Irwin."

"Very well, I will!" he snapped.

"And I want you to withdraw your threat of imprisoning her friends."

"Why the devil should I? That debt was entirely legit."

"Legal perhaps, but still underhanded. You lured them to your Faro table and staked them well beyond their means to pay. But regardless of how the debt came about, they should have the funds to repay you shortly. If not I will cover the debt in full."

When O'Rourke continued to glare, Heath smiled amiably. "I could have brought a draft from my bank today, but my 'firebrand,' as you call her, is rather proud and independent and wishes to handle the problem on her own, so I won't interfere unless absolutely necessary. But one way or another, Mr. O'Rourke, you will be repaid."

O'Rourke shook his head in irritation. "I don't want your blunt, milord."

"Then what do you want?"

"Fanny. I want Fanny."

Heath settled into the proffered chair after all. He had suspected something of the sort. "Would you care to explain?"

O'Rourke's grimace was part vexed, part rueful. "I've been head over ears for Fanny since the first time I saw her. I was her first protector, in fact."

"But she didn't return the sentiment."

The gamester's mouth twisted bitterly. "Not back then. Even when I offered to make her respectable and wed her, Fanny turned me down cold. She was sixteen and wanted the grand life I couldn't give her at the time. I'm rich as Croesus now and could set her up in comfort for life, but she still won't bite at matrimony. Says she doesn't want me for a husband, even though she'll be whistling a fortune away. I fancy it's because she thinks herself too good for the likes of me. But I know I can make her see reason if I keep after her."

"So you are using that debt as leverage to persuade Fanny to return to you," Heath mused.

"Yes. I don't care about the blunt. And I wouldn't really send those old bawds to prison. But you see why I don't want you settling their debt. If you pay, I'll have no chance to convince Fanny to wed me."

Heath gave a brief nod. He could at least sympathize with the man's dilemma, since he'd been trying earnestly to convince Lily to marry *him*. But sympathizing was not the same as condoning.

When O'Rourke continued, his tone was more congenial. "You seem to be a reasonable gent, milord. Surely we can come to a mutual agreement?"

"I believe so, since my terms are simple."

"I won't hurt Fanny again, you have my word."

"Good. And if you mean to continue trying to win her hand in marriage, you will accomplish it without threatening her friends. This afternoon you will write to Fleur and Chantel and inform them of your willingness to wait for repayment for as long as they require. And you will be gracious about it."

"Very well, milord," O'Rourke said reluctantly. "I suppose you leave me no choice."

Heath smiled. "That was precisely my intention, Mr. O'Rourke. I am gratified that you are such an astute businessman."

Lily heard from Heath that afternoon, but his brief missive only reported that he had dealt with the problem of O'Rourke. Lily couldn't feel entirely satisfied by the news. She had wanted the brute severely punished for hurting Fanny but suspected Heath had let him off with merely a stern warning.

An hour later, however, Fleur and Chantel received an effusive apology from O'Rourke, saying that he regretted causing them distress and that he would no longer insist on immediate payment of their debt, so Lily had to be content with that.

And truly, she *was* grateful to Heath for helping her friends avoid the threat of prison. And for being willing to protect Fanny against O'Rourke. She was even more grateful for what he'd done for Betty and Peg. Seeing his gentleness when he'd consoled the sobbing prostitute had nearly melted Lily's heart. Heath had promised the girl she would be safe in her new life, and Lily trusted that it would happen.

Yet he apparently didn't want gratitude for his kindness, since he declined Fleur's special invitation to dine at the boardinghouse that evening. Lily couldn't help but believe that *she* was the cause of his refusal. He was deliberately avoiding her, it seemed.

And while his seductive games had once driven her to distraction, the cessation was now highly unsettling, since she worried about the reason for his retreat—the possibility that he had taken a mistress. The notion was beginning to trouble Lily greatly. She couldn't help wondering how Heath was occupying his time these days, couldn't stop picturing him in some perfumed beauty's arms, satisfying his carnal needs with the same sensual tenderness he had shown *her* . . . perhaps at this very moment.

Unable to curb her vivid imaginings, Lily tossed and turned sleeplessly the entire night. By Saturday morning, she decided she needed to talk to someone who could understand her dilemma. Thus, when Tess came to London on business for one of her charities, Lily eagerly invited her to stay for luncheon.

They settled in the small garden at the rear of the

house, shielded from the bright summer sunshine by the shade of an elm tree.

Lily began by telling Tess about Lord Claybourne's recent generosity, but it wasn't long before she found herself confessing her mixed feelings about the possible end of his courtship.

Tess's first response was surprise. "I thought you would be pleased if he is no longer set on pursuing you. Isn't that what you wanted all along?"

"I *am* pleased," Lily assured her. "I mean . . . I will be very glad if he is no longer interested in claiming me for his marchioness."

"So what has made you so melancholic?"

"I don't know exactly." Lily shrugged. "I suppose I am just frustrated at being confined here with so little to do. I feel I cannot leave London until our friends' debt is paid and they are out of danger. And Roslyn's wedding to Arden will be held at St. George's on Tuesday, so of course I want to remain here for that and the dinner Marcus is giving in their honor the night before. And there is still the uncertain outcome of my game with Lord Claybourne. The two weeks we agreed to will be over on Monday. He earned another point yesterday for giving one of our boarders a home at his family seat in Kent, so he has nine points thus far, nearly enough to win. But he may have no desire to finish the competition."

"Is that what concerns you? You have become attached to him, and you don't want your game to end?"

Lily hesitated. "Perhaps 'attached' is too strong a word. But I do admit that I am exceedingly attracted to him."

When she fell silent, Tess fixed her with a penetrating

look. "Is there more you aren't telling me, Lily? What did he do to make you so attracted to him? Kiss you?"

Lily hesitated; Tess knew her too well. "What we did was far more intimate than kissing."

"More intimate?"

"Yes. And I discovered that I liked it—very much."

Tess frowned a little. "You didn't let him make love to you?"

"No. I am still a virgin. He wouldn't go further until I agreed to marry him. But the truth is . . . I wanted to go further, Tess." Lily's voice lowered to a bare murmur. "Claybourne says that I don't want to remain a spinster all my life, and it is partly true. I want to know what it is like to lie with a man, with *him*. I want to know about passion, about pleasure."

"So do I," Tess said with a soft sigh.

Lily gave her a quizzical glance. "You wonder what making love would be like?"

"Yes, I have for quite some time. But my scruples always kept me chaste. Lamentably so," she added with a wry grimace. "I could have given myself to Richard before he went off to war and was killed, but I saved myself for marriage. I regret that more than you know, Lily. I wish I had enjoyed our time together when I had the chance."

Reaching across the table, Lily took her friend's hand. "Oh, Tess, I am cruel, speaking of passion and lovemaking when you lost your betrothed. Please forgive my thoughtlessness."

Tess summoned a cheerful smile. "There is nothing to forgive, dearest. I am done with mourning. It has been two years now, and I cannot keep wallowing in grief and sadness—nor would Richard want me to. I realize I must live my life, despite my loss."

"Yes, you must," Lily agreed warmly. "And I suspect you haven't given up your desire to marry and have a family."

"No. I want a husband and children someday, even if I cannot have Richard." Her gaze grew distant. "I don't know if I will ever love so deeply again. They say that true love only comes once. . . ." Tess suddenly looked back at Lily. "But enough about *me*. It is your future that is in question just now. What is it you want, Lily? Do you even know?"

Lily gave a rueful laugh. "Well, if I am *truly* honest . . . I would like to have Lord Claybourne for my lover."

Tess hesitated. "You won't consider marrying him?"

"No, but I might consider becoming his mistress. Are you shocked, Tess?"

"I cannot say that I am. But there could be serious consequences."

It was Lily's turn to sigh. "I know. It isn't fair that gentlemen are allowed to have as many lovers as they wish, but ladies can be ruined by a mere hint of indiscretion."

"Indeed," Tess agreed. "But that is the way of the world."

"Still," Lily mused aloud, "if I thought I could keep an affair secret and avoid scandal, I wouldn't hesitate. If I never plan to marry, it matters little if I lose my innocence."

"I suppose not."

"And an affair with Claybourne wouldn't last long— I would make certain of it. I won't risk becoming so enamored of him that I wouldn't want to end it."

"Would it be so terrible if you fell in love with him?"

"*Yes,*" Lily replied emphatically. She never wanted to feel the misery and pain that came with loving someone. Never wanted to be enslaved by her love for a man. For too many years she had witnessed her mother's anguish. Her mother had loved her father at the beginning of their marriage, and look where *that* had lead.

Lily shook her head firmly. Her greatest regret was that she couldn't save her mother from such misery. But she could save herself. All she had to do was to keep her emotional defenses strong.

Admittedly, she had come to respect Heath a good deal in the short time she had known him. And she was supremely grateful to him for aiding her friends even when she'd been so reluctant to accept his help. But she would not let respect and gratitude affect her heart.

Indeed, an affair with Heath needn't be anything more than the pursuit of physical pleasure. She could satisfy her burning curiosity about passion. Furthermore, making love to Heath would hopefully put an end to the frustrated cravings that had plagued her so relentlessly of late. It might also serve to keep him from seeking comfort in the arms of another woman.

Most importantly, if she offered to become his paramour, he might give up the notion of matrimony for good. At least if she took so drastic a step, Heath would see how adamantly determined she was to refuse his marriage proposal, even if he did win their game and the right to publicly court her.

The thought was interrupted when Tess spoke. "Sometimes it is wiser to follow your heart, not your head, Lily."

"Not in this instance."

"Well, then . . . if you want Claybourne for your lover, I think you should act now. If there is one thing I have learned, it is that life is too short, and you are foolish to sit passively on the sidelines while it passes you by."

Again Lily nodded, in full agreement with her friend. It was time to take her fate into her own hands. She had been fighting her desire for days now, and she wanted to end it.

Despite her decision, however, she lacked the experience to set an affair with Heath in motion. Lily's mouth curved as she laughed inwardly at herself.

"The thing is, Tess . . . I wouldn't know how to begin. I cannot ask Fanny for advice, for she will only tell me that I should wed Lord Claybourne. I don't even know how I can manage to be alone with him."

"That shouldn't present a problem," Tess replied. "You may use my rooms at the Darnley Hotel. It is very quiet and discreet, and you can wear a veil and pretend to be a widow."

Tess stayed at the Darnley whenever she had to remain in London overnight, Lily knew.

"So the next question is *when*," Tess added thoughtfully.

Lily pursed her lips, realizing that time was running out. Their game would be over in three more days, but she didn't want to wait until then. Yet how would she contrive an opportunity to see Heath if he was set on avoiding her? He was certain to be at Marcus's London home Monday evening for the dinner in honor of the bridal couple, however. . . .

"I expect he will attend Marcus's dinner. You are coming, aren't you, Tess?"

"Yes, I wouldn't miss it."

"I plan to remain there afterward and spend the night," Lily added, "so my sisters and I will have some time together before Roslyn marries."

"Then it must be before Monday. Perhaps tonight."

The thought that she might be with Heath tonight sent a shocking little thrill through Lily. "But how do I persuade him to meet me at the hotel?"

"We will think of something," Tess said confidently. "And of course you will have to take precautions against pregnancy. There are methods. . . . One of your friends here should be able to advise you."

Lily's brow furrowed. She hadn't thought that far ahead, although now that she did, Peg seemed the logical choice to counsel her about such intimate details. Even so . . . "How do you know about such things, Tess?"

Faint color warmed her cheeks at the question. "I have had this same discussion with Fanny, in the event I decided to take a lover myself."

Lily's eyes widened a little. It seemed surprising that Tess would have considered something so scandalous since she was the epitome of a genteel lady. Yet her next words were even more startling:

"If Claybourne is concerned about dishonoring you, Lily, you may have to be prepared to seduce him."

After a surprised moment, Lily gave a soft laugh—not so much at the idea of seducing Heath, but that Tess had been the one to suggest it.

It was a relief, however, to have her decision made. She would become Heath's lover, even if she was required to act as his seducer.

She wondered how he would respond when *she* was the pursuer for a change.

Amusement curled the corners of Lily's mouth. It was difficult to think of herself as a brazen femme fatale and Heath her victim. Even so, the endeavor should prove vastly interesting.

Chapter Fourteen

❧

Seducing him was more difficult than I expected.
Lord Claybourne can be a very stubborn man.

—Lily to Tess Blanchard

Lily's stomach felt highly unsettled as she waited in her borrowed rooms at the Darnley Hotel for Heath to appear. She'd written to him directly after luncheon, asking him to meet her here at ten o'clock tonight, yet she wasn't certain he would come.

She was seated facing the door, at a small table near the hearth, although she hadn't touched a bite of the sumptuous supper the hotel staff had served a short while ago. She was too aware of the curtained bed at one side of the chamber to have much appetite.

When a quiet knock sounded at the door, Lily gave a start, but she wet her dry lips and bid entrance. Her heart began thudding in recognition even before Heath stepped into the room and slowly shut the door behind him.

He looked supremely handsome dressed in formal evening finery, Lily saw, taking in his burgundy coat, silver embroidered waistcoat, and gray satin knee breeches. His gaze swept over her own attire—a modest, high-necked gown of sapphire silk. She had kept on her veil to maintain anonymity before the servants, and that was what Heath studied the longest before finally speaking.

"What do you mean by asking me here, angel?"

Removing her veil, Lily summoned a welcoming smile. "I wanted to thank you properly for your generosity. You refused Fleur's invitation to dinner last night."

"I had a previous engagement last night."

"Oh?" she asked casually. "You were not simply avoiding me?"

His gaze remained enigmatic. "No. I attended a musicale hosted by Lady Beldon—Marcus's aunt."

The disclosure raised Lily's curiosity more than it should. "I suppose Lady Eleanor was there as well?"

"Of course. Lady Beldon is not only Eleanor's aunt but chaperone also. Nell lives with her."

"And tonight? Did you have a prior engagement this evening?"

Heath's gaze narrowed. "I was at my club. What does it matter to you, sweeting?"

"I was simply curious," Lily prevaricated.

"What of you? I trust you mean to explain what you are doing alone in a hotel, unchaperoned by a maid. Do your friends even know you are here?"

Lily shook her head briefly. "No, I made no mention of it. I allowed Fleur to think I would be staying at Marcus's house tonight, helping Roslyn with her wedding plans—which is certainly not the case." Her smile turned impish. "Roslyn doesn't want my help, I suspect because she is afraid I will try to talk her out of marrying her beloved duke. Won't you join me?" Lily added, gesturing toward the empty chair at the table.

Although Heath's penetrating regard never faltered, at least he moved a few steps closer. "I am not hungry."

"Well, I am. I couldn't eat a bite all evening, I was so anxious."

That much was true. There was a quaking excitement inside her that set all her nerves on edge.

Heath did not appear to share her excitement, however. On the contrary, he looked impatient. "Why don't you come to the point of your invitation, Lily? What the devil are you up to?"

She swallowed. "Well, the thing is . . . I have a proposition to put before you."

"What proposition?"

His tone was as un-loverlike as possible, Lily noticed, her lips trembling with nervous amusement. "I know it is normally the gentleman's prerogative to initiate an affair, but . . . I want you for my lover."

His brows snapped together. "Is that so?"

"Yes. You were right, Heath. I don't want to remain a virginal spinster all my life. And that is all your fault. You gave me a mere taste of passion when I want the full experience. But you have tantalized me long enough."

"You don't honestly expect me to deflower you?" he retorted. "You are supposed to be a lady."

"True," Lily agreed, a humorous smile hovering around her mouth. "But you know I have never conformed to the proper rules of society. And you said you wanted me in your bed."

"As my wife, not my paramour." Heath's frown deepened. "What is this, Lily? Your next move in our game? Because Fleur and Chantel are likely to take away points from my total if they learn I have despoiled you?"

She shook her head. "I have no intention of telling

them. And this has nothing to do with the game. It has to do with desire." Lily stood slowly, holding his gaze. "I want you Heath. I want to be your lover."

Unmoved, he crossed his arms over his chest. "You know my terms, Lily."

She pursed her lips thoughtfully. "Tess warned me that I might have to seduce you."

At her blithe admission, one dark eyebrow shot up, but otherwise he didn't respond.

"Although I suspect," Lily went on, "you won't like it if I ape all those other women who have chased you from the time you were out of short coats." As she spoke, Lily reached up to pull the pins from her hair. She was gratified when Heath's eyes followed her movements as she let down the dark tresses and combed them out with her fingers.

"Don't you want me, Heath?" she asked in a pouting voice.

"You know damn well I do."

"And I want you. So what is the difficulty? I am willing, even eager to become a scarlet woman."

"I have no intention of making love to you until you agree to wed me, you know that."

"Why not?"

"I won't risk getting you with child, for one thing."

"Ah, but I have a solution. Sponges soaked in brandy or vinegar are deemed most effective, I am told. Peg gave me some to use tonight."

His gaze sharpened, but he stood there obdurately, his jaw set.

Bending, Lily drew off her evening slippers one by one. Then reaching behind her, she unfastened the hooks at the back of her gown. When she let the garment slip to the floor and stepped out of it, she was left wearing only a delicate lawn chemise and silk stockings.

Sensation danced over her skin as Heath's golden gaze fixed on her breasts. Her nipples had hardened and the rosy aureoles showed through the thin fabric of her chemise. When his gaze dropped lower, she knew he could see the shadows of the dark curls below her belly. The desire that flashed in his eyes was unmistakable, and it encouraged her a measure.

With a casualness she wasn't feeling, she leaned down and undid the ribbons of her garters, then slowly peeled the silk down her legs.

"Lily, stop right now." The command was low but husky.

"I don't believe I will, Heath. If you won't make love to me, then I shall have to be the aggressor."

A muscle jumped in his jaw. He was making an obvious effort to resist the temptation she presented, Lily realized.

When Heath didn't speak, she moved around the room, turning down the lamps until only a faint glow remained from one on the bedside table. While there, she drew back the bed curtains. Then silently, she went to the door to lock it and withdrew the key.

Turning, she dangled the key from one finger provocatively. "You will have to take this from me if you want to escape."

"Lily . . ." There was exasperation in his voice along with a faint note of dismay. Yet he didn't look as if escape was on his mind. Instead, he stood rooted to the floor, watching her every move.

His eyes had darkened with hunger, Lily saw. It gave her the confidence she had lacked until now. Tossing the key in the direction of her discarded gown, she crossed to Heath, then reached up and began to untie his cravat.

"Lily, devil take you. . . ."

She laughed softly. "You may swear at me all you want, but I intend to have my way with you."

Her laughter affected Heath more than anything else she could have done. He stared back at Lily as she unwound his cravat from around his neck. A teasing smile graced her lips, while her eyes were innocent and full of deviltry at the same time.

That look enchanted him, sending a hot rush of need straight to his loins, even before she slid her fingers down his waistcoat to probe the firmness of his burgeoning erection beneath his evening breeches.

"Do you really think you can resist me?" Lily murmured tauntingly. "Do you even want to try?"

Her big dark eyes sparkled with repressed laughter and something more: desire. She had been truthful when she said she wanted him. The realization aroused Heath even more than her tantalizing touch.

"I understand that seduction is an art," Lily was saying as she knelt before him. "And I know firsthand that you are a consummate artist. So I hope you will forgive me if I am not quite as skilled at pleasuring you as you are at pleasuring me."

When she unbuttoned the front of his evening breeches so that his sex sprang free, Heath muttered another oath and growled in a low voice, "Lily . . . I am not made of stone."

"I should hope not," she murmured, curving her fingers lightly around his cock. "Although this *is* rather like granite."

Then she began stroking him . . . cradling the thick

shaft of his manhood, grazing the blunt head with her fingertips, cupping the heavy, swollen sacs beneath.

At her boldness, Heath sucked in a harsh breath. He had never seen Lily like this. She had taken complete control, playing the enchantress, determined to seduce him. Her willfulness not only delighted and tempted him, it jolted him with stronger emotions he couldn't begin to sort through just now. It was a struggle simply to remember why he had to resist her sensual assault.

"Am I doing this correctly?" Lily asked innocently, gazing up at him. "You had best advise me, or I might inadvertently hurt you."

He didn't reply except to curl his hands into fists at his sides. Then her touch grew even more brazen, her fingers wrapping around his turgid length, sweeping slowly up and down, squeezing, kneading gently.

Heath's jaw locked and his entire body went rigid as he fought for control. Lily's erotic caresses made him throb with heat. And when she leaned forward and pressed her lips to the crest of his arousal, it jerked eagerly.

He gave a low, strangled sigh as she closed her lips over the swollen head, tasting him with her tongue. A rush of fire flared through him, destroying the last vestiges of his resistance.

Tangling his hands in her hair, Heath closed his eyes and let his imagination take over. He could almost feel his shaft gliding slickly between the feminine folds of her sex. . . .

The fire built inside him as Lily went on suckling him, plying him with warm caresses of her tongue and lips, laving and pulling, coaxing a shudder from him.

Heath finally yielded before he exploded. With a low

groan, he grasped Lily's shoulders and pulled her up. The satisfied smile on her lips gave him absolutely no choice but to haul her close and seize her mouth in a hungry kiss. He couldn't possibly stop himself.

And in truth, he didn't want to stop himself, Heath thought dazedly, drinking in her breaths as their tongues fiercely tangled. His strategy of keeping away from Lily seemed to have succeeded; she had come to *him* this time. Not only was she offering herself to him willingly, she was the pursuer, bent on his seduction—a huge step in their courtship war. And he intended to let her win this particular battle.

Lily would share his bed one day, it was inevitable. Even though she hadn't yet agreed to wed him, she would soon. And claiming her body now would only hasten the day when he could make her his wife.

With that calming reflection, Heath forced himself to slow down. Although he was still breathing hard, he broke off their kiss and divested Lily of her chemise. Then he stepped back a short distance, the better to see all of her.

In the soft glow of lamplight, she looked like a cherished fantasy. A cloud of vibrant chestnut tresses framed her face and drifted about her shoulders, while her skin gleamed pale gold. Her disheveled look entranced him, but it was the sight of her luscious body that made his blood pound. Her high, ripe breasts. Her narrow waist. Her sweetly curving hips. Her slender legs. He wanted to explore the silken mass of her hair with his hands while he tasted every inch of her creamy skin. Yet he held back his impatience as he let Lily undress him.

When he was completely naked, she moved closer, into his arms. All her amusement seemed to have faded.

Instead, she held his gaze solemnly, her hands roaming over his body as if she was hungry to touch him—which only made Heath hungrier.

In turn, he skimmed the undersides of her breasts, cupping her fullness. Lily made a breathy sound as he palmed the soft mounds in his hands, a sound that became a whimper when he thumbed her taut nipples. He was mesmerized by the lure of her bare skin, yet he wanted more. Much more.

"Come," Heath said hoarsely, taking her hand.

He drew her to the bed and lay back upon the sheets, pulling Lily down on top of him. But then he let her take the lead again. Her dark, fragrant hair fell in a silky curtain around their heads, then teased his skin as she bent and pressed passionate kisses over his jaw, his throat, his chest.

Heath welcomed her eagerness, reveled in the erotic friction between their bodies as she rubbed herself against the hardness of his erection. But then suddenly she stilled and raised her head, her expression uncertain for the first time this evening.

"Heath . . . I know I haven't the experience of your other women," she began before he abruptly cut her off.

"Hush," he ordered, softly smiling. "You have all the experience either of us needs."

And there were no other women any longer, Heath added silently. Not since their first kiss in the barn loft. There was only Lily. She was lush and alive and more desirable than any woman he had ever known.

With one deft and powerful twist of his body, he rolled her under him. He was utterly captivated by her, he thought, gazing down at her. He was enchanted by her fire and softness, her glowing eyes, her marvelous mouth. . . . God, how he wanted her. Yet he had to remember her virginal state.

His fingers trailed down her body to the apex of her thighs, gliding through the curls to find her feminine cleft. She was already hot and swollen for him, even before he brushed the sensitive bud that was the center of her pleasure and began stroking with exquisite tenderness.

He made her arch and shiver against his hand, but when he lowered his head to kiss her, this time it was Lily who stopped him.

"Heath, the sponges . . . on the bedside table."

Her breathless reminder brought some semblance of sanity to his mad rush to take her.

Nodding, he sat up and reached for the pouch on the table, which contained several small sponges with strings attached. Wetting one from the vial of liquid, he probed her warm, silky folds with his fingers and pressed the sponge slowly, carefully inside her woman's passage.

Lily gasped and tensed her muscles, but Heath murmured a quiet reassurance, so that when he stretched out to cover her again, she was gazing up at him trustingly.

Bracing his weight on his forearms, he nestled his body in the cradle of her thighs and parted her swollen sex with his phallus.

"I may hurt you," he warned, his tone regretful.

She smiled faintly and reached up to touch his face. "It's all right," she whispered.

The tenderness he felt for her deepening, he stared down into her lovely face and gently, very gently, eased the head of his cock into her quivering flesh.

Lily held her breath but made no sound. With exquisite care, Heath pressed forward again, pushing inside her a fraction of an inch.

When a wince flashed across her features, he halted and feathered light kisses over her forehead, her cheekbones, her lips, wanting to kiss away the pain. After a moment he could feel her body begin to relax again, so he slowly slid in further, his long, thick arousal stretching her flesh, filling her. When at last he sank in the entire way, he held completely still so Lily could grow accustomed to his throbbing fullness.

She was tight, wet, fitting him like a glove, enveloping him in glorious heat . . . blissful for him but not for her yet, Heath knew. Impaled on his hardness, Lily remained rigid beneath him, her breath coming in shallow pants.

After another long moment, however, her body softened as if the discomfort had faded. And when several more heartbeats passed, she stirred her hips, tentatively, testing.

"Better?" Heath asked.

The hint of a smile that wreathed her lips told him what he wanted to know, even before she whispered, "Much better, thank you."

He began to move then, withdrawing the slightest measure, then carefully gliding upward once more. It wasn't long before he felt her shiver of aroused excitement and her hips began to move of their own accord.

Hot, urgent longing clamored inside Heath at her instinctive motion. He wanted to bury himself inside her fiercely, again and again, but he held back. Instead he kept up the careful, deliberate rhythm, coaxing her, pleasuring her slowly and sweetly, claiming her with endless tenderness.

And Lily responded. Her skin was flushed with passion now; her breath was ragged, but not from pain as he thrust gently into her melting flesh. In another few moments she was whimpering feverishly, her nails digging into his shoulders as she matched his rhythm.

Clenching his teeth, Heath struggled to maintain control, his own breathing rough as he moved inside her. But only when she was on the brink of climax did he hasten the pace, sliding free only to plunge again. Lowering his head, he captured her wild moans with his mouth but never stopped moving as she writhed and strained beneath him.

Then suddenly she jolted against him, arching her spine helplessly, her harsh cries muffled by his lips as the tumult broke within her. Trying desperately to keep his savage need in check, Heath used all his skill to prolong her ecstasy as wave after wave of rapture convulsed her slender body.

But her fierce abandon was his undoing. A great shudder surged through his frame as at last he surrendered to his need for her. With a hoarse moan of his own, he let himself fill Lily with the desire that he'd felt from the first moment of meeting her.

His body clenched and spasmed with the same blazing heat she was feeling as he plunged into pleasure so intense and raw, it seared.

As the firestorm receded, they lay there together, weak with the aftershocks. Finally easing his weight to the side, Heath drew Lily into his arms, wrapping his body around her trembling one, soothing her shivers, calming her.

When she exhaled a ragged sigh, he brushed her temple with his lips and breathed a sigh of his own.

The contentment he felt was indescribable. He had marked Lily for his own. She belonged to him now. They had fully consummated their union, and there was no going back. In truth, he thought of her as his bride.

Elation flooded through Heath, along with a primal possessiveness.

What surprised him, however, was how powerful his response to her had been. He'd never experienced lovemaking quite like that before. Never felt that liquid fire pouring through him.

Lily had felt it, too, he was certain. She had met him fiercely, giving as passionately as she did everything else. Her vibrancy made him feel intensely alive, filling him with exhilaration and something very much like joy. . . .

"Now perhaps you will believe me," he murmured against the crown of her head, "when I say you are a woman of great passion."

Sated and boneless, Lily pressed a kiss against his bare shoulder. "I think you give me too much credit. You are devastatingly adept at lovemaking."

His laughter came quietly against her hair. "You will soon become adept yourself."

That could very well happen, Lily reflected, if they made love again. And she certainly wanted to. Passion was as thrilling and wonderful as Heath had promised it would be.

Recalling the magic of it, Lily sighed once more. He had appeased the aching need deep within her, shown her pleasure beyond her wildest imaginings. She had felt part of him with their bodies joined, skin against warm skin, flesh against naked flesh, hardness against softness.

And now, when he enfolded her more tightly in his arms and stroked the curve of her hot cheek with a soothing finger, Lily shut her eyes, savoring his tenderness . . . the intimacy, the bliss of lying here with him like this.

Suddenly she found herself swallowing against the tightness in her throat. That threatening ache had returned, along with an odd, yearning sensation that spread out from the region of her heart.

This would never do, Lily warned herself. She couldn't allow Heath's tenderness to overwhelm her emotional defenses. She only wanted his passion, nothing more.

Determined to break the spell he had cast over, Lily pressed her hands against his chest to loosen his embrace.

"So," she commented casually, drawing back a short way to gaze up at him. "If you approve of my carnal abilities, does this mean you will consider me for the position of your mistress?"

Chapter Fifteen

❧

He refused my offer to become his mistress out of hand.

—Lily to Fanny

Lily felt Heath stiffen at her question. All his languidness had flown, she realized as he fixed her with a measuring stare.

"You cannot possibly think I would set you up as my mistress," he finally responded.

"Actually, I do think so."

A scowl wreathing his handsome features, Heath sat up in bed, absently propping the pillows behind his back. "Have you taken complete leave of your senses?"

Lily dimpled up at him. "I believe I am in possession of all my faculties, my lord. At least the ones that still remain after you obliterated them just now."

"Lily, damn it all . . ."

"Your swearing at me is becoming rather repetitive." She pushed herself up to brace her weight on one elbow. "I want to be your *chère amie,* Heath."

He shook his head in disbelief, then said very slowly, as if speaking to an extremely dimwitted child, "But *I* do not want you for my mistress, sweeting. I won't settle for less than marriage."

"And I won't settle for marriage, especially after

tonight . . . now that I know what making love to you is like. It was even better than you claimed it would be. I am certain the role of your mistress will be significantly better than that of your wife."

"No, it won't be," Heath said tersely. "And it is unworthy of you even to suggest it."

Lily arched her eyebrows. "Unworthy? Why? I think it is the perfect solution to our impasse."

She rose so that she was kneeling beside him. Immediately his gaze drifted down to her bare breasts, then abruptly lifted again when she continued:

"A mistress has numerous advantages over a wife, Heath. Chiefly the independence to be her own woman without the misery. I will be free to leave an affair if I choose, just as you will. You won't have to be saddled with me for life."

"I have told you, I *want* to be saddled with you."

"But you won't consider my wishes at all?"

"Certainly I will consider them."

"Then why won't you at least think about my proposal?"

"No," Heath repeated adamantly. "It's out of the question."

With that staunch declaration, he rose from the bed and went to the washstand, where he wet a cloth from a ewer and washed his loins. When he strode naked back to the bed, Lily found her gaze riveted on his beautiful, muscular body—until he commanded her to lie back.

Warm color suffused her face as he carefully washed away the traces of seed and the pink tinge of blood from her thighs and the area between. Lily drew a shaky breath at the intimate gesture, but Heath's touch was completely perfunctory, not seductive in the least.

Neither was his tone as he returned the cloth to the washbasin. "You can't have considered the consequences of your proposition, Lily. You would lose all respectability if you became my light-o'-love."

"Our affair would have to be kept secret, of course."

"We could not keep an arrangement secret for long. And until then, we would have to sneak around to avoid scandal. You couldn't go about town with me, or be seen anywhere in public. You would have to hide in the shadows, just as you do now."

Heath crossed to the bed again, but this time he sat beside her. "I won't be content with a few stolen hours together now and then. What kind of life would that be for us? What kind of future would we have? We most certainly couldn't have a family without marriage."

"I forgot," Lily murmured, reluctantly meeting his gaze. "You want heirs."

"Eventually, yes. What about you, Lily? Are you telling me you don't want children?"

She wasn't able to say any such thing, but her desire for children was not strong enough to overcome her objections to matrimony. "Not if it means I must marry."

His gaze searched hers. "Why this sudden turnabout? Why this insistence on our becoming lovers before our game is even over?"

He was completely serious, Lily realized, deciding she owed him the same seriousness. "The truth is, I don't want you taking another woman as your mistress."

He stared at her for a brief moment. "I don't want any other woman for my mistress. I want you."

"You say that now, but as soon as the marriage lines are dry, you may change your mind."

A muscle twitched in his jaw. "I won't argue with you

or offer vows of fidelity when you won't believe me anyway."

"I won't argue with you, either, Heath. But I mean to persuade you to listen to me." Giving him a soft smile, Lily raised her fingers to his lips. "I know I have a long way to go before I can hope to satisfy a man of your vast experience and expertise, but I think I could become skilled enough in time. You could teach me what I need to know."

"You already satisfy me, Lily. And I suspect you would make the best mistress I have ever known. But I am not interested."

She reached down and lightly touched his flaccid member. "At least let me show my appreciation for your generosity . . . how grateful I am to you for helping my friends."

Her offer caused his gaze to narrow. There was real anger in his eyes as his fingers closed about her wrist and held her hand away. "I won't even dignify that with a reply."

Standing abruptly, Heath retrieved his clothing and began to dress.

"You are leaving?" Lily asked in dismay.

"Yes, and so are you." Bending, he picked up her gown and tossed it to her. "Put this on."

Distractedly Lily clutched the garment to her naked breasts. "But I thought we would spend the night together."

"We don't have that right. We aren't legally wed."

"Heath . . . I want to make love to you again."

He shot her a dismissive glance. "What you want is beside the point. I'm not touching you again."

Lily raised her eyes to the ceiling in exasperation. "I

have already lost my virtue to you. It hardly matters now how many times we make love."

"It will matter to you tomorrow. You will be tender and sore enough as it is."

Her gaze went to the table where the dishes were still in their covers. "We could at least stay long enough to partake of supper. I dislike for all that food to go to waste."

"The hotel can return it to the kitchens and serve it to their staff. Get dressed, Lily. I am taking you home."

Finally accepting that she wouldn't sway him, she flounced off the bed. "Very well. But you cannot take me to the boardinghouse."

"I certainly am not taking you to Marcus's. He would have my liver if he knew what we had done tonight."

"Heath—" she began before he cut her off.

"That is the end of it, Lily. Get dressed."

Highly miffed, she pulled on her gown and struggled to fasten the hooks while various thoughts spun in her head. The evening had been an abject failure . . . except that she now was fully a woman and Heath had become her lover for a few magical, enchanting moments.

She couldn't regret that, Lily reflected with a small, secret smile. Even if he obviously did.

She wasn't prepared to give up just yet, though. By now Heath should know her well enough to realize she wasn't the sort of woman to surrender after one little defeat. He would be her lover again. She just needed to determine how to overcome his objections.

Despite her resolve, Lily was actually a little relieved that Heath broke his unyielding silence as his carriage halted on the street near the boardinghouse.

"I intend to call upon you tomorrow afternoon. At one o'clock, if that is convenient."

She debated refusing, but that would defeat her own purpose. "Very well, one o'clock."

"Wear a pelisse and your veil. We will be taking a drive."

"Oh?" Lily asked curiously.

"I have something to show you."

Heath refused to expound further as he helped her down from his carriage and escorted her to the rear tradesmen's entrance. Lily felt strangely disappointed when he bid her a terse good night and remained waiting for her to go inside. But it was his unexpected anger that took her aback. That, and the sense that she had gravely disappointed *him*.

If she hoped she would avoid detection by the household, however, she was soon proved wrong. Just as she was about to mount the rear service stairs, she spied Fanny coming down the corridor toward her. Surprisingly, Basil was directly behind her.

"May I speak to you a moment, Lily?" Fanny called out.

"Yes, of course."

Basil halted beside Fanny. "I will leave you two ladies to your own devices. If you need me, Fanny, I am at your service."

"Thank you, Basil," Fanny replied with a soft smile. "I am glad we had our little coze."

When he gave her an odd glance in return, it was almost a wince—which puzzled Lily. There were definite undercurrents of tension between Basil and Fanny, yet not the exasperation and irritation they usually roused in each other. Apparently they were no longer at daggers drawn, at least for the moment. And as Basil turned away, heading for the stairs, the look of desire and longing in his eyes was unmistakable.

Musing over the cause, Lily followed her friend to the parlor. The lamps were lit, so she surmised that Basil and Fanny had been making use of this room just now.

"What are you doing here, Fanny?" she asked as they settled into chairs. "I would have expected you to be occupied on a Saturday evening."

"I came seeking company, but you were not here." Her tone was almost accusatory.

Lily hesitated, not wanting to confess exactly where she had been. "Could not Fleur and Chantel have sufficed?"

"They are out with Lord Poole, celebrating."

"Celebrating?" she echoed.

Fanny nodded. "It seems Lord Poole has rekindled his former ardor for Chantel, so he insisted on paying the entire gambling debt of thirty thousand pounds to Mick O'Rourke."

"Why, that is splendid!" Lily exclaimed. "It means they are no longer in danger of imprisonment."

"Yes," Fanny said glumly. "But Mick still will not accept that I don't wish to marry him. He called on me at my home this afternoon and offered me his entire fortune if I would agree to become his wife. He was quite unhappy when I refused."

Stiffening involuntarily, Lily leaned forward in her chair. "That brute did not hurt you again?"

"No. This time he was the perfect gentleman."

Lily surveyed her friend carefully. Either Fanny's bruises had healed, or they were artfully concealed by cosmetics. Yet she still look disturbed.

"But . . . ?" Lily prodded.

Fanny grimaced. "But Mick made a nuisance of himself. He wouldn't leave my house, so I had no choice but to take refuge here. I was supposed to entertain one of the Prussian ambassadors this evening. Mick cost me a pretty penny, let me tell you. At this rate, he will put me out of business—which no doubt has become his aim."

Lily scowled. "He is trying to coerce you to marry him?"

"I suspect he doesn't see it that way." Fanny sighed. "I like him well enough, but I have no desire to wed him. And he makes an extremely poor patron. He is far too possessive." Fanny suddenly frowned. "What of you, Lily? I was told you were spending the night at Lord Danvers's home with your sisters. Imagine my surprise to find you sneaking into the boardinghouse."

"I was not *sneaking*," Lily protested. "I merely saw no reason to advertise my precipitate return."

"You were with Claybourne, were you not?" When Lily looked at her in surprise, Fanny sent her a sardonic smile. "His lordship's carriage drove past on the street, and I recognized his crest on the door panel."

"My being with him is hardly a crime, Fanny."

Her friend sighed. "No, but I worry about you. Just what have you been doing with him, darling? The flush on your cheeks suggests you have gone past mere courtship. You have become lovers, have you not?"

"Well . . . yes," Lily confessed, not wanting to lie. "Tonight was our first time, in fact. But you needn't worry. It may come to nothing. I offered to become Heath's mistress so he would abandon the notion of winning my hand in marriage, but he decidedly refused."

"Oh, Lily." Fanny sounded less shocked than dismayed.

Lily gave her a quizzical glance. "What is the matter, Fanny? You of all people should understand my desire for independence. The position of mistress will allow me freedom I could never have as his wife."

"I know. But I feel guilty for leading you astray. I have been such a wicked influence on you. You would never have made so scandalous a proposition to Claybourne but for your friendship with me."

Lily was truly puzzled. "You aren't to blame whatsoever. And since when did you suddenly become so prim and proper?"

"Since you conceived the abominable idea of following in my footsteps. Trust me, Lily. You don't want to be any man's mistress. You do not want that life."

"I am not proposing that I enter your trade, Fanny. Just that I limit my relationship with Claybourne to an affair instead of marriage."

"Even so, I think you would be making a dreadful mistake."

Falling silent, Lily searched her friend's beautiful face. There was more to Fanny's objection than met the eye. There was real distress in her tone, along with a genuine sadness. She had recently spoken of being lonely, Lily remembered. . . .

"Fanny, dearest, what is troubling you?"

Lily was startled to see Fanny bite her lower lip as if holding back tears. When one spilled over, Lily sprang up from her chair and went to kneel before her friend, taking her hands in a light grasp.

"Come now, what did I say to make you cry?"

"It . . . was not anything you said." Fanny dashed a

hand over her welling eyes. "It is nothing, truly. I am simply feeling sorry for myself."

"Why, Fanny? Because you are lonely?"

Pressing her trembling lips together, Fanny gave a shaky nod. "I suppose so. And because of all of the uncertainty with Mick. If I were wise, I would accept his marriage proposal."

"You can't possibly believe that marrying that brute would be wise."

"At least I would have financial security as Mick's wife."

With effort, Lily managed to keep herself from scoffing. "You are just feeling vulnerable because you contributed all your savings to pay off the first ten thousand pounds of the gaming debt."

"Perhaps, but I know what my fate will be when I grow old and lose my beauty. I see the streetwalkers in Covent Garden, scrounging for their livelihoods, barely able to put food in their bellies." Fanny shuddered. "I don't want to become like that."

"Your circumstances are very different, Fanny. You are the toast of London."

"For the moment, I am. But Fleur and Chantel were the reigning queens of their era, and look at them now. They are all alone. Well . . . Chantel has Lord Poole now, but that may not last long." Fanny sniffed inelegantly. "When my old age comes, I will have no one. I have been spurned by all my family and former friends—except you and your sisters, of course."

Lily felt her heart twist at the bleakness of her tone. "You know you will always have us. And you have several other close friends. Fleur and Chantel are like family to you."

"Yes, they are my family now. But it is not the same as having a husband and children."

"You want a husband and children?" Lily asked in surprise.

It took Fanny a moment to answer. "I believe I do, Lily. I try to convince myself that I am happy in my current life, but I want more. I wish I could be with just one man . . . a husband I could love. I wanted the gay life of a Cyprian, but I would give it all up for true love."

Lily scarcely knew what to say. Fanny had always condemned love as a foolish weakness, but perhaps that was due to her profession; courtesans could rarely afford the luxury of love.

Fortunately she wasn't required to reply just then since Fanny emitted a bitter little laugh. "Perhaps I have merely been dwelling too much about husband-hunting because of my book. The publisher is pleased with the manuscript, did I tell you?"

Lily had almost forgotten about Fanny's efforts to supplement her income as an author. "No, you said you were finishing the final corrections," she murmured.

"*Advice to Young Ladies on Capturing a Husband* by an Anonymous Lady," Fanny recited. Her lips curled in a sad smile. "I am most definitely not a lady any longer. And it seems rather arrogant of me to presume I could advise anyone about securing a husband when I cannot even fend for myself."

Lily squeezed her friend's hands. "You are being much too hard on yourself. You gave Roslyn excellent advice on how to arouse a gentleman's ardor, and because of it, she will be marrying the Duke of Arden."

"But I had little to do with them falling in love. Arden

lost his heart to Roslyn because of her brains and her charming nature, not to mention her beauty."

Patting Fanny's knee, Lily rose to her feet. "Well, I imagine you are right about one thing. Your spirits are depressed just now, so you are allowing yourself to wallow in self-pity. We will have to find a way to bring you out of your melancholy. What sort of husband do you want, Fanny?"

She looked up distractedly as Lily returned to her own seat. "I beg your pardon?"

"Perhaps you should take your own advice and capture a husband. And I am willing to help if I can."

Fanny's eyes widened. "You, Lily? *You* are willing to help me acquire a husband?"

Lily smiled. "I know. It boggles the imagination and violates every independent principle I possess. But I cannot bear to see you so despondent." She let her expression turn serious. "What about Basil?"

Fanny's brows drew together in a frown. "What about him?"

"You are fond of him, despite the constant rows you two have."

"Not fond enough to *marry* him, for heaven's sake! Are you daft? Basil is the most insufferable, provoking creature alive."

"To you, he is. But I suspect he is being deliberately vexing because he wants to gain your attention. Otherwise you would completely ignore him."

Obviously disbelieving, Fanny shook her head. "Basil is vexing because he is Basil. He doesn't think of me in an amorous way in the least. . . ." Her certainty faltered. "Does he?"

"Well, I cannot claim to know his feelings, but I have

seen the way he sometimes looks at you when you aren't aware of it. I expect he would worship the ground you walk on if you gave him the slightest encouragement."

Her jaw dropping, Fanny stared at Lily as if the possibility had never occurred to her.

"Do you have even the slightest romantic affection for him?" Lily asked. "You enjoy his company, I am certain—because of your common childhood memories if nothing else. You and Basil were fast friends when we were growing up."

"I suppose I do enjoy his company," Fanny said thoughtfully before her mouth quirked with irony. "At least with Basil I can be myself instead of always being on my guard. He doesn't see me only as a prize possession or a commodity for sale."

Lily had to agree. Fanny was sought after by half the men in London, but Basil was not bowled over by her beauty or her aura of excitement and glamour. "You can be a real person around him," Lily stated.

"Yes," Fanny said slowly. "With all my patrons I must be witty and flattering and artfully alluring at all times."

"But with Basil you can say precisely what you want to say."

Her smile was faint. "Indeed. I can be as cross and temperamental and irritable as I choose. But that is simply because he doesn't care enough about me to be concerned with my feelings."

"He cares," Lily assured her.

"I believe you are mistaken. Basil couldn't think any worse of me than he does. He profoundly disapproves of my profession, that much is certain."

"Because he is jealous of all the men you must be

with. But if you were willing to change professions . . ."
Lily let the thought linger for a time while Fanny pondered. Then: "If you believed that Basil truly loved you,
Fanny, could you possibly return his regard someday?"

Fanny thought over the question for a long moment
before replying. "Astonishingly enough, I might." But
almost immediately she followed with a scoffing sound.
"I must be mad to find Basil appealing. No doubt I want
him simply because he doesn't want me."

"He *does* want you, Fanny. That is abundantly clear
to me, if not to you."

It was a perfect case of opposites attracting, Lily reflected. Fanny was gay and lively, a pleasure-seeker
down to her satin dance slippers, while Basil was earnest
and studious and serious most of the time. "He would
cure your loneliness, at least."

Fanny's laugh held a sharp note of humor. "Perhaps
so—because we would fight all the time. No, Lily. It
would never serve. I could never marry Basil. In any
event, we would starve on his income. I have very expensive tastes, you know. He is a mere law clerk who
earns barely a pittance."

"But he may have greater ambitions, Fanny, and his
future prospects could be quite handsome. He could
perhaps take a position as secretary to a nobleman who
is involved in politics. The House of Lords is always
passing laws governing the country. And to write those
laws, someone must have knowledge of our legal system. Why not Basil? He could earn a significantly higher
wage as a peer's secretary than as a clerk."

"I suppose so." Fanny worried her lower lip. "But it
wouldn't be enough to support an expensive wife. No, a

marriage with him is out of the question. It would be a disastrous mismatch."

"I am not convinced of that," Lily replied. "But you needn't make up your mind this moment. You should, however, think about what Basil means to you."

"It might prove a cure for my doldrums at least," Fanny quipped, obviously in higher spirits. Suddenly she straightened. "How did we manage to change subjects so radically, Lily? We were speaking of you and Lord Claybourne."

"I would much rather discuss you and Basil," Lily said lightly.

"I still believe you should consider Claybourne's proposal of marriage. You may never find a better match."

That might indeed be true, Lily thought, falling silent. Heath would make a better candidate for her husband than any man she had ever met. She had to concede they were well-matched, at least. If she were not so adamantly set against marriage. . . .

"In all seriousness," Fanny continued, "I might make a similar observation about you. You seem to enjoy his lordship's company a great deal. Did you enjoy his love-making also?"

She did enjoy his company, greatly, Lily admitted to herself. And her enjoyment of his lovemaking was beyond question. She had never known such pleasure as Heath had made her feel. She couldn't deny, either, that she had relished the closeness she had known with him tonight. The tenderness. The sharing.

She had felt a sense of feminine power as well. Heath was not the kind of lover to dominate or command or take selfishly. Instead, he had led her to experience the kind of enthralling fulfillment she knew few women ever experienced.

He had treated her as fully his equal even as he tutored her untried body. He had taught her the pleasure of giving someone else pleasure. The joy of surrendering to him as a woman, of meeting his passion with her own. She no longer feared his tenderness, Lily realized—which should have been a warning in itself. . . .

Again Fanny broke into her silent reflections. "Having Claybourne for your husband could satisfy more than your physical desires, Lily. You could have a good future with him. Trust me, you don't want to find yourself all alone in your old age."

It was the same argument Winifred had made recently, Lily remembered.

"Can you honestly say," Fanny pressed, "that you are completely happy as you are now?"

She wasn't *unhappy*, at least. There were times when she felt a little . . . empty. Lily frowned. Did she truly feel empty? No, of course not. She led a very fulfilling life, even if she *had* been lonely without her sisters during these past weeks since coming to London.

"I am perfectly content to remain single," she finally said.

Fanny sighed. "Well, then you should take care not to become too close to Lord Claybourne. Passion can lead to love, Lily. If you don't want to risk losing your heart, you would do best to break off all intimacy with him."

Lily's frown deepened. "I may not have a choice. He is very close to winning our game, and if he does, I agreed to allow him a formal courtship."

"Just because you are required to share his company

doesn't mean you must share his bed. It would be a grave mistake to continue."

No doubt Fanny was right, Lily acknowledged. If she continued as Heath's lover, she risked surrendering her heart to him. And it could prove disastrous if she were to fall in love. For then she might actually agree to marry him, and she would be trapped in wedlock with no way of escape, just as her mother had been.

She knew how seductive Heath's powers of persuasion could be. How captivating his allure. No doubt it had been unwise of her to make love to him tonight—

"At least promise me you will give up this fool notion of becoming his mistress," Fanny urged.

Lily nodded slowly. "Very well," she said, realizing the wisdom of that advice. "I promise."

She would end her affair with Heath before it had even begun, even if just now her heart and body yearned to do otherwise.

Chapter Sixteen

✤

You were right to warn me, Fanny. Intimacy with him is far too dangerous. I must put an end to our affair before it is too late.

—Lily to Fanny

Since Heath refused to disclose the intended destination of their drive the following afternoon, Lily's first indication was the cries of gulls and the scents of brine and fish. And when she peered out the carriage window, she could see the River Thames.

He had brought her to the London docks, she realized to her surprise and puzzlement.

His silence continued until the carriage halted on the quay before a large, two-masted brigantine.

"Are you planning on taking a voyage?" Lily asked as he handed her down.

"Not immediately, no," Heath replied cryptically.

The day was overcast but pleasant, and a light breeze fluttered her veil and pelisse as he escorted her up the brigantine's gangplank. The ship seemed to be deserted—or at least Lily spied no one on board.

"Where is the crew?"

"They have been dismissed for the afternoon. We are alone except for a pair of sentries. Come, let us go belowdecks."

Highly curious, Lily followed Heath across the gleaming oaken deck to a hatch and descended a ladder to a narrow corridor. Moving forward, he led her into what looked to be a passenger cabin that boasted rather rich appointments. Polished brass and mahogany adorned the bulkheads, while a luxurious brocade counterpane covered the spacious berth. And in the filmy light flooding through the open portholes, she could see a map spread upon the small table that stood in the center of the cabin.

When Heath shut the door behind her, Lily lifted her veil and turned to face him, one eyebrow raised. "Do you mean to keep me on tenterhooks forever, or will you tell me why you have brought me here?"

"I wanted to show you the ship, since it is my gift to you."

Lily blinked. "You want to give me a ship?"

Crossing to the small writing desk in one corner, he opened a drawer and pulled out a thick sheet of parchment. "This is the deed of sale, Lily. The final transactions were made two days ago. You can see that ownership is in your name."

When he handed her the deed, she studied it distractedly, realizing that her name was indeed recorded as owner. But two days ago? If that was so, Heath had to have begun the purchase proceedings some time before that, possibly even at the start of their game. It was hard to believe he had gone to such lengths. . . .

"A *ship*?" she repeated, looking back up at him. "A suitor normally gives small gifts such as books or flowers. This is far too costly and extravagant."

His smile was indulgent. "Actually the *Zephyr* was not overly costly. I purchased her for a good price, since I have connections in the shipping industry. I believe I mentioned that I've funded several scientific explorations? The *Zephyr* was built last year but has taken her maiden voyage and proved herself seaworthy."

Lily's own mouth curved wryly. "Whatever the price, it is still inappropriate, Heath. But of course, expense makes no difference to you. You know very well this will likely put you over the total points needed to win our game."

"I am not doing this to win our game, angel."

"No? Then why?"

"To show you that I understand your need for independence. You told me that you have always aspired to go adventuring. This is your chance."

When Lily merely gaped at him, Heath added casually, "I am an adventurer at heart, just as you are, so I sympathize with your need for freedom. Now with a ship of your own you can sail nearly anywhere. You can travel the world and explore to your heart's content, as you always dreamed of doing."

Feeling a little dazed, Lily searched his face, her brow furrowed.

"You said you wanted a life of adventure," Heath prodded when she remained silent.

"I did at one time," she admitted. "But not now. I gave up that dream when I came to London."

"You gave it up?"

Lily nodded. "I realized I must make a choice. I will no longer have the means to afford travel since I plan to spend my modest fortune on my new cause, helping needy women avoid a life of prostitution. In fact, I am thinking of starting a home for poor women and unwed mothers. I hope to better their lives if I can, and improve their sad conditions so they won't be trapped in lives they abhor. Even if our boarders no longer need my help now, there are many destitute and desperate women who do."

"I see," Heath responded, regarding her solemnly. "But you needn't give up your dream of adventure, Lily. As my wife, you can both see the world and help needy women. It is one of the prime advantages of wedding me."

Lily's laugh was strained. "But the disadvantages are rather significant. I would have to wed you first."

Heath shook his head. "Wedding me is not a condition of accepting my gift. Naturally I would like to accompany you on your voyages, but that is your choice."

She held up the deed. "What is this then, a bribe to persuade me to accept your proposal?"

"No. It is just as I said. I am offering you the means to fulfill your dream. Granted, I would also like you to see that our life together could be a grand adventure. And for you to realize that your fears about maintaining your independence after our marriage are unfounded. As my wife, you wouldn't be under the thumb of a dictatorial husband. You could live your life very much as you choose."

She hesitated a long moment, torn by conflicting emotions. "You know I cannot accept something so outrageously expensive. It would make me too indebted to you."

Heath shrugged. "The decision is entirely up to you, sweeting. You can sell the *Zephyr* and donate the proceeds to one of Miss Blanchard's charities if you wish. Or use it to start your home for unfortunate women."

Lily swallowed, feeling that odd little ache in her

throat again. She was greatly touched by his generosity. And dismayed as well.

Heath understood her yearning. Before becoming involved with the women at the boardinghouse, traveling the world had been her deepest desire. She still longed for adventure, even though an even greater desire had supplanted it in her heart. And his offer was so very tempting.

As if reading her thoughts, Heath took her hand and led her to the table where a map of the world was spread out. With a sweeping gesture, he indicated the various continents and oceans. "Where would you go first if you could?"

Reluctantly Lily glanced down at the map. France lay there beckoning. And Italy. And Spain. And the Alps. And countless other places she longed to see. During the many years of wars with Napoleon's armies, those countries had been far too dangerous for visitors, but now the wars were over. . . .

"I could take you there," Heath murmured, his low tone all too beguiling.

Wistfully, Lily trailed her forefinger over the map, letting her touch linger on the Mediterranean. In her mind's eye she could picture the splendid beauty she had only read about. Azure seas. Dazzling sunlight. Pristine beaches. Palm trees gently waving in the warm breeze.

"Thank you, but no," she finally said with a regretful sigh.

When she handed the deed back to Heath, he merely laid it on the table. Then he reached up to untie the strings of her bonnet, removing it and her veil.

Lily gave him a quizzical look. "Heath . . . what are you doing?"

"I am undressing you."

She froze. "I thought you said you wouldn't make love to me again."

He gave her a lazy smile as he made short work of the pins holding her coiffure in place. "I changed my mind."

A small thrill ran through her. "But you don't want to risk making me *enceinte*."

"True." From an inner pocket of his coat he withdrew a small pouch that Lily recognized. It held the sponges Peg had given her.

"I kept this from last night," Heath informed her.

Her heart began racing. "Does this mean you have reconsidered allowing me to become your mistress?"

"No, but you are welcome to be my mistress as well as my wife. You can be as passionate and wild as you want—and respectable at the same time."

"Heath . . ." she began in protest, but he took her face in his hands and kissed her once, slowly. The tender gesture left her spellbound.

"I mean to take you on a map of the world, Lily. Surely you can comprehend the symbolism."

She couldn't respond; her throat was suddenly too dry.

His fingers threaded in her hair, arranging the tresses to his satisfaction, so that they flowed over her shoulders.

"I intend to show you what our marriage could be like," he murmured. "How pleasurable it could be."

He stood there waiting for her decision, his golden gaze intimate, knowing, caring. The ache of longing spread to Lily's chest. She had known Heath had an ulterior motive for bringing her here. She also knew she shouldn't dare make love to him again. Fanny was right;

she had to end their intimacy before she did something so foolish as fall in love. Heath was becoming more irresistible each day, and the danger had only increased the moment he brought her on board the ship to show her his amazing gift.

Fighting her desire, Lily took a step back. "I don't think it would be wise of me to let you."

He stepped closer. "When have you ever let wisdom dictate your actions? You want me, Lily. Just as I want you."

That was certainly true. She needed only to look at Heath and her body responded. Already moisture had pooled between her thighs.

And then he kissed her and she forgot to breathe. Lily pressed her own hands against his chest, struggling for willpower, yet his arousal tempted her, vanquishing the voices of reason clamoring in the back of her mind.

Perhaps she could have him once more, Lily told herself. Just one last time. And then never again . . .

As if sensing her struggle, Heath tightened his embrace, his lips claiming and wooing. Giving a small sigh of defeat, Lily returned his kiss helplessly.

For a time, he seemed satisfied with her response, but after another few moments he broke off and began silently to undress her. His fingers expertly unfastened the hooks of her gown and removed it and her undergarments—her corset and chemise, her slippers and stockings—until she was bared completely to his gaze.

"It always amazes me, how beautiful you are," he said, his voice low and husky.

Lily felt herself flushing with warmth at his intent perusal, and she was glad when Heath finally began to shed his own clothing.

When at last he was naked, she drank in the beauty of his finely honed, athletic body. His rigid manhood jutted out from his loins, the length of him proud and hard. Lily felt her own loins clench painfully.

When she met his wantonly beautiful gaze, a tangible desire shimmered between them, filling the very air.

Heath's eyes had darkened, she saw as he moved toward her and stopped barely a few inches away. Her heart thudded erratically, beating a wild pulse in her throat. With his body so very close, she could feel the heat of him.

He drew a line down the silky hollow between her breasts, then feathered the tips with the backs of his fingers, making her gasp at the sparks he kindled in her so effortlessly.

"Feel how hard your nipples have grown."

She couldn't help but feel it. Her nipples had instantly tightened, betraying her arousal, while her breasts felt heavy and swollen.

But she wanted to touch him, too. Lily reached up to caress Heath's chest. His skin was hot and smooth, the sinewed muscles rippling beneath her fingertips. Then he took over again, gathering her against him until her breasts nestled against the broad wall of his chest, her stomach against his hard flat one. The warm, velvet pressure of his erection sent a rush of hunger through her, kindling a heavy ache deep in her lower body.

Her breath faltering, Lily made no protest when Heath lifted her up and set her on the table facing him. And she yielded willingly when he laid her back upon the surface.

The map was beneath her, and the parchment felt cool

and rough against her skin. Yet Heath's gaze was hot and very male as he surveyed her nakedness.

Nervously Lily wet her lips. She was lying there wantonly exposed to his brazen scrutiny. The heat of his gaze as he looked at her made her heart race wildly— and so did his warning:

"I mean to arouse you, Lily. I'll make you so frantic with pleasure, you can't bear it."

He started with his hands. Stepping between her parted legs, he reached up to cup her breasts, molding their softness, teasing the nipples that had pebbled into jutting peaks.

Lily sighed at the sweet spasm of desire that arrowed down to her loins, deep in her center. When his hands moved over her body, his palms skimming lightly, she found herself arching against his caresses, seeking more of the delicious pleasure he was arousing in her. Everywhere he touched, her skin seemed to burn.

She was restless and feverish by the time Heath brought his mouth down to hers. His tongue delved deep inside, exploring, while his hands stimulated her breasts, gently kneading, his thumbs stroking the sensitive buds.

His taste, his scent, his touch filled her senses. Lily trembled at the feel of him . . . the eroticism of his kisses, the warmth and strength of his hands . . . the hard length of his body pinning her to the table . . . the thick rod of his straining arousal teasing her throbbing, feminine warmth.

She gave a helpless moan as an aching tightness coiled inside her. All she could think about was how Heath's splendid arousal would fill her.

Another sensual shiver rippled through her when his

mouth left hers to trail down her throat. Palming her breasts so they were mounded in his hands, he covered a nipple with his hot tongue, laving the sensitive tip, drawing it against his teeth.

When she whimpered, Heath lifted his head briefly. "Do you want me to suckle you, sweeting?"

"Yes," Lily rasped, her fingers clutching in his silky hair. Anything to bring his mouth back to her breasts.

To her immense relief and gratification, Heath obliged, taking one of her aching nipples and sucking it into the hot wet haven of his mouth.

A frisson of fiery sensation sparked inside her as he suckled her. His mouth was a searing flame upon her bare, aching breasts, while his hands explored her with the same bold seductiveness.

Lily shuddered at the tumult assaulting her. Heat waves spread like velvet shimmers throughout her body until she felt light-headed and liquid with arousal.

Moments later she felt his hand move between her legs. He cupped her woman's mound, his touch sexually possessive, and dipped lower to find the wetness there. Then brushing the point of her pleasure with his thumb, he slid a long finger deep inside her, into the slick, steamy heat of her.

Anticipation screamed through her senses as another streak of fire ignited deep and low inside her.

"Heath, please . . ."

She could feel the rush of her own blood, could feel the tremors shivering through her.

"As you wish, love."

His hands parted her legs farther and slowly smoothed up the insides of her naked thighs. Holding them spread wide, he bent down to her belly. Her pulse jumped in a frenzied dance as his lips moved lower, seeking and finding the very core of her.

At the first touch of his mouth, she gave another whimper.

"Yes, sweet angel, let me hear you."

His voice had become a hoarse murmur, but shortly he fell silent in order to attend her, his tongue rimming the sleek cleft of her femininity and finding the tiny bud hidden there.

Lily gasped even as she put both hands in his hair to hold his face between her burning thighs. His palms continued molding the ripe swells of her breasts as his hot mouth worked its enchanting spell on her sex. Scalding hot, his tongue stroked her, every long flick sending shafts of pleasure spiraling through her, increasing her already intense arousal.

When his lips closed over the bud, sucking in a kiss, the sensation rocked her. Yet Heath went on laving her slowly, savoring, teasing, as if he were engaged in a sensory feast.

Lily clenched her teeth against the delicious torment yet held his head in place with two tight fists as his sinful mouth caressed her in a devastating assault on her senses.

A heartbeat later, his tongue slid inside her. Her breath caught on a sob, and she raised her hips, desperately arching against his ravishing mouth.

His mouth wasn't enough, though. She wanted them joined, wanted to have him deep within her. She needed—*craved*—an end to the savage longing Heath had created in her.

Her hands were actually shaking when she tugged on

his hair, urging him higher. At her silent plea, he raised his head.

"Now, Heath . . . take me now."

A faint smile wreathed his lips as he made use of the pouch's contents and slid a brandy-soaked sponge inside her.

A sigh rasped from Lily's throat as he positioned himself between her thighs once more, his arms braced on either side of her, his hardness a hot brand against her center. Lily could only think of the enchantment to come, how it would feel to have that swollen length thrusting inside her, filling her. She could feel the heat of his rigid flesh probing her soft folds. . . .

To her dismay, Heath hesitated, remaining poised above her, his gaze smoldering as it played over her face. His eyes had taken on a slumberous look, the golden depths darkening into something both primitive and powerful.

He continued looking deeply into her eyes as he slid forward, entering her slowly, gliding into her yielding, wet flesh. Lily gasped at the feel of him, huge and hot and urgent, stretching her open. But there was no pain. Only the promise of great pleasure.

Her breath streamed out in a shaky exhalation at the exquisite feeling of being filled by him, by his throbbing heat. When he drove forward all the way, locking them together, she felt deeply, thoroughly possessed.

Still holding her gaze, Heath lowered himself to cover her with his hard body. His hands cupped her breasts, erotically kneading as he began moving inside her.

When he withdrew only to thrust even more deeply, the intense pleasure made them both shudder.

Lily's heart wrenched with exultation at Heath's ardent response . . . the awed expression that flashed in his eyes as he claimed her. The womanly part of her was thrilled by the depth of his need, but then her own powerful need took control of her body.

She rocked against him with desperate yearning, her inner muscles tightening at the white heat scalding her. Her breathing grew erratic and ragged as his hard, straining form moved against her, branding her with his desire.

Her whimpers turned to moans as her own hips began moving in a rhythm that was ancient, mindless, elemental. She could hear Heath whispering praise for her passion all the while. He was more demanding now, plunging inside her, sending her into a frenzy of need. She felt frantic, unable to get enough of him.

Lily tossed her head wildly, her helpless cries spilling from her throat and filling the hush of the cabin.

Even so, the shattering, searing explosion caught her by surprise. With a scream, she sank her teeth into the raw silk of his bare shoulder as ecstasy ripped through her.

Heath followed right behind. His head thrown back, his neck corded, he drove into her one final time. A hoarse groan burst from him as his climax erupted in a powerful stream.

Lily absorbed his fierceness, her body clenching again and again around him as the firestorm took them both.

In the aftermath, Heath collapsed upon her, his breath as tortured as hers. They clung to each other bonelessly as the fire slowly receded.

The last shimmers of passion were still glowing inside Lily when Heath finally lifted his head. He looked as jolted as she felt, his eyes dazed yet tender as he surveyed her flushed face, her swollen lips.

"Did I hurt you?" he rasped.

"No," she said hoarsely, offering him a dreamy smile. "Not in the least."

"Good." His arms tightened about her for a moment, crushing her naked breasts to his chest. Then keeping her legs wrapped around his hips, Heath lifted her up and carried her to the bunk, where he laid her down.

Searing tenderness filled him as he stretched out beside Lily's warm supple body and drew her close. He was still breathing hard after his powerful climax, still shaken by what had just happened between them.

No woman had ever demolished his sense of reality as Lily did. When he had come inside her and felt her shatter around him, he had splintered in a thousand fragments.

And Lily had experienced their passion as intensely as he did, Heath was certain. She had been pure desire, uninhibited and wild.

Hearing her soft sigh, he held her closer. This was what he craved, he thought, his fingers twining in the dark chestnut strands of her hair. Lily warm and weak from his lovemaking, clinging to him, her heartbeat as uneven as his.

A fierce joy engulfed his heart at the memory of how incredible it felt to be buried inside her. How right it seemed. The strength of his response still startled him.

This was new to him, though, this overpowering need to be with one woman. He had never wanted anyone the way he did Lily.

But then he'd been slightly off kilter since the first moment of meeting her.

And now? Heath wondered. He had to acknowledge that Lily mattered to him in a different way than any woman ever had. She was everything he wanted, everything he desired.

Curious how he'd never thought he needed anyone before Lily. But the sense of completion she gave him only made him realize what he had been missing all this time.

It was not only being with her, sharing her life, that could fulfill him, either. He wanted to be as intense and passionate about life's endeavors as she was.

A quiet smile touched his mouth as he recognized the maze of emotions running through him: Possessiveness and tenderness. Awe. The need to cherish her always. Love.

He was in love with Lily, Heath admitted, marveling at the realization. The feeling had been stealing over him for days now. His pursuit of her might have started as a challenge, but he had fallen hard for her.

And winning her hand in marriage was no longer a game to him.

His smile faded as reality reared its taunting head. He considered Lily his wife now, yet she continued to fight him tooth and nail. Somehow he would have to make her accept the inevitability of their marriage.

He would redouble his efforts to woo her, Heath promised himself. It was now imperative that he make Lily fall in love with him.

She wasn't willing to give him her heart yet, he knew. Yet a moment ago when he'd looked deeply into her eyes, he had caught a fleeting glimpse of something hopeful, something infinitely fragile in the dark depths.

But then passion had taken over and rendered them both mindless with pleasure.

One thing was certain, however, he swore as he wrapped her more tightly in his arms.

He wasn't going to let her go.

Ever.

Chapter Seventeen

❧

It frightens me that he has won the game, since he now has three more months to court me. How can I possibly resist him for so long?

—Lily to Fanny

As expected, that evening when Lily confessed to Fleur and Chantel about Heath's latest gift, they were not only delighted but impressed by his romantic gesture. How many suitors gave their sweethearts a ship?

The courtesans happily awarded Lord Claybourne another point, bringing his total to ten, and proclaimed him the winner of the game, which sent a surge of panic flooding through Lily. The thought of Heath courting her for three more full months alarmed her, since she couldn't trust herself to be able to resist him for so long.

The past fortnight had proven how vulnerable she was in the face of his persistent pursuit. No matter how determined she was to keep her heart's defenses intact, Lily feared she would eventually lose the battle.

She did *not* want to fall in love with Heath and be tempted to accept his marriage proposal.

Somehow, despite his victory in the game, she had to convince him that she didn't desire him either as a suitor or lover or husband, Lily reflected, trying to calm herself.

Meanwhile she would have to keep him at arm's

length. Most certainly she couldn't risk being alone with him ever again. She knew exactly where such intimacy would lead—as today's encounter on board his ship had decidedly proven.

Yet she was honor bound to share his company for part of each day, starting tomorrow evening at the dinner Marcus was holding for Roslyn and her duke.

In dire need of assistance, Lily waylaid Basil directly after supper and begged him to escort her to the dinner the next evening.

Regrettably, Basil looked at her as if she had gone daft. "You know I don't care for fancy dinners and such. And wedding celebrations are the worst."

"Yes, I know," Lily agreed, "but I don't want to be alone with Lord Claybourne."

"Why not?"

"Because I might do something I would forever regret. Please, Basil, you have to help me," Lily implored. "It won't be too difficult. All you need do is stay by my side for the evening."

Basil eyed her the same way he'd done when they were children and she had led him into some risky escapade, before he finally emitted a long-suffering sigh. "Very well, but you owe me yet another favor, Lily."

"Yes, of course, whatever you ask. You are a true gentleman."

She kissed Basil's cheek in gratitude, overlooking his flush as she turned away and headed for the writing desk in the parlor. She had to send a note to Marcus informing him to expect an additional guest at his dinner. And she had to review her strategy to keep Heath at a distance.

Tomorrow evening, Lily vowed, she would ignore his

presence as much as possible and behave with total aloofness. If she was required by politeness to respond to him, she would be perfectly bland and boring. She would not smile or laugh, and she would certainly not allow Heath to provoke her as he was so fond of doing.

Even so, she dreaded the coming encounter. Basil would be her only ally, for she couldn't count on her sisters to take her side when it came to love and matrimony. Not when they were so much in love themselves. Lily still planned to stay the night at Marcus's town house after the dinner so that she could be with her sisters, and so that the next morning she and Arabella could help Roslyn dress for her wedding day.

Lily spent Monday afternoon packing a valise— including the gowns she would wear to the dinner and the wedding—and was ready at five o'clock when Marcus's carriage came to collect her.

Roslyn and Arabella had arrived just ahead of her, and Lily was glad that the bustle of settling into their rooms and having a sisterly coze precluded her dwelling much on Heath.

Moreover, she didn't want to say or do anything to spoil Roslyn's happiness. Roslyn was positively glowing with joy, which made her delicate beauty seem almost incandescent. Thus, Lily prevaricated when questioned about her own welfare, not wanting to mention her courtship troubles. Whenever the conversation veered too close to Lord Claybourne, she steered it away again.

Fortunately Basil arrived early for the dinner in a hired hack. Having already dressed, Lily was there to welcome him and take him into the drawing room, where the company would gather before dinner. So she had time to remind Basil of his promise to remain by her side throughout the evening.

When Arabella and Marcus joined them, followed by Roslyn and Arden, Lily introduced Basil to the two noblemen, explaining that Mr. Eddowes was an old family friend. And she chimed in occasionally when Arabella and Roslyn reminisced with Basil about their childhood days together in Hampshire.

Lady Freemantle appeared shortly after that. Quickly, Lily led Basil across the drawing room to admire a portrait by Gainsborough so she wouldn't have to endure Winifred's vexing machinations. Even so, she couldn't help feeling agitated as she waited for a certain handsome marquess to arrive.

She sensed his presence the moment he walked in. Heath's broad-shouldered form seemed to fill the drawing room, while his magnetism was a powerful lure for all her feminine sensibilities. And when Lily locked gazes with him across the way, the hint of a smile he sent her held an intimacy that made her feel as if they were the only two people in all the world.

She found it nearly impossible to look away, and just as difficult to keep her greeting to a mere nod when Heath approached her. But she responded in monosyllables when he spoke to her. And as soon as possible, she turned her attention to the other guests, dragging Basil with her.

She spent the next ten minutes quizzing the bridegroom about his plans to visit Arden Castle in Kent for the first leg of his wedding journey with his bride. Afterward the duke would take Roslyn to Paris and then travel on to Brittany to visit the former Lady Loring, where Victoria had settled with her new French husband. Lily was constantly aware of Heath, however, and where he was at any given moment.

Then Marcus's sister, Lady Eleanor Pierce, arrived, along with her elderly aunt, Lady Beldon. The vivacious raven-haired beauty kissed Marcus affectionately on the cheek before she sought out Heath and gave him the same fond salutation.

It was absurd to feel a sharp twinge of jealousy at the sweet gesture, Lily knew, yet she couldn't help it. Especially when Lady Eleanor stood there laughing delightedly up at Heath.

Recalling her plan, Lily focused her attention on Basil, pretending to hang on his every word. It dismayed her a little, therefore, when Lady Eleanor brought Heath over to join them and then somehow managed to draw Basil aside, leaving Lily alone with the very man she had earnestly hoped to avoid.

"Will you permit me to take you in to dinner?" was Heath's first remark.

"That is kind of you, my lord," Lily said in an offhand manner, "but Basil has already offered. You and I won't be seated together at dinner, either."

"I suppose you made certain of the seating arrangements?"

"Well . . . yes."

"Then I will settle for sitting beside you during the wedding tomorrow."

"I have promised to sit beside Basil tomorrow," Lily hastened to say.

Heath arched an eyebrow. "You have two sides, do you not? I will sit on your right, and he may have the left. I believe I have earned the privilege. Fleur informs me that they have deemed me the winner of our game."

"Yes, they have," Lily said despondently.

"It will be our first time to be seen in public together. Somehow it seems fitting that we will be attending a wedding together."

"We will not be attending *together*," she pointed out. "I will be riding to the church with my sisters."

"As you did for your eldest sister's wedding. I remember the moment you arrived. You captured my attention with your laughter." Heath smiled as though it was a pleasurable memory.

"Oh? I don't particularly recall meeting *you* then," Lily lied.

His eyes sparkled with humor. "You wound me, darling. Am I really so forgettable?"

He was no such thing, she thought, trying to ignore the devilish charm dancing in his eyes.

"You cannot say you have forgotten our first kiss in the barn loft, or any of the kisses that followed."

"My lord!" Lily hissed in a repressive undertone, glancing around to see if he had been overheard.

"Are we back to 'my lord' now? What have I done to earn such disdain?"

"You can hardly object to the term," she retorted. "You know that 'my lord' is the proper form of address when we are in polite company."

"I can accept that as long as you call me by my given name in private."

Somewhat agitated, Lily looked away, searching for Basil.

"Do you expect Eddowes to come to your rescue?" Heath asked curiously. "What is he now, your protector?"

"Of a sort," Lily replied, aware of the desperation in her thinking.

"You seem very fond of him."

"I am indeed. We have known each other since we were in leading strings."

Heath reached up to touch her chin, bringing her gaze back to his. "I think you have grown a little fond of me, too, Lily."

She couldn't issue an honest denial, no matter how much she wanted to. "Against my better judgment," Lily murmured, finally looking straight at him. "But simply because I hold you in affection doesn't mean I wish to marry you or spend the rest of my life with you."

"*Do* you hold me in affection, sweeting?" Heath asked, his tone a tender tease.

Lily pressed her lips together. "That was a slip of the tongue. I consider you a friend, nothing more."

"I think we have gone far beyond mere friendship. I have been inside of you, remember?"

"Will you stop that!" Lily demanded in frustration.

Thankfully, she was spared from further provocation when Marcus's butler, Hobbs, appeared and announced that dinner was served.

Even more thankfully, Heath made no effort to approach her again that evening. Instead, he spent much of the time with Lady Eleanor—an unexpected turn of events that strangely unsettled Lily.

The image of them laughing together stayed with her as she tossed and turned in her solitary bed that night, no matter how much she tried not to think of Heath with the lively, lovely Lady Eleanor.

Lily woke late the following morning, weary and

bleary-eyed, but she made a concerted effort to be cheerful when she and Arabella gathered in Roslyn's bedchamber to help her bathe and dress. It was not too difficult since Roslyn's high spirits were infectious. Lily couldn't help but be sad, however, that she was losing her other sister.

Roslyn eventually noticed her melancholy and commented on it. "Lily, I know you would rather I didn't marry Drew, but I love him dearly. More than I thought it was possible to love anyone."

"That is quite obvious," Arabella interjected with a fond smile at Roslyn, "from the way you look at him. And he spent the entire evening gazing adoringly at you. It is frankly remarkable to see the elusive, cynical Duke of Arden wearing his heart on his sleeve for all to see."

"I don't object to you marrying him if you are happy, Rose," Lily said, feeling her throat ache with love for her sister.

"I *am* happy, truly. I can only wish you the same happiness, Lily, with a man as wonderful as Drew."

A wonderful man like Heath, Lily found herself thinking. *A man who was tender and generous and gentle and strong. . . .*

For a fleeting moment, Lily caught herself imagining that she was the one preparing for her wedding day just now, eager to become Heath's bride. Doubtless, it was her unsteady emotions making her harbor such foolish musings. She should know better.

With a deliberate effort she shrugged off her nonsensical reflections and managed a laugh. "Your idea of happiness and mine are quite different, Rose. I would not be happy as a wife. But I must say that I am highly envious of your trip to Paris and Brittany. That is kind of Arden to take you to see Mama."

"Indeed. But he realizes how much it means to me after we were estranged from her for so long." Roslyn shook her head. "We are on much better terms with Mama than Drew is with his mother. And I admit I am very glad that the duchess will be remaining here in London after our wedding."

Lily understood her sister's sentiment, since she'd heard how cold and haughty the Duchess of Arden was. "The duke told me last night that you mean to remain at Arden Castle for the first week of your wedding journey."

"Yes. Drew wants to have his family home to ourselves for a time, so he gave his mother an ultimatum— and she promised to make herself scarce for the duration of our visit to Kent."

Arabella nodded in sympathy. "And you won't have to endure the duchess's company much after you are wed."

"Fortunately not," Roslyn agreed. "We will be living here in London most of the year since Drew has so many obligations to Parliament and the government."

"Well," Arabella interrupted briskly, "we had best stop chatting and get you dressed, or you will be late. You don't want to keep your groom waiting at the altar for long. Lily, will you ring for Nan so she can arrange Roslyn's hair? We could do it ourselves, as we did for years, but with so much of the ton sure to be in attendance, she must look worthy of being a duke's bride."

A large number of the ton was indeed present at St. George's church in Hanover Square, Lily saw when they arrived. And most of those wedding guests were amazed to see the illustrious Duke of Arden willingly don the shackles of matrimony to marry Miss Roslyn Loring, whose family had such a scandalous past.

The baroque splendor of the church provided a regal setting for a society wedding. With her elegant golden beauty, Roslyn made the loveliest bride imaginable, and Arden seemed her ideal match with his fair hair and strikingly handsome features. Indeed, their union seemed like the perfect ending to a fairy tale.

Lily spent much of the lengthy ceremony trying to calm her unsettled nerves. She was much too aware of Heath sitting beside her, and too aware of how his proximity would look to the ton, rousing speculation that there would soon be a third wedding in the Loring family.

She spoke to Heath as little as possible, not only because she wanted to discourage his suit but because of the tightness in her throat. When at last the ceremony ended and Lily said her final farewells to the bride and groom, the threatening sting of tears only increased.

Mutely she accompanied the other guests as they left the church to gather on the massive Corinthian portico and see off the newlywedded couple in the duke's coach, which was adorned with white roses and satin ribbons and pulled by a team of six white horses wearing plumed headdresses.

Heath stood beside Lily, watching as the carriage drove away. Basil had disappeared somewhere in the crowd, although she hadn't noticed his absence until this moment. Fanny was speaking to Arabella while waiting for her own carriage.

Glancing up at Heath, Lily swallowed against the

ache. "Well," she murmured, her voice husky with unshed tears, "I believe I have fulfilled my obligation to you for today, my lord—spending time in your company."

He merely looked at her for a long moment. Then to her startlement, he took her elbow and escorted her back inside the church.

Perplexed, Lily went along reluctantly as he led her down a maze of corridors. When they reached a deserted chamber that appeared to be a clerical office, Heath shut them inside, then turned to face her.

"That is the problem between us, isn't it Lily? You see me merely as an obligation."

She regarded Heath uncertainly, wondering what his objective was in bringing her here. "Since you asked . . . yes. I am obliged to endure your formal courtship since you won the game. Yet I agreed to the terms, so I am prepared to honor my word."

"But you would rather be drowned in boiling oil."

"Well, to be quite candid—"

His mouth curled with irony. "Are you ever otherwise?"

"To be honest, Heath," Lily began again, trying to keep the desperation out of her voice, "your courting me continues to be pointless. I will never wed you. And I don't believe you truly want to wed me."

"You are gravely mistaken, Lily." His searching eyes were vibrantly intense, disturbingly aware. "I want to wed you more than ever . . . because I have fallen in love with you."

Lily drew in a sharp breath, certain she hadn't heard him correctly. "You cannot mean that."

"Of course I can. I love you, Lily. Rather intensely, in fact."

The desperation she felt increased to panic. How could she keep her heart safe when he was saying such tender things to her?

"You do not love me, Heath! You couldn't possibly. You have known me for barely two weeks."

"It has been much longer since we first met. And even then I knew you were very special. Someone who might prove to be my ideal match."

"But love?" Lily shook her head earnestly. She wouldn't believe that Heath really loved her. She couldn't let herself. "I just cannot credit it."

His bright eyes held hers, never wavering. "Do you want to know why I fell in love with you, sweetheart? Because you are vibrant and passionate and full of life. You make *me* feel alive. You make me feel joyous and exhilarated. With you I look forward to each new day as an adventure. *That* is why I love you."

He gave a soft laugh. "I have been looking for you my entire life, Lily, even though I never realized it. And once I found you, I had no choice but to love you."

At his confession, Lily felt a helpless dismay wash over her. She didn't dare listen to Heath's beguiling words. They were too seductive. Too dangerous. They made her heart too vulnerable.

She had to return their argument to a logical footing at once, she thought frantically.

"You want me as your wife because you want heirs," she insisted.

"No, Lily. I once thought I could be satisfied with a marriage of convenience because we are compatible in so many ways. But I was wrong. To be happy, I need a real marriage with you. I want a family with you, children. A future. But most of all I want your love. I am not asking for that now. I think in time it will come. But for now I will be satisfied if you simply give me a chance."

Stepping closer, Heath curled his hand against her cheek. "You fill a void in me I never knew existed, Lily. And I believe I can fill that same void in you. I could be a good husband to you."

Her gaze was caught helplessly in his as he stroked her cheek with his thumb. Lily wanted to protest. That fierce yearning was stirring inside her again, and she knew it would only lead to pain and heartache. . . .

When she determinedly managed to push away the tender feelings and draw back abruptly, Heath sighed and lowered his hand. "You will have to come to the same conclusion on your own, Lily. The decision to marry me must be yours, because you want to. Because you want to spend the rest of your life with me. Because you can't imagine any other choice. That is how I feel about you, Lily. I can't imagine living my life without you."

"And I cannot imagine living my life *with* you, Heath," she said rather desperately. "You know I plan to never marry."

"Because you fear being hurt." His eyes delved deeply, intently into hers. "I cannot guarantee that I will never hurt you. I can only swear that I will never betray you or abandon you. But you will have to take me on faith. I cannot make you trust me, any more than can I make you believe my feelings for you."

Clenching her fingers together, Lily retreated another several steps. "I don't believe you truly love me," she repeated fervently. "Noblemen of your ilk don't fall in love."

Faint amusement touched his mouth. "Try telling that to Marcus and Drew."

Knowing she was losing the debate, Lily groped for an even more desperate argument. "Even if you did fancy yourself in love with me, you cannot promise me fidelity forever. My father was disastrously unfaithful in his marriage, and you could be just like him. I couldn't trust that you would give up your myriad lovers for my sake."

Heath's gaze was intense, clear, and suddenly ruthlessly focused on hers. She could see he was struggling to keep his emotions in check, and his tone held a rough edge when he replied. "Even if you question my honor, you should have more confidence in your own abilities. Any man who can command all that fiery passion of yours in bed will likely never stray. Fidelity is one thing I can promise you."

Lily shook her head again. "It doesn't matter how many promises you make, Heath. I won't risk it."

His jaw hardening in frustration, he raked a hand through his hair. "Your cherished independence will be cold comfort when you are old and gray. You were not meant for spinsterhood."

She raised her chin stubbornly. "I was willing to be your mistress, but you turned me down out of hand."

"Because carnal pleasure is not enough for me. For you, either, I am sure of it. And that *is* something I can prove to you."

Her regard turned uneasy. "What do you mean?"

Closing the distance between them, he reached up to cup her left breast. Lily jumped at the unmistakable sizzle of lightning his touch engendered. As her nipple sprang to taut life, she drew back, shaken, and turned away in alarm, blindly reaching for the door.

She had grasped the handle when Heath wordlessly moved to stand behind her, drawing her back against his body. She felt the warmth of his thighs against the backs of her legs, even through their clothing.

His voice dropped to a rough murmur. "Shall I prove my claim, sweet Lily?"

"No, don't—"

"I think I should." He molded himself to her body, triggering a surge of heat deep inside her. "I could take you right here, you know . . . from behind, so that I wouldn't even have to see your face."

When he lifted her skirts, Lily went rigid, feeling the sudden kiss of cool air on her bare thighs, her exposed buttocks. She couldn't believe Heath was acting this outrageous way. It would be scandalous to make love in a church.

His wickedness shocked her, but his coldness shocked her even more. Yet she was powerless to pull away, and she remained mute as his hands slid softly over the globes of her buttocks, even when his knee eased her legs apart.

When his fingers trailed up her inner thigh to brush against her silky folds, though, Lily gasped, her stomach clenching as she felt those long, strong fingers caressing her. When he teased the bud of her sex, Lily gritted her teeth, fighting that part of herself that hungered for him. It was shameful, how much she wanted him.

Then he slowly slid a finger inside her and nearly buckled her knees. She pushed back against him helplessly, locking her jaw to hold back her moan of need, her hand gripping the doorknob as if her life depended on it.

Yet he was right, Lily realized in some distant part of her mind. Carnal pleasure was not enough. His touch was detached, passionless, calculating. Nothing like the tender lover she longed for.

His voice was just as remote when he spoke again. "I don't believe I will take you this way after all. You see, angel . . . if all I wanted was nameless, faceless sex, any woman would do."

Withdrawing his finger from her, Heath let her skirts fall. Lily shivered with disappointment and shame, but it appeared he wasn't done with her.

He kept his body pressed against hers while his lips found her ear. "I could make you scream with pleasure, Lily. But in the end, all that would be engaged are our bodies. It is your heart and mind I want. Your very soul."

A sharp ache escalated in her chest while absurd, ridiculous tears pricked at the back of her eyes. She bit her lip hard because she didn't want to cry, but Heath went on, his voice harsh and low.

"It is *you* I want, Lily," he repeated. "Not any other lover. Not any other woman. Not any other wife. But I intend to grant your wish. I am through chasing you and beating my head against the walls you've erected. Unless you agree to wed me, I intend to keep away from you."

His hands reaching up to lightly grasp her shoulders, he eased her away from the door and opened it, then stepped out into the corridor. But he glanced back over his shoulder at her, his eyes dark as night and bright as fire.

"What we have between us is unique and very rare,

Lily. Only a fool would throw it away. I never took you for a fool, but perhaps I was wrong."

He left her standing there, staring after him. He couldn't have unnerved her more if he'd shaken her. She felt dazed, dismayed, miserable.

Which was supremely foolish. Heath shouldn't have the power to hurt her. But he had walked away, Lily acknowledged, feeling the hot sting of tears behind her eyes.

Becoming aware of her weakness, she dashed furiously at the dampness. She wouldn't cry over a man as her mother had done so frequently. Indeed, there was no reason for her to cry. This was exactly what she had wanted, hoped for! For Heath to leave her entirely alone.

She had been right to refuse his offer of marriage; right to reject his dubious declarations of love. She couldn't deny that a sharp pain had settled in the pit of her stomach, but there would be far worse pain in store if she allowed herself to be drawn into loving him.

Wiping her eyes one last time, Lily took a shaky breath and left the room in search of Basil.

"Where the devil have you been?" he demanded when she found him outside on the portico. "You told me to remain beside you—"

"Never mind, will you please just take me home?"

His gaze narrowed. "What is wrong, Lily? Have you been *crying*?"

"Yes, because I am sad at losing my sister. But nothing is wrong. Indeed, everything is utterly perfect."

She kept telling herself that during the entire drive back to the boardinghouse, no matter that she couldn't make herself believe it for a single moment.

As soon as they entered, however, Lily was jarred from her emotional turmoil.

Something was wrong, she realized as Ellen came rushing up to her in agitation. Apparently the chambermaid had been watching for her arrival.

"Oh, Miss Loring, Miss Delee wants to see you right away!"

"What is the matter, Ellen?" Lily asked, somewhat alarmed.

"I don't know exactly, but I think it has to do with Miss Irwin."

"Where is Miss Delee?"

"In her sitting room upstairs."

"I will go to her at once," Lily said, turning away quickly.

She hurried up the stairs with Basil hard on her heels. When she reached the sitting room, she found Chantel wringing her hands and Fleur pacing the floor. Another distraught woman was seated on the sofa, her face splotched with tears.

Fanny's dresser, Joan Tait, Lily realized as she entered.

"Thank God you are here, Lily!" Chantel exclaimed, while Fleur's head snapped up.

"Where is Lord Claybourne, Lily?" Fleur demanded urgently. "We need him at once!"

"Why?" Lily asked in bewilderment, looking from Fleur to Chantel and back again. "What has happened?"

"That dastardly O'Rourke took Fanny, and we need Claybourne to rescue her!"

Chapter Eighteen

❧

For a nobleman Lord Claybourne is exceedingly fearless and daring, even heroic.

—Lily to Fanny

"He took Fanny?" Lily repeated, her stomach clenching with dread.

"Yes," Chantel replied hoarsely. "That devil abducted her in broad daylight. Tait saw it all."

Trying to control her alarm, Lily turned to Fanny's dresser. "Tell me exactly what happened. You saw Miss Irwin being abducted?"

Gulping back tears, Joan Tait nodded vigorously. "Yes. Just as Miss Irwin returned from the wedding a short while ago. Mr. O'Rourke's carriage was waiting on the street in front of the house—I saw him from an upstairs window when his coach door opened. Then two hulking footmen jumped out and pushed Miss Irwin inside, and the coach drove off right before my very eyes."

"She didn't go willingly?" Lily asked, wanting to be certain.

"No, Miss Loring. I heard her cry out for help."

Basil clenched his fists in fury. "That *bastard*. If he has harmed her, I swear I will kill him."

Lily felt a similar sentiment. Fear and fury warred inside her as she imagined what Mick O'Rourke might be doing to Fanny this very moment. "How long ago was this, Tait?"

"Perhaps twenty minutes. I came directly here—I didn't know where else to turn."

When the dresser started weeping again, Chantel patted her shoulder comfortingly. "You did exactly right. Lord Claybourne will help."

"I am not waiting for Claybourne," Basil declared, spinning on his heel and heading for the door.

"Basil, stop!" Lily exclaimed. "You cannot go off half-cocked. We need a plan."

"My plan is to find O'Rourke and cut out his liver."

Lily shook her head, thinking furiously. "They are right. Lord Claybourne can help us." Although she wasn't certain he would be *willing* to help her after their acrimonious parting barely an hour ago. But she knew Heath would be more capable of dealing with O'Rourke than she and Basil were.

Basil wasn't of the same mind, obviously. "*You* go fetch him, Lily. I am riding to O'Rourke's gaming hell to find Fanny."

"He won't be naive enough to take her there. Not when he knows that is the first place Fanny's friends will look for her."

"But that is the best place to start," Basil insisted. "You find Claybourne and meet me there. I mean to save Fanny from that devil's clutches," he growled as he stalked from the room.

Basil would likely head to the mews to fetch his horse, Lily conjectured, so it was up to her to find Heath—

"I need your carriage," she said quickly to Fleur.

Joan Tait lifted her head. "I have a hack waiting on the street, Miss Loring. It will be faster if you take it."

"Thank you, I will," Lily said before swiftly following after Basil.

She would go to Heath's home first, Lily decided as she hurried down the staircase. And if he wasn't there, she would search the gentlemen's clubs next. Or perhaps he might even be with Marcus, still celebrating after this morning's wedding.

Heath's mansion in Bedford Square, Lily discovered a short while later, was elegant and imposing. And the Claybourne butler was even more stately, looking down his haughty nose at her when she identified herself and asked to speak to the marquess.

Calling at a bachelor's establishment was rather wanton for a young lady, Lily knew, especially when she wore no veil to help disguise her features. But her urgent tone of voice must have made an impression on the august servant, or perhaps he recognized her name, for he admitted her at once and showed her to a sitting room while he excused himself to go in search of Lord Claybourne.

Heath appeared moments later, much to Lily's relief.

"Thank heavens," she murmured, aware of how glad she was to see him. He had taken off his coat and cravat but still wore his formal wedding attire.

His expression was quizzical at first, but it darkened as Lily quickly told him about Fanny's alleged abduction by O'Rourke.

"I warned him . . ." Heath said dangerously, a muscle pulsing in his jaw.

"Basil has gone to O'Rourke's club to try and discover her location, but it may be all for naught. Please, Heath, will you help us rescue Fanny?"

He looked impatient at her request. "Need you even ask?" Abruptly he turned and strode from the room.

"Where are you going?" Lily said, hurrying after him.

"To fetch some weapons."

"I have a hack waiting."

"Good. It will save me the trouble of having my own carriage harnessed. Go wait for me there, Lily."

Grateful that he hadn't hesitated, Lily obeyed and returned to the hack. In a very few moments, Heath appeared. He had donned his coat, although his cravat was still missing. And he carried two small cases that Lily suspected contained pistols, and one long case that looked familiar from her fencing lesson with him.

Behind him were two strapping footmen who climbed up on the rear perch of the hack.

"Reinforcements," Heath said brusquely as he joined Lily inside.

The small cases did indeed hold pairs of matching pistols, she saw when Heath opened them, but the longer one contained extremely sharp rapiers rather than the buttoned practice foils she had used with him for their bout.

During the drive to Bond Street, Heath carefully primed and loaded each of the guns. His jaw was set in anger, and he spoke little on the way.

Lily tried not to let his silence bother her. She couldn't let herself dwell on Heath's remoteness when she was so dreadfully worried about Fanny.

When the hack eventually slowed and came to a halt before a tall brick building that must be O'Rourke's gaming club, she bestirred herself to say, "I want to come with you."

Heath hesitated but then nodded grimly. "Very well, but you will let me take the lead."

They had barely descended from the carriage, however, when they heard shouts from the vicinity of the front entrance door. Lily's heart leapt to see Basil being thrown unceremoniously out of the gaming hell. He tumbled down the short flight of steps to land in a heap on the sidewalk, while the door slammed shut behind him.

Giving a gasp of alarm, Lily ran to him, but she wasn't required to help him up. Instead, Basil lunged to his feet, his fists clenched with rage as he glared at the entrance door. He was sporting a bruised eye and a bloody nose, and he was livid.

He would have rushed back into the club, but Heath clamped a calming hand on his shoulder, preventing him. "Hold there, Eddowes. Pistols can be far more persuasive than fists."

Upon seeing the loaded weapon Heath held, Basil let his shoulders sag. "Fanny isn't there, nor is O'Rourke. But his bloody bruisers wouldn't say where she was taken."

"Perhaps they will tell me," Heath replied, making for the door.

Lily followed immediately on his heels. Her friend's beating had lit the fire of anger inside her, and she was ready to strangle O'Rourke and his minions with her bare hands.

The door swung open the instant Heath knocked. The large, burly man standing there wore a fierce scowl and had raised his fists threateningly, as if he'd expected

Basil to return. But the sight of a pistol pointing directly at his chest made his eyes widen in alarm.

Glancing back at Lily, Heath withdrew a handkerchief from his coat pocket and handed it to her. "Why don't you accompany Mr. Eddowes to the carriage?" he advised. "I expect I won't be long."

Then with a lethal smile at the doorman, he gestured with the pistol. The servant backed away carefully, and Heath stepped inside, shutting the door quietly behind him.

Basil immediately started sputtering in outrage at being denied his revenge. Lily felt like doing the same, yet she wanted more to stop him from charging back inside and suffering even more damage to his battered face.

Telling herself she could trust Heath to handle the matter, she corralled Basil back inside the hack, then climbed in after him. Yet she was still worried for Heath. She hated to think of the danger he might be in, facing those brutes alone, even if he *was* armed.

For the next interminable five minutes, Lily kept peering out the carriage window while applying the handkerchief to stop her friend's nosebleed, alternating between fretting silently and trying to reassure Basil that Lord Claybourne would succeed in discovering where Fanny had been taken.

Her confidence was soon rewarded. When Heath appeared, he was unscathed. He gave directions to the driver and then settled inside across from Lily and Basil.

"I persuaded O'Rourke's lackeys to tell me where he might be found," Heath explained as the hack moved forward and picked up a rapid pace. "It appears he recently built a private residence in Marylebone, and yesterday sent several of his servants there to ready the house for habitation. He intended to be gone for the next several days."

Marylebone was a district just north of London, Lily knew, not too distant from Heath's own town house.

"So Fanny is likely being held there?" she asked.

"That seems a reasonable assumption."

"How do we rescue her?" Basil demanded.

Heath shifted his attention to the younger man. "I would rather you allow me to handle it."

Basil's jaw hardened. "No, my lord, I cannot do that. I could never forgive myself if Fanny came to harm while I stood idly by." His voice lowered to a rough whisper. "It is bad enough knowing that bastard could have brutalized her by now."

"If he has, he will pay for it," Heath said grimly. "But there is a possibility the dresser mistook what she saw for an abduction."

"A *slim* possibility," Lily muttered. "It is much more likely that O'Rourke is a true villain."

"I agree," Heath replied. "Which is why we will take adequate precautions. Reportedly the house is in a quiet neighborhood, so we will halt a distance down the street and proceed on foot. There is no need to alert O'Rourke to our arrival."

Basil scowled. "But you mean simply to knock on the front door?"

"That is the usual method of gaining entrance to a house," Heath said dryly. "Although I don't plan on knocking in this instance. I intend to walk in and take him by surprise."

"What if the door is locked?"

"Then I will break a window."

"You realize O'Rourke could have an army of bruisers guarding Fanny?" Lily warned.

"True," Heath responded. "So we will go in armed. I will approach the front and my two footmen will cover the other exits to cut off any escape routes."

Basil still looked skeptical. "I cannot believe you will just waltz up to the house as if you are paying an afternoon call."

Heath raised a quelling eyebrow. "Would you prefer that we burst in shooting? That could lead to hurting innocent bystanders, perhaps Fanny herself."

The wisdom of his argument prevailed with Lily, and even Basil eventually nodded his head slowly.

"As you wish, my lord, but I mean to help," he insisted.

"So do I," Lily seconded.

Heath gave a grimace as he regarded her for a long moment. "I have no doubt that you are daring and fearless, sweetheart, but I would rather you remain in the carriage. You could put yourself in danger—"

Her scoffing sound cut him off. "It is all very well for you to play the hero, but I cannot because I am a woman?"

"I don't want to see you hurt. The thought makes my blood run cold."

At his admission, Lily felt her defenses soften. Yet she wasn't swayed from her determination. "Heath, Fanny is my friend, and if she is in trouble, I mean to save her. I am not remaining behind like a useless ornament. Besides, you may need more than your two footmen to rescue her."

Raising his eyes briefly to the carriage ceiling, Heath

gave a sigh of resignation. "Very well, but you will do *exactly* as I say, both of you."

"Yes, of course," Lily said quickly, fearing he would change his mind. "And Basil will also." When Basil kept his lips shut, Lily prodded him with her elbow. "Say you will do as Lord Claybourne tells us."

"All right, I will!" Basil agreed under duress.

He lapsed into morose silence as Heath explained his plan, but Lily listened carefully to his every word, determined not to put Fanny in any more danger than she might already be in.

Lily's stomach was curled into knots by the time the carriage began to slow. They were traveling along a wide avenue, in a stylish and obviously wealthy neighborhood. Most of the houses were opulent mansions and had the look of newness about them.

When the hack halted, the driver jumped down to open the door and let his passengers out. "Number Twelve is just up ahead, yer lordship."

Lily's glance followed the coachman's pointing finger. The elegant terrace house he'd indicated was built of gleaming white stucco. The classical decoration and Corinthian columns proclaimed it to be a creation by John Nash, the architect who frequently designed houses and parks for the Prince Regent and other wealthy aristocrats.

Acknowledging the driver's information with a brusque nod, Heath handed loaded pistols to his two footmen and another to Basil, keeping the last for himself. Lily was armed with a gleaming rapier. When earlier she'd tried to protest Heath's choice, he had threatened to leave her with the carriage, saying she could defend herself better with a rapier than with a single shot pistol, and he didn't want to have to worry about protecting her if they encountered resistance.

Lily had had no choice but to promise to remain behind him at all times, where it was safer.

She waited as his servants and Basil moved off quietly, intent on sneaking around to the sides and rear of the house. Then stealthily she followed Heath to the front entrance.

To her great surprise, the front door proved to be unlocked. O'Rourke evidently was not expecting company so soon, if at all, Lily surmised.

She obeyed when Heath silently motioned for her to stay back and then slowly swung the door open. The entrance hall was deserted, she saw as she craned to see over his shoulder.

But no sooner had Heath stepped inside when a shout sounded from his left. Their intrusion had been spotted, Lily realized, for O'Rourke had indeed posted guards.

A muscular hulk of a man came charging down the corridor at Heath, his fists swinging, but Lily's attention was drawn upward, to the head of the staircase.

"Heath, up there!" she exclaimed an instant before a second brute aimed a pistol directly at Heath and fired.

Fear for him crowded in her throat, but Heath managed to leap back just in time to avoid being shot. The bullet whizzed past him to lodge harmlessly in the wall beside his head, to Lily's vast relief.

Heath's own aim was much more accurate. Discharging his pistol, he hit the bruiser who stood on the upper landing. The man gave a cry of pain and clutched his shoulder before sinking to his knees and tumbling down the stairs.

The blasts reverberating in her ears, Lily tightened her

grip on her rapier and pushed her way inside the entrance hall after Heath. By that time the brute on her left had nearly reached him. Heath braced for the impact, but the guard barreled into him.

Lily flinched as both men went crashing to the floor, Heath's empty pistol skittering across the parquet. When the brawny man rose to his knees, his powerful fists swinging at Heath's face, Heath rolled to one side and leapt to his feet. The guard did the same and charged full force—although this time his blows were countered as Heath met the assault with blows of his own in an effort to defend himself.

Gunpowder smoke stinging her eyes, Lily raised her rapier and surged forward, desperately wanting to help Heath if she could. But there was no opportunity to strike without endangering him; they were moving too fast.

It was alarming, having to watch the two men pummel each other in a savage struggle for physical domination.

The macabre dance showed no signs of ending. Both men were breathing hard as they punched and jabbed and weaved and fought. Then one mighty fist connected with Heath's cheekbone, snapping his head back and nearly lifting him off his feet.

Lily cried out, feeling as if the blow had struck *her*. Then strangely, time seemed to slow. She was sixteen again, stunned with fear as her father's fists assaulted her mother. She was unable to breathe, her heart pounding in horror.

But she was no longer that helpless girl. Shaking herself, Lily gave a fierce shout, this one filled with rage and fury as she lunged toward the guard, brandishing her rapier. Startled, he whipped his head around, searching for the threat.

The distraction gave Heath the time he needed to regain his footing. Muttering curses, he went on a fierce offensive, delivering an onslaught of rapid blows to the guard's face. A lucky one felled the brute to the floor, and he went down hard, grunting in pain.

It was then that Lily heard the explosive sound of a gunshot coming from somewhere at the back of the house. She froze for another instant, looking to Heath for instruction.

"Go!" he shouted to her as his opponent lunged to his feet with a bellow.

Lily obeyed. Heath still had to deal with the guard, but it looked as if he might win this fight while Basil might be in deep trouble, as might Fanny—

Fear for her friends urged Lily on as she raced down the hall toward the rear of the house. Even before she reached what looked to be a study, she heard the sounds of fighting.

Skidding to a halt, she took in the scene from the doorway. The stench of gunsmoke in the air suggested that Basil had shot at O'Rourke and missed, but then the two men had come to blows.

Basil once again was getting the worst of the contest, his fists flailing wildly at O'Rourke while Fanny watched in horror, one hand held over her mouth.

Before Lily could act, O'Rourke hit Basil's jaw hard, knocking him halfway across the room. When Basil careened into an oaken desk and slumped to the floor with a sharp cry, O'Rourke began dragging a struggling Fanny toward the open French doors.

A chill squeezing her ribs, Lily rushed into the room,

shouting for him to stop as she charged after him, rapier raised.

Startled by her ferocious shriek, O'Rourke glanced over his shoulder, a scowl darkening his face when he spied her. But he didn't let go of Fanny.

Instead he picked up the nearest weapon at hand, a bronzed bust of some Greek god, and threw it at Lily with all his might. Although Lily tried to dodge the heavy object, her momentum carried her forward too fast, so that the bust struck her shoulder.

The pain nearly made her drop her rapier, but the distraction gave Fanny an opportunity to thwart her abductor. Thrusting out one foot to tangle with O'Rourke's legs, Fanny tripped him and shoved hard, sending him stumbling back into the room.

Her clever action gave Lily time to recover her balance. Lifting her rapier again, she swung it hard at O'Rourke, managing to crown him on the side of his head with the hilt guard. He fell to the carpet to land with a satisfying thud and lay there without making another sound.

Weak with relief, Lily moved toward a trembling Fanny and hugged her tightly. The two of them were half sobbing, half laughing when Heath burst into the room.

Lily's relief deepened when she saw that he was safe. His breathing was still harsh after his fistfight, and there was a bloody gash on his cheekbone, but he had proved the victor in his battle, just as she had.

She wanted to go to him right then—to put her arms around him and to tend his injured face—but Fanny needed her more. Holding on to her friend, Lily let herself drink in the sight of Heath safe and sound.

When his worried gaze searched her for injuries, she gave him a fleeting smile. "Fanny and I are fine," she said thankfully before nodding down at O'Rourke. "I don't believe that villain can say the same."

His attention shifting, Heath crossed to O'Rourke's prone body and bent to examine him.

"You didn't kill him, I see," Heath murmured to Lily.

"No," she admitted. "I only bashed his skull a little."

"Remind me never to get into a fight with you, angel."

Before she could reply, she heard a groan from the far side of the room. Basil was stirring from his stupor.

Fanny noticed him at the same time Lily did. Disengaging from their embrace, they headed toward Basil, but Fanny moved past Lily and reached him first. She knelt down beside him, while Lily did the same on his other side, Heath moving to stand behind her.

Opening his eyes, Basil gave a start to see them all looking down at him in concern, but then his gaze riveted on Fanny.

"Fanny . . . God, are you all right?" he demanded in a croaking voice.

"Yes," she said, smiling softly down at him. "In truth, I seem to be in much better condition than you are."

"O'Rourke?" he asked, trying to see beyond her.

"He is unconscious for the moment. You saved me from him, Basil," Fanny added in a tender tone.

"I hardly saved you," he retorted. "O'Rourke darkened my daylights."

"You most certainly did save me. You fought him and stopped him from taking me."

Basil gritted his jaw, obviously furious at himself for his failure to conquer O'Rourke. But when he started to rise, the effort made him groan once more and raise a hand to his bloody temple as if his head ached.

"Lie still," Fanny urged, cradling his head gently in her lap.

Lily's heart went out to poor Basil, his face bloodied and bruised, his pride injured. Hoping to distract him, she took the opportunity to ask Fanny what had happened. "Tait feared that O'Rourke had abducted you."

"He did," Fanny said, her lips compressing into a tight line. "He caught me off guard and forced me to accompany him here."

"Did he hurt you?" Lily demanded, her anger rising all over again.

"Nothing beyond a bruise or two on my arms," Fanny replied. "And I don't believe Mick meant me harm. He claimed he wanted to show me the beautiful house he had built for me. . . ." She gestured around the room, indicating the luxurious decor. "This was to be my gilded cage. Mick intended to keep me here until I agreed to wed him. He already had a special license and had bribed a vicar to perform the ceremony."

"You cannot wed that bastard!" Basil exclaimed in outrage.

"Trust me, I won't," Fanny assured him with feeling, lightly stroking his forehead as she gazed down tenderly at him.

Looking dazed by her regard, the wounded Basil reached up and cupped his hand around her nape and drew her mouth down to his for a long, unexpected kiss.

Fanny froze for an instant, then returned the pressure with surprising urgency, causing Basil to wince in pain from his split lip.

When she hurriedly drew back, she seemed unaccustomedly flustered.

"Forgive me," Basil muttered, his face turning red. "I should not have done that."

Lily, diverted by the tender moment, was surprised when Heath reached down and took the rapier from her. But O'Rourke was regaining consciousness, it seemed.

Climbing to her feet, she followed Heath over to the prone man.

Heath went down on one knee but kept the rapier point between them as he prodded O'Rourke's shoulder to wake him. After an interval, O'Rourke slowly opened his eyes and pushed himself up on one elbow.

Shaking his head groggily, he squinted up at Heath, but then he spied Lily and shot her a look of intense dislike. "I knew that she-devil would be the death of me."

Heath's grim smile held no amusement. "She very well could have been. And you were foolish not to heed my warning."

"Oh, I heeded it, milord. I just considered it worth the risk of dying if I could have Fanny."

The twist of his lips was bitter as he glanced across the room at Fanny, who still held Basil's head in her lap. "I thought I could make her see reason. That she would come to love me once we were wed." O'Rourke gazed longingly at Fanny for another moment before finally looking away, his expression one of anguish. "But I can see I was mistaken."

Heath kept his gaze focused on O'Rourke. "I advised you of the consequences if you laid a finger on her again, remember?"

Grimacing, O'Rourke met his gaze and nodded reluctantly. "Aye, you did. So what will you do with me now?"

"Deliver you to the authorities. You will be fortunate if you don't hang, but perhaps you will only wind up in Newgate Prison."

Handing the rapier to Lily, Heath hauled O'Rourke to his feet and proceeded to bind the man's hands with his own cravat. O'Rourke offered no resistance, though. All the fight had gone out of him.

When Heath finished, he turned to Lily and said in a low voice, "You should take the hack and see Fanny and Eddowes home."

"What will you do?" she asked.

"I'll commandeer O'Rourke's carriage and escort him to the Bow Street Magistrate's Court to lay charges against him."

"Very well."

When her gaze shifted, a pang of dismay shot through her. Heath's cheek was still bleeding from the gash his opponent's meaty fist had inflicted.

"Heath, you are hurt. Your cheek . . ."

She raised her hand gently to his face, but he drew back, avoiding her touch. "It is no matter."

Just then his two servants appeared, reporting that all the bruisers had fled, including the one his lordship had shot. They had abandoned their employer when confronted with superior force.

Heath gave his orders to the footmen, who led the prisoner from the room. His head bowed, O'Rourke didn't so much as glance at Fanny, although she followed his retreat with an odd mix of anger and sadness on her beautiful features.

When O'Rourke had gone, Lily returned her attention

to Heath's injured cheek. Reaching down, she lifted the hem of her gown of pale green silk—the same stylish confection she had worn to Roslyn's wedding that morning, which was now stained with Basil's blood—and tore a strip from her chemise.

"Here," she said, raising the linen to Heath's face. "You gave your handkerchief away."

To her puzzlement, Heath again pulled back abruptly, as if he couldn't bear her touch. He took the scrap from her, however, and pressed it to his wound. "See to Eddowes, Lily. He needs your compassion more than I do."

His cool tone took her aback. Lily regarded Heath in silence, trying to hide her own emotional turmoil: Gratitude that he had been willing to help her when she desperately needed him, without question or pause. Awe that he had risked his life to save her friend. Relief that he'd emerged relatively unharmed. Nerves from the danger they had faced. Pain from his coldness.

For the space of a heartbeat, she stood there awkwardly, wanting to say something more to Heath. But as soon as she nodded in agreement, he turned and followed his servants from the room, leaving Lily to stare after him, feeling strangely as if she had just been delivered a powerful blow to her chest somewhere in the vicinity of her heart.

Chapter Nineteen

❧

I never thought it would hurt this much to lose him.
—Lily to Fanny

At their wits' end with worry, Fleur and Chantel were overjoyed to have Fanny home safely—and appalled by Basil's trouncing. The elderly courtesans fussed over him even more than they fretted over Fanny, settling them both in their cozy sitting room and fortifying Basil with pillows, hot tea, and a liberal dose of brandy.

When Basil looked embarrassed by their coddling, Fanny assumed control of his nursing, bathing and tending his wounds and bandaging his right hand herself.

He endured her tender attentions with more fortitude, yet he still seemed dismayed by her concern. No doubt, Lily suspected, because he thought his physical injuries made him appear weak in Fanny's eyes, even though she and the Cyprians praised his heroism numerous times.

Lily was also extremely proud of Basil, although she wasn't quite as profuse in expressing her admiration just then; in part because her nerves were still unsettled from their brush with danger, her emotions still shaken after watching Heath risk his life for her sake. She badly wanted to see him again, to reassure herself that he was all right. Yet she knew there was an even greater reason for her present agitation. The truth was, she couldn't bear the way they had parted.

To distract herself and Basil as well, Lily kept him company for the remainder of the afternoon, reading to him from Byron's latest epic poem, *The Prisoner of Chillon,* and engaging in a half-hearted argument over that scandalous lord's latest exploits abroad, all the while pretending an interest she didn't feel. But she kept a close eye on the door, hoping Heath would arrive soon.

However, when he at last appeared at the boarding-house that evening to check on Fanny and to report on O'Rourke's arrest and incarceration, Lily had no chance to be alone with him, since Fanny asked to speak to him privately.

They left the sitting room together, and when Fanny returned, Heath was not with her.

"Lord Claybourne took his leave already?" Chantel asked, sounding disappointed. "But we wished to ask him to stay for dinner so we could properly thank him."

"Yes, his lordship has gone," Fanny answered. "He said to convey his apologies but he had business that required his attention."

Lily felt her stomach sink further. She knew exactly why Heath had left without even saying farewell: because he was shunning her.

Not stopping to debate the wisdom of her actions, she sprang up from her seat to go after him.

There was no sign of him below in the entrance hall, Lily saw when she reached the first floor landing, so she quickly ran down the stairs and flung open the front door.

He was just climbing into his coach, she noted with

relief. When she called to him, he froze for a long moment, before finally turning and walking slowly back toward her. Even from a distance she could tell that his face was completely shuttered, not an encouraging sign.

Lily hurried down the steps and along the sidewalk so that they met halfway, out of hearing of his coachman and footmen. When Heath halted before her, though, the sheer remoteness of his expression gave her a chill.

Lily stood gazing up at him helplessly, wondering what she could say to take that awful coldness from his eyes. At least the gash on his cheek didn't seem too serious now that it had been cleaned and was no longer bleeding.

After a long moment she broke the strained silence by offering rather feebly, "You gave us no chance to thank you for saving Fanny."

The humorless curl of his mouth resembled a grimace. "I have told you more than once, Lily, I do not want your gratitude."

"Well, you have it. You saved my friend, and I am profoundly grateful to you."

"Fanny has already thanked me adequately enough. Now, if you are quite finished . . ." With a curt bow, he took a step backward, as if preparing to turn away.

Dismay spearing through her, Lily stopped Heath by laying an imploring hand on his arm. "You are just leaving like this?"

"What reason do I have to stay, Lily?"

That sinking, tightening feeling in her stomach only intensified, especially when his voice dropped to a rough murmur. "It is clear we are at a total impasse, Lily. I cannot make you trust me. I cannot make you love me. So I am declaring an end to our courtship."

When she mutely searched his face, Heath added with cold dispassion, "Come now, this is what you wanted all along. You should be glad I am giving you your wish."

But she wasn't glad at all! She didn't want him walking away like this, severing even a chance of friendship between them. And the thought of possibly never seeing him again was more than she could bear. "Heath, please . . . I did not mean that we should—"

"*Enough.* There is nothing more to be said."

The finality in his tone roused a painful constriction in her chest. Then wordlessly, Heath turned and headed for his coach, once again leaving Lily to stare after him.

Yet this time the ache in her heart felt as if it might never go away.

Walking away from Lily just now was one of the hardest things he'd ever done, Heath reflected as his coach drove off. He hadn't even wanted to come here tonight, let alone speak to her in private.

His frustration with Lily was balanced on a knife's edge, and he wasn't certain he could control his primitive urges. He wanted to take her by the shoulders and shake some sense into her. He wanted to make her accept his marriage proposal. He wanted to hold her and protect her and love her forever. . . .

His reaction was driven by fear, Heath knew. The gut-deep fear that Lily might never give him the chance to love her as she deserved to be loved.

She believed that marriage was a prison for wives, that love was a destiny to be feared. Her irrational phobia frustrated the hell out of him because it was a fight he couldn't win.

It wrenched him inside that Lily couldn't let herself

trust him. Which was why he had forced himself to walk away. If he continued making it easy for her to avoid the issue of marriage, she would have no reason to reevaluate her refusal.

He was taking the biggest gamble of his life, but he was determined to push her to decide what she truly wanted.

Remembering her huge dark eyes just now—the stricken look he'd seen there—gave him a measure of hope. Her dismay had seemed very real. And it was certainly possible that the adage about absence making the heart grow fonder might apply in her case.

But would his absence be enough to make her reconsider her answer?

He ardently wanted it to be so. Rescuing her friend this afternoon had only proved to Heath what he already knew: that he and Lily were ideally matched. She had faced danger at his side without flinching. His lovely spitfire was a magnificent woman, one he wanted beside him for the rest of his life.

But he couldn't compel her surrender. He couldn't demand that Lily's feelings for him equal what he felt for her.

Thus, he had hit on a new plan. Yet he didn't have faith it would work.

Meanwhile, he had another frustrating matter to deal with—namely Fanny's decision to bargain with Mick O'Rourke rather than send him to prison for her abduction.

During their interview a short while ago, Fanny had laid out her arguments: Mick hadn't really hurt her when he'd kept her captive in the beautiful house he had built solely for her. Nor could she overlook how kind and generous he'd been to her at the outset of her career as a courtesan. She actually *was* fond of him in a nostalgic sort of way. But certainly not enough to marry him as he wanted.

Perhaps she could work out a deal with Mick. She wouldn't press charges against him for her abduction in exchange for his promise to leave her alone in the future, in addition to a significant monetary settlement. Yes, he had made that same promise before—to Lord Claybourne himself just last week. But this time Fanny felt certain Mick had finally accepted that his love wasn't returned.

If he agreed to her offer, he would be spared a trial and perhaps years of prison, or even worse, deportation or hanging.

Fanny had asked Heath to escort her to Newgate in the morning, so that she could put the question to her former lover.

Heath intended to honor Fanny's plea, not because he thought it was the best course, but because he didn't want Fanny going there alone and making a bargain she would come to regret. He needed to be convinced that O'Rourke would honor his word this time.

Moreover, Heath reflected grimly, dealing with Fanny's troubles had the advantage of taking his mind off the fear and frustration engendered by his damnable stalemate with Lily.

Another fitful night of tossing and turning left Lily feeling morose and restless when she woke. And vexingly, her low spirits continued the entire morning and into the afternoon. The boardinghouse seemed overly quiet after the tumultuous events of yesterday, but she had politely declined Fleur and Chantel's invitation for a shopping excursion on Bond Street, courtesy of Lord Poole.

Settling in the parlor downstairs, Lily tried to occupy herself by reading, but she discovered that concentrating on a printed page was nearly impossible. Her emotions were in too much turmoil.

She was still struggling against her uncharacteristic depression when Peg Wallace sought her out just after luncheon.

The girl was beaming with shy happiness as she shared her good news. "I came to thank you, Miss Loring, from the bottom of my heart. Madame Gautier offered me a position as her assistant, and the pay is substantial enough to allow me to leave the Royal Opera. I gave notice last night."

"Why, that is wonderful, Peg," Lily responded warmly. "I am so pleased for you."

"And Betty Dunst sent word that her employment at Lord Claybourne's estate is 'wonderous fine.' Those are her exact words. She is aiding the third gardener in the conservatory. You are a true angel, Miss Loring."

At the undue praise, Lily laughed faintly. "I am no angel, Peg, I assure you. I only wanted you both to have better lives."

"And you made it possible. No one else cared enough to help us. You *are* an angel—and so is his lordship. Will you please thank him for me?"

Lily's smile faded. "I will be sure to tell him when I see him again."

If I ever see him again, she added to herself once Peg had gone.

Lily wasn't certain that would happen. She was only

certain that Heath's withdrawal had left her feeling forlorn and miserable. She already missed him after barely a day.

A wretched sign, Lily thought, wincing. If she was feeling so distraught after so short a time, how could she bear to end their relationship altogether?

But Heath was giving her no choice. Her only course would be to accept his proposal of marriage, and she couldn't bring herself to risk it.

What she would do with her future instead, however, remained the question.

Since her childhood she had wanted to travel and explore, to lose herself in a world of excitement and adventure. But now she had a different desire. Now she very much wanted to start a home for unfortunate women.

Helping those poor girls escape a life of poverty and prostitution could become a passion for her, Lily knew. Her own life had always seemed rather superficial and shallow before, but now she had the chance to do something truly meaningful, something she would find greatly fulfilling.

Even if it might not totally fill the emptiness she was feeling at just this moment.

And where she would live was yet another question, Lily reminded herself. She couldn't stay here at the boardinghouse with Fleur and Chantel forever—and in truth, there was no reason for her to remain, since her friends were safe from O'Rourke's threats of imprisonment.

Admittedly, returning to Danvers Hall to live with Arabella and Marcus held little appeal, although Lily knew they would gladly welcome her. But not only would she feel sadly de trop, she believed the newlyweds deserved time to themselves if their union was to have the best chance of prospering.

Perhaps, Lily mused, she could move in with Tess— her lovely house in Chiswick had ample room. Chiswick would be close enough to London for her to carry out plans for starting a charity home for women. And living quietly in the country might allow her the chance to recover from her heartbreak. . . .

There, she had finally said it, Lily acknowledged, shutting her eyes. She had admitted that her heart was breaking. All because Heath intended to cut her out of his life.

Realizing how pitifully weak that made her seem, Lily shook her head while fiercely chiding herself. She could *not* let herself wallow in this deplorable state, pining after a man who didn't want her. Yearning for his friendship, for his touch, for the simple joy his nearness brought her.

No, Lily vowed fervently, she had to regain control of herself and her pathetic emotions. Which meant that she couldn't stay here, where she would constantly be reminded of Heath. She had to make a fresh start. And she would have to keep so busy, she would be too tired to dwell on her loss.

Jumping up from her seat, Lily left the parlor, determined to go upstairs and pack so that she could be ready to leave for Chiswick first thing in the morning.

She had just reached the entrance hall when she encountered Fleur and Chantel as they arrived home from their shopping expedition. Despite the courtesans' entreaties to join them for tea and help them to entertain

Lord Poole, Lily politely declined rather than endure their blithe cheerfulness.

To her dismay, however, she made little progress on her vow to dismiss Heath or her heartache from her mind while she was packing.

Then a short while later, Basil startled her by rapping hard on her open bedchamber door and stalking into the room without even waiting for her to bid him entrance.

"Women! I will never understand them!" he exclaimed, flinging himself into the single chair.

"What is wrong?" Lily asked, a little disquieted by his vehemence and his appearance as well. Basil looked rather pitiful, with his face swollen and bruised and his left eye turning a vivid collage of black and purple. His scowl made the effect worse.

"Fanny! *She* is what is wrong. She is damned wrongheaded, not to mention stubborn and foolish."

"What has she done?" Lily asked in puzzlement.

"She paid me a call at work—to check on my injuries, she said. But in fact it was to explain. She wanted to tell me herself before I heard it from someone else."

"Heard what, Basil? Will you cease this roundaboutation before I throttle you?"

Lily's threat seemed to capture his attention, for he slumped over in his seat while clutching his hair as if wanting to pull it out by the roots.

"Fanny agreed to withdraw the charges against O'Rourke if he would return the thirty thousand pounds to Lord Poole and the ten thousand Fanny paid him at the start, plus give Fleur and Chantel another twenty thousand pounds to provide them security in their old age."

Lily stared at him, wondering if she had heard correctly. "Do you mean O'Rourke is *not* going to prison for abducting her and holding her prisoner for the better part of an afternoon?"

"That is exactly what I mean!" Basil grumbled. "That bastard will be set free tomorrow. Claybourne arranged for his release this afternoon."

"He just let O'Rourke *go*?" Lily repeated in disbelief.

"Yes! Fanny talked Claybourne into it. She wrapped him around her little finger, the way she does every other poor sod of her acquaintance."

"But O'Rourke threatened her life! And his servants nearly killed Lord Claybourne!"

"I know that! But she has conveniently dismissed O'Rourke's villainy. She claims he has learned his lesson. And he has sworn to provide financially for Fleur and Chantel. If you ask me, I think Fanny elected leniency because she loves that bastard. There is no other excuse for her madness."

The disgust in Basil's voice couldn't hide the underlying bitterness. He was greatly upset, Lily knew. Even more because he was envious of O'Rourke than because he wanted to see the gaming hell owner pay for his crimes.

Lily understood the deep hurt Basil felt. She might not have two weeks ago, but she did now. She'd gained a newfound sensitivity over the past fortnight, because her recent love affair with Heath had made her much more sympathetic to the trials and tribulations of lovers.

"I am very sorry Fanny set O'Rourke free, Basil," Lily said in a calmer tone. "But I don't believe it is because she loves him."

"Then *why*?" The question was a plea for understanding, and his tone held an edge of anguish, although Lily knew Basil would be embarrassed if she took note of it.

"My guess is that she earnestly wants to provide for her friends. Twenty thousand pounds is a significant fortune. If Fleur and Chantel are the least frugal, they will be set for life. And Fanny will no longer need to worry for their welfare. Instead, she can see to her own."

"How is her welfare made better by championing that villain?" Basil's hands clutched harder in his hair before he shook his head furiously. "Blast it all, I have had enough! I can't bear to watch her any longer."

"What do you mean to do, Basil?" Lily asked warily.

"I will return to Hampshire as soon as I can arrange it. I'll give notice to my firm tomorrow."

Lily hesitated a long moment. "You would leave London right now?"

"Yes!" he practically hissed. "I cannot stay here any longer. It is *stupid* to torment myself this way. I can never have Fanny. I have to accept that."

"You love her."

The glance he shot Lily was full of misery. "Yes, fool that I am. I have loved her for years. Why do you think I followed her here to London? I wanted to be certain she was safe and happy. I wanted just to be near her. But I can't bear sharing her with other men."

Seeing his anguish, Lily softened her tone even more. "I don't think you should give up, Basil."

"Why not? What would be the point of remaining?"

"Because I know Fanny is extremely fond of you."

Basil continued to scowl while shaking his head. "Any feelings she has for me are brotherly, just as yours are. She doesn't love me as a man. And she wouldn't wed me if she *did* love me."

"Basil, believe me, Fanny's feelings toward you are *far* from brotherly. I am absolutely sure of it."

His gaze arrested on Lily. "They are?"

"Most definitely. She told me so herself last week. And that was *before* you risked life and limb to rescue her. I have no doubt that your heroism helped to melt her heart even more."

"Do you truly think so?" he asked as if not daring to believe.

"Indeed I do," Lily replied. "Fanny hasn't seen this valiant side of you until today, as I have. But now she knows that you have hidden depths that any woman would admire."

That gave Basil pause. "I suppose I do have a hidden depth or two."

Lily smiled at the surprise in his tone. "Of course you do. And I suspect her concerns about matrimony are based more on practical matters. Fanny thinks she cannot afford to marry you. She doesn't know how she would earn a living. But if she no longer has to support her friends because of O'Rourke's settlement, then she can curtail her expenses significantly. And she has her savings back now, thanks to her bargain with O'Rourke. If you could find employment that provides a higher income . . . Well, then, a marriage between you is not beyond the realm of possibility."

When a fragile hope shone in his eyes, Lily pressed harder. "So you see, if you leave now, Basil, you will never know what might have been between you and Fanny. You must stay awhile longer, no matter how painful it is at the moment."

His clutching fingers releasing his hair, Basil slowly nodded. "I think you may be right."

"I know I am right about this," Lily insisted.

Basil sank back in his chair, deep in thought. Then suddenly he took notice of the valise Lily had laid out on the bed and the neat piles of clothing that were stacked beside it.

His brow furrowing, he glanced back up at her. "Why the devil are you packing?"

The question made Lily recall her own troubles, but she tried to keep the despair from her voice when she replied. "I am returning to Chiswick in the morning. I plan to live with Tess for a while."

"You are leaving London?"

Lily shrugged as she went back to folding the last of her gowns. "Why not? I have done everything I came here to do and more. I will be perfectly content to leave."

Which was a blatant falsehood. She was immeasurably happy that things had worked out so well for her friends, but otherwise she was perfectly miserable.

"You just told me *I* could not leave," Basil said slowly. "I think perhaps you should take your own advice."

Lily couldn't meet his gaze as the ache in her throat returned. "The two circumstances are very different."

She felt Basil eying her. "Are they, Lily? I think our circumstances are closer than you are willing to admit."

Turning, she sank down onto the bed. It was true, she thought bleakly. She had insisted that Basil needed to remain in London, and so did she.

She couldn't leave Heath. She couldn't bear to just walk away.

She bit her trembling lower lip as she stared down at the carpet.

When she remained silent, Basil's tone became more insistent. "What *are* your feelings for Claybourne, Lily?"

Her feelings? How did she answer that complex question? Her feelings for Heath were . . . complicated. Intense. Confused. Overwhelming. And in the end, so very simple.

"Come now, you made *me* bare my soul."

She nodded faintly. Basil was one of her oldest, dearest friends, and she wouldn't try to deceive him, even if she had been doing the same to herself for quite some time. But she couldn't fool herself any longer.

She loved Heath.

She was dreadfully, desperately, painfully in love with him.

Sometime in the past fortnight, the walls she had so determinedly built to protect herself had tumbled down, leaving her vulnerable and defenseless to his passionate enchantment.

She had fallen in love with her determined suitor.

The expression on her face must have satisfied Basil, for he softened his tone. "If you love him, will you accept his marriage proposal then?"

Her fingers clenched on the gown she held. "I never thought I would marry," she murmured hoarsely.

A week ago she had been afraid to give herself to Heath in marriage, afraid to make the irrevocable commitment that would bind her to him for life.

"Not all men are brutes like your father was," Basil said quietly.

Lily lifted her head, searching his sympathetic eyes.

Basil understood her greatest fears. He had been the one to keep her company when she hid out in the stables during her parents' battles, or rode hell for leather across the countryside in an effort to forget. He had been the one to console her when she'd threatened to kill her own father for his brutality toward her mother.

"I know that," Lily said shakily.

"Claybourne is not like O'Rourke, either, even if he does know how to use his fists."

That was also true. Heath was no brute. He was a strong man who used his might carefully and wisely, and only when necessary.

And sometimes violence *was* necessary, Lily thought, remembering the satisfaction she'd felt yesterday when she'd felled O'Rourke to prevent him from taking Fanny. She would have liked to do the same to her father all those years ago when he was beating her mother. . . .

"So what are you worried about?" Basil asked. "Claybourne isn't the kind of man to hurt women, and you know it."

She did indeed know it, Lily admitted. Heath would never physically hurt her. Heath, who had been so tender and passionate with her. So protective, so generous.

But what about emotionally? What if she married him? He would own her completely then, heart and soul and body.

Basil, however, still was fixed on the physical threat a husband might present. "You can damn well hold your own with any man, Lily, you know very well." His half-hearted smile was self-deprecating. "Unlike me. You are no weakling."

Lily tore herself from her own reflections in order to protest. "Basil, you are certainly no weakling. Claybourne has had years of training in swordsmanship and fisticuffs."

Basil nodded reluctantly. "I know. He fences at Angelo's salle and strips with Gentleman Jackson."

"Yes. And you have not had the luxury of a nobleman's life of leisure, as he has. Besides, you ride nearly as well as he does, and your mind is every bit as sharp."

Basil looked rather pleased by her observation. "So is yours, Lily. You are a match for him in so many ways."

Lily looked away. "I am not denying that."

"Then what is stopping you from wedding him? He would make a good husband for you."

She couldn't deny that, either.

"Are you afraid he doesn't return your sentiments?"

Lily swallowed. "Yes, I am afraid. Heath said he loved me, but what if he doesn't truly mean it? Even ardent declarations of love from a man can prove false. Have you forgotten Arabella's first fickle suitor, Viscount Underwood?"

"Claybourne is nothing like that sorry weasel," Basil said dismissively. "And I doubt he would say he loved you if he didn't mean it." Basil paused. "Do you *want* him to love you, Lily?"

"More than anything," she said softly.

She had told herself she only wanted Heath's passion, but she wanted his love. So much that it hurt. Lily felt a stab of longing so fierce that she pressed her hand to her stomach to ease the pain.

At her silence, Basil shrugged and rose to his feet. "Well, Lily, only you can conquer your fears. *You* have to decide if the risk of marrying Claybourne is worth the gain."

He left her to her tumultuous thoughts then. Alone in

her bedchamber once more, Lily found herself staring blindly out the window.

Could she summon the courage to trust Heath that completely?

On the other hand, did she truly have any choice? Even if being married to him might lead to pain, being without him would be infinitely worse.

Since their parting yesterday, she had felt more alone than she'd ever felt in her life. She already missed him so much that she ached with it.

She knew Heath was right on that score at least: spinsterhood would be cold comfort. She didn't want to be alone and lonely for the rest of her life. Empty. The way she felt now.

There were also numerous other reasons to accept Heath's proposal, Lily reminded herself. Most of which he had already argued with her before.

Unless they married, they could never have the intimacy she craved. They would be compelled to keep to the shadows, stealing a few precious hours now and then to be together. They could never have children, a family.

Passion was all they would ever have. And passion, no matter how pleasurable, wasn't enough for happiness. Heath was right about that, too.

And what of her fear of being treated as chattel? Even as the thought crossed her mind, she dismissed it. As Heath's wife, she wouldn't be shackled to him. He wasn't likely to suddenly start controlling her and dictating to her and ordering her about. Not if he truly loved her. Rather, he would be her husband, her partner, her companion, her soul mate.

And if she truly loved him, if she truly trusted him, she

would swallow her fears and take the risk of marrying him.

She *did* love him, she had no doubt whatsoever. Heath had made her dream dreams she hadn't even known she wanted. Made her yearn for a future with him. He had touched something deep inside her. Something warm and wonderful and enchanting.

You make me feel alive, he had told her only yesterday. *You make me feel joyous and exhilarated, as if each day is a new adventure.*

Which was exactly how she felt about him.

So, yes, Lily decided, a soothing feeling of calm settling over her. She was ready to take the risk and wed Heath. She was ready to trust in his love.

Turning her head, she glanced at the clock on the mantel, wondering where he could be found just now. She needed to tell him of her change of heart right away.

She might have to grovel a bit to make him forgive her, Lily suspected, remembering how cold and remote Heath had been when he had left her for the last time. But she would make him see that she regretted taking so long to come to her senses and to know her own heart—

"Lily?" Chantel's shaky voice broke into her thoughts.

Lily looked up to discover that Chantel had silently entered her bedchamber. Her face was pale, and she was clutching something to her chest.

The newspaper, Lily realized distractedly. "What is it?" she asked, suddenly concerned.

"You need to see this. . . ."

Without another word, Chantel crossed to her and handed her the newspaper. It was this evening's edition of *The Star* and was opened to the society page.

"There," Chantel said hoarsely, pointing to an announcement halfway down the page.

The Marquess of Claybourne, Lily read, *has the great pleasure of announcing his betrothal to Lady Eleanor Pierce, sister of Lord Danvers and niece of Viscountess Beldon. The nuptials will take place next month at the family estate of—*

The newspaper dropped from Lily's nerveless fingers while the blood drained from her face. She tried futilely to catch her breath as she told herself there must be some mistake. Surely Heath was not planning to marry Lady Eleanor, even though it said so here in stark black and white—

"I don't understand," Chantel said plaintively. "I thought Lord Claybourne wanted to marry you, Lily."

"So did I," she rasped.

"He won your game. He has the right to court you now. So why is he engaged to wed someone else?"

She knew the answer. Because she had turned him down too many times. And she was now paying the price. Heath had decided he no longer wanted to marry her.

A surge of panic slid up her spine. Heath had decided to marry Marcus's beautiful, vivacious sister instead.

He must have asked Lady Eleanor very recently, perhaps this morning or even yesterday. That was the only way he would have time to place the announcement in this evening's paper.

Lily brought a trembling hand to her mouth to silence the anguished cry she wanted to utter. She had no one to blame but herself, she knew. She had refused Heath's offer of marriage countless times, until he had finally come to accept that she meant what she said.

He had given up his pursuit of her entirely, just as he'd warned he would.

She squeezed her eyes shut as the reality of what she'd done sank in. She'd had the promise of a lifetime of happiness within her grasp, and she had thrown it all away.

How would she live without Heath? How could she bear it?

Fear tightened in her chest until her heart hurt.

"Do you know the most painful irony?" she whispered to herself. "When at last I understand my heart's desire, it is too late."

She had been so determined never to trust him, never to open her heart to him, that she had lost him. *Dear heaven . . .*

A sense of desperation washing over her, Lily shook her head in denial. She couldn't lose him! She wouldn't let Heath go without a fight.

Lily rose abruptly to her feet, clutching the newspaper to her bosom.

"Where are you going?" Chantel exclaimed to her retreating back.

"To find Lord Claybourne," Lily said fiercely. "He will not marry Lady Eleanor! He will only wed *me*!"

Chapter Twenty

❦

He is my heart's desire. I know that now at long last.

—Lily to Fanny

Desperation beset Lily all the way to Heath's house in Bedford Square and only escalated when she arrived. A jaunty lady's phaeton stood out in front, the dashing pair of grays held by a liveried groom.

Wondering if the phaeton belonged to Heath's new betrothed, Lady Eleanor, Lily descended from the hack and forced herself to approach the front door, where she applied the knocker.

At least the Claybourne butler recognized her and admitted her without question. Yet the hollow ache in her stomach intensified when she was shown into a different room than before—a large masculine chamber that was obviously the master's study.

Lady Eleanor was there, lounging on a plush leather sofa while reading, her legs curled comfortably beneath her as if she belonged there as mistress of the house.

Utterly dismayed, Lily halted on the threshold, wondering if she should turn and flee before she was noticed. But then the butler announced her, and she had no choice but to step into the room.

Heath was seated at a massive desk, writing with a

quill pen. Upon Lily's entrance, he raised his head and studied her for a long moment. She couldn't read his expression at all; his face was completely enigmatic, just as it had been yesterday.

Lily's heart sank even lower, if that were possible.

She barely heard Lady Eleanor say in a pleasant tone, "Miss Loring, how good it is to see you again."

Striving futilely for composure, Lily murmured a polite reply as she curtsied. But she immediately turned her attention back to Heath. "Might I have a word with you in private, my lord?"

Still watching her, he shrugged his powerful shoulders. "Why in private? I doubt you have anything to say to me that Eleanor cannot hear."

Lily regarded him with mingled anguish and frustration. "I saw the announcement of your betrothal," she finally said.

To her surprise and vexation, Lady Eleanor replied for him. "I gather you have some objection to our betrothal, Miss Loring?"

"Yes . . . I do." As she faced the raven-haired beauty, Lily clenched her fists, girding her loins, so to speak. "You cannot have him, Lady Eleanor. He is already spoken for."

Eleanor's eyebrows shot up. "You are laying claim to my dear Heath?"

"*I am,*" Lily said fiercely.

The soft smile of satisfaction that touched Eleanor's lips was utterly puzzling. "I told you so," she said cryptically, glancing over at Heath. "You owe me that magnificent chestnut stallion of yours."

He nodded briefly. "Whatever you wish, minx," he

replied, never taking his eyes off Lily. "Now, if you don't mind . . ."

Eleanor laughed at his thinly veiled prodding. "Very well, I know when I am unwanted. I will leave you two to sort out your affairs."

Rising, Eleanor collected her book and pelisse and reticule without another word, but as she passed Lily, her smile was warm and kind, and she murmured, "Good luck," as if she truly meant to wish Lily well.

Bewildered, Lily turned back to Heath. He had risen to his feet but remained behind his desk. She took a step closer, her heart thudding, her knees weak, her stomach tied in knots.

"What did she mean?" Lily asked unsteadily, "when she said 'I told you so'?"

"It is no matter. Why are you here, Lily?"

His tone was hardly encouraging. She hesitated a long moment before replying, "To put an end to your betrothal. You cannot marry Lady Eleanor."

"Why not?"

"Because *I* want to be your wife."

The interval before Heath spoke seemed interminable. "Indeed. What caused your change of heart? I seem to recall asking you to marry me numerous times, and you refused every time."

"I know." Lily tried to swallow, even though her throat was dry as dust. "But I realized . . . I love you, Heath."

His expression never changed, except that his gaze seemed to sharpen. "I don't know that your love will be enough, Lily."

"N-not enough?" she repeated, her voice quavering.

"I told you, I want your trust as well."

"You have my trust, Heath." Words crowded into her throat but weren't even close to being adequate. "I know I was wrong to fear you. You would never deliberately hurt me."

His expression softened the slightest degree. "How gratifying that you finally comprehend that."

Lily nodded in agreement. "I have been a fool, I know that now. You were right. What we have is unique and rare. Something so perfect comes along once in a lifetime. I cannot throw it all away because of fear."

"It would indeed be foolish of you."

"Yes. Yesterday . . ." She hesitated several more heartbeats before she found her voice again. "Yesterday you said you loved me. Do you love me enough to give me a second chance?"

Her heart leapt at the warmth that suddenly shone in his eyes, even though he didn't answer her directly. "I find your nervousness very endearing, sweetheart."

Fear and hope tangled inside Lily. "I am not nervous. I am *terrified* that I am too late."

"So this is a proposal of marriage?" he asked as he moved out from behind the desk and came to stand before her.

"Yes."

Heath pursed his lips thoughtfully. "So say the words, Lily. I have done my fair share of proposing. I believe it is your turn."

There was tenderness in his eyes, along with a faint hint of amusement. He was enjoying her repentance, Lily realized with a stab of exasperation. Yet he deserved to hear her abject apologies. "Do you want me to get down on bended knee as well?"

"No, a simple proposal will do."

"Will you *please* marry me, Heath?"

"Tell me why I should."

"Because I love you dearly, and I don't want to live without you."

His gaze continued to measure her. "I thought you were adamant about maintaining your cherished independence."

"I was—but independence is not worth having if I am miserable. And I am utterly miserable without you. My life would be painfully empty if I lost you." Lily held his gaze determinedly. "I want you for my husband, Heath. I want to spend the rest of my days with you, as your wife."

At last he gave a brief nod, as if satisfied. "Then I accept your offer."

The relief that flooded through Lily made her knees nearly buckle, and so did Heath when he took a step closer and bent to kiss her.

His lips touched hers, unexpectedly gentle, unbelievably wonderful. He tasted familiar and precious and oh so dear— Yet he stepped back before Lily could even raise her hands to his shoulders.

Turning away, Heath went to his desk and picked up a document, which he held out to her. Curious, she crossed to him and took it before proceeding to read.

It was a special license to marry, with Heath's name designated as the applicant, and her name written in as the prospective bride.

Lily looked up at Heath in puzzlement. "I don't understand. I thought you were betrothed to Lady Eleanor."

He shot her a look too bland to be innocent. "Because

I wanted you to think that. But the announcement you saw wasn't genuine."

"Not genuine?"

"Not at all. And you received the only copy. The publisher of *The Star* is a friend, and I prevailed upon him to print a single copy with that announcement proclaiming my engagement to Eleanor. I know how much your courtesan friends enjoy reading the society gossip in the papers, so I trusted they would find that item and inform you."

Lily stared at Heath in disbelief for a long moment before flinging the license on his desk. Her hands went to her hips while her eyes narrowed in vexation. "You *tricked* me into thinking you intended to marry Lady Eleanor? Of all the despicable, underhanded, deceitful things to do!" she sputtered. "You frightened me half to death!"

With a smile lighting his eyes, Heath hardly looked contrite. "Turnabout is fair play, love. You frightened the devil out of me, vowing you would never marry me no matter what I did."

"So you *pretended* to want someone else?"

"I hoped to force your hand. If anything could make you come to your senses and realize your feelings for me, I thought it would be jealousy. And Eleanor was kind enough to play along."

Lily poked her forefinger into his chest, hard. "You are a dastardly villain, Heath Griffin!"

In self-defense, he caught her wrist and held her hand away. His gaze burned into hers, hot and amused and challenging. "You left me little choice, stubborn little hellion that you are. What else could I do? Professions of love send you into a panic, and coercion only makes you dig your heels in more fiercely. I couldn't force you to accept my hand, Lily. You had to choose freely."

He brought her fingers to his lips, pressing a light kiss to her knuckles. "But I was never going to let you get away from me. I love you too much to ever accept 'No' as your answer."

Lily's ire faded at the fervency of his tone, at the possessiveness and tenderness and warmth she saw dancing in his eyes. Suddenly she felt as if she could breathe again. She had not lost Heath after all. He loved her and was willing to forgive her for her obstinacy.

"You are still a beast," she muttered, even though a smile threatened to break out on her mouth.

He favored her with his own familiar enchanting smile. "Perhaps, but this should prove to you how much I love you. Would I have gone to so much trouble if I didn't?"

"I suppose not," Lily admitted grudgingly. "So I shall contrive to forgive you."

He reached up to touch her face, his thumb caressing her cheekbone as he stared into her eyes. "So you will marry me?"

Her heart moved into her throat at the love she saw shimmering there in the golden depths. "*Yes*, Heath. I will marry you, and gladly."

"Thank God. I was running out of hope." His arms coming around her, he drew her close and rested his cheek on her hair. "I could never live without you, Lily. I could never be happy alone, now that I know what happiness is." He laughed softly. "I thought I was perfectly content until I met you. I never realized how much I was missing until then. I haven't been the same man since I kissed you in that stable loft."

Lily felt the same way about Heath. He filled all the empty places in her heart and in her life.

She leaned into the warm, solid strength of him, cherishing the feeling of holding him, of knowing he belonged to her from now until forever. "I am profoundly grateful that you didn't give up on me."

She heard the smile in his voice when he replied. "You should know by now that I can be as stubborn-minded as you. It just shows how well-matched we are." He paused. "But you have changed me—for the better I think."

"What do you mean?"

"Because of you, I was obliged to face some unpleasant truths about myself. More crucially, I realized that if I wanted to win your love, I needed to be worthy of you."

Still not comprehending, Lily drew back to search his face.

Heath's expression was surprisingly intent as he continued. "You see, everything has always come easily to me. I never had to work for anything I wanted. And then I met you. You were the only thing I ever desired that I couldn't have just by snapping my fingers. You made me go to extraordinary lengths just to be near you."

He gazed down at her solemnly. "And then I came to know you, Lily. I saw your dedication. I saw how fiercely passionate you were about helping your friends. It made me feel humble, angel. Until then, life was always something of a game to me. I never thought much about others, about the servants in my employ, about young girls who are forced into prostitution. But because of you, I realized that life is not just a game. And that with all my wealth and resources, I can do more to help the plight of the less fortunate."

"You have already helped tremendously," Lily replied earnestly. "You gave Betty and Peg entirely new lives."

"It isn't enough. But I mean to do better in the future by putting my wealth to good use. I began by contributing to some of Tess Blanchard's charities. And I want to help you found a home for destitute women so they don't have to sell their bodies in order to survive."

"Oh, Heath . . ." Lily felt her heart melt, even though she was a little stunned that she could have made such a difference to his perspective on life. "You did not have to go to such lengths for me."

"Yes, I did. I want to be good husband to you, Lily. I want to share your passion."

Her heart gave a great surge of gladness. "I have no doubt you will be the best husband any woman could ever hope for." Lily gave him a teasing smile as she reached up to wrap her arms around his neck. "I know very well that you are not the worthless libertine that many of your noble peers are."

He grinned. "I am gratified you think so."

"And I agree that you are my ideal match. You are bold and fearless and daring. I greatly admire those qualities in a man—and I insist on having them in my husband."

"Then I am in luck."

Suddenly serious, Lily shook her head. "No, the luck is *mine*, Heath. I don't know that I deserve you, but I love you deeply, and I will try my best to be a good wife to you."

"I intend to make very certain of it, sweetheart."

The words were provocative, while the teasing light had returned to his eyes, reassuring Lily as much as his next tender declaration: "I love you, Lily. I will never stop loving you."

She arched an eyebrow, not wanting to show her uncertainty. "And if you should come to tire of me?"

"That will never happen in a million years."

As if determined to prove his assertion, Heath cupped her face and claimed her mouth in a cherishing kiss.

With a sigh of joy, Lily responded to his caress with all the fervency she possessed. Her senses seemed starved for him, it had been so long since she had last kissed him, last touched him. His ardent passion banished the last of her fears and kindled her desire to a heated urgency—

To her dismay, however, Heath abruptly broke off and peeled her arms away from his neck. "Not so fast, love. We need to settle some issues before we indulge in pleasure."

"What issues?"

"When you will actually marry me, for one."

Breathless and frowning, Lily allowed Heath to lead her over to the sofa. "The date matters little to me," she said once they were settled with his arm around her.

"It damn well matters to me. I want to hold the ceremony as soon as possible—this week, before you decide to change your mind."

She smiled up at him. "I promise you, I will never change my mind."

"I'm not risking it. Do you want a large wedding like your sisters had?"

"Heaven forbid." Lily mimicked a shudder. "I would

much rather save the expense and contribute the funds to establishing our new women's home. The same goes for wedding gifts. You needn't give me any exorbitantly lavish presents like that ship, Heath."

"Very well, no more lavish gifts . . . as long as you agree to accept the *Zephyr* as a token of my love."

Her smile turned impish. "I think I could be persuaded. I am not so stubborn as to refuse your most alluring offer to sail the world with you. I once dreamed of having a life of excitement and adventure, but I was willing to give up that dream when I discovered my new cause."

"Fortunately as a wealthy marchioness, you can do both."

"Yes," Lily agreed with an amazed laugh. "I can do both."

"And anytime you feel the need to escape the shackles of matrimony, you will have the ship at your disposal. You can leave me whenever you wish, at any time, for any reason."

Lily's expression sobered a little as she finally realized the significance of Heath's gift. "So that is why you gave me the ship," she said slowly. "Not to win points in our game, but so I would have the means to escape. So I would feel free to leave if I risked wedding you."

"Yes, sweetheart," Heath answered.

She cocked her head, considering him. "I doubt I will ever want to escape you, my dearest Heath. And I don't want to sail anywhere without you. But thank you."

"You are quite welcome. Now . . ." he said, changing the subject, "where would you like to go first? I suggest we take our wedding trip to the Mediterranean. We can visit your mother in Brittany, if you like."

"Oh, Heath, I would love that. I have always wanted to see France. And Italy and Spain—"

"Whatever my beautiful bride desires," he said gallantly.

His lips lowered to hers to bestow a lingering kiss. Lily sighed in delight at the heart-soaring thrill his tender gesture gave her.

"So we are agreed?" Heath asked when he allowed her up for air. "We will marry on Saturday. We can hold the wedding on board the *Zephyr* and have a man of the cloth perform the ceremony."

"Saturday should serve well enough. It will allow us time to call Roslyn back from *her* wedding trip with Arden. I don't think she will object, since they didn't intend to leave Kent until next week. I want my sisters to attend my wedding, Heath. And Winifred and Tess. And Fanny, of course. And Fleur and Chantel."

"Of course, since they played such a large role in bringing us together. And I would like Eleanor there as well."

Lily's gaze sought his. "As long as she relinquishes any claim to you, she is welcome."

One corner of Heath's beautiful mouth quirked upward. "There was never any question of my marrying her. You have no reason to be jealous, although I admit to being gratified. I think you could become fast friends with Eleanor if you gave her the chance."

"I like Lady Eleanor exceedingly well now, but I was ready to run her through when I thought you meant for her to take my place."

"No one could ever take your place, my enchanting virago."

"Good," Lily said firmly. "For I have absolutely no intention of sharing you."

Heath gave her a considering look. "I trust I have no reason to be jealous of your friend Eddowes?"

"Basil?" Lily almost laughed. "Not in the least. Basil is like a brother to me. Besides, he is head over heels in love with Fanny."

"I suspected something of the sort when he kept risking a pummeling in order to save her."

"I do hope they are able to solve their difficulties and find happiness together," Lily said softly.

"Is that so?" Heath asked in a voice laced with amusement. "Pray don't tell me that *you* intend to turn matchmaker, angel."

She felt her cheeks coloring. "At least now I can understand Winifred's compulsion to bring couples together."

Heath chuckled. "I would say you have been transformed as much as I have."

"More so."

Exhaling a dreamy sigh, Lily leaned her head on his shoulder. Love had changed her, very much for the better, she believed. The protective shell around her heart had melted, all because of Heath's relentless, unwavering pursuit of her. He had steadily chipped away at her defenses until she had no choice but to surrender.

And now the love she felt for him was powerful and irrefutable.

No one could be as fortunate as she, Lily thought, wordlessly raising her mouth to his. She had the love of an amazing man, and the promise of a remarkable future together.

Just as silently, Heath favored her with the kind of soul-deep kiss she had grown addicted to. His enchanting mouth possessed hers thoroughly, making her feel the dizzy rush of desire and need she only knew with him.

When she reached up blindly to untie his cravat, though, Heath stayed her hand. "What do you think you are doing, sweetheart?"

"I want to make love to you," she said huskily. "I thought to give you a wedding gift. Myself."

He held her hand away. "That is a gift I will treasure always, but I won't accept it until we are irrevocably married."

"Heath," she began, her tone exasperated and imploring at the same time.

"I am as impatient as you are, but I am not letting you seduce me until you are my bride."

"I am perfectly willing to let *you* seduce *me*."

"You will have to be satisfied with kisses until Saturday."

"Only kisses?" Highly disappointed, Lily assumed a pout. "You know it will be torture, waiting until our wedding night."

A devilish gleam entered his hazel eyes. "The wait will be worth it, I promise you."

"Indeed?" She trailed a tantalizing finger over his lower lip, but Heath refused to surrender.

"We will have a lifetime of wedding nights together," he insisted.

"Very well," she finally conceded. "But I intend to hold you to your promise."

"I trust you will, love. Until then"—Heath surprised

her by reaching up to pull the pins from her hair—"I mean to see how inventive we can be with mere kisses."

The magical warmth of his smile set her pulse soaring. And when he bent to capture her mouth again, laughter and desire welled up in Lily in equal measures as she gave herself up to Heath's enchanting caresses.

Epilogue

You were right, dearest Fanny. My happiness does lie in marriage to Lord Claybourne. A lifetime of love and fulfillment with the most wonderful man I know. What more could I ever want?

—Lily to Fanny

I am thrilled by your happiness, my dear Lily. If my new book is successful, the income may be sufficient to allow me to seek my own happiness in marriage. Who knows? Perhaps I shall turn to writing fiction and become an authoress. The accounts of how you and your sisters found true love would make delightful tales.

—Fanny to Lily

London, August 1817

On the quarterdeck of the *Zephyr,* Heath regarded his bride of three hours with pride and affection. Lily looked incredibly happy surrounded by her family and friends, her dark eyes big and bright with humor and excitement.

How he loved those glowing eyes, Heath reflected. How he wanted to kiss that luscious mouth . . .

Despite his impatience to have his bride all to himself, however, he would have to wait until the wedding guests departed the ship. At the moment they showed no desire to leave. They were too busy drinking champagne and offering congratulatory toasts and sharing entertaining tales about the newlyweds.

Laughter abounded, in part because the small guest list fostered an intimacy to the gathering. The marriage ceremony had been a simple affair in comparison to Drew's lavish society wedding a mere few days earlier. And the celebrations afterward—a luncheon served on deck by Heath's capable staff—were quite modest, nothing like the enormous wedding breakfast and ball at Danvers Hall following Marcus's wedding, which had been held in the village church at Chiswick two months ago.

But Lily deemed the arrangements perfect. The nuptials had been performed by the vicar from Chiswick, the same clergyman who had married Marcus and Arabella. And viewing the myriad ships anchored on the Thames and docked at the quay only increased Lily's anticipation of their wedding journey, which was to begin next week.

Much to Heath's amusement, his new wife had made a point of drinking a mere half glass of champagne, claiming that she wanted no repetition of her shameless behavior in the stable loft the first time they'd kissed. Lily was determined to remain circumspect, despite the scandalous vocation of several of the guests.

Fleur and Chantel had eagerly attended, along with Fanny and Basil. The elder courtesans had spent much of the past hour crowing over their success in uniting the bridal couple, while Lady Freemantle had taken credit for bringing them together in the first place.

Her ladyship looked smugly delighted now as she exclaimed in her booming voice, "You know all I ever wanted was your happiness, dearest Lily."

"I know, Winifred," Lily replied, fondly embracing her friend. "Which is why I forgive your meddlesome attempts at matchmaking."

"Humph," Winifred said archly. "I make no apologies for my meddling, young lady. If not for my encouraging Lord Claybourne to follow you to Hampshire—where I falsely believed you to be hiding, I might add—you would likely not be married now. You were so adamantly set against imprisoning yourself in matrimony, he was forced to take drastic steps to pursue you."

"I admit," Lily said, laughing, "that I was greatly mistaken about matrimony being a prison."

She glanced beyond her friend, searching for Heath. When she located him a few yards away, the smile she sent him was pure sunshine, golden with warmth.

Heath found himself gazing back at her, spellbound. Her impact was like a blow to the chest, straight to his heart. And as their gazes touched, a wave of tenderness washed over him so strong it made his knees weak.

Just then Marcus and Drew joined him.

"So now you are one of us," Marcus drawled in an amused voice as he clapped Heath on the back. "I seem to recall not three months ago you adamantly protesting that the marriage noose was too restrictive to your freedom."

Heath chuckled. "You were right, old friend. It only took meeting the right woman."

"We all three learned that lesson," Drew added with wry humor yet no trace of his former cynicism. "Although it *is* rather remarkable that we managed to find our ideal wives, and that they happened to be sisters."

When the three noblemen turned to admire the beautiful Loring sisters, Heath knew his friends' feelings for their respective ladies were very similar to his own for Lily.

"Yet I had to work for *my* bride," Heath reminded them. "I had the devil of a time convincing Lily even to allow my courtship."

"Then it was extremely fortunate," Lady Eleanor interrupted as she moved to her brother's side, "that you didn't give up, Heath. You and Lily are perfect for each other."

Grinning, Heath gave Eleanor a bow of acknowledgment. "And I have you to thank for helping Lily to come to her senses by pretending a betrothal to me."

Marcus's look was teasing as well as he put a brotherly arm around Eleanor's shoulder. "What was that, Nell? Your third betrothal?"

She made a humorous face. "I suppose so, even though this engagement was a total fabrication and only lasted a few hours."

Marcus turned to Heath. "I trust you used discretion in having that false announcement printed?"

"I did. The publisher and his printer are sworn to secrecy, with their palms well greased."

"Good," Marcus replied. "If word got out about yet another broken betrothal of Eleanor's, it would only cement her reputation as a jilt and make it even harder for her to wed. And unlike Lily, she doesn't wish to remain a spinster for the rest of her life. Isn't that so, minx?"

Eleanor nodded cheerfully. "Yes, dearest brother. I would very much like to find true love as you and Heath and Drew have done. I have not given up hope. Miss Irwin's book, which reportedly advises young ladies on how to catch a husband, is to be published soon. Perhaps it will help me to find my ideal mate."

Lady Freemantle overheard her comment and called over to her. "If you need any assistance, Lady Eleanor, I am just the person you need."

"Thank you, my lady," Eleanor said with a smile. "I will keep your kind offer in mind."

Fanny joined their conversation then. "Lady Eleanor, I would be pleased to let you read my book in advance. If you find my advice beneficial, you might suggest its purchase to your genteel friends."

"I would be delighted to read and promote it, Miss Irwin."

"Thank you. I am hoping the proceeds will be profitable enough to allow me to become an authoress full time."

When Fanny glanced at Basil, whose face was still discolored from his beatings, the tender look they shared only confirmed Lily's suspicion that they wanted a future together. Heath had promised Lily he would do his part to help their love affair progress, beginning with finding a more profitable post for Basil than law clerk. Thus far he had three possible positions in mind.

And Basil already looked the part of a nobleman's secretary. The elderly courtesans had taken him in hand, intent on turning him into a fashionable gentleman. Under their direction, Basil had shed his clerkish aura along with his homely attire. Now dressed in an expertly tailored frock coat and pantaloons and shiny Hessian boots, he carried himself with far more confidence, more manliness, even, as if he planned to be the equal of a beautiful Cyprian like Fanny.

The crowd shifted a little just then so that Tess Blanchard could move closer to Heath. "I wish to thank *you,* Lord Claybourne, for your generosity to my causes. We are fortunate to have such a magnanimous benefactor. You may be pleased to know I have located a house that might do very well for your needs."

"Oh?" Winifred broke in. "But his lordship already has a magnificent house—several of them, in fact."

Lily replied for Tess. "We plan to start a home for needy women, Winifred. A place where desperate girls can find refuge and learn various skills that will allow them to seek respectable employment."

"How admirable," Winifred exclaimed, eyeing Heath in approval.

"I cannot take the credit," he said, holding out his hand to Lily. "My lovely bride came up with the idea."

Taking his hand, Lily moved to stand beside him. "But you are making it a reality. It is extraordinary, how willing you are to champion my cause."

When the conversation moved on, Heath bent to murmur in Lily's ear so that only she could hear. "That is what love does to a man, wife of mine. Makes him willing to slay dragons for his lady."

Lily's eyes danced as she gazed up at him. "Are you offering to slay my dragons, husband?"

"If you should need me to—although you are fierce enough to do your own slaying in most instances."

"I shall take that as a compliment."

"It was intended to be," Heath said, pressing a light kiss on her temple.

He did indeed mean his comment as praise, Heath thought, watching Lily blush at his intimate gesture. He wouldn't change a thing about her, most certainly not her passionate nature. She would face villains with fists swinging, but she would be standing at his side. And she would love him with a fierce loyalty, he had no doubt.

He felt the same way about her. The love he felt for Lily was intense, ungovernable, while desire echoed fiercely in his heart.

Winifred happened to notice Lily's flushed cheeks and boldly called the company's attention to the fact that it was Lord and Lady Claybourne's wedding day. "I believe we should take our leave and allow the lovebirds some privacy," her ladyship said in her own blunt style.

Heath agreed wholeheartedly, yet it was nearly half an hour later before the wedding party broke up for good. By then his servants had finished packing up the remains of the celebration and loading the tables and chairs into wagons.

One by one the guests said their farewells to the bridal couple. Arabella and Roslyn were the last to go. Rather surprisingly, tears shone in Lily's eyes as her sisters embraced her.

"Please don't cry, dearest," Roslyn implored, "or you will have me doing the same."

"Nonsense," Arabella said fondly. "Neither of you has any reason for tears. Lily, it isn't as if we are abandoning you. We will see you in less than a fortnight in Brittany."

Arabella and Marcus were planning a voyage to Brittany as well, so that the three sisters could hold a reunion with their mother. Both Roslyn and Lily had wed since Victoria and her French husband had visited England earlier this summer and attended Arabella's nuptials.

"I know," Lily replied, dashing the moisture from her eyes.

She let her sisters go eventually but stood watching as their husbands escorted them safely down the gangway to the quay to settle in their waiting carriages.

"Are you still sad about losing your sisters to matrimony?" Heath asked curiously.

Slipping her arm through his, Lily managed a bright smile. "No, not now. It is just that we are all beginning new lives apart from each other. But I cannot be sad when I have you."

She stood at the railing another moment, watching as the carriages pulled away. Heath, however, watched *her.* He had frequently imagined Lily at the bow of this ship, sunlight burnishing her dark chestnut hair as it streamed out behind her in the wind. There was little wind just now, but the sun brought out the shimmering copper and gold in the strands.

When Heath dropped a kiss onto the crown of her head, Lily turned to look at him with an adoring glance. "You needn't worry about my happiness, Heath. I could not be any happier. And I have no doubt that our wedding voyage will be the first of many wonderful adventures together."

"It will be if I have any say in the matter."

Reaching up, Lily entwined her arms around his neck. "Do you know what I think?"

"No, sweetheart, what do you think?"

"That love will be the grandest adventure of all."

"I could easily be persuaded to agree."

He captured her enchanting smile with a kiss and drew her close. It had been far too long since he'd last held her this way.

"Shall we go below to our cabin, my lady?" Heath murmured when he eventually broke off.

Lily raised a teasing eyebrow. "Oh? What did you have in mind?"

"I mean to seduce my bride. I promised you a memorable seduction on our wedding night, did I not?"

She felt a surge of heat at the desire she saw shimmering in his eyes. "Indeed you did. So why are we tarrying here?"

Of one accord, they turned to cross the deck. Her blood pulsing with anticipation and excitement, Lily allowed Heath to lead her below. By the time they reached their cabin, her heart was thudding against her ribs.

And the moment he shut the door behind them, they were in each other's arms.

"At last," Heath rasped before taking her mouth with the same fervency Lily was feeling. She responded fiercely to his every touch, his every kiss, his demanding lips, his masterful arms. With every breath she took, she wanted him more.

They were both wildly out of control as they shed their clothing . . . and then they were naked, gloriously naked.

Heath's eyes blazed with desire, with love, as he urged Lily to the berth. They fell together onto the silken sheets, locked together in a sensual tangle, so fierce yet so tender. A shower of heat bathed them when he came into her body and became part of her.

Lily shuddered as Heath filled her to overflowing. The powerful feeling pulsed deep inside her—a happiness so sweet and rare, it felt like shimmering sunlight. She was full to bursting with joy and wonder. And as her body shattered, she carried Heath with her.

When it was over, they clung to each other, breathless and sated, glorying in their joining.

Finally Heath muttered an exhausted oath in her ear. "Damn, but I meant our consummation to go slowly. That was hardly a seduction."

"No," Lily agreed weakly. "It was a conflagration."

They laughed softly into each other's mouths as they kissed again. Then, easing his weight from her, Heath rolled onto his side and gathered Lily to him with heart-melting care.

"It was worth the wait," he murmured hoarsely after another long interval. "I never realized that carnal pleasure could be so satisfying."

"Mmmm," she agreed dreamily.

It was true, Lily thought as she lay with her cheek against his heartbeat. Their passionate lovemaking as husband and wife was more satisfying, more thrilling, more joyous than as mere lovers.

And while she lay there savoring his warmth, another realization struck her: She was bound to Heath now, yet she had never felt so free. She had found freedom in his arms, much to her amazement. He had taught her about trusting. He had taught her the power of love.

She had no doubts now that their union would prosper. Heath was her husband; her friend and lover for always. The man whose smile could control the rhythm of her heart.

Lily pressed her lips tenderly against the warm bare skin of his chest. Nothing in her life had ever seemed this natural, this right. And when Heath's arms tightened around her, she sighed at the magic of being treasured by such a special man. She was loved, deeply loved.

No woman could ask for more.

"Have I told you how thankful I am for your persistence?" Lily murmured at last, lifting her head so that she could see his face.

"Not lately, wife. Why don't you tell me again?"

"I *am* thankful, Heath. I am profoundly grateful that you would not give up on me. And even more grateful that you came to love me."

His eyebrow arched. "I have told you countless times, I don't want your gratitude . . . but in this case, I will make an exception."

Slipping his hand behind her nape, Heath favored her with an alluring male smile—that same wickedly charming smile she had come to cherish. "But now, my lovely bride," he said provocatively, "what of this seduction I promised you?"

Lily flashed him a saucy smile. "Perhaps we should hold a contest to see who can best seduce whom."

"I am more than willing to compete," Heath agreed huskily, bringing her mouth closer to his. "But be warned, angel, I intend to win."

Giving a laugh of elemental satisfaction, she bent her head. "I wouldn't have it any other way."

Don't miss all three enthralling novels in
The Courtship Wars trilogy by
Nicole Jordan

To Pleasure a Lady

Marcus Pierce is a strikingly handsome aristocrat with a
wicked reputation. So when he inherits guardianship
of Arabella Loring and her two sisters he immediately
declares his intention to marry them off. But defiant
Arabella sparks frustration—and something deeply
erotic—in Marcus. And it isn't long before an
extraordinary game of seduction begins. . . .

To Bed a Beauty

Clever and charming Roslyn Loring realizes that to win
her future husband's devotion, she must learn the secrets
of kindling a gentleman's ardor. And she finds a willing
tutor in Drew Moncrief, the Duke of Arden, a notorious
rake whispered to be London's most magnificent lover.
But as Drew begins schooling Roslyn they discover how
easily lessons in pleasure can become lessons in love. . . .

To Seduce a Bride

Spirited beauty Lilian Loring believes that love is too
risky a venture and marriage is best avoided entirely—
even if her unwanted suitor comes as deliciously
packaged as Heath Griffin, the Marquess of Claybourne.
But for Heath, victory in their game of passion means
nothing less than winning Lily's elusive heart. . . .

 Ballantine Books